About the Author

Originally from East Brunswick, New Jersey, Myranda Marie now lives in Central Florida with her husband of thirty years, Jim, their son, Nick, Banshee the Pitbull and two cats; Harmony and Jake. A true creative; Myranda not only writes but paints, cooks and redesigns furniture. Her philosophy has always been; do what feeds your soul. Jobs do not define your life; passions do. When the world around us becomes daunting and uncomfortable; create a better place. Paint your scenery; write your story, and redesign your surroundings. Myranda Marie's first publication, *Ordinary Heroes* gives her readers hope in people and faith in connections in a time when our reality seems so divided, and relationships become increasingly difficult to sustain.

"*Ordinary Heroes* is a manifestation of unity, acceptance and selflessness. We simply need to welcome the signs from the Universe." – Myranda Marie

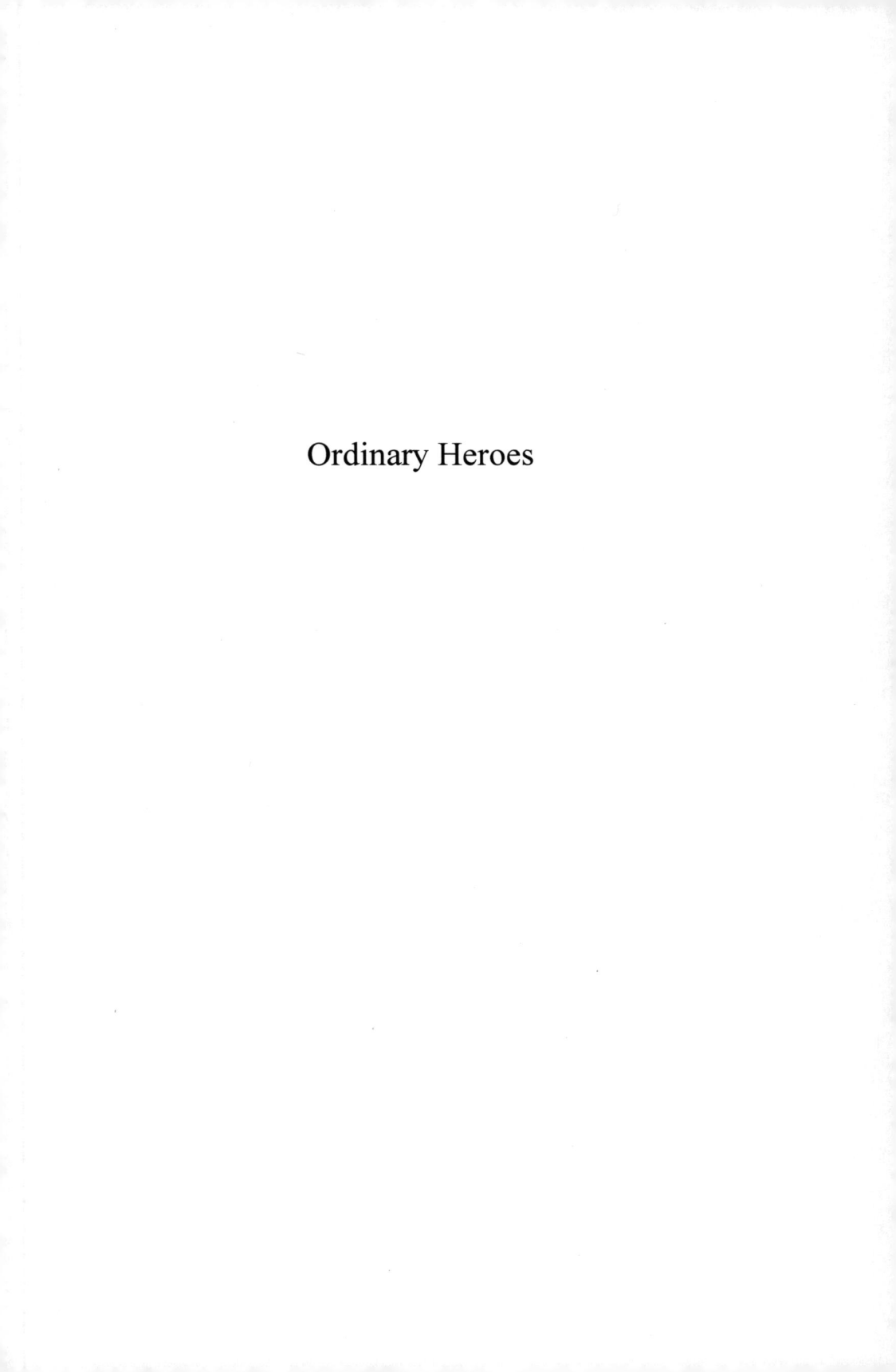

Ordinary Heroes

Myranda Marie

Ordinary Heroes

Vanguard Press

VANGUARD PAPERBACK

© Copyright 2024
Myranda Marie

The right of Myranda Marie to be identified as author of
this work has been asserted by her in accordance with the
Copyright, Designs and Patents Act 1988.

All Rights Reserved

No reproduction, copy or transmission of this publication
may be made without written permission.
No paragraph of this publication may be reproduced,
copied or transmitted save with the written permission of the publisher, or in
accordance with the provisions
of the Copyright Act 1956 (as amended).

Any person who commits any unauthorised act in relation to
this publication may be liable to criminal
prosecution and civil claims for damages.

A CIP catalogue record for this title is
available from the British Library.

ISBN 978 1 80016 733 9

This is a work of fiction. Names, characters, businesses, places, events and incidents are either the product of the author's imagination or used in a fictitious manner. Any resemblance to actual persons, living or dead, or actual events is purely coincidental.

*Vanguard Press is an imprint of
Pegasus Elliot Mackenzie Publishers Ltd.*
www.pegasuspublishers.com

First Published in 2024

**Vanguard Press
Sheraton House Castle Park
Cambridge England**

Printed & Bound in Great Britain

To my son, Nick: Thank you for always reminding me that life isn't about the expectations of others, but rather the connections we make that inspire us to create expectations for ourselves.

Acknowledgements

I wrote a book! I couldn't have come this far without the support of my husband and son tolerating so many take-out dinners when I couldn't stop writing. Many heartfelt thanks to Norma; my dear friend who not only believes in me but is a true inspiration; her kindness knows no bounds. I must thank my family and friends for serving as templates in character development; and for those people in my life who have been less than kind for the same. I am most grateful for my guardian angels; of which I have many. However, it was my Gram and Pop who gifted me with the love of words, writing and reading. They taught me about healthy expression and to advocate for myself as well as for others.

Introduction:

She walked on to the stage as she had so many times before. Her audience filled the auditorium with thunderous applause; so loud, in fact, she couldn't hear her own thoughts. It never gets old, and never ceases to invoke feelings of empowerment as well as humility. She stepped to the podium and adjusted the microphone; the crowd quieted.

"Thank you all for being here with me today. Each time I am blessed with the opportunity to speak; I develop a greater sense of gratitude. This life; this purpose, was meant for me; given as a gift from some higher power. It's nothing short of a miracle that I am standing here, speaking to all of you. So many people had to go through so many things in order for my life to have the meaning and purpose it has today. I know you came today to hear my story, but what I want to tell you is that everyone's story is bits and pieces from the stories of those who have in some way influenced our lives; both positively and negatively. Our Universal connections to each other, as humans are not always perfect, but they are always necessary.

Her audience once again broke into deafening applause. She was sure she'd heard someone whistle from the back of the auditorium. The energy in the room was indeed palpable and required the opportunity to be expressed. She waited a moment before continuing to speak.

I was eight years old when my father was murdered. He was a drug dealer who was killed for a few dollars and fewer hits of whatever he was peddling that week. Honestly, I didn't miss him; I'm not sure I even cried when the police came to the door to inform us of his demise. He wasn't the kind of dad a little girl needed in her life anyway. I think I feel sorrier now; when I reflect on that time than I did as I lived through it.

Two years later; my mother O.D'd. I came home from school one Friday afternoon to find my mother face down, laying in her own vomit; unresponsive. I went to the neighbors apartment and asked for help. She called 9-1-1, but my mother had been dead for hours. The neighbors took me in that night, they had told the authorities they'd contact my family; but

I had no one. I heard the woman talking to her husband about 'putting me to work'. She said I'd be easier to control than the others. I was ten, and I was afraid of what she meant, so I ran away. I had nothing but a small backpack with a few articles of clothing, a toothbrush and a stuffed bear I managed to take with me from my house before the police locked me out.

For three years, I was able to survive on my own; homeless but not helpless. I got by with a little help from some very kind people. No one came looking for me, no one cared. I would do chores and odd jobs for food; sometimes shop owners and restaurant workers would let me sleep in their businesses or cars. No one wanted to 'get involved' but some were compassionate enough to manage the occasional good deed. I was grateful; and shared any food, clothing or useful item I was given or found with others like me; kids on the street with no home; and no one to care for them.

One day while taking trash to a dumpster in an alley behind several businesses that often gave me food in return, I heard a noise. It was a high-pitched whimpering coming from inside the dumpster. Barely tall enough to look inside, I flipped the lid and jumped up onto the rim. When I looked down, I saw a pair of soulful eyes looking back up at me. Someone had thrown a puppy into that dumpster. I remember stacking some discarded junk up on the side so I could climb in and rescue this poor animal. I did get him out. It took a while, but with determination and no regard for the fact that I now smelled like garbage; I rescued my best friend. For the next few months, I focused on caring for Harry. I would feed him even before feeding myself. I snuck him into public restrooms and bathed him in sinks until he became too big to lift. I named him Harry after a beloved character from the only book I owned. I remember one of the nice shop owners bringing that book for me. He held it out and said, " You can have this; that is if you can read." I took the book and wanted to smack him with it. Instead, I thanked him and as politely as I could, reminded him that I was homeless, not stupid. However, his inquiry was warranted; and I hadn't been in a classroom for several years. I kept my brain engaged by reading old newspapers, magazines, and even people's discarded mail that was left in their recycling bins. I knew I had to be able to read if I wanted to have a job someday, and all I could think about was taking care of Harry. Will; meet Way!

One night; while I slept in a tent with four other kids, someone reached in and grabbed Harry. By the time we could get out of the tent, they were gone. I searched everywhere; I hadn't slept in days and spoke to everyone who would stand still long enough to ask if they heard or saw anything. I asked around the shops where I usually scrounged for food; hoping the people who worked there would recognize Harry if they saw him. No one had.

Finally, a young man who used to live on the streets as well told me to go see Nate. He told me where to find him, and he was my best bet for getting Harry back. Nate is what I call an Earth Angel; *My* Earth Angel. She paused for a brief moment and blew a kiss into the audience. By everyone's best guess; Nate was seated in the front row.

"You know some say that my luck changed because of what I had been through as a young child. That's not true; luck has no role in my story. If it had, more kids like me would be filling more auditoriums like this one. I was not unique, but I was strong. Was I a victim? Mmmm… Probably, by definition. But what I endured happened long before I knew what a victim was. The only thing I was sure of was surviving, and not by any means. I wouldn't work for the dealers; for fear of being killed. I wouldn't live with strangers; I was safer on my own. The stories from the other kids were chilling and gave me nightmares. People can be cruel. Hurt people; hurt other people. I never looked back on the hurt inflicted on me; just forward. It never occurred to me to cause pain, in any form to any being. I just wanted to continue to move away from pain. Somehow I knew the only way to do so was to be aware of the consequences of my own actions. I guess I was a pretty progressive pre-teen having an in-depth grasp of the law of Karma. Well, Namaste to me!"

Her audience burst into laughter. She took the opportunity to move from the podium and sat on the top of the stage steps just above the orchestra pit. She motioned to the right of the stage where a young man emerged with a portable headset.

"Ok, can everyone hear me? I still have a little more time with all of you, and my feet are killing me in these heels. If you don't mind, I'm going to sit here for the remainder of our time together."

There was a chorus of barely audible voices; not one objecting to her surrendering to her sore feet.

"Before I take a few questions from you; I have one of my own to ask. There is no right or wrong here' but I ask you to think about your answer. Is this *my* story? I know you're all here today to hear MY story. But, what happened here today was simply this; I delivered to you, my perspective of a small, but significant part of a story. Everything I told you, and everything you have yet to hear is only a fraction of what happened in my life to get me here today. This very day; this very moment has become a part of all our stories because we are here, experiencing it together; think about that.

We are all connected. It is human nature to live for and with others. Our connections fuel our experiences. Those who connect with bad people have bad experiences as they placed themselves on that bad path. Some choose to connect with good people, and well, you're all intelligent beings, you can figure out rather easily what happens when good, positive and healthy connections are made. My most momentous connection came from a near tragedy; someone suffered an injury but saved my life. I often wonder where I would be if she didn't have the munchies that night."

Her audience giggled in unison.

"Those of you who have read my book know what I'm talking about. If you haven't read it yet, well, there's your incentive."

A little more sedate laughter.

"Remember to consider yourself; this is your life. Don't be afraid to say no to a relationship of any kind that feels wrong; negative and toxic. There is no such thing as being disrespected and hurt out of loyalty. Don't be afraid to ask for help. Not everyone will tell you they don't want to 'get involved'. Even the smallest effort from another person can lead to great things. If this were not true; I would not be here with you today. Fear is debilitating; Faith moves us forward.

Each morning I wake up and ask God or the Universe or my Guardian Angels; or whoever may be listening to make the signs clear. Allow me to follow the right path and afford me the opportunities to help others see their paths as well. Remember, the smallest gesture can create the most powerful change. Standing on a stage telling my story is a small gesture. I choose to tell it to anyone who wants to listen, because it may become a significant part of someone else's story. Just as a million minor details in the lives of so many incredible people influenced me; they had no idea. An entire group of random people chose to do what they did; say what they said; move where they live; speak to whom they made connections with in order for me to stand before you; right now. Let's take a moment to recognize the one major act of heroism that set my life on the path to you. I'm talking about my superhero; my very best friend and my personal moral compass. Wanna know more? Yes, you guessed it; read the book!

Those who had already read it; applauded. Those who hadn't yet became inspired.

I learned to look at life instead of back at it. Had that dirtbag not taken Harry that night, I would likely not be here today. That awful man changed my life; he probably saved it for the first time. I know how crazy that seems, but that horrible event placed me on the path that led me here. Seriously, let's be real for a minute. How long do you think a kid of thirteen would have been able to survive on her own without somehow being influenced by the negative forces in this insane world? Maybe, with the grace of God, I would have managed to stay alive; but would I have given in to crime? You know hunger leads to desperation; your fight or flight kicks in when you feel as though you may not survive. Desperate people do desperate things; don't they? My options would have included stealing; dealing, and selling my body and soul. What an awesome life that would have been! So many young people give in to those options, to survive. When our basic needs aren't being met, it is our nature to substitute them for what is available. We need love; if no one loves us, we seek attention from others; acceptance; a sense of belonging. We need shelter; if we are living on the streets with no protection from the elements; no security; we follow the first person who takes an interest in us wherever they lead. If we are hungry, and there is no food for us; we will work for sustenance; it won't matter what we are doing, as long as we do not starve. The moment we show our vulnerability; the vultures swoop in and pick us clean. I am fortunate and ever grateful that the first people to take an interest in my well-being were, and are exemplary human beings. I strive to emulate their natural nobility.

Asking for help does not make one vulnerable; choosing to accept help from the wrong sources does. If you take only one thing away from your time with me today, please let it be this; No one deserves to be hurt, miserable, neglected, used, or abused because they are expected to be loyal to their abuser. *No one*! Even if you have made huge mistakes; you can choose to move away from them, and not allow those mistakes to define you forever. If you have stolen from someone; then move forward and give. If you have hurt someone; take every opportunity to soothe others. Be the cycle breaker, not the misery maker. You're all getting it, right?

Her audience cheered.

Now, before someone asks; I will tell you. I did get Harry back. But you'll have to read that part of our story on your own. I will meet you all in the foyer in a few minutes to take some questions and sign some books. Please consider buying one, as all proceeds go to our foundation which provides much-needed assistance to homeless kids as well as their dogs. I think you'll find my book worth the twenty bucks; so please pick up your copy of *Ordinary Heroes.*

She stood, holding her shoes in one hand and with the other, she waved and blew a kiss; this time to everyone in the audience. Yes, there was an immediate and unanimous standing ovation. There usually was.

Part 1
Wanda the Wonderdog:

Fiona Lasher had just returned home from a three-week stay in Florida. She needed the break; the distraction from her first and rather epic heartbreak. Even after talking it all out with her grandmother, she was still unsure as to how and why everything that seemed perfect in her life fell apart. Grams offered comfort and a sympathetic ear, but she too felt as though there was a piece of this puzzle either missing or simply didn't fit.

Being with Grams in Florida was less than cliche as she lived right between the theme parks and the beach in a real neighborhood where all the houses actually looked different from one another. There were no gates, or strict rules, just the most beautiful homes nestled among the Cypress, Palm, and Mimosa trees. Grams' house looked like a resort in itself, complete with a pool, beautiful gardens, and six bedrooms, always ready for her visitors; her family. No shuffleboard, bingo, or Early bird specials in the cafeteria, just endless choices of fun and relaxation. Fiona envied that life. Someday she would live in the sunshine as well, but for now, she was back to her reality, back home in New Jersey with her mother and Wanda. She loved her life, her home, and her mother, but dreamed of bigger things; better things. She longed to have something more to look forward to; more than just an entry-level job, and community college.

The rain stopped, although temporarily. Fiona's mother said it had been raining constantly for more than a week. The roads were flooded, and the ground was swampy and spongy. The humidity made her clothes stick to her body and her long hair plastered itself to her neck and cheeks. Still, the break in the depressing rain prompted her to get out of the house, even for a few minutes. She called for Wanda and grabbed her leash.

The distinct sound of Wanda's nails clicking on the wood floors as she scrambled to the back door made Fiona smile. The Pitbull Aussie mix was oddly beautiful and always attracted attention with her merle markings and one blue and one brown eye. Her coat was short like a Pitbull and her smile was nothing short of comical, but it was her intelligence that made her so unique. Wanda had instincts that would rival any self-proclaimed psychic. She was her once-in-a-lifetime best friend and Fiona missed her while she was away. A little time together, just walking and enjoying her company was long overdue.

Fiona called to her mother in the other room to let her know they were headed out. Her mom responded that she had just heard more thunder in the distance so make it quick, which was fine because her intention was to walk down to the pizzeria at the end of her street and back, just to breathe and stretch. Thirty minutes should be enough time to beat the return of the rain; she hoped.

Wanda didn't necessarily need her leash as she never strayed more than two or three feet from her companion. Nevertheless, it was always a good idea to take it anyway, just in case. It was unlikely that a stranger would be walking down her road this afternoon, and everyone in her very typical suburban neighborhood knew Wanda; trusted her and most of her neighbors even looked forward to seeing her. But, better safe than sorry; so the leash stayed off, but they had it if they needed it.

Fiona walked slowly, letting Wanda sniff every blade of grass for the six blocks to the back lot of the restaurant. As they approached the pizzeria; about one hundred yards before the corner of the road; Wanda started her exciting prancing thing; a signature move reserved for when she wanted to bolt toward something or someone either familiar or curious. Once she realized what had Wanda so eager to leave her side, she made a slight hand gesture giving the dog permission to go. Wanda enthusiastically headed for the back door of the pizzeria where their friend Nicky stood, just inside the doorway, sucking on his cigarette. Nicky's family owned the little pizza joint that had over the years become a very popular place to hang out, get good food and feel at home. He literally grew up making pizzas and his friends grew up right there with him.

"Well, hello pretty lady; and Fiona," he quipped as he sat on the back step to snuggle with Wanda who seemed to flirt with Nicky every time she saw him. It was sheer gratitude; but honestly if dogs flirt; this was how they did it. It was Nicky who saved Wanda almost eight years ago, and she never forgot his kindness.

While playing in the parking lot behind the pizzeria, eleven-year-old Nicky heard the cries of an animal in obvious distress. He searched everywhere, calling out hoping the animal would keep responding until he could locate it. Finally, Nicky jumped up on some crates and peered into the dumpster where he saw a filthy, scared, malnourished puppy desperately trying to climb her way out of her dire situation. Nicky dove in and scooped her up; and ran all the way to what would later become Wanda's forever home.

Fiona remembered that day so well. She and Nicky had been neighbors and best friends all their lives, and that day was the first time she had seen him so distraught. Even as a toddler, Nicky had the most positive disposition and was always a pleasure to be around. Nothing ever knocked him off his game, until that day. He stood in her doorway holding the puppy; shaking and sobbing and pleading with her mother to help them. His mother and sister were both back at the pizzeria and Nicky knew better than to bring the pup into the restaurant. He knew exactly who to go to for help.

Susan Lasher quickly ushered them both inside the house to assess the situation, only to find it wasn't as critical as it seemed.

"This pup needs a bath, a good meal and lots of love, that's all; she's going to be fine thanks to you." There wasn't even a discussion about keeping her; it was already decided the moment Nicky presented that dirty little squealing dumpster diver at their front door. So, it's not a wonder that Wanda has a love for him like no other; he is her person.

"Give me Wanda's leash." Nicky reached out his hand waving his fingers in the 'let's have it' motion.

Confused by the request, but with no reason to question his judgment; Fiona handed the leash to Nicky who proceeded to hook it to Wanda's collar then threaded his hand through the loop and gently pulled her a little closer to him. She waited silently for an explanation, assuming there was one; finally, Nicky looked up from Wanda, still holding her firmly to his side.

"Carter's here; up front, in the lot, with all his stupid friends. They've been here for about an hour, just hanging out and eating pizza on that nasty picnic bench. I'm afraid if Wanda sees him or hears his voice, she will bolt, and then one of us will have to go get her and deal with all that bullshit."

Fiona sighed deeply.

"Thanks for telling me; I think we will head back anyway. I can hear the thunder getting louder; more rain is on its way." She tried to seem unbothered by the fact that he was literally around the corner from where she stood; that if she was quiet enough, she may hear the sound of his voice for the first time in months; or maybe catch a glimpse of him if he were close enough to the side of the building. But inside, she shook; her heart raced, and her stomach turned; even felt a bit dizzy for a split second.

Nicky knew her better than anyone and could sense her anxiety despite her efforts to stay calm and unaffected by his news.

"Hey, wanna hang out later? I'll come by after work; we can watch movies or something. I mean I haven't seen you in weeks, let's catch up, ok?"

"Yes! That would be amazing." She reached for Wanda's leash as Nicky wiggled it free from around his wrist. But without warning, Wanda uncharacteristically bolted toward the road. She and Nicky both screamed for her attention; expecting the dog to obey and come right back, but she didn't. As they ran toward the front lot, they could hear Wanda frantically barking; and the distinct sound of a woman screaming. "Help!" over and over. Fiona called back, assuming it was Wanda that startled the woman on the road, "She's friendly! Don't worry, we're coming." But the woman stood frozen in fear and continued to scream for help.

Fiona and Nicky quickly caught up to Wanda, begging her to move away from the woman, but she continued to bark and stomp her front paws in the water which had pooled in the road due to the debris from the storm blocking the drainage ditch. The water was level with the road, ladened with fallen branches, clogging the culvert. Fiona knew there was a ditch in front of the pizzeria, and quickly surmised the water's depth. She called for Wanda again for fear of her beloved dog getting too close and falling in. The woman was frantic and finally managed the words, "My son."

Three-year-old Joshua Frye had been out for a walk with his mother; and playfully splashing in puddles, as children often do. Joshua's mother had no idea the ditch and water were so deep when she let her son enjoy the aftermath of all the rain. Joshua stepped into the ditch and got caught on a branch which caused him to lose balance and land face down into the water. He struggled to free himself, but the water moved him even further into the culvert which his mother couldn't reach. She instantly panicked.

"Oh, dear God, there's a child in the water!" Nicky took his cell phone from his pocket and screamed. "I'm calling 911!"

Fiona turned in the direction of the parking lot where familiar faces, once true friends stood watching as if it were all happening for their entertainment. She caught his eyes and begged, "Help me!" He hesitated; looked to his group of miscreants as if seeking their permission to do what he knew was right. It turned her stomach. Carter's new girlfriend had taken out her phone and began to video the struggling toddler, commenting to her friends that she was 'live' on social media.

Fiona stepped down into the drainage ditch to get closer to the child. Nearly knee-deep in water, she reached Wanda who had managed to get her leash close to the little hand that was desperately stretching, and finally grabbed hold. Wanda backed herself up; stepping slowly and methodically as if she knew that hand could lose its grip if she wasn't careful. Crying and silently pleading with God for help, Fiona coaxed her dog back out of the flooded gully, "Come on baby, you got this, you're my superhero, Wanda, come on sweetie!"

Fiona felt his hand on her shoulder, then her elbow, in an attempt to support her as she backed away from the tangled debris. It wasn't the right time or place, but her body responded to his touch instinctively with chills. She looked up and nodded as she steadied herself with his help. He spoke.

"I'm going to be in big trouble for this."

She was shocked by his statement, her eyes widened, and the chills were suddenly gone; "For helping to save a kid?"

"No, for helping *you* help save a kid." She stepped back from this man she once trusted with her own life as if she just discovered he was the villain in a horror movie. What an absurd thing to say; how could Carter be associated with people so who were so obviously heartless?

Wanda had successfully pulled the small child from the watery culvert and Nicky was wrapping him in the flannel shirt he had tied around his waist. She could hear the little boy's mother sobbing and thanking them. The sirens from the approaching emergency vehicles grew louder and closer; then an ear-shattering clap of thunder. Lightning cracked; right where she stood in the water at the edge of the road; the saturated earth gave way and she slid further into the pooled debris. Fiona felt a unique sensation from the charge; like time stopped for just a few seconds. Right before she blacked out; she saw his eyes and felt his hands reach around her waist.

Grab a Tissue

Anthony {TC} Cooke sat at his desk staring intensely at his computer screen. Anyone passing by would easily assume he was engrossed in his work and was not to be disturbed at this level of extreme focus. One would speculate that the founder and CEO of a leading tech. The corporation would have plenty of important things to keep him occupied throughout the work day; but in this case, on this day, at this moment, one would be wrong.

Anthony Cooke was dedicated to the discovery, development, and implementation of non-invasive medical procedures and devices; among other things. His mission statement always included *there's a safer way of helping people.* Cooke Industries was world renowned and quite famous; maybe even a bit notorious for their cutting-edge technological advancements in the medical field, and the latest to come out of their labs was under scrutiny by everyone from Big Pharma to the SPCA. But none of that mattered to Cooke; he had 'people'' that were paid to worry about his company's reputation, and it was his job to worry about its integrity. However, at the moment, he was obsessing over some rather old and in his words, 'oddly interesting' social media posts having nothing at all to do with his actual job. It seemed as though there was a miraculous rescue about four years ago, involving a child and a dog; somewhere in a small town in central New Jersey, and Anthony Cooke couldn't turn his attention away from the myriad of posts and comments.

Cooke or TC to most was not only a brilliant man but entirely colorful as well. His personality vacillated between that of a teenage boy to someone rivaling, maybe even surpassing the intellect of Nickola Tesla. TC wasn't stereotypically eccentric, or even allowably flashy for a billionaire. He was a nice guy with a big brain and access to any and every resource known to man. The people who worked for him were loyal, happy, and content. It was as though TC and his wife; Laurel built this gigantic family business instead of a billion-dollar tech corporation. The only people who didn't like TC were of course his rivals; and calling them rivals was generous considering no other company, no other brilliant mind could come close to Anthony Cooke and Cooke Industries.

Still staring at his computer screen, TC reached out and waved his hand over a small glass panel inside his desk. The glass turned green, and a disembodied voice asked for a name.

"Laurel," he replied, then added. "Please."

The voice responded, "Calling Laurel."

Much like her husband, Laurel Cooke was certainly not a stereotypical billionairess socialite, but she was by definition an eccentric. She was classically beautiful by anyone's definition, and truly had no idea how much her looks influenced the way people perceived her. Laurel was never one to care much for outer aesthetics and chose to look within to see a person's true spirit; which she could admit was not always something she chose to see. She rarely passed judgements though, but rather engaged or steered clear once she established a connection with those she came in contact with. Her inner circle was small, and her family and few friends meant the world to her, especially her husband. They met almost twenty-five years ago, purely by coincidence while vacationing in Ocho Rios, Jamaica. It was love at first sight according to both of them. When TC asked her after just hours of meeting her to be with him forever; Laurel didn't hesitate. She had fallen in love with his spirit; and she knew together they would do miraculous things; and have continued to do so.

Laurel had just stepped onto the patio from her studio where she was working on redesigning a vintage cedar chest. She had sanded the original finish and just began to give it a fresh coat of paint when the alert sounded throughout her home; another disembodied voice chimed, "Laurel, you have an incoming call from TC, care to accept? "

"Of course."

"You are connected."

"Helllloooooooo," she sang into the room as she walked back through the patio doors.

TC answered, "Hey there, are you free for lunch?"

Laurel could tell by the tone of his voice that his invitation had some sort of business attached to it and was not a simple and leisurely proposition to spend the afternoon together. It didn't matter, the sound of his voice made her smile, despite its inflection. However, she knew all too well that a working lunch with her beloved might result in a tension headache for the rest of the day. Being married to someone who never, ever stops thinking can be quite taxing no matter how much you love them.

Laurel rolled her eyes, and took a breath, affording herself a few seconds of contemplation before answering. TC already knew she would have lunch with him, it was simply a matter of details.

"Where are we having lunch? Let me guess, the deli in your building?"

TC wanted to be less predictable, but of course, that was his plan.

"Did you roll your eyes when I asked you to lunch? I felt like you did. I think I heard them roll," he joked.

"Oh, maybe, you know my eyes have a mind of their own, rolling is an involuntary response when my brain needs a second to engage, or switch gears. It's nothing personal, they roll for lots of people and lots of reasons; you aren't exclusive."

"You're just making shit up; but I love you and your eyes. Can you be here around one?"

"I will be there, love you too." She waited for the chime indicating he had disconnected from the call before leaving her studio to get ready for their lunch date.

Laurel called for car service, asking to be picked up in thirty minutes. She then proceeded to change out of her paint splattered clothes into a pair of faded jeans, vintage concert t-shirt from the eighties and her favorite red sneakers. Being forty-something didn't mean you had to give up feeling like a kid; or dressing like one. She was not one to worry about looking impressive or maintaining any sort of public image. Her philosophy had always been, *people judge you no matter what you do, it's unavoidable. So, be the best you, for you and their judgements won't matter. If they like you, great, if not, that's just fine too.*

Laurel was just grabbing her jacket from the hall closet when that familiar chime sounded again and 'the voice' informed her that her car had arrived. Cooke Industries had their own private car service with three hubs; one in the city under their corporate building, one just blocks from their home on Long Island and the other positioned on the fringe of New Jersey to accommodate airport runs. TC loved to drive, but not in the city; he felt it was best left to those who were able to navigate without stress, and anyone who didn't mind driving in the city, deserved to be handsomely compensated for said skill. Cooke's car service was always available for employees and business associates as well as friends who may need a lift. Cooke's cars also provided additional employment opportunities to those already holding positions within the company. Most of the drivers were part time, working around their full-time positions for extra money. TC loved this idea when Laurel suggested it several years ago. She had a knack for mutually beneficial solutions.

Laurel stepped outside and stopped on the front porch before walking down to the street. She went through her mental checklist; "doors locked, keys in handbag, phone in pocket, sunglasses in hand, now on face, ready, set, go." She was pleased to see Charlie get out of the driver's side to walk around and open her door for her. Laurel liked all the drivers, but somehow young Charlie Wheeler had a special place in her heart. Just out of college, Charlie was one who worked two jobs with Cooke to help his family while planning for one of his own someday in the near future. He was engaged to be married next June. He and his fiancée Kay both lived with Charlie's mom; grandmother and his two younger sisters. It wasn't always easy, but he never complained, never called out sick, and had a kind word for everyone. Charlie was the embodiment of gratitude, and Laurel just loved his energy. They greeted one another with huge smiles and a quick hug. Charlie opened the door for Laurel and made an exaggerated gesture with his arm to usher her in.

Once they were under way, he informed her that he had called ahead for a downtown traffic report. The dispatcher said it was fairly mild with no detours or delays on their particular route. Pleased to hear the good news, Laurel quipped back with, "Well that's wonderful and makes your job easier, but I'm meeting the boss for lunch, and if I'm late, well then he will simply have to wait."

Charlie was all too familiar with the quirky dynamic between TC and Laurel. He admired it and hoped he and Kay would have that kind of relationship when they married. The Cooke's were his positive example, his role models. Charlie's mom was amazing, but his dad had been absent for most of his life, leaving them even before he knew that his mother was pregnant with his youngest sister. Charlie's mom always told her children to be grateful, not resentful. Growing up without a father is so much better than growing up with one who didn't want to be there in the first place.

Laurel was impressed by Charlie's mom, and it was no wonder he was so positive and gracious. She loved hearing Charlie prattle on about his family while he drove. There were so many crazy anecdotes and tales of teenage sister drama to keep Laurel entertained even on longer drives. Sometimes, listening to Charlie made her a little melancholy. Her maternal side was very strong despite not having children of her own. She regarded Charlie as well as many others who worked for them and with them as her family and sometimes it felt strange to remember they had real families of their own.

As promised, traffic was light, and they made great time getting downtown. Charlie asked if he should wait around to drive her back home after lunch. Laurel thought for a few seconds and told him to go ahead about his day; she may just hang around to do some shopping this afternoon and catch a ride back home in the evening with TC. They waved one more time before Charlie got back in the car, and Laurel disappeared behind the ominous glass doors of the Cooke building.

It wasn't an easy or quick task to walk through the gigantic lobby of the Cooke building to the deli, not for Laurel anyway. She felt compelled to say hello to everyone working on the first floor as she came into their vicinity. First stop was of course the reception area to check on Rae and ask her how her dad was doing after his heart attack last month. Rae happily reported that Dad was doing well, and thanked Laurel again for the food she had sent over to Rae's family the first week her father was home from the hospital.

"Oh, honey, it was our pleasure," Laurel assured her. "Your Mom had enough to worry about; she shouldn't have had to cook as well. If there's anything you need, just call me or let Jaime know. We're here for you."

Next stop, the concierge desk to check in with Jaime. The two women exchanged empathetic gripes regarding TC and his obsession with deli sandwiches and black coffee as well as a few other oddities such as his occasional need to walk out and go to the movies by himself in the middle of the workday. Jaime had been with Cooke Industries for nearly fifteen years. She and Laurel became fast friends when they first met in college, sharing so much in common. Laurel even refers to Jaime as TC's "work wife" as she's the one who literally keeps him on track when his thoughts begin to fixate, and his day-to-day work schedule seems to be a lesser priority.

Laurel walked behind the enormous desk to hug Jaime and the women made plans to get together over the upcoming weekend.

"We'll see you and Joe on Saturday then; around four?"

"Perfect, see you and TC then; let me know what you want us to bring." Jaime blew her a kiss as Laurel made her way closer to the deli where she speculated TC was waiting, but certainly not patiently. A few more waves hello as she passed by; and one last stop at the doors of her destination. Ralph stood at the greeter's podium waiting for Laurel to make her way in. He was happy to see her as it had been a while since her last visit. He stretched out his arms and stepped around the podium to embrace his friend. Laurel quickened her step to receive the hug from Ralph she had been anticipating all afternoon.

"So good to see you Miss Laurel," the older gentleman said as he hugged her tightly and sort of swayed back and forth. Laurel felt a little squished; and probably rolled her eyes, but Ralph's warmth outweighed his strength, and she knew he genuinely adored her and TC. He called them his heroes. Ralph was one of the best humans ever created and helping him was not about heroics as much as knowing the right thing to do and having the resources and ability to do it.

Ralph's deli was iconic thirty years ago. People from all over would make his place a must visit destination when dining in the city. His space was small, and back then it wasn't unusual to find a line forming outside his door to get one of his famous sandwiches. TC had been one of Ralph's best customers for as long as he could remember. Even as a kid, TC who grew up in the city would walk to Ralph's to pick up dinner for his family, or sometimes to just sit with a soda and talk to Ralph about food.

But times changed, and soon the old-world style of Ralph's became less desirable to tourists and his local patrons simply weren't enough to keep him in business. What most people didn't realize was that Ralph's deli had been donating food to people in need in his neighborhood for years. It hadn't been a financial concern for the small business until the local economy changed drastically. The building had been sold and his lease was up for renewal. The new rental terms had more than tripled his monthly means, leaving Ralph no choice but to close his doors. Laurel remembers the day she and TC stopped in for sandwiches to go and were greeted by Ralph's red and swollen eyes. He told the pair he would be closing at the end of the month and how sorry he was for letting them and his other customers down. TC knew that Ralph's concern was for those in need more so than the despair of losing his business. He knew his old friend worried for hungry children and the homeless who knew where they could get a good meal.

That night TC couldn't sleep. He kept thinking about his buddy Ralph and how unfair life can be. How circumstances beyond one's control can change their path and the paths of others just like that. He paced the floors and ranted about an unjust society, greed and the best pastrami in the world. Laurel let him get it all out, hoping he would happen upon the obvious solution in that massive brain of his. But sometimes simple and obvious elude TC. He was clearly overthinking on Ralph's behalf, and in Laurel's opinion, taking entirely too long to find a solution.

Laurel couldn't handle another minute of seeing her husband in such a state of distress and finally offered her thoughts on the subject. Laurel was the perfect yin to TC's yang; simple and obvious were usually first in her thought process.

"You want pastrami; right? Ralph wants to serve you pastrami, yes?"

"Yes, well, yes, but he wants to save his deli, I mean, he can't afford that ridiculous rent, it's not like I can just go to his house and ask him to make me a sandwich every day at lunchtime, can I?" he took a breath and continued. "And what about those people who counted on old Ralph for help? What will they do, and Dear God, how will Ralph deal with not being able to help them?"

"Ok, so, no, you may not go to that man's house every day. But you're missing the obvious here; just bring the man and his pastrami to *your* house; or rather you're building." She smiled when she realized her proposition got his attention. Laurel continued to prime the well knowing TC would eventually go with the flow and put that plan in action immediately.

"Let's move the deli to the first floor; there's plenty of room and renovations couldn't take more than a few weeks. We can send Ralph to visit his children in Pennsylvania while we get everything in order. Cooke Industries can offer him free rent for let's say the first three years, and then start low, let it ride for the next three, and so on, considering it won't cost us much more than the renovations to make this happen. Or you can offer him a partnership; that may be a win for both of you."

TC's thoughts began to focus, "I'm with you, but what about the people he fed in his neighborhood?"

"I have an idea for that as well, let's set up some sort of foundation; we can use donations to buy extra food for the deli, have Ralph prepare meals that he can take home with him every weekend and distribute to his regular recipients; maybe even extra for people around here; you know that would be amazing."

The rest is Cooke Industries history as they say. The deli where they currently stood was thriving; and the 'Can you Cooke?' foundation attracted many generous donors who care about the people of their city; the children in their own neighborhoods and now, people in need nationwide. Ralph's is more than TC's favorite place to eat, it's the literal keystone of a nationwide campaign to eradicate hunger with more than six thousand participating food establishments, currently.

Ralph finally let Laurel out of his bear hug and personally escorted her to the table where TC had been waiting. The elderly gentleman pulled her chair for her and then handed her a linen napkin to place on her lap. He slapped the table rather loudly and said, "Enjoy my good friends!" before returning to the kitchen.

Laurel looked around the dining room, "It's busy today."

"Yeah, I thought maybe I'd need a reservation; so, I asked Jaime to secure a table." TC seemed pleased that the deli was doing so well; but then again, it was rare to have empty tables on any day, especially at lunchtime. He continued, "That was some hug you got from Ralph; he missed you."

Laurel laughed, and pointed to her lapel, "I think he got some mustard on my jacket too." She took the napkin from her lap and dabbed a corner in her water glass before attempting to wipe the stain away.

The server came to the table to take their order.

"What can I get you folks today?"

Laurel said hello and asked the woman if she was new; she said she'd only been working there for about two weeks. Laurel continued the conversation asking how she liked it so far, and the woman told her it was the best job she had had in a long time. Neither TC or Laurel felt the need to introduce themselves, saving this new server the anxiety of waiting on the owners of the company she was working for. They both politely placed their lunch order and left it to fate whether someone would tell her who they actually were.

Laurel took a sip of her water and figured she would jump right into the reason she had Charlie drive her into the city on thirty minutes notice in the middle of the week, "So, why are we having lunch today? And don't give me some made up crap about wanting to spend time together, or romantic nonsense; what's going on in that chaotic mind of yours?"

TC had to laugh. He knew that she read him so well; he knew she was already ten steps into his agenda.

"OK, I was looking around on social media for stupid crap because I was having one of those mornings where I didn't want to think about nanotechnology or thermal imaging, and I came across a bunch of posts from like four or five years ago about Wanda the wonder dog."

Laurel nearly spit her water across the table, "I don't even want to know what keywords you were searching to find those posts!"

"Right? It's crazy, I know, but there were literally hundreds of posts about it. But one picture in particular caught my attention, and I can't seem to shake the feeling that I may have found a freaking treasure here. Look!" he handed Laurel his phone with the photo he was referring to already displayed on his screen. Laurel stared at it for a long time; minutes perhaps, as it held her attention. She studied it; every aspect, trying to pinpoint what exactly had TC so intrigued. It wasn't easy putting herself inside his mind, but she could, on occasion anticipate what had his neurons firing with all cylinders.

The photo was of two people: a young man and woman. They were soaked from the rain, standing near a road. She was looking up directly into his eyes and he into hers as he embraced her like he was holding his whole world in his arms. It was beautiful, hopeful and sad all at the same time. Laurel kept looking, every little nuance of the image may provide the clue as to why TC wanted her to see it. Then she noticed this ever so slight anomaly in an otherwise monochromatic image. There was a strange but distinct glow between them. The image of the woman appeared to be outlined in a faint blue hue. Similarly, the young man's image emanates a reddish color and between them was a noticeable violet. Laurel speculated the occurrence was a fusion of what, their individual auras? Some type of life force inadvertently captured in the photo. She had only seen something similar once before, just once.

"I see it," she declared as she looked up to meet the wide-eyed stare of her husband.

"So, I'm not crazy?"

"Well, that's still up for debate, but if you're asking if I think it's comparable to the first time we saw this "colorful convergence," in a photograph; I do, I think it's the same phenomenon."

"Laurel, I have to meet them. I need to find them."

"OK, let's find them." Laurel knew better than to advise her husband to simply let this go. Once TC had an idea, he had no choice but to see it through.

By this time, their lunch had been served; Laurel had a vague feeling that she at least acknowledged the server when she came back to the table; but couldn't be sure. She thought their fixation on TC's phone would be construed as rude behavior and planned on apologizing with a huge tip, and of course some genuine words of gratitude. The couple ate in silence for a few minutes, enjoying their food; the company and of course turning that image over in their minds; time and again. Finally, Laurel spoke, "Jaime and Joe are coming by on Saturday; should we ask Ralph to send something over, or are you in the mood to fire up the grill?"

TC looked up from his plate, "Huh? oh, sorry. Yes, let's grill. We haven't done that in a while." Clearly, TC was still preoccupied, but at least this hadn't yet escalated to obsession; yet!

Laurel sighed, knowing she would be taking on the task of finding the young couple in the photo; sooner than later.

"I was going to do some shopping while in town, but now I'm thinking I could go up to the office with you after lunch and start searching for information on the photo instead. I would just need a desk to work from, and maybe a fresh pot of coffee; I work cheap."

"OK, if you want to, that would be amazing."

"Sure, it probably won't take much, I mean with social media; finding people is rather easy. They were probably tagged along with others who know them in some of the posts from that day. It's just a matter of narrowing it down."

TC wiped his mouth and placed his napkin on the table, indicating he was finished with his lunch, as if the completely empty plate wasn't obvious enough. Their server was standing by waiting for some signal to approach. TC was evidently finished, and it was the perfect time to ask if the couple in fact needed anything else before receiving their check.

"Is there anything else I can get for you this afternoon?" She was very polite, and her voice was pleasant despite the weary look in her eyes. The server smiled and held the check behind her back as if not to seem as though she was rushing them.

Laurel answered, "No, I couldn't eat not one more bite, but thank you," she looked up to read the servers nametag, "Silvie."

"Then I will leave this with you and be back in a moment to take care of it for you," Silvie said as she gently placed their check at the edge of the table.

"Wait, I will save you a few steps," TC said as he picked up the check and handed it back to her along with his credit card. Silvie took the check and told them she'd be back in a jiffy. Her choice of words made Laurel giggle a bit, "jiffy," who even says that anymore?

When Silvie returned to the table, she handed the receipt to TC to sign, along with his credit card.

"I noticed the name on your card, any relation?" she joked as she gestured in a circle, referring to the building they were in, and the name on its door.

TC signed the receipt as Laurel watched, making sure he left a generous tip for Silvie. He handed it to her and answered, "Relation? Well, sort of, I guess you could say that." Laurel then took the opportunity to apologize for their behavior and told Silvie they had hoped she didn't think them to be rude; they were just very focused on their conversation this afternoon. Silvie simply replied that it was a pleasure serving them today and she hoped they enjoyed the rest of their day.

The Cooke's left the deli and headed up to TC's office as Silvie handed the signed receipt to Ralph. She just then noticed the very large sum in the tip column and immediately told Ralph there had been a mistake; and to not enter the amount until they could alert the customers of the error. Ralph glanced quickly at the receipt and entered the information into the computer. The cash drawer popped open, and he took two one-hundred-dollar bills from it and handed them to Silvie, "No mistake sweetheart, this is for you."

She took the money; still a bit confused, but within seconds, the pieces fit together for her, and she realized who exactly her last customers were. Ralph noticed the tears in her eyes as she excused herself to the restroom.

Up on the twenty first floor, Laurel settled in at a desk in a small vacant office down the hall from TC's. It was quiet; away from the other offices on the floor. She wondered why this office was not in use but was grateful to have a little privacy while she scoured the internet in search of information on what she was now calling "the convergence couple".

She had just started making progress, following virtual breadcrumbs from the posts she found from that particular day. TC was right, there were many; and all from different perspectives. It was hard to precisely piece together exactly what happened, as most of the posts were self-involved. The original posters seemed more concerned about becoming internet famous themselves than the safety of the little boy; the dog or the couple standing in the road. Several times while reading the comments and captions, Laurel found herself shaking her head and rolling her eyes in disbelief. How in the world can people be so clueless?

TC stopped in to check on Laurel's progress. He had a coffee cup in one hand and a folded piece of yellow paper from a legal pad in the other.

"How's it going?"

"Well, not bad actually, I have a pretty solid lead. One of the photos shows the sign on the front of the building they must have been nearby. It's a pizza place, Pete's Pies, and just our luck, they are a registered participant in 'Can you Cooke?' So, I grabbed their info from our database for the foundation and sent them an email. I simply asked if anyone still working there may know how we could get a hold of a young woman that was present the day of the rescue. I included my personal email and my cell number; hopefully, someone will respond soon."

"Hey, that's great, I knew I had the right woman for the job."

"Haha."

"Oh, yeah, I almost forgot; Jaime sent this up a few minutes ago. It's from Silvie, our server at lunch today. I figured you'd like to read it but do yourself a favor; go get a tissue, I know how you get." He handed her the single sheet of yellow legal paper and walked back up the corridor to his own office. Laurel assumed he was teasing her about needing a tissue, opened the paper and just began reading.

Dearest Mr and Mrs Cooke,
I wanted to thank you for your generosity. I honestly thought there was a mistake in the tip amount, but Ralph assured me it was not a mistake, and that the money was truly for me. I am so grateful; you cannot imagine.
What you may not know, is that you have already helped me, and my family get through a very trying time. I've been a single mom to two children for a little over three years. My ex-husband made some bad decisions with his own lifestyle, and I could not subject my kids to any of it. We left with what we could carry and came to the city to stay with friends. I figured it wouldn't take me long to get back on my feet, but life found it necessary to continue to challenge me. It wasn't until I was asked to come in and speak with my oldest son's teacher about his lack of focus that I finally admitted I needed help. His teacher feared the reason behind his lack of focus was due to malnourishment. She checked with the teachers of my other kids and discovered they all had similar issues. I was doing my best, but I admit, there were plenty of days my kids left for school hungry. My son's teacher put me in touch with someone from 'Can You Cooke?' so we could get placed on a meal plan. Ralph's deli was the closest location, and I began picking up food for my kids several times a week. One day Ralph asked me what hours my kids were in school. I told him from seven to two, approximately. He then offered me a job in the deli. At first I declined, thinking I was no more than a charity case at this point in my life and I felt unworthy of the opportunity. Then one day while standing at the service entrance waiting for my food, I met another server who told me it would be great to work together; she said we would be good friends. I had no idea at the time that Ralph sent her out there to make me feel more comfortable. He's a smart man, it worked. Not only do I have a great job now, but I can also still get meals when we need them through 'Can You Cooke?' and that other server and I did become good friends. We are both single mom's and are looking to share an apartment with all our kids; hopefully, we will find one soon.

So, thank you again for all that you do, not only for my family, but for so many people who just need someone to care. May God always bestow His blessings on you and yours,
   Silvie

   Damn it, Laurel thought to herself, *should have listened to TC and grabbed some tissue.*

Don't I know you?

While having her second cup of coffee Laurel formulated a plan to find the couple in the social media photo that TC had discovered the day before. She heard the all too familiar chime, followed by 'the voice' as she affectionately referred to the smart house automation. Laurel never bothered to give it a name like some people chose to do, but simply responded to it as an innovate entity in her home. It was creepy enough without giving it a specific identity.

"You have an incoming call from a verified number belonging to Pete's Pies."

"Oh, right, yes, please connect." Laurel sort of jumped up as if there were someone actually entering the room.

"Hello?" a man's voice opened the conversation. He sounded pleasant and apprehensive all at once.

"Hello," she responded. "Who am I speaking with please?"

"Um, this is Nick La Salle; I'm the owner of Pete's Pies; I got your email regarding an old photo taken in front of our place. Please forgive me but I am completely confused."

"Oh, I'm so sorry Nick, my intention was not to be confusing, I'm interested in contacting the couple in that photo, are you perhaps the young man in the picture?"

"Oh, God no!"

Laurel could tell that his response was quite spontaneous and likely unintended.

"Well, then Nick, I didn't mean to insult you," she said with a little nervous laughter.

"Oh, no ma'am, you didn't, I mean, I'm not, but I know the guy, well at least I used to know him, now he's just not the kind of guy you want to be mistaken for, you know?"

"I do; and I am sorry, Nick. He may not be in your favor, but do you know how to reach him, or the young woman in the picture?"

"May I ask why?" His voice went from being awkwardly nervous to overly protective.

"Of course; it's kind of a long story, but if you have time, I am happy to clarify my intentions."

"Honestly, ma'am, this is a bit of an inconvenient time, I'm the only one here right now and there is a lot to do in the morning in a restaurant. Would it be possible to schedule another call?"

Laurel recognized being blown off as if she were an annoying telemarketer and thought quickly, "I have some time today, are you open for lunch? I could come by; have some pizza and hopefully put you at ease. I can tell you're very leery and rightly so. If someone was randomly asking about my friends, I would be apprehensive as well."

"We are open for lunch; we start serving at eleven. Actually, closer to noon would be better, I have staff scheduled in the kitchen and dining room by eleven thirty. That would give me time to talk."

"Nick, thank you so much for getting back with me, I will see you later then." She thought about waiting for him to hang up but decided to just leave it where it is. 'End Call'.

Her next task was to call for a car. She asked if Charlie was available for a long drive out of the city. He was and would be there to pick her up by ten thirty. She then called TC who was in a meeting. Her voicemail simply said, "On my way to Jersey, see you tonight, love you."

Charlie was a bit early, but that suited Laurel just fine. She had no idea how long it would take to get there, even though GPS estimated seventy-four minutes. As usual, her driver greeted her warmly and made sure she was securely in the back seat before starting their journey. They chatted about everything from the weather to his little sister punching her classmate for calling her pretty.

"Yep, she popped him square in the jaw."

"I know you're a proud big brother, but what did your mom say? I'm thinking she wasn't as pleased as you are."

"Nope, she told Erika that we don't go around punching people, especially people who are trying to be our friend. But I think a little part of Mom was like, 'that's my girl'."

"Oh, Erika is in sixth grade now? It's only going to get worse from here on in. Buckle up big brother."

Charlie agreed. It wasn't easy being the father figure and big brother; they aren't always in agreement when it comes to the serious stuff, like discipline. He continued to regale her with stories of the girls' antics, his mom and of course Kay. Laurel listened intently as she truly did care for Charlie and his family. She cared so much so that sometimes she would silently and privately question his relationship with Kay, thinking he deserved someone, well, different.

At first, Kay seemed perfect for Charlie. But Laurel had a sense about people and the last few times she was in Kay's company, she felt something 'off' between them. Even now, as Charlie spoke of her, his voice didn't have that same harmonious tone as it used to when he would even mention her name. Laurel hated to think the magic had faded so quickly for the young couple. Maybe it was her imagination; she was being overly protective herself. She knew she had no right and would never voice her unsolicited opinions to Charlie, but secretly Laurel wished someone would.

"It looks like we're almost there; maybe another ten minutes or so. Would you like me to wait in the car while you have your lunch meeting?"

Laurel told Charlie she wanted to meet with the proprietor of Pete's Pies in regard to new developments within 'Can You Cooke?' and its policies. She explained that this young man offered a fresh perspective and could really be an asset. Something that important should be discussed in person, always. She was a bit embarrassed to tell him the real reason behind their trek to New Jersey. It did seem odd to be chasing down information regarding an old photo of complete strangers on social media because TC had a hunch they were something special.

Charlie simply agreed and asked if it would be feasible for him to check out a vintage toy store nearby that he had heard about in one of his collectors groups. They would be less than twelve miles from the store, and it would be amazing to have the opportunity to do a little shopping. He also expressed his concern for leaving Laurel in a strange place alone, and of course offered first to be on standby in the parking lot.

She was flattered that he would think of her first, even though that was literally in his job description but gave her blessing on the toy store excursion.

"When would you have the chance to be down here again any time soon? It's like fate that I had business so close to the store you'd like to visit, right?"

"Thank you so much, Laurel. You know I will be on coms and can get back to you within minutes. Do not hesitate to contact me; Ok?" He spoke to her as if he were *her* older brother. That made her smile and warmed her heart.

"I will totally do that, but my guess is, I'll be just fine. I mean look at this place, it's perfectly safe and inviting." She rolled down the back window to get a clearer look at the establishment as they turned into the parking lot. Charlie's GPS announced, "You have arrived at your destination." Laurel was being optimistic in her initial assessment of Pete's Pies. It was slightly run down and rather dank from the outside. But Laurel wasn't intimidated, she knew she would be just fine on her own, she'd been to dives like this before.

She asked him to please stay in the car. It seemed pretentious to have her driver come around and open her door for her when she was clearly physically capable of doing it for herself. Charlie reluctantly agreed. He turned his head toward the back seat and tapped on his right ear, indicating he had his com link in and turned on. Laurel showed him her own earpiece in her hand and then intentionally placed it in her ear before exiting the car. She smiled and tapped her own right ear.

TC was a big fan of coms. The tiny earpieces were the most efficient and quickest way to get a hold of someone; especially if help was needed. Laurel preferred to use her cell phone, but today she decided the earpiece was a good idea. Although the pizza place and its owners had been vetted through her foundation, one could never be too sure of anything, and safety was always a priority with Cooke Industries. She adjusted the com link with Charlie's contact as well as TC's, just in case of a real emergency; although she couldn't imagine what that would be.

Charlie told her he would be back within the hour, but if she needed more time, just to let him know. It wouldn't break his heart if he had a little more time to browse the vintage toy shop. Laurel agreed and closed the car door. She stood in front of the building as Charlie pulled into the street and drove away. She was trying to see the exact perspective of the photographer, whoever he was that day. But things did look quite different, and it was truly a stretch to determine where they were standing four, almost five years ago. The trees were cut down near the parking lot apron; and the culvert had been completely restructured. Her guess was that a change had to happen so another accident didn't occur. Laurel glanced down at her watch; eleven-fifty-seven. She was right on time.

Laurel pulled open the heavy wood door, noticing the 'Can You Cooke?' sticker near the handle. Each participating 'Cooke' restaurant displayed a sticker indicating their place was one that provided free meals to those in need of a little help. Laurel was so proud to see it prominently placed on the front door. It was satisfying somehow to see her work, her ideas, her own heart and soul being implemented in real life. Much to her surprise, the front door led her directly into a bar rather than a dining room. There were two people sitting inside, enjoying their midday libation. No tender stood behind the bar, and it was eerily quiet. The only sound came from a television in the corner reporting the local weather; and even that was on a low volume setting. Laurel took a seat at the bar and waited. A young man appeared from behind a swinging door across the room, "Hey, can I help you?" He sort of called out to her rather than play the part of restaurant greeter.

She widened her eyes, partially in disbelief, but mostly due to the lack of natural light in the room.

"Yes, please. I'm here to see Nick, and I'd like a menu as well."

The young man came into the bar area fully and walked toward Laurel.

"Sorry about that, I'm Nick." he extended his hand, she shook it. "Honestly, I didn't think anyone would show. I figured you for a prank or something. But you're here, so please, let's go into the dining room and get you some lunch. The bar is so damn depressing, isn't it? "

"Well, as far as bars go, I have been in more well-lit establishments; but this one seems to be just fine too." She was being polite, and Nicky knew that. He ushered her through the swinging door into a very cozy dining area. It was a little cliche for a pizzeria, with its grapevine wallpaper and red checked tablecloths, but very clean and cozy with much better lighting.

He finally did offer her that seat at one of the tables for two in the corner and waited for her to sit before taking the chair across from her. Laurel thought, rather than a bunch of small talk, her host may better appreciate a more direct exchange. She took a deep breath, opened her mouth to begin her explanation as to her inquiries when Nicky cut her off; "Don't I know you?"

Of course, Laurel expected this; and although she preferred to keep as low key as possible, she was one of the most photographed faces in Cooke Industries. She appeared in magazines, online publications and tabloids several times a week. Just as she was about to formally introduce herself to Nick; Laurel was again interrupted. This time by a woman peering around the corner from what Laurel assumed was the kitchen.

"Nicky, I'm sorry to bug you, but Dinah is here." The woman sort of loudly whispered in her attempt to not be invasive. She was, by Laurel's best guess, in her mid-thirties; but it was very hard to tell for sure. She was definitely related to Nick, as the resemblance was obvious even from the quick glance Laurel managed of her face. Maybe his mother, but more likely an older sister. Laurel figured she'd ask before they got into the real reason for her visit; and she was not only curious but genuinely invested; family businesses were sort of her thing.

"Great," Nick answered. "Those containers to the right of the fridge are for her; all of them." The woman just smiled in their general direction and disappeared back into the kitchen.

"Sorry about that. Um, it's a big take-out order for a friend of ours. I guess Linda didn't know all those containers were going." He continued, "Dinah has offered to take care of a few kids from our neighborhood while they're on summer break from school. She does it voluntarily; knowing the families can't afford camp or daycare. So, we made a deal; twice a week Pete's provides lunches for all her charges. This really helps Dinah, who pays for everything for those kids from her own pocket. Today is the first day she's picking up such a big order; I probably should have given my sister a heads up!" He laughed.

Suspicions confirmed.

"Oh, is Linda your sister? I should have known, there's quite a family resemblance."

"Most people think she's my mom. Linda hates that," he smiled slyly.

"I think it's awesome that you work together. Does anyone else from your family work here as well?"

"Our mother comes in sometimes; she's what she calls semi-retired. But Mom can't seem to stay away from the kitchen for too long. She likes to come in and cook something special; usually on the weekends, so we can offer an 'off menu' option. It depends on the mood she's in, or what she's personally craving that day. My mother is so used to cooking for a lot of people, she'd never just make something for herself. And, I think she gets a rush from people complimenting her on her cooking skills."

Laurel found her segue and extended her hand across the table, "Well, speaking of cooking, I'd like to officially introduce myself; I'm Laurel Cooke, and it's really great to meet you, Nick. Thank you for having me today."

Nick La Salle was feeling a bit starstruck as he shook hands with *the* Laurel Cooke. He admired her, so not only for her philanthropy but her abundance of grace and void of arrogance. Laurel Cooke was as genuine as they come, and everything she had accomplished benefitted so many people; so many that Nick knew personally. He also admittedly loved her look. Somehow Laurel managed to appear ten years younger than her age of forty-three, and she did so without trying. Everything Nick knew about Laurel, he admired and now here she was, in his dining room, about to eat his food and have a conversation with him. He suddenly felt special. In his mind, he was in the company of royalty.

Laurel contemplated her next sentence, hoping to break the awkward silence rather quickly, but thankfully Nick began to speak.

"I am so sorry I didn't recognize you right away Mrs Cooke; I should have, I mean I think you're amazing and I know everything about you and your work. I read everything; and right now, I'm babbling like a huge ass because you're here, like right here."

Her eyes widened; still not sure if it was her turn to speak, she gave Nick another few seconds to either continue or offer some non-verbal cue that it was her turn. He leaned in over the table as if to ready himself to receive orders for a secret mission. That was her cue; and although she did need his help; it was hardly the secret mission she feared he was hoping for.

Instead, she offered a little more small talk, "Thank you Nick, you're very kind. I am sort of glad you didn't recognize me right away, actually. I would rather make a friend than an impression."

"Oh, Mrs Cooke, you have made both today."

"Laurel, please. Call me Laurel, we're friends now, right?"

Nick responded enthusiastically, "Absolutely!"

Still feeling elated, Nick abruptly jumped up from the table. Laurel thought to herself; this may turn out to be a long afternoon as she couldn't seem to find a way to start the conversation and explain to Nick the real reason for her trip to New Jersey. There was so much more she wanted to accomplish and at this point; she simply hoped for the chance to do so.

"First order of business; *Lunch,*" Nick declared.

He stuck his head inside the kitchen and said something to who Laurel assumed was Linda. When he returned to the table, he asked, "Would you prefer pizza, or would you trust me with my recommendation?"

"I trust you. I'm sure whatever is prepared for me today will be amazing." Just then, she heard Charlie's voice in her ear. "Can you grab something for me to go? I could totally go for some pizza."

"Oh, for Pete's sake!" she had to laugh at her unintentional pun, and before answering Charlie, she asked Nick if there was in fact a Pete.

Nick waited for Laurel to quickly inform Charlie that he had plenty of time before having to return to pick her up, and she would place a to go order for him. She apologized to Nick for the interruption; explaining that her driver was at some toy store not far from there, and he wanted to make sure he had time to shop before returning to drive her back to the city. Nick told her he was familiar with Bonham's Vintage Toys and although he wasn't into collectibles, his inner child did enjoy the occasional trip to the store.

"Yes, to answer your question." Nick continued, "There *was* a Pete. He was my grandfather. He and my grandmother started this business together right after they got married. He had been saving most of his life to open his own restaurant; it was his dream. When my grandparents met, they were both working summers at the shore in a restaurant; he was a cook and grandma was a server. It was a match made in seafood heaven, I guess. The rest is pretty self-explanatory," Nick said as he looked around the dining room.

"I love everything about that story," she said, and genuinely meant it. "As a matter of fact, it does remind me as to why I wanted to speak to you about the couple in the photo." She was really hoping to get things back on track before her lunch was served.

"Right, the reason you're here." Nick blushed, "I'm so sorry; I keep getting distracted."

"You're fine; it's nice getting to know you; but I do hope you can help me connect with the couple."

"Oh, well, first of all, they are so *not* a couple, well not for a long time anyway. They weren't even a couple when that picture was taken. Please understand, I'll do my best to help you, but their story isn't mine to tell; I can tell you about the girl though. No disrespect Mrs Cooke, but I have to protect her privacy when it comes to the relationship."

Laurel was well aware that Nick wanted to be a part, even ever so small of what she was asking; but she was impressed by his loyalty to his friends. Although she wanted to know more about the relationship between the couple in the photo, she admired Nick's integrity too much to press the issue.

"I'd be grateful for whatever you feel comfortable telling me, Nick."

He continued, "The girl, well she's my best friend. We grew up together. Our moms actually met when they were pregnant with us, right here in this pizzeria. My mom was working, and her mom was just craving pizza that day. So, we were friends even before we were born. There is nothing I wouldn't do for her."

As Nicky spoke of the young woman, Laurel could sense the love he had for her. It wasn't at all romantic; but brotherly; sincere and protective. He went on to tell Laurel the story about the day he found baby Wanda in the dumpster, and how that dog bonded them even closer together, and how grateful he was for her selflessness and willingness to share Wanda with him, even though he couldn't care for her every day. Listening to the Wanda story gave Laurel chills and an even deeper desire to meet 'her'. It was time she asked for a name, at least.

"Your friend, does she have a name?"

"Oh, oh my God, yeah, of course, sorry. Her name is Fiona. Fiona Lasher."

Fiona Grace:

Fiona made the left onto Brook Street from Main. *Almost home,* she thought. It had been one of the longest days at the end of the longest week of her life and she was looking forward to just relaxing with Wanda, watching a cheesy movie and bingeing on some junk food. Maybe she'd call down the street and have a pizza delivered. She pulled into the driveway and noticed her mother's car wasn't there. Fiona guessed she was either still at work or had stopped for groceries on her way home.

She went inside, threw her handbag and jacket on the hall table just inside the back door and called for Wanda. Her wonder dog was almost twelve and her hearing wasn't what it used to be; Fiona called for her a second time. Tick, tick, tick; the sound of Wanda's nails on the wood floor paced slowly these days; but at least she was responding. Fiona bent down to rub Wanda's face.

"Hey baby, how was your day? Better than mine I hope." She couldn't help but notice the grey hairs around Wanda's muzzle had begun to migrate all the way to her eyebrows, seemingly overnight.

"Oh, my beautiful old lady; I love you." She rubbed Wanda's ears and asked if she needed to go out. The dog responded with a rather enthusiastic butt wiggle and pushed past Fiona's legs to the back door. She opened it for her old friend and went out with her. Fiona sat on the back steps just breathing in the evening air while Wanda explored the yard and took care of business. She thought of the day when she'd come home, and Wanda wouldn't be there to greet her. It was an awful thought; why would it even enter her mind?

"Ugh, how morbid of me" she said aloud.

"What's morbid?" Fiona's mother was just coming around the corner of the yard as she heard her daughter talking to herself.

Fiona leapt to her feet; obviously startled by the sound of her mother's voice.

"Jesus Mom, you scared the shit out of me, I didn't know you were there!"

"Sorry love, why are you being morbid?"

"Oh, I was just thinking about Wanda. She's getting so grey. I wish dogs lived as long as people so we could be together forever. It's just been a bad day; I don't know what's wrong with me." Fiona's eyes were filled with tears.

"I'm so sorry. Let's go in and talk about how we can salvage it; maybe with a pizza?"

"I was thinking the same," she admitted.

Wanda sidled slowly up the back steps and stood at the door; it was time to go in and relax. Once inside, Wanda headed straight for the sofa; took a few minutes to work up the stamina, then jumped up and settled into the corner of the sectional.

"She has the right idea," Mom said to Fiona, pointing into the living room.

"Go get comfy Mom, I'll order the pizza and meet you on the sofa in a few." Fiona pulled her cell from her handbag and dialed Pete's; Linda answered on the first ring.

"What can we do for you this evening?"

"Hey, Lin. It's Fiona. I need our usual and by any chance do you have a delivery guy tonight? I know I'm like a minute away, but I just want to throw on sweats and not worry about leaving the house. It's been a long and lousy day."

"Hi, Fee. Yeah, Mike is delivering tonight, I'll send him down when your pie is ready. Oh, wait, hang on, Nicky wants to talk to you. I hope tomorrow is brighter. See you soon."

"Hey," Nicky sounded out of breath. "Oh my God, Fee. You're never going to believe what happened here today. I have to tell you. I wanted to call you this afternoon, but we actually got busy as hell. I mean, I would have, I swear." Nicky didn't even skip a beat. "Fiona, this could be life changing; for you." He let out an enthusiastic, "Ahhhhh," and kept going; "I know I won't get out of here until probably midnight, but I'm coming over; just stay up, I promise it will be worth it."

"Ok, you certainly have my attention. I'll hang out down here; and leave the back door unlocked. Just come in and wake me up in case I fall asleep on the sofa." As much as Fiona loved Nicky and enjoyed their late-night chats, she was almost sorry something great happened to him today of all days. It would have been her plan to just go to sleep early.

"Gotta go; later, love you."

"Love you t… oo." Nicky had already hung up before she could get the words out.

Susan came back downstairs; her face washed, hair in a ponytail, wearing her pajamas and slippers. She looked like a teenager ready for a slumber party.

"Ok, now your turn. Go get comfy, and I'll find something for us to watch on TV; oh, unless you'd rather talk."

Fiona got off the sofa, picked up her shoes and headed up the stairs.

"Oh, I do want to talk to you, Mom, eventually. But for tonight, let's just chill and watch a movie. I think I need to decompress." Fiona was well aware that not only was she being a bit dramatic but wallowing as well. And although there was something oddly comforting about the mood, she was beginning to wish it would go away sooner than later. She was on her own nerves.

Susan Lasher knew her daughter well enough not to feed into the melancholy, but rather treat it exactly as it was; temporary.

"Works for me."

Fiona decided rather than just changing her clothing; she'd jump in the shower while she was upstairs. The idea was to literally try and wash this day from her, both mentally and physically; and to some degree, it worked. She was feeling a little more herself. As she was digging through her dresser for some clean sweats and a T-shirt she heard the doorbell. Pizza! This day does have the capacity to not completely suck; she thought. There were still a few hours left to find some joy, and certainly she would find joy in a pizza box from Pete's Pies.

Fiona's mother was already settled in on the long side of the well-loved blue sectional sofa that took up most of their modest living room, with Wanda curled up at her feet. The pizza box was on the coffee table in front of her along with two large plastic bags, a bottle of soda and two plastic cups, paper plates and an entire roll of paper towels.

"What's in the bags?" Fiona asked, taking her place on the shorter side of the sofa next to Wanda who was now wide awake and curiously sniffing in the direction of the food.

"Nicky sent over a ton of goodies; he really hooked us up!" Susan seemed pleased at the opportunity to use that phrase correctly. "There's fried zucchini, some kind of pasta, garlic bread and I haven't opened the container in the second bag yet. My guess would be calamari, or at least I'm hoping it is."

Fiona sat up, "Do we need silverware?"

"Nope, there's plasticware in there too. He thought of everything. Did you mention you had a bad day, because it's just like Nicky to find a way to try and make you feel better. He loves you."

"I know he does. Actually, he did most of the talking, and has something important to talk to me about. He'll be here after the kitchen closes. I told him I'd stay down here and leave the back door open. I'm just hoping I can stay awake. I did however mention my day to Linda, so it is likely she gets the credit for this comfort food feast."

"Awe, just like old times. I probably won't be awake by the time he makes it over here so let him know I'm grateful for the food, whether it was his or Linda's doing."

"I will, promise." Fiona had already unpacked the bags and busted open the take-out containers. She filled her plate while Susan selected a movie for them to watch while they ate.

"I figured we could start with this one, and there are two more movies I found that we haven't seen yet."

"Mmmm... Hmmm," Fiona agreed with a mouth full of fried zucchini; her favorite.

Susan loved rom-coms. She allowed herself to become immersed in their unrealistically romantic story lines and exaggerated acting. Fiona preferred horror and mystery genres, but never minded indulging her mother's movie choice. More times than not, the two women would end up predicting the next scene before it happened; reciting a line they assumed was coming and finding flaws with the characters who were written to be practically perfect. It became their ritual more than just traditionally watching the movie, which made them more entertaining than the writers even intended. Rom-coms were, by nature, very predictable.

"Ohhhh, see?" Susan pointed to the television screen and waved her fingers; That's the guy she ends up with; I guarantee it!"

"Ha, you're probably right. The nerdy guys always get the girl, don't they?"

They made it through the first movie and about twenty minutes into the second; before Fiona realized her mother was sound asleep. She reached over and gently shook Susan's foot, "Mom," she whispered. "Mom," a little louder. "Mom, go to bed, it's late."

Susan sat up, "Oh, good Lord, was I sleeping?"

"Yeah, it's getting late; go to bed. I'll see you in the morning."

"Are you coming up?" Susan stretched and rubbed her eyes. "Oh, that's right, Nicky is stopping by. Well, tell him hello, and I hope you can stay awake. Love you."

"I'll make it. Love you too."

Fiona watched as Susan padded up the stairs; and couldn't help but feel lucky to have her mom as her best friend. She thought for so long that all mothers and daughters were as close as the two of them; like her mom and Grams; and her aunts and cousins as well. She had no idea until she was in about fifth grade that some moms weren't like hers; and some daughters weren't the kind of kids their moms necessarily wanted to be friends with. Fiona knew that all families weren't 'traditional'; hers certainly wasn't. But still, she remembered feeling sad for her friends; knowing the mother/daughter dynamic wasn't the same in every home. Now, dads was another story.

Fiona had met her father several times. He's a pleasant man who lives in Arizona with his wife and three children. She knows he works as a real estate agent, lives in a nice house with a pool and a trampoline in the backyard. She thinks they have a dog, or at least they had one at one time or another. She knew his last name; Montgomery and was grateful she had been given Mom's last name instead. The last time Fiona saw her father was about six years ago. She had come home from school one afternoon to find her mother at the dining room table, having coffee with this rather good-looking man who seemed vaguely familiar. He was wearing jeans, a red polo shirt and brand-new Adidas sneakers. Fiona remembered thinking they had to be new; they were so clean and white. It took Fiona a few seconds to realize who he actually was. He spoke first, "Hey Fiona, it's great to see you." He was genuine, and somehow not at all nervous or awkward.

"Oh, likewise." Unlike her father, Fiona felt entirely awkward. She was hoping for some sort of cue from her mother, and when it didn't happen, she had to say something; but 'likewise'? What seventeen-year-old says likewise?

"Do you have a few minutes to sit with us?" Mom asked.

"Uh, sure," still feeling like she was experiencing some out of body phenomenon; Fiona sat in one of the empty chairs on the side of the table, near her mother.

Susan seemed so at ease; "Mark stopped by to say hello. He had some family business in New Jersey and wanted to catch up."

"That's nice." Fiona was relieved that her mother referred to her father as Mark and not something off the wall, like. "Your dad."

Mark cleared his throat; "Yeah, I'll be leaving tomorrow, just here for two days, but I was hoping to see you both before I went back to Arizona, I'm really glad I caught your mom at home."

Fiona unintentionally found herself staring into space while Mark spoke. She heard his voice, but the actual words were incomprehensible. Mark was quick to recognize her lack of interest which left him a bit uneasy as he began to babble about her having two half-sisters and a half-brother. He said his oldest daughter resembled Fiona and she should connect with her through social media; Lainey Montgomery; well Elaine, but everyone knows her as Lainey. It was either the word sister, or her name itself that snapped Fiona back in the moment. She smiled and politely told Mark she would look her up.

He didn't stay long; and when he got up to leave, Mark kissed her mother on the cheek. It was sweet; brotherly, but sweet. He extended his hand to Fiona. She shook it; and as she did, he pulled her in closer and hugged her around the shoulders with his other arm; again, sweet, appropriate, and genuine. Mom had been right all his time. Mark was a really nice guy; and he cared for them, maybe not as his family, but more than general concern. Fiona found him interesting.

Later, when she questioned her mother; the answer was the same as it had always been.

"We were good friends in high school who shared a moment and made you. We loved one another, still do, but more like brother and sister; we weren't *in* love." Mom told her about the shore house their friends rented the summer after graduation; the celebratory drinking which led to the irresponsible sex; which lead to having to tell Mark three months later she was pregnant just after he met the love of his life; his now wife, Pam. It was an easy decision to let him go live the life he deserved; even though he did do the right thing and offered to be with them; be a father and a husband. Susan knew if she made Mark stay, he would spend his whole life trying to do the right thing, but with a broken heart and she cared for him enough to want him to be happy.

"It really was a no-brainer, Fiona. I had all the love and support I needed from Grams and my sisters. I had no doubt you'd grow up knowing what it was to feel loved and safe and wanted. And, I knew that Mark had fallen in true love with Pam. I have to say, he chose well. I don't know if I could have been so gracious and understanding if I were her. When we told her I was pregnant; she took it like a trooper."

Something about that part of the memory; brought Fiona back into focus, back to reality. She picked up her phone and checked the time. It was only quarter to eleven; she had at least an hour before Nicky came by. She wondered if there was anything new on Lainey's social media accounts and decided to take a look. It had been a while since she had given the Montgomery's a thought. The last time she stalked her half-sister's accounts was when she found the pictures of the yard with the pool and the trampoline and a dog. There was also a 'congrats' post with a picture of Mark and Lainey captioned, "Dad sold another one; someone book us a vacation!" Mark was wearing a polo in the photo just like the one he was wearing the last time Fiona saw him. The logo read *'Red Door Realty'*.

Lainey Montgomery was an avid poster on social media. She proudly shared everything from pictures of her food to positive affirmations. She had strong political opinions for someone so young and to Fiona's surprise, leaned toward a conservative viewpoint much like her own. It certainly wasn't fair to assume, given Lainey's young age of eighteen that she would view politics from a more liberal standpoint. It also wasn't fair to be surprised that she had any political interest at all. Fiona tried her best to remain unimpressed. She feared the more invested she became in Lainey, the more she would want to know her half-sister. Admittedly, she thought Lainey was cool. She was just about to close the screen on her phone when she noticed a picture of an elderly woman and three children. It was posted recently; but given Lainey's propensity for posting the picture was further down in the feed. Fiona clicked on the photo to read the caption. *Rest in Peace Grandma Grace; we will miss you.* She felt her eyes well with tears as she touched the screen with her fingertips. Grandma Grace was gone, and Fiona hadn't even known she existed. For a moment, she wondered why her mother would give her that woman's name; but she also felt a strange sense of pride to be Fiona Grace.

Fiona leaned her head back; and closed her eyes. Part of her wanted to reach out to Lainey but what would she even say?

"Hi, I'm your half-sister from New Jersey. I have wanted absolutely nothing to do with you since the day I found out about you, but I'm feeling sorry for myself today and figured I'd screw up your day too." Probably not the best way to establish that relationship. Besides, if Mark suggested years ago that Fiona look Lainey up; then she must know about Fiona as well and has never tried to make contact either. Fiona supposed they had more in common than either of them knew.

Wanda stirred; stretched and inched her way closer to Fiona from the corner of the couch where she had been sleeping all night.

"You need to go out, girl?" Fiona asked as she patted Wanda on her head. Three staccato thumps from Wanda's tail indicated that indeed she could use a trip to the back yard. "Ok, ok, let's do this." They both stretched again and made their way to the back door. Fiona flipped on the porch light and screamed. Instinctively, Wanda began barking as she slammed her front paws on to the window.

"Holy shit, it's me!" A very startled Nicky stood at the door, frantically trying to identify himself and calm both girls down. Although Fiona was expecting Nicky, it was unfortunate timing that he had stepped up to the door the very moment she turned on the light.

"Hang on," Fiona told him as she reached for Wanda's collar and guided her back down on all fours.

"It's ok sweetie, it's Nicky." She waited until Wanda realized there was no threat before opening the door. Although the dog loved Nicky as her own, she went directly into protective mode when she heard Fiona scream and may have continued to react before recognizing her friend.

Nicky stepped back to let the girls out, "Jesus, you scared the hell out of me."

"Uh, you scared us first," she said, giving him a swat in the arm. Wanda seemed embarrassed as she stood at Nicky's side with her head down, giving him a few apologetic licks on the hand. Nicky reassured his buddy, "It's ok sweet girl, you were doing your job. This is your house, and you were protecting it. I'm so proud of you." He scratched her behind the ears and waved his hand in the direction of the yard. "Go do your thing, Wanda, everything is ok now." He turned to Fiona, "I told you I'd be here around this time."

"Yeah, but your face was unexpectedly right there as I hit the light; it was a horror movie worthy moment."

"I think I'm insulted."

"You know what I mean. I do love your face; just not when it's staring at me like that through the door. I have to say though I'm pretty impressed with Wanda's reaction. Not bad for an old girl. I was feeling sorry for myself and rather sad before thinking that she is getting older and my time with her is running out, but tonight she proved there's a lot of life left in her. I feel so much better."

Nicky agreed, "If I were an intruder, I would have totally thought twice about entering this house. She really hit that door hard; like she meant business for sure. And don't think about Wanda's age, she'll be with us for a while, yet. You'll see." Right on cue, Wanda sidled up to Nicky and looked at him with her crazy mismatched eyes; she no longer seemed so threatening. Once in the house, Wanda stopped in the kitchen for a quick drink of water before returning to the exact spot she had been before; curled up in the corner of the sofa.

As they settled in on either side of Wanda, Nicky asked Fiona if she and her mom enjoyed their dinner.

"Yes, so much. Thank Linda for the goodies; and Mom loved her calamari." Fiona did think the small talk was a little strange considering when Nicky was telling her they needed to talk, he sounded as if he were about to explode. But she was so tired she figured it would be better to let him work it out his way. She didn't want to seem as though she was rushing him because she was desperate for some sleep, even though that's exactly what she was feeling.

Nicky kicked off his shoes and got comfortable. Wanda inched a little closer and put her head on his leg. She sighed deeply and closed her eyes.

"She loves me so much," he gushed as he gently stroked Wanda's ear. "I am her favorite person."

"You smell like food! Of course, she loves you."

"That is *not* why she is snuggling with me and not you."

"You can tell yourself that, but the truth is, women find men who smell like food very sexy." Fiona took a deep exaggerated breath in. "Yum, you smell like oregano and garlic. No wonder Wanda is snuggled so close; I mean I could totally curl up in your lap right now too."

"Funny, Fee… so should I be telling Rob that he has competition?"

Fiona grabbed a cold slice of pizza still left in the box and shoved it in her mouth.

"Ummm, Hmmm," she answered, shaking her head in agreement. Nicky couldn't contain his enthusiasm any longer and finally began telling Fiona all about his lunch with Laurel Cooke, and her interest in finding and speaking with Fiona. She listened politely; and decided to wait until he was finished recounting his afternoon before letting him know, she was not only uninterested, but skeptical.

Laurel Cooke had her own version of the afternoon and couldn't wait to tell TC all about her Jersey excursion. She began with her impression of Nicky and Pete's itself. "He's a great kid; lots of ambition and so much compassion."

TC was much more interested in what Laurel found out about the couple in the photo; but being it wasn't very much and knowing he'd be rather disappointed; she chose to focus on the positive aspects of her afternoon.

"We should drive down for dinner one night, I know you'd love it. The food was surprisingly good for a hole in the wall pizza joint. I loved the tacky decor, and the best part is, its family owned and operated. I got to meet Nick's sister too. Lovely woman."

It had been a long day for TC; the kind he dreaded; meetings and mergers; decisions and debate. He would have preferred spending the day in his workshop, discovering new ways to automate everyday mundane tasks. For a while, he was obsessed with prolonging human life' and the technology he originated had become a controversial topic within several industries. Cooke Industries board of directors advised TC to 'take a break'. from advancing the tech for now. The only thing TC took a break from was telling anyone what he was working on. He did inadvertently stumble across another application for one of his brainstorms, which would improve the quality of life for so many people with physical and even mental detriments. TC had become rather obsessed with running virtual simulations and would have preferred doing just that instead of listening to the board prattle on about the bottom line. However, it was an unfortunate necessity that left TC exhausted; yet his curiosity surrounding the couple in the photo hadn't diminished a bit.

Laurel continued; "I invited the kids here tomorrow. I thought maybe we could get to know Fiona a little before assuming she's interested in our theories. Jaime and Joe are coming over; remember? Should we also see if Charlie and Kay are free as well?"

TC shrugged, "If you want; I'm just having a hard time tolerating Kay these days. Charlie is family, and I thought she was perfect for him; I think I'm reconsidering my first impression."

"Well, it's really not your call, is it? Charlie is in love, and if he's happy, we need to be happy for him; for both of them. Besides, it will be good to have people closer to Fiona's age here; kind of representing us. I think Charlie and Kay will make us look more normal. The last thing I want is to scare her off; thinking we're a couple of psycho stalkers."

TC smiled at his wife; she had the most amazing heart, and he rarely disagreed with anything she wanted. Laurel had this gift for orchestrating scenarios that almost always lent benefit to everyone she involved. It was like she could see all the potential outcomes of any situation and adjusted to create the best one. He called her his intuitive genius. Between Laurel's undeniable gift of human comprehension and understanding and his aptitude for technology and business; the Cooke's were like two sides of the same coin. A rare phenomenon; indeed but certainly not exclusive; and they were determined to prove that.

"I'm looking forward to tomorrow; we could both use a relaxing afternoon with good friends and new acquaintances. But for now; I'm going to bed; care to join me?"

Laurel followed her husband into the bedroom. She knew just by his body language, that he was exhausted, although his implications seemed intimate, he needed to sleep.

"Sleep now, play tomorrow," she whispered as she kissed him on the cheek. TC didn't object.

Nicky had fallen asleep on Fiona's sofa; but not before telling her he had already accepted Laurel's invitation. At first Fiona protested; loudly and emphatically; but after realizing how excited Nicky was about spending tomorrow with the Cooke's; she gave in. Nicky picked up his phone and sent a text, which was answered rather quickly. He messaged Rob that they would be ready by eleven; and to pick them up at his house.

Cooke-Out

Rob Rosen wasn't the kind of guy who believed in fate, destiny; or divine intervention until two years ago when the strangest of circumstances led him to Nick La Salle. He grew up on Long Island, not far from where the Cooke's live, ironically. The Rosen house was always the gathering place for friends; with its large backyard and built-in pool; not to mention the basement equipped with air hockey and a vintage pinball machine.

Rob's parents often travelled for business and he and his sister spent most of their childhood in the care of their grandparents. They were a close and loving family who believed in supporting one another; their hopes, dreams, lifestyles and career choices. Rob's grandparents were all too accommodating when they were asked to move in and help raise Rob and his younger sister Sarah when their parents' business began to grow. If there is in fact a perfect childhood; Rob and Sarah experienced it.

During his first year in college; Rob had taken a part time job driving for a car service. It was mostly airport runs and pre-nuptial pub crawls, but he realized quickly that he had a true calling as a driver. Rob felt most comfortable behind the wheel of a town car; knowing he was responsible for the safety of his charges. He was proud of his zero-incident record; and began to save his money in hopes of buying his own car, or maybe two. It didn't take long before Rob was registering his own car service, *Safe Travels* as a new business.

While on a run to Atlantic City, one Saturday afternoon; Rob's car experienced some mechanical issues. He managed to get his car off the highway and drive to a safe place before it broke down completely. Rob called a towing service and then to one of his drivers to bring another car; so his customers could resume their trip. He had noticed the pizza place across the street from the lot where he managed to settle the car and asked his clients if they'd prefer to wait inside. They agreed. While waiting to be seated, Rob spotted Nick across the bar. There was something about him that made it impossible for Rob to ignore. He walked over to Nick and explained his situation.

"Pardon me; I'm sorry to interrupt, you seem very busy. My car broke down across the street and I have my clients here with me; would it be ok for us to wait in here while a replacement car is delivered?" He sounded very professional for someone that just got weak in the knees at the very first glance of Nick La Salle; dirty apron and all.

"Oh, man, that sucks. Look, I don't know much about cars, but I do know how to make people feel better." Nick's smile completely did Rob in. He tried his best to remain cool and professional as Nicky pushed open the door leading from the bar into the dining room. "Come on in; let's see if we can't make your day a bit brighter."

Rob motioned to the couple still standing by the front door to follow him and Nick into the dining area. Nick seated them at a table on the far wall, under the plastic grapevines and vintage amber colored sconces. He asked if anyone would like something to drink and the couple eagerly ordered midday cocktails, explaining that they don't get a lot of days off together, and were on their way to Atlantic City, so why not start the party now? Nick looked at Rob; who became instantly and visibly flustered as he ordered a soda; "I'm driving."

Nick returned with their drinks and ducked into the kitchen. Within minutes he was back with several appetizers for his three guests to share.

"I didn't know what you'd like, so I brought a little of everything, on the house. But, please let me know if there's something else you'd like." The young woman picked up on the obvious vibe between Nick and Rob. She would have liked to think the VIP treatment was for her and her boyfriend, but it was evident that Nick was out to impress their driver. After her first cocktail, she broke the ice for them.

As Nick leaned over the table asking if everything was to their liking, the woman spoke, "Everything is wonderful, thank you, and I hope I'm not being too presumptuous, but you two would make an adorable couple! I think you should exchange numbers before we have to leave. Our car should be here shortly, so if I'm right, and I think I am, you two better figure out how to stay in touch. Better yet, make a date!"

Her boyfriend looked mortified; "Wine makes her chatty; sorry guys."

Nick laughed out loud.

"No apologies necessary; and I agree." He glanced at Rob who basically wanted to hide under the red and white checked tablecloth. "Would it be cool if I took your number? I don't get much time off, but maybe we could work something out. You could always come back here and let me cook dinner for you."

Rob Rosen knew that the best decision he'd ever made was giving Nick his number that day. Two years later, they were still together; and in love. Their relationship just made sense. When Nick asked Rob to drive to Long Island with him and Fiona; he had no idea that Rob had planned a special date for the two of them. It was going to be a surprise; now it will have to wait. This trip to the Cooke's seemed so important to Nick and Rob didn't want to disappoint him.

At eleven a.m. sharp, Rob pulled into Nick's driveway. His business had been reduced to one car and one driver, Rob himself. He still accommodated his regular clients, but since moving to New Jersey to be near Nick, Rob had been giving driving lessons full time to pay the bills. But he kept his original town car in pristine condition and still enjoyed driving her more than anything.

Fiona and Nick walked over to the car, and Rob opened the back door for Fiona. She wasn't sure if that was a residual response from his work or if he was really just that much of a gentleman; she leaned toward the latter. As soon as Rob opened the door, Fiona could smell the coffee waiting for her in the cup holder. She turned to Rob.

"You are an angel, you know that?"

"I do. And I already know of a few decent places to stop on the way if you have to pee, so enjoy your coffee."

"You thought of everything!"

"It's my job, ma'am," Rob teased.

Fiona settled in the back seat while Nick joined Rob up front. He adjusted the radio station; and took a long sip of his own coffee while Rob began to navigate through their little town toward the highway.

"We should be there in about an hour and a half, provided we don't have to stop more than once," Rob announced as he peered back at Fiona through the rear-view mirror.

"Haha, sure, blame the girl for having to stop to pee. I bet one of you has to go before I do."

"Wager?" Nick challenged.

Rob laughed.

"Let's just get there, ok kids? Honestly, don't make me regret this."

Admittedly, Fiona was anxious about going to the Cooke's. She wasn't excited like Nick, or indifferent like Rob; but apprehensive and skeptical. Although she was aware that it was her they wanted to meet, she was doing this more for Nick than anything; and she was sure Rob felt the same way. When Fiona and Nick were younger, she would imagine the day when she would have to share him with someone. She knew eventually they would both find people to love and who loved them; romantically. Nick deserved the very best that humanity had to offer; and she feared her reaction if he fell in love with someone not worthy of his kind heart and beautiful soul. He had a few short-lived romances in the past; but before she could find a way to express her concerns; Nick would end the relationship, citing the very same issues Fiona noticed as his best friend. Then, Nick and Rob met. It was several weeks before Nicky asked Fiona to meet him. He was sure Rob was 'the one' and Fiona's impression would either confirm or contrast that of his own. Either way, Nick knew the two most important people in his life; outside of his family had to meet; sooner than later.

Her impression was surprising, not only to Nick, but Fiona herself. Rob won her over almost immediately. Fiona loved Rob's quiet confidence, his style and manners. He had a great smile, dressed well and could hold a conversation on just about any subject. She remembered thinking; if she were to hand pick someone for Nick, she couldn't have done any better than Rob. Hell, if he were straight, she'd totally date him.

"We're about ten minutes out; you made it with no stops," Rob called back to Fiona who was still sort of daydreaming in the back seat.

"Oh, actually, could we stop? I mean, I really don't want to walk into Cooke's house and be like, 'nice to meet you, where's the bathroom?'"

"Seriously, Fee? we're almost there." Nick was visibly excited and eager to get to the Cooke's, but Rob took pity on Fiona and her request was granted. He pulled into a fast-food restaurant parking lot just a few minutes from the Cooke's neighborhood. She jumped out and ran toward the side door.

"Hurry up!" Nick shouted out the window

"That's not going to make her go any faster, you know?" Rob was always the voice of reason. "I'm sure she's just as excited as you are, but maybe a little nervous too. You've already met Laurel Cooke. Poor Fiona has absolutely no idea as to what to expect. Cut her a little slack today, ok?"

"You have a point. I wasn't thinking about her; just myself which is totally unfair."

"Yeah, considering if it weren't for Fiona, you would have never met Laurel or been invited to her home."

"OK, I get it, I'm kind of being an ass."

"Kind of?"

Within minutes, Fiona was safe and sound in the car, and they were back en route. Nick apologized for rushing Fiona, which in her opinion was totally unnecessary. She knew Rob told Nick to do so. As they pulled onto the street; Fiona wondered if they had the right directions.

"Um, are you sure we're in the right neighborhood?"

Rob checked the GPS on his phone.

"Yeah, this is the only Ryder Drive in town. We're in the right place; and that's the house," he said, pointing to the right just ahead of them. Rob pulled the car up to the curb in front of the house just as Laurel appeared from the side, struggling to wheel a trash can down to the street.

"There she is!" Nicky squealed. "That's Laurel Cooke, and she's taking her own trash out."

"Jesus, Nick, calm down, don't make me sedate you." Rob teased.

Nicky jumped out of the car and offered his assistance to Laurel, leaving Rob and Fiona behind. Fiona leaned over the front seat; "Were you expecting something different? Because I was. This house, this neighborhood all seems so normal."

"Yeah," Rob agreed. "Very un-billionaire-ish."

Nick's struggle with the trash can on wheels was nothing short of comical. His nervous energy was evident, and Laurel felt it necessary to try and put him at ease.

"Nick, thank you so much, I fight with that damn thing all the time, and lose. It looks like you got the best of it today. I appreciate it, believe me."

Fiona opened her door and got out of the car. She stood still for a minute, hoping Nick would collect himself long enough to make introductions; but he was once again, starstruck and had appeared to have lost his mind. Fiona gave a sheepish wave in Laurel's direction and cleared her throat.

"Hi, um, I'm Fiona Lasher."

Laurel walked down to the car.

"Fiona, it's great to meet you; thanks so much for coming," she politely extended her hand, and Fiona shook it. Laurel seemed a little confused and finally asked. "Who drove?"

"Oh, Rob. Oh my God, where are my manners?" Nicky tried desperately to pull it together, but his excitement had overwhelmed his ability to function normally.

"Is Rob joining us?" Laurel asked

"Well, I didn't want to assume that it was ok to bring a plus one, and Rob offered to drive because he knows the area, so he's going to go visit with his sister for the afternoon. She's only a few minutes from here. Rob actually grew up on Long Island."

Laurel opened the passenger door and stuck her head inside the car.

"Rob, I assume?"

"You have assumed correctly," he answered. "It's nice to meet you, Mrs Cooke."

"Laurel," she corrected. "Rob, why don't you go get your sister and bring her back with you? We have plenty of food and would love for the both of you to join us."

Rob was so calm and confident.

"Thank you, Sarah would love it. And frankly, it would be better if I were here to keep Nick in line. I love him, but he can be a little overwhelming, especially when he has an audience. I'll be back shortly and thank you again, Mrs Cooke."

As Rob drove off to pick up his sister, Laurel ushered her other two guests into the back yard, through the side gate. The front of the house was certainly deceiving; although perfectly manicured, it was fairly non-descript and blended in well with the other homes on the street. However, what lay beyond the side gate was another story entirely. Fiona felt like she had just stepped into a fairy tale! Her first thought was, *I want to live like this, someday,* Fiona couldn't be sure she didn't say that out loud.

The pool was certainly the focal point of the yard, which was vastly larger than one could imagine from a first impression from the front of the house. It was perfectly framed in grey stone; Fiona wasn't entirely sure what type, but it was gorgeous. The far side was walled with the same stone, and at closer inspection; she noticed the built-in benches along the wall; each flanked with giant potted plants. To the left of where they were standing was a waterfall, and to the right, of course, a basketball net and diving board. If the pool wasn't brilliant enough; the outdoor kitchen and lounge area would certainly take anyone's breath away.

Fiona managed to speak. She turned to Laurel who was asking Nicky to text Rob and have Sarah bring a swimsuit.

"Oh, your yard is astonishing! It belongs in a magazine."

Laurel laughed; "It was. Several years ago, we hired a friend's son to do some landscaping upgrades back here. He had just started his own company after working in landscaping since he was mowing lawns at the age of twelve. He asked us if he could document the work with photos for his marketing materials and of course, we were happy to help. So the photos were not only used for his website portfolio, but were posted on his social media pages. He's a smart kid and follows several home and garden publications; one of which took an interest in our yard pics. They contacted Kurt; my friend's son," she clarified. "And asked if he'd be interested in being interviewed. It was such an amazing opportunity for him; and the magazine had no idea the photos were of our yard. Once they found out; the interview turned into a feature! Needless to say; Kurt is a busy guy these days."

"I love everything about that story," Fiona admitted. "I don't follow every Laurel Cooke or Cooke Industries story like Nicky, but he has told me time and again that there are so many like this one; written about you and your husband. You two are charmed, that's very impressive." As she continued to look around the back yard, discovering something amazing with every passing glance; Fiona found herself feeling awestruck and comfortable at the same time. It was an unfamiliar sensation she hadn't counted on.

Laurel didn't want to have that conversation with Fiona just yet. She simply smiled and offered to introduce Fiona to her friends and of course TC. They made their way from the garden area to the outdoor kitchen where everyone had gathered; drinks in hand and engaged in conversation. TC emerged from the open French doors with several trays of grill ready food balanced on his forearms. A young man jumped up and offered his help, taking the top two trays from the stack.

After the polite introductions, Fiona made her way to an empty lounge chair apart from most of the guests. She figured it would be best to remain an observer until Rob came back with Sarah; then she'd have someone to talk to. Nicky had already joined in the festivities as if he knew these people for his entire life. Fiona loved that about him and being a rather self-conscious person; she was grateful for him and his ability to make friends and fit in no matter where they were or who they encountered. Still, she found herself in extraordinary admiration today. It takes true talent to fit in so quickly here; in a billionaire's home; with their likely billionaire friends.

As she watched Nicky slowly and methodically take over at the grill under the guise of showing TC a few tricks; Fiona began to relax. She sat back a bit in her lounge chair and took off her sunglasses, hoping to get a little tan on her face while she sat poolside in this amazing resort worthy yard. Within seconds, a shadow blocked the sun from Fiona's face. She put her sunglasses back on and looked up to see a young woman, about her age standing over her. She was taller than Fiona with bleach blonde hair and long neon orange fingernails. Fiona's first impression was that this girl would be so pretty if she wasn't trying so hard. Before she could say anything, the young woman spoke; "Hello, who are you? Do you work for the Cooke's? Are you related ?" The young woman held her cell phone in her hand, flat out as if she were waiting to record Fiona's response. In reality, it was probably her long nails that were responsible for the awkward phone posturing.

"Oh, hey, I'm ummm Fiona; it's nice to meet you," she paused, hoping the woman would

at least reciprocate and tell Fiona her name, but she just stood waiting for Fiona to finish answering her questions with her head curiously tilted to one side. Fiona thought she looked a little like Wanda when she heard a weird noise. Not for any other reason than to try and break the awkwardness; she continued, "I was invited; well, my friends and I were, by Laurel. No, I'm not related, nor do I work for the Cooke's. And your name is?"

"I'm Kay," she answered, offering her hand in such a position, Fiona wasn't sure if she was expected to kiss it, or shake it.

"Well, again, it's great to meet you Kay." Fiona knew it wasn't exactly proper etiquette to not ask Kay about herself in return, but she feared if she asked, Kay would spend more time answering than Fiona was willing to listen. So, instead, she just smiled stupidly and as luck would have it, Fiona spotted Rob and Sarah coming into the yard from the side gate. "Oh, excuse me; my friends are here." She jumped up and practically sprinted over to Sarah and Rob.

Sarah met Fiona half-way and almost knocked her off balance when she hugged her.

"Oh my God! It's been forever, I am so glad to see you! And what the hell is all this about?" Sarah asked, lowering her voice.

"I'm not sure; but I am so happy you're here. Come sit with me. Besides you guys and Nicky, I really don't know anyone," Fiona whispered to Sarah as they made their way back to the lounge chairs. "Well, except for that blonde girl over by the bar; she spoke to me; not sure why and really not sure yet if she's even friendly or how she fits in here. So, yeah; let's hope Nicky is getting the scoop for us." Fiona gestured toward the kitchen area where Nicky had just about completely taken over the grill and was evidently charming everyone around him, including TC Cooke himself.

The girls sat down together away from the group while Rob went over to let Nicky know he had returned. The scene was typical' with the guys near the grill and the women seated near the bar and dining table. Sarah and Fiona chatted about their expectations of this gathering as opposed to what it was in reality. The guests all seemed very comfortable; and not at all pretentious; well other than Kay and her neon nails. Sarah spotted Laurel and another woman walking toward them.

"Heads up," she whispered.

The two women approached; Laurel was carrying a tray with drinks and the other balanced two trays of snacks; one in each hand. Fiona immediately noticed Laurel's friend was adorably petite; and physically the exact opposite of Laurel herself. She couldn't have been more than five feet tall; with dark hair, cut in a bob falling just around her chin. She wore little round sunglasses; in complete contrast to Laurel's oversized frames; jean shorts and pale blue sleeveless collared polo. She carefully placed the trays on a side table between Fiona's chair and a little potted palm tree, which Fiona later found out was actually a banana tree.

The women sat down across from Fiona and Sarah; and introduced themselves.

"Hi! I'm Jaime; and you must be Sarah and Fiona." Both girls smiled and nodded. She offered up the snacks and asked if there was something else they'd prefer.

"I'm sure Laurel has whatever you might be craving somewhere in that kitchen. She tends to over buy even for small get-togethers like today."

Sarah reached for the cheese and crackers; "This is perfect; thank you." Fiona thought to herself, *Oh, to be eighteen again and not have a worry in the world.* She admired Sarah's ease and confidence in the company of strangers. She was more like Nicky in that respect than her own brother, who had now joined the grill group but was standing quietly to the side in complete admiration of his boyfriend and his ability to work a crowd.

Laurel spoke; "Fiona, can I get you anything before I plop my tired ass down for a bit?" Fiona laughed; and realized Laurel's humor had relieved some of her anxiety; she joked back, "Plop away, I'm good!"

The four women made small talk about the weather, food and their dream vacations. Sarah kept looking over her shoulder at the pool. No one was swimming; but she was eager to get into one of the oversized floating rafts and work on her tan. Laurel noticed her distraction.

"Did you bring a suit?"

Sarah lifted her T-shirt exposing a floral bathing suit underneath, "Yep!" she exclaimed, knowing she was about to have her wish come true.

"Be our guest!" Laurel gestured toward the pool. "That's what it's there for, please enjoy. But, fair warning, as soon as the first person goes in, everyone usually joins. You won't be alone for long. Enjoy the peace while you have it."

Sarah kicked off her sneakers and quickly pulled off her shirt and shorts.

"That's OK, as long as I get one of those rafts," and with those words, she jumped in.

"Fiona, I am so sorry again. I screwed up by not mentioning the pool when I spoke to Nicky about you coming to hang out with us today. I'm pretty sure I have something that would fit you if you don't mind borrowing a stranger's clothes." Laurel was aware there was at least a two-size difference between her and Fiona but offered anyway.

"Oh, I'm ok for now, thank you. And I don't mind the borrowing thing; so maybe later I could take you up on that?" Fiona turned to watch Sarah climb up into the raft and settle herself without capsizing. She looked like a postcard from a tropical island resort.

"Whenever you'd like." Laurel sensed Fiona's envy for her young friend. "Just let me know when you're ready. We have two more rafts in the shed, so that too can be you!"

"Thanks, I appreciate it. But would it be ok if we just got down to it; I mean, I'm all for getting to know you and your friends, but you have to know that my curiosity is killing me. Nicky told me that you wanted to meet me and ask me about the incident almost five years ago with the little boy and my dog. No offense but it all seems a little crazy; why now?" Fiona surprised both women with her candor. They had her pegged as quiet and shy and were unsure as to how to approach the conversation. Laurel seemed relieved that Fiona broke the proverbial ice.

Jaime stood. "OK ladies, this is my queue; I will leave the two of you to chat."

"Please stay." Fiona looked up at Jaime who didn't stand much taller than Laurel seated. "I'm totally fine with you being here too. I mean, there's really nothing personal or secretive about that day." She wanted to tell Jaime that she felt more comfortable with her than Laurel but decided to keep that to herself.

"OK, but if at any point you want me to find a better place to be, just give me a sign. Or just tell me to get lost. That would work too." Jaime sat back down and put her legs straight out in front of her on the lounge chair. She leaned back and took a deep breath in; and on the exhale, she made that sound; the one everyone makes when they're relaxed. "Ahhhh – oooooo!"

Laurel slid her own chair closer to Fiona's. She tucked her legs up underneath her and slouched to one side.

"OK, here we go. First of all, forgive me again for procrastinating. I didn't want to intimidate you by jumping in your personal life only a few minutes after meeting you. I, well, we got the impression that you were more of a private person."

Fiona laughed.

"I'm not. I'm actually very outgoing; I just have this God-awful job that I hate. It stifles me; makes me feel dead inside, and I think I just needed a minute to remember who I am outside of that hellhole." She continued, to the bewilderment of Laurel and Jaime; Fiona was indeed very outgoing and outspoken as well. "You know, I was just about to tell my mother last night that I am ready to quit, but Nicky and his 'Oh my God, you'll never guess where we're going...' sort of distracted me."

"How long have you and Nicky been friends?" Jaime asked. The continued small talk was unintentional; she was genuinely interested.

Fiona was all too happy to answer, as their story was a really good one.

"Well, our mom's met when they were pregnant with us, so I'd have to say more than forever. We live around the corner from one another, so we grew up in each others homes; went to school together, even vacationed together with our families."

"That is so cool. So, really you two are more like siblings, yes?"

"Exactly. And being I don't have any siblings of my own, I'm glad the Universe blessed me with Nicky. Oh, well I just lied. I do have siblings, two sisters and a brother but we have never met. Long story; maybe for another time."

Laurel was encouraged by Fiona's remark, *maybe for another time*. She took it as a positive sign that Fiona wasn't so uncomfortable as to want to leave and never see them all again.

"Fiona, do you still have contact with the young man in the photo? I asked Nick and he deferred to you. He said it wasn't his story to tell. I have to say, I admired him for that. He has a lot of respect for you; obviously."

"He's the best! But honestly, it is his story as well; I wouldn't have minded if he did tell you. So, what exactly do you want to know about Carter?"

"I did know his name is Carter, but that's all I know about him. Anything beyond his name will be news to me."

She rolled her eyes, but no one could tell from behind her sunglasses. Fiona continued; "Carter Wyatt. He was my boyfriend a long time ago, and Nicky's friend," she sighed deeply indicating her touch of melancholy at the very thought of what once was. "I'm actually surprised Nicky didn't offer more of the Carter story. He does have a tendency to enjoy the sound of his own voice."

"Oh, I can relate. TC can be the same way."

Fiona laughed, "And they say women talk too much. I'm sorry, but in my experience, the men can certainly hold their own."

"So, you two were a couple when that photo was taken?" Laurel asked as she pulled up the picture on her phone. "Is Carter a talker as well?"

"No, actually, we had been broken up for several months by then, and no, Carter is rather quiet. The day that photo was taken, he and his idiot friends happened to be in the parking lot of Pete's. Wanda spotted the boy and went running to the road. I had no choice but to follow her. Otherwise, I would have done anything to avoid having to see him and his friends that day. It was a total coincidence that we were both there."

"I don't believe much in coincidences," Laurel said as she handed her phone to Fiona. "If that wasn't you in the picture, how would you describe the couple?"

Fiona took the phone from Laurel's outstretched hand. She quickly glanced at the photo she had stared at a million times since it was posted. She knew exactly what Laurel was seeing, and why she'd assume they were still a couple on that day. Fiona gave Laurel her phone back; took her sunglasses off and placed them on top of her head. She thought this was one of those conversations better had with actual eye contact. Somehow, it would lend to its honesty; it's authenticity. She presumed her audience; like others before them, would dismiss her feelings as nothing more than the residual feelings of her first love.

Fiona leaned even further back in her lounge chair; took a few deep breaths and grabbed a drink from the tray Laurel had brought over.

"Are these adult beverages, by any chance?"

Jaime answered her; "Oh, yeah. They're loaded."

Fiona took a huge sip of her bright orange drink through the yellow and white striped straw.

"So good," she said. "It tastes like vacation."

"I know this whole situation is weird, Fiona. I appreciate you indulging me in my curiosity. I think drinks are just what we all need right now. We can talk about Carter a little later." Laurel chose a glass of her own and knocked back almost half its contents in one anxiety driven gulp. All three women giggled; clinked their glasses together and finished their drinks. Laurel turned toward the grill area and held up her empty glass, shaking it to make the ice cubes clink against the sides. "Babe," she called out to TC. "A little help."

TC walked over to his wife, bent down and kissed her on the top of her head. He picked up the tray with the empty glasses.

"Another round, ladies?" TC was a very endearing man; the kind of person you want to know. He had an energy about him that was infectious; and his smile was so genuine, Fiona found herself searching for something to say that would make him smile again, just to absorb his warmth. It did occur to her that she may have a bit of a crush on him and if she did in fact say anything, it might just be ridiculous rambling. However, that orange drink had kicked in and lowered any inhibitions she may have had.

"My compliments to the bartender; they are amazing," she said, gesturing to the tray of empty glasses. Well, it certainly wasn't quote-worthy, but her comment did make TC smile, so mission accomplished, and with a low embarrassment factor.

"I'm glad to see you aren't opposed to day drinking, Fiona. We don't do it often, but when we do; it's nice to know everyone is enjoying themselves. Ladies, I will return with your refills shortly." TC turned on his heels and headed toward the house, butler style.

"He's kind of awesome," Fiona exclaimed, trying not to sound as awkward as she felt. Laurel and Jaime agreed with her sentiment. She figured it was time to get back to the subject of the day, but before diving back in the deep end, so to speak, she turned her attention to Sarah; still floating aimlessly around the pool by herself.

"Sarah is so relaxed, I'm envious."

Jaime giggled.

"She looks like an ad for sunscreen."

"Yes, she does, I would totally buy that brand," Laurel agreed.

Fiona took a second to recollect; and mentally ready herself to tell her new friends the story of Carter Wyatt. She couldn't help but smile, just thinking about how they met.

"Laurel, I'm not sure what you're looking for, or expecting from this story; but if at any time, you realize it's not what you had hoped for; just stop me; otherwise, I may talk forever, especially if we keep drinking."

Laurel assured her that she had no hidden agenda; and her story was, no matter how it went, exactly what she wanted to hear. TC had returned with fresh drinks. He sensed the change in energy, from just a few minutes ago when the women were relaxed. The levity had morphed to an intensity that seemed palpable. He left the tray; and simply placed his hand lovingly on Laurel's shoulder before returning to his other guests.

Fiona smiled and readied herself.

"Two weeks before my fifteenth birthday; my mom and I went to the salon to get our hair cut. My usual stylist wasn't there so they put me with a new girl. I was just getting a trim, so it didn't occur to me to care until she told me that my hair was the color of dirty dishwater. I remember instantly feeling like an ugly freak. OK, let's take into consideration that I was an emotional teenage disaster; but my feelings were crushed with one stupid comment from someone who really didn't matter to begin with." Fiona sensed that her audience was politely listening, but a bit confused. "Please, stay with me, I'll get there in a minute."

"We're with you," Laurel assured.

"Well, on our way home, I begged my mother for highlights for my birthday. At first she said no; but I told her what the stylist had said about my hair color, and eventually she agreed. She did say we wouldn't be going back to that girl to have them done. Anyway, when we got home, I wanted to tell Nicky that my mom said yes to highlights, because I told him everything, I still do, so I ran down the street to Pete's. I was sweaty and out of breath when I got to the back door to the kitchen. As I was running in, Carter was walking out to take trash to the dumpster. Yes, as you may have guessed, we collided! The trash bags went flying from his hand and I fell back right on my ass."

She waited a minute while Jaime and Laurel finished laughing. Fiona took a long swill of her second cocktail and continued, Suddenly, she was ten years in the past; reliving the best time of her life.

"Damn it!" Fiona yelled as she struggled to her feet. She looked up into the face of a stranger who was obviously annoyed with their first meeting.

"Jesus, what's your hurry? You are going to get me fired!" Carter began picking up the trash that had been strewn about when one of the bags opened as it hit the ground.

"Wait, you work here?"

"Well, it's either that or I enjoy wearing dirty aprons and taking other people's trash out for kicks."

Fiona wrinkled her brow and rolled her eyes.

"Since when?"

"Not that I owe you an answer, but this is my first week, so thanks for making me look incompetent." He had collected the debris and was walking toward the dumpster when Nicky poked his head out of the back door.

"What the hell Fiona? Why are you yelling?"

Fiona pointed toward Carter.

"He knocked me on my ass." Of course in hindsight, Fiona realized her dramatics made it seem as though Carter struck her to the ground intentionally. She was certainly not concerned with preserving his job or his reputation.

Nicky just shook his head. He was all too familiar with Fiona's flair for exaggerated expression and although he hadn't known Carter for very long, he couldn't imagine the guy just throwing a girl to the ground. Without a word, Carter walked back inside the kitchen and got back to work.

Fiona made a face.

"So where did he come from?"

Nicky told her they met at a party two weekends ago. They got to talking and Carter told Nicky he was looking for a job. He was turning seventeen in six months and wanted money to buy a car. As luck would have it, Nicky's mom had just mentioned wanting to hire someone in the kitchen a few nights a week and on weekends. Nicky told Carter to come in and meet his mom who hired him on the spot. He also told Fiona that Carter was a good guy and they had become friends, so she needed to stop being weird. Carter would be hanging out with them as well as working at Pete's, so she'd better get used to him.

In truth, Fiona's first impression was that Nicky and Carter were into each other; so, she swore to be good; and get to know Carter before passing any more judgement. She went on to tell Nicky all about her pending highlights and all the other changes she wanted to make in her appearance once she officially turned fifteen. Her excitement lasted just long enough for Mrs La Salle to notice Nicky's absence. She stuck her head out of the kitchen door.

"Oh, hey Fee, how are ya' honey?"

"I'm great! I'm getting highlights for my birthday," she yelled over her shoulder as she set off through the side lot on her way back home.

Nicky turned to his mother.

"Why are girls so weird?" Mrs La Salle told her son she had no good answer for that question. They both returned to the kitchen and Nick apologized to Carter for Fiona's attempt at causing trouble. Carter smiled. "She's adorable."

"Just, no! Off limits man, not her."

Carter seemed perplexed.

"Are you into her? Cause, I thought…" his voice trailed off as if in search of the right way to complete that sentence.

Nicky clarified.

"Oh, haha, no, you thought right the first time. I'm not into her, she's like my sister. I'm kind of protective when it comes to Fee, and besides, I think she thinks your gay too," he teased.

Carter just couldn't seem to get Fiona off his mind. He knew there was an almost two-year age difference, but it didn't seem to matter, and he secretly hoped he would see her again soon. Each time he was working a shift in the kitchen: he found himself lingering just a few extra minutes outside when he took the trash out, thinking that lightning may strike twice, and she'd come running through the parking lot like the day they met. Two weeks had gone by; and Carter couldn't stand it any longer. Despite Nick's warning, he decided to ask about Fiona.

"Um, so Nick, I know you said off limits, but what's up with your girl Fiona?" The boys were standing at the counter in Pete's kitchen, prepping for the Friday night dinner rush. Nick ignored his friend's question for a few minutes. Finally, he turned to Carter; and took pity on his new friend.

"Tomorrow is her birthday. There's a party at her house; bring a gift. I'll meet you here around seven; we can go over together. I'll get Linda to cover your shift."

"Cool."

Two drinks in and Jaime squealed.

"Oh my God, you guys were so cute. I love this story, tell us more, please?" she glanced over to where the guys were still gathered; trying to imagine Nick La Salle ten years ago in the throes of teenage angst.

Laurel chimed in; "I just need to know; did you get your highlights?"

Jaime added.

"Oh, and did he bring a gift?"

Fiona was pleasantly surprised with their interest; and felt inspired to continue in spite of her suspicions that the intrigue was primarily fueled by alcohol consumption.

"Yes to the highlights; and yes to the gift. He brought me flowers," she smiled; remembering the feeling of getting flowers from a boy for the first time. She told the women that having her hair done made her feel as though she had finally transitioned from a child to a woman. But that paled in comparison to having a boy bring flowers for her birthday.

"Roses?" Jaime assumed

"Ha; well, no. He was sixteen and working for minimum wage and saving for a car. No roses: they were an assortment of all white flowers with three calla lilies. Really pretty. I remember my mom being impressed, so I knew they were nice. Remember; I had nothing to compare them to. I couldn't have recognized crappy flowers from nice ones; flowers were flowers before that night."

"OK, but still, kind of romantic; right?" Jaime was gushing a bit. Fiona could tell she had a sweet story of her own as she seemed to be relating on such a personal level. It made Fiona feel less like a lovestruck child and more like one of the girls.

"It was romantic. I also got my first real kiss that night. It was totally unexpected; but I'll get to that in a minute. Anyway, the thing about Carter that made me take notice was his ability to find his place among my friends and family. He and Nicky served food; cleaned up; and Carter definitely worked the room. My aunt couldn't believe we had just met. He literally came to my party as my future boyfriend; like he knew we would be together. I know that sounds creepy; but it wasn't. At the end of the party, he and Nicky were ready to leave. Carter asked me if he could see me for a minute in the kitchen. I followed him in, and he opened the back door. "Come outside with me?" So, I did. Wanda, my dog came out with us; and Carter sat on my back step petting her. I sat down next to him. We just sat there for ten minutes, not saying anything. I remember feeling like I belonged there; in that moment, with Carter. Finally, he turned toward me; and just stared into my eyes. That's when I noticed how insanely green they were. I stared back; not sure what else I was supposed to do. Then he kissed me. I felt that kiss everywhere. After a few minutes, he stood up and thanked me for having him at my party. We went back inside; Carter got Nick and they left. I swear my entire life changed that night.

"Oh my God, Fiona, you're killing us here." Jaime sat up and pulled herself to the edge of her chair. "So, he didn't ask to see you again, or anything? He just left?"

"Yes! I was really confused too; but I felt like if I never saw him again, that moment on my back steps was so worth it," Fiona sighed. "However, I found out later that he wanted to talk to Nicky first before asking to see me. I guess he wanted his blessing," she joked. "That next weekend, Carter left a note in my mailbox asking if I would be interested in seeing a movie together. The note said 'check yes or no' with little drawn boxes next to each option. It was really cute. I checked yes and put the note back in my mailbox. The following day there was another one that said.

"See you at six."

One of the guys near the grill shouted into the yard.

"Food is ready!" His exclamation pulled the women from Fiona's past into the present.

Jaime stared down into her empty cocktail glass.

"Girls, we really should eat something."

Laurel and Fiona noticed their own empty glasses and burst out in laughter. Laurel agreed.

"Yeah, food is a great idea. Are you ladies good with taking a lunch break?"

"We better," Fiona agreed, feeling grateful for the temporary detour off of Memory Lane.

The Seduction of Carter Wyatt

Fiona wished she knew the details surrounding their breakup. She made light of that particular part of the story when asked to recount by Jaime and Laurel. Fiona alluded to the sudden lack of interest on Carter's part being her fault.

"I think I may have been holding on too tightly. It was our first love; first relationship and I should have known it wouldn't last; they almost never do." Fiona spent too much time filling in the blanks with every imaginable scenario; wishing she and Carter had the opportunity to break up properly; with explanation and closure. The truth was; Carter's immaturity lent to his ability to be easily influenced. He made so many bad decisions. He loved her, and never thought his choices would upend her life; their relationship until it was too late.

"I'm dying for pizza! Wanna go to Pete's tonight?" Carter asked. His friends, Eddie and Keith both looked at him like he had lost his mind. Neither answered him but went back to working on their current project.

Carter Wyatt had an aptitude for fixing cars. Not only was he mechanically inclined, but he loved it. Everything about being in a garage; the smell, the grease, the challenge of rebuilding an engine, or the thrill of hunting down original parts to complete the life-sized jigsaws that lay in pieces waiting to be restored. He and his friends spent many Saturday afternoons in Mr Daly's garage. It was a dream come true for this group of amateur grease monkeys. Mr Daly was a car aficionado; a collector and a high-end vehicle specialist for the past thirty years. Having five daughters not at all interested in mechanics; he was all too happy to have Carter and his friends hang around the garage in their spare time. He affectionately called the boys, his T-Birds, referring to characters from the movie Grease. Mr Daly found his reference more witty

and more amusing than the boys did.

He had a particular interest in Carter, who had been dating his middle daughter, Meg for the past few years. Mr. Daly was determined to make

Carter his apprentice and groom him to take over his business someday. But of course, he would first have to convince Carter to marry Meg because that's what she wanted more than anything. Somehow he knew it was immoral to continue to bribe Carter to stick around; but what Meg wanted, Meg got, and she wanted Carter.

The seduction began several years ago when the Daly's met Carter and his friends at a swap meet. Mr Daly had taken his latest restoration to the car show; and asked three of his daughters to accompany him for the day. He knew pretty girls attracted men, and Mr Daly was not above using his daughters to drum up interest for his business. Carter, Eddie and Keith were in awe of the Daly entry in the car show; a fully restored 1974 Ford Mustang Mach One. The young men were more enthralled with the car than the girls; and Mr Daly knew they didn't have the resources to be buyers or even clients; hell. it would be shocking if they drove any car at all, never mind a classic or luxury. However, Meg fell in love at first sight; and made it obvious to not only Carter, but his friends and her family as well. Mr Daly quickly and methodically befriended the boys. He enticed them with an invite to see his personal garage and showroom.

"Come by any time, guys, I think you'll flip out when you see my setup."

Ironically, Mr Daly's efforts to get the boys to his home were primarily driven by Meg's interest in Carter, who of all three was the least interested and the most skeptical. He preferred to spend all his free time with his girlfriend, and although he had a healthy interest in cars and an aptitude for mechanics, Carter was also great at reading people, and something seemed 'off' about the Daly family. Nevertheless, it couldn't hurt to check out Mr Daly's garage and Eddie and Keith were already hooked.

Each time the guys visited Mr Daly's garage, his middle daughter made sure she had a reason or two to walk out from the house. His four bay garage was loaded with tools, toys and technology; fascinating the teens as if they were touring a museum. They found themselves looking forward to the next time they could spend the day interacting with the mechanical apparat and picking Mr Daly's brain. They also found themselves in anticipation of Meg's next appearance in the garage, as her attire became increasingly more alluring. Meg played the gracious host and brought cold drinks and snacks to her father and his new young friends. In reality, Meg Daly wasn't the type to serve anyone; but more the type to expect everyone to serve her. However, Carter was a tough nut to crack, and she kept creating ways to capture his attention.

One particular afternoon; as the boys were about to leave, Meg called out to Carter; "See you tomorrow?" He told her he wouldn't be around for a while, that he was taking extra shifts at work to save for something special. He didn't tell her that he was saving to buy his girlfriend an engagement ring. The thought of Carter not coming around sent Meg into panic mode. She shot her father a look of desperation and Mr Daly thought quickly.

"Carter, that's too damn bad, son. I'm sorry to hear you won't be around much. I was going to surprise you, but I'll just tell ya'. I was able to get a hold of some nice upgrades for your car. I was hoping we could all work on it together. I planned on giving you one of my cars to get around while we made yours into a showpiece. Imagine your little Maverick all shiny and new; I mean you deserve to drive in style, my friend."

Carter stayed quiet while his friends enthusiastically tried to convince him to rethink his decision to stay away. He felt his heart begin to race and his head pound; admittedly, he was conflicted. Mr Daly sensed his hesitation and sweetened the pot, "I guess this is a good time to mention too, I was hoping to offer you a job as a mechanics apprentice."

Eddie and Keith were jumping around the garage, yelling and calling Carter the luckiest man in the world. Their disregard for Carter's current job and of course his relationship was disheartening and a bit disrespectful. Free pizza paled in comparison to the opportunities and perks they would have as Carter's friends once he began working for Mr Daly. Yes, the boys were thinking of themselves and had no concern for Carter's best interest; he knew that and tried to keep a clear head amidst the excitement. However, the temptation was overwhelming; and much to Meg's delight, he stayed. Carter turned to Mr Daly; "Ok, let's talk."

Fee-Nix Rising

Fiona pulled on the heavy, oversized glass door leading into the Cooke building. A doorman came running over to her as she stepped inside and apologized for leaving his post. He explained while catching his breath that someone in the lobby had asked for his help with directions, and he walked over to offer his assistance just as Fiona was coming in.

"It's perfectly fine; no worries. I handled that door like a pro, right?"

The doorman laughed and thanked her for her understanding. He told her his name was Pat and he was looking forward to holding the door for her on her next visit. His charm made Fiona blush, and his obvious flirtation left her feeling more hopeful than she already felt. She wondered as she made her way through the extraordinarily grand first floor to the concierge desk if Pat accepted tips; which would certainly explain his enthusiasm. She made a mental note to ask Jaime when she saw her.

As Fiona approached the concierge desk; which looked more like an intergalactic space station, she heard Jaime call out her name. Fiona waved and made her way over; trying not to be distracted by the myriad of street vendors set up in this luxury lobby. She was in awe of the artwork; handmade jewelry, pottery and baked goods. There was an entire street fair set up around the shops and restaurants residing within actual walls. Jaime came out from behind her enormous desk to hug Fiona.

"Hey, I'm so glad you're here."

Fiona, still wide-eyed, hugged her new friend and asked about the vendors.

"This is the coolest thing I've ever seen! Are there like assigned areas for each vendor, or is it first come, first serve?"

Jaime gladly explained to Fiona how the vendors came to be.

"One day about two years ago, one of our security guys noticed this man in the lobby setting framed artwork against that far wall," she pointed toward the left of the front doors. "Anyway, he asked the man to please leave. The man was nice, but he refused to exit the building at the guard's request. He said it was too cold to stay out in the street, and he needed to make money to feed his dog. The security guard figured he was a little crazy, but when he looked closer, there was actually a dog sitting in the corner next to a stack of paintings. James, the security guy, tried to explain to the man that he couldn't panhandle, and never mind have a dog in the building. Anyway; as luck would have it for this guy, TC was walking through the lobby on his way out and saw two men conversing. He asked what was going on, and they both explained, offering their own side of the story. TC told the guy he was welcome to sell his wares in the lobby and told James to go get the guy and his dog something to eat."

"That's amazing." Fiona was in awe.

"Wait; there's more, you're gonna love this!" Jaime continued. "TC calls Laurel and tells her about the painter in the lobby. She calls me and asks me to estimate how many vendors we could accommodate comfortably on the first floor. I told her at least thirty; maybe more. Laurel shows up a few hours later and spends the afternoon sitting on the floor with this painter and his dog, talking about who knows what. Later, we find out that she hired him to coordinate a street vendor association; complete with space assignments and a rotating schedule for those who wanted it. So, within a week or so, we had this cool set-up; and thanks to Laurel's marketing skills, people from all over were visiting our building to shop from the vendors. If that's not cool enough; the painter was given an office and access to two suites on the fourth floor to use as he saw fit. He decided the suites would be best utilized for vendors who had been sleeping on the streets; especially during the winter. He used the money from his new salary to buy beds, blankets, pillows and pet beds. Now; he not only coordinates our vendors but has created a non-profit to pair homeless vendors with dogs; for company as well as protection. He spends so much of his time finding more permanent accommodations for our vendors and other homeless people in our area."

Jaime tapped her right ear and spoke into thin air, "Chris, are you available to come to the concierge desk ?" She shook her head and asked Fiona to give her just another minute before they went to lunch. Within minutes a man in his mid-thirties, dressed in jeans and a sport coat joined them. He leaned against the desk and asked Jaime what he could do for her.

"Chris, I'd like you to meet Fiona. She was just asking about our lobby vendors."

He smiled and extended his hand.

"Fiona, it's great to meet you; are you an artist?"

"Ha! No, I wish I had even a fraction of artistic ability, but sadly, I can't even draw straight lines."

Chris laughed.

"Well Fiona, I just started hosting creative expression sessions on the weekends. Mostly for our street artists, but you're welcome to join us any time. I bet you have talent that you haven't discovered yet. Just grab the info from Jaime, and I hope to see you again." He apologized for having to 'run-off', but he was waiting for a call and better get back to the office.

Fiona was so impressed. She thanked Chris for the invite.

"Um, before you do, can I ask, how's your dog?" It was a little awkward, but Chris was all too eager to tell her that Loki was upstairs, resting in style in his bed under Chris' desk. Jaime told Chris that Fiona was a dog person too, and he should look up 'Wanda the Wonder Dog' when he had a minute.

"Will do," he said as he turned in the direction of the elevators. "Again, nice meeting you Fiona." He called out and waved over his shoulder.

"OK, ready for lunch ?" Jaime once again tapped her com. "Hey guys, hold down the fort. I'm on my lunch break. I'll be in the deli if you need me, but you won't, I'm sure."

Jaime led the way across the left side of the first floor and around the corner, right into Ralph's Deli. The two women waited just inside the door for a minute or two. The deli was exceptionally busy, and no one came to seat them. Jaime made polite excuses on Ralph's behalf and stepped into the dining area to look for an available table. Just then, a young man came running, literally running toward them. He leapt over a chair that hadn't been pushed back under its table and jumped in front of them.

"Miss Jaime! I'm so sorry! Busy here today! Just the two of you?" he didn't give her a chance to answer. "I have a table, right this way please."

Jaime followed the young man across the dining room to a table for two in the far corner. He pulled out her chair, and then Fiona's. He told them a server would be with them shortly and ran off as quickly as he ran up on them a moment ago.

"Wow; I wish I had his energy! Was it me, or did everything he say to us sound like an exclamation?"

Jaime took a sip of her water; "Ha, yeah, he's a good kid. His mom works here too. He's been bussing tables for a few months now. If you overlook the obvious ADHD factor, he really is quite endearing."

"Oh, I wasn't judging; I am jealous of his energy and enthusiasm." Fiona took the linen napkin from the table, unfolded it and placed it in her lap. "So, what do you recommend?" she asked.

Jaime asked Fiona to trust her; she had already called in their lunch order.

"I wasn't sure how much time I would have without being interrupted by work; so I called ahead and ordered a little of everything."

"Great, I'm famished."

"I'm just really glad you accepted my invite and were able to come into the city today."

"Oh, I love the city; and I was really happy to get your text. I mean, I thought we all got along so well last weekend; and I was hoping I wasn't just hallucinating."

Jaime laughed.

"You were not hallucinating. Laurel and I both agreed that you fit in so well with our craziness. She thought we might have been a bit much for you and worried you wouldn't want to hang out with us again. You know, I didn't tell Laurel I asked you to meet for lunch. I kind of wanted to fill in some blanks for you before you jump to conclusions about Laurel and TC."

"I was just about to ask you if Laurel was joining us. It would have been fine, but I am glad it's just us today; I do have some questions for you."

"Hold your questions; I bet I answer them all even before you ask." Jaime sat back in her chair, almost smug; but Fiona preferred to think of her as self-assured. She had no doubt that Jaime was more than capable of providing the answers to her long list of questions. Fiona was also relieved that Jaime was willing to do so.

"First things first," she began. "What did you decide about that crappy job you were complaining about?"

"Ah, yes," Fiona offered. "My own personal hellhole. Actually, I went home that night and talked to my mom about it. Monday morning, I went in and gave my notice. My boss was such an ass, he told me to leave immediately, and no notice was necessary. He said he was on the verge of firing me anyway. I know that's a huge lie, he's just that much of a jerk."

Jaime seemed pleased.

"That's so good to hear; no one should be miserable every day. What exactly did you do there?"

"I was supposed to be working in social media marketing but what I actually did was send emails and make coffee." She sighed, " It sucked. The worst part is that I stayed as long as I did. I got that job days before Carter decided to walk away from us. Somehow; I felt like that stupid job was my punishment for whatever I did wrong to make Carter just disappear." Fiona took a sip of water and cleared her throat, "Crazy, I know. But I was a kid, and I had just gotten the wind knocked out of me."

"Not crazy, Fee. Not at all. I'm just really glad you still don't feel that way. You're meant for greater things, and everyone loves a good comeback story. It's so exciting to think of you now beginning to write yours. And… I get to be around to see the rise of the Fee-Nix. Get it?"

"I do get it, and I'm so ready to rise from the ashes, so to speak. Thanks for the vote of confidence. One step at a time though; first I need to find another job. My mom is wonderful, and she offered to help me out for a while, but I need to work. I need to feel useful in this life, you know?"

"I do, and…" Jaime was cut off by the sudden appearance of a very loud man with plates of food in both hands.

"Hello, my ladies," Ralph greeted them before realizing he hadn't yet made Fiona's acquaintance. He placed the platters on the table between them and handed each of his guests a small salad plate. "Enjoy, my ladies."

"Um Ralph, this is Fiona; she's a new friend."

"Good to know you, Fiona, I have a special dessert I keep secret for new friends, so save room." Ralph shook his finger at her as if he were scolding her. Fiona found him adorable. Jolly and sweet; like Santa. As Ralph disappeared back into the kitchen, Fiona told Jaime her thoughts on Ralph and his similarities to Santa.

"You do have a knack for reading people, don't you? Ralph is not only a real-life Santa in so many ways, but he also plays Santa for us at Christmas time. He hands out gifts to all our employees and meets with underprivileged kids at our annual fundraiser."

"I can totally see it," Fiona admitted.

The women ate their lunch with a bit of small talk; as Jaime contemplated the best way to approach the more serious subjects. As if on cue, Fiona asked, "So, you and Laurel were roommates in college?"

Jaime jumped on the chance to talk more about Laurel.

"Yes, we met during orientation. She was behind me in line when they were assigning dorms, and because of my challenges with height," Jaime ducked her head for effect to make herself seem even shorter. "Laurel was able to look directly over my shoulder. She noticed we had the same room assignment and tapped me on the arm. She introduced herself, but she was so quiet; and a little awkward. Honestly, my first thought was, *oh no!* But, I decided in that minute we had to be friends. No one wants to live with someone they dislike. So, I found things we had in common and started there. We both love art and music; oh and clothes, especially shoes. Unfortunately, we couldn't borrow from one another, but we had a blast treasure hunting in local vintage clothing shops."

It quickly became evident to Fiona that Jaime regarded Laurel more like a sister than a friend. She could feel the love and warmth in her words. Their friendship was not unlike her own with Nicky. It was nice; she wanted to know more.

"Most girls were jealous of Laurel. She was so pretty without even trying; and kind to everyone, which made her beautiful on the inside as well. But the best part of Laurel is, even now, she has no idea how extraordinary she truly is. Her gift for helping people to help others is nothing less than a phenomenon. It's like having a database in her brain of all the people she meets; what they need and want. Laurel has the ability to access that information and pair it with someone who can either help or needs help. Crazy, I know. But, I've seen her do this time and again with so much success and reward."

Fiona was more than intrigued; "Is that why she wanted to meet me? Does Laurel think I need someone's help?"

"Well, yes and no. It was actually TC that came across the photo; while looking for something else entirely. He noticed the colors; and took it as a sign. I'm not sure what he thought he found, and I don't think he quite knew either; which is why he put Laurel on the case, so to speak."

"Um, what colors?" Fiona seemed confused. It was the first time anyone mentioned colors in reference to that photo.

"Let me show you something, Fiona. And when I do, you tell me if you're as curious as TC was when he noticed your picture. I think you'll find this interesting." Jaime took her phone from her handbag and began scrolling through her photos. She had taken a picture of the original of TC and Laurel when they first met, and had it stored in her phone specifically to show Fiona when she had the chance.

"Here, take a look." Jaime passed her phone across the table to Fiona.

She reached over and tapped the screen; "Tell me what you see. You know, I took this picture. This is where TC and Laurel met. We were all on vacation; I think it might have been winter break; definitely our junior year."

Fiona studied the image of the photo for several minutes. It was TC and Laurel seated at what looked to be a table in a restaurant. They were very tan; wearing sunglasses and there were tropical plants in the background. Fiona looked at Jaime with evident confusion.

"Keep looking; I promise, if you don't see it in another minute, I'll let you off the hook."

"The only weird thing I can pinpoint is the glow right above their shoulders, where they touch one another. Maybe from the sun behind them? Or a reflection from the glassware on the table?" Fiona handed the phone back to Jaime.

"Mmmm... Good eye; but I can't agree with your explanations for two reasons. First, there are several other photos taken at the same time of either Laurel, or TC alone, and none have that same glow. Second, and most importantly; the blue glow is closest to Laurel and the yellow, TC. The green color is the convergence of both primary colors. It's as if the picture is telling us; when two people are meant to be; they converge energy, or auras, or whatever, to create a new energy; stronger, brighter, and more beautiful when those people are together."

Still feeling perplexed, Fiona had to agree.

"Well, after seeing them together in person with my own eyes, I'm sure you're on to something. The Cooke's are an obvious match made in Heaven. It isn't a stretch to believe that their connection was somehow captured in the picture. Did you use your phone?"

Jaime had to laugh.

"Uh, we didn't have smartphones back then. Most people didn't have a cell phone at all, let alone anything high-tech. I think TC had a flip phone or some sort of primitive device. I took that picture with a big old clunky digital camera. I was so proud of that thing. *"Ah, OK. So, that wouldn't count for an accidental filter application."* Fiona mused. It was a final attempt at a more reasonable explanation. Even though she believed in auras and energies. She feared this had more to do with the picture of her and Carter. It seemed more comfortable to try and blame the camera or the photographer.

"Nope, it's not the camera because your photo *was* taken with a phone, and the very same thing showed up. Jaime had scrolled back to the photo of Carter and Fiona." She handed the phone back to her friend. "Again, I will ask you; tell me what you see. It should be easier this time, you know what you're looking for."

Fiona was right; this wasn't just about the photo of the Cooke's. She looked down and let out an involuntary, albeit loud gasp, which drew the attention of several others around them. Jaime smiled and announced.

"She's OK, really."

"OK, I see it. I do have to wonder why I'm red and Carter is blue. Oh, and I should tell you, I totally blacked out right after this picture was taken. The water I was standing in had been charged by lightning; I wonder if that has any significance?" It was still barely conceivable to Fiona, after everything that happened, she and Carter were somehow meant to be.

"I think you're missing the point." Jaime continued, "TC believes that he and Laurel were destined to be together. He would think so even without the photo; but all these years, he felt they had actual proof of soulmates, twin flames or kindred spirits; whatever you'd like to call two people who are meant to be together. Now, he finds the same proof in your photo. I know you don't know him like I do, but believe me, he's not going to simply write this off as a coincidence, or try and find a reasonable explanation. This is why we want so desperately to know what happened between you and Carter; we think; yeah, I said we, that the two of you are soulmates, for lack of a better term."

Fiona was visibly emotional. Her eyes welled with tears and her hands trembled so that she had to place her glass back down in front of her.

"You know; five years ago I would have agreed with all of you; and your kindred spirit theory. But, the last thing Carter said to me; that day, moments before someone took that picture, broke my heart so badly; I fear I would never be able to love him like I once did," she went on to tell Jaime how she pleaded for his help, and his hesitation to do the right thing only because she was the one to ask. His worry was that he'd somehow upset Meg by being anywhere near her, even if to save a child. She also explained the photo; he grabbed her only to prevent her from slipping backward into the water. It wasn't meant to be a romantic moment; but she felt their connection when he touched her, so momentarily; and then it was gone forever. "I should have been over him, but that day my heart broke all over again."

Jaime took a deep breath and exhaled slowly. She closed her eyes for a few seconds, hoping when she opened them, Fiona wouldn't be upset any longer.

"I am so sorry, Fee. I never meant for our conversation to upset you; never mind hurt you."

"Oh, Jaime, I know that. I'm OK, really. You didn't hurt me; Carter did," she wiped her eyes with the linen napkin that had been resting on her lap. "Is there anything else you'd like to know?"

"Oh, God, Fee, I'm not going to make you talk about him anymore. I feel awful."

"It's OK, honestly. Maybe I needed this."

"May I ask just one more question?"

"Of, course. But I bet I can guess what you'd like to know. You're going to ask me if I've seen him since that day."

"I was going to ask, but I'd rather you be OK than to ever know the answer."

"I am OK, and I will gladly tell you. Yes, I have, several times in fact. We only live about ten miles from one another. It's hard to avoid people in our area as everyone shops and eats in the same places. We aren't technically a 'small town', but our options are limited." Fiona rolled her eyes. "It's not too bad when I see him and his friends from a distance, or when I'm with my mom, or Nicky and Rob, but when I run into them and I'm alone; it's like I'm fourteen again, and just showed up for school in my underwear."

"Them? You said run into them. Is he always with his friends?"

"Basically. I did see Carter with just his girlfriend a few times. It was much harder to ignore; seeing him with Meg is like witnessing an accident. As much as I wanted to, I couldn't turn away. Believe me, it was rather embarrassing."

"Ah, that was going to be my final question. There's a girlfriend. That sucks."

Fiona acknowledged the irony of their lunch conversation. Jaime had said she was sure to answer all of Fiona's questions about the Cooke's. As it turns out; she was the one offering the answers for Jaime.

"Yes, I suspect she's the magician that made him disappear; but ultimately; it was his decision, I know that."

"Is she anything like you?" Jaime asked.

"Um, I'm not sure. I don't know much about her; by design, of course. The little I do know is superficial. She and I are nothing alike if you count physical appearance and style. Honestly, she reminds me of that girl I met last weekend at Laurel's; the one with the nails."

"Oh, Kay," Jaime clarified, then added. "Ohhhhh Kay... oh no." Jaime's eyes widened. "Look, I'm really not into gossip; but when it comes to Kay, I will say this, something isn't right between her and Charlie. She's changed since they first met; and not for the better. Maybe I'm being cynical; but if and when it hits the fan with those two, you'll know what I'm talking about."

"I have a feeling I already do, but like you, I'd rather not speculate. I've had too many people gossip about me in the past few years. I always found out and it always feels horrible. No one deserves that,"

Jaime was already certain that Fiona was meant to be a part of the Cooke's family; but after hearing the sincerity in her voice as she chose to not contribute to the possible pain of someone she didn't even know; or much care for, it was clear she had to convince Fiona to become a part of the team.

Ralph made his way back to their table and asked if they would like anything else. He almost seemed disappointed when they declined.

"No special new friend dessert today?"

Fiona had forgotten about his offer.

"Oh, I am so sorry; lunch was so amazing, I couldn't stop myself from eating everything," she gestured to the nearly empty platters on the table. "Please forgive me." She gave Ralph her best puppy dog eyes.

"It's OK, Miss, I will have it ready to go for you, how's that?"

"Fiona; Ralph, her name is Fiona." Jaime knew he had forgotten by the way he addressed her.

Her name amused the man.

"Oh, like the firebird, that's you, firebird."

"Oh." Fiona quickly got the reference. "Yes, like a Phoenix." She shot Jaime a look. "Jaime called me a Phoenix, just before lunch was served. Ironic."

"Oh yeah, I did, I called you our Fee-Nix," she said, accentuating the FEE part of the word.

Ralph wiped his hands across his apron before extending his right hand to Fiona.

"So happy you enjoyed your lunch Firebird. I will bring dessert to go and TC's bag to you Miss Jaime. Give me a minute."

Fiona called out to Ralph, "Would you be so kind as to bring the check too?"

Ralph shook his head and made his way back to the kitchen. Jaime told Fiona that lunch was taken care of; not to worry.

"Thank you, Jaime, you didn't have to do that."

"I didn't. But you're very welcome. This was great. Um, would you happen to have a little more time to hang around this afternoon, or are you in a hurry to get home?"

"No hurry; the train runs all night. Why what's up?"

"Well," she began as she stood and collected her things. "I have to bring TC his lunch; I thought you might want to tag along and get the Cooke Industries ten-cent tour."

"Sure, let's do it," Fiona agreed. Ralph had returned with three bags. He placed them on the table near Jaime. "Big one for the big guy," he said pointing straight up, indicating the top floor where TC's office was located. "And, for you and Firebird, dessert to go." He blew a kiss in their direction as he walked away.

"Oh, Jesus, is Firebird going to be a thing?" Fiona joked.

"Not if it annoys you."

"It doesn't. Not at all. I've never been given a nickname before, well other than Fee."

The two women made their way upstairs. Jaime had once again let her whereabouts be known through the comlink in her ear. Fiona's curiosity got the best of her.

"Does everyone use those?" she asked, tapping on her own ear for reference.

"Not everyone. TC was instrumental in the development of this particular model. It's very efficient and user-friendly. It's great for those of us that don't have a traditional desk job. Although I am usually downstairs; I walk around this building all day. Two-way radios are cumbersome, and cell phones suck when you don't have pockets. TC likes toys; and tech, so we get to play with a lot of cool things. Our coms can be programmed according to any phone list. In other words, we can create lists using people's cell numbers and sync the coms to them. Right now, mine is synced to a list of Cooke's administrators; TC, James in security, Chris, and a few others."

"Well, that's fun!"

Jaime motioned for Fiona to follow her; "This way," she directed once they exited the elevator. The halls were wide and brightly painted. Fiona noticed the individual offices were only partially enclosed; and by glass panels. She could faintly hear music coming from multiple directions; and someone was singing aloud to the right of where they were standing. Fiona looked through the large glass wall to see a woman maybe in her fifties; staring at her computer screen, singing along to whatever tune was emanating from her earbuds. There was a large flower arrangement on the corner of her desk; it was fresh, maybe recently delivered. She motioned to Jaime.

"Now, that's what I call enjoying your job."

Jaime smiled and tapped lightly on the glass to get the attention of the woman in the office. She looked up from her monitor and gave Jaime a very enthusiastic wave.

"That, my friend is Emma Cooke; TC's sister. She works with our interns and heads our scholarship program."

Fiona squinted in an attempt to find a family resemblance, but it was tough to determine from where she was standing. Jaime continued, "Emma basically raised TC; that's a story for another time though. If you ask me; the family resemblance isn't physical as much as it is intellectual." Jaime had taken notice of Fiona's squint. They took a few more steps forward, passing several offices much like Emma's; cheerful and bright."

Jaime stopped just outside a small corridor entrance.

"Let's see what the boss is up to, shall we?" The corridor was a bit deceiving. Fiona expected to turn into a hallway; but as they rounded the corner, it opened up into one very modest office suite.

"Huh, not what I was expecting," She admitted.

TC emerged from behind the only door in the office. Fiona suspected it was the restroom; and refrained from asking where he had just come from.

"Hey kids, how was lunch ?" TC sat on a small sofa near the far wall. He was wearing jeans and a T-shirt much like the one she saw him in when she visited his home last weekend. He definitely had a unique style for the CEO and founder of one of the largest tech companies in the world. His sneakers looked brand new, and Fiona noticed when he sat; he wasn't wearing socks. She saw no real relevance in her observations, but found them curious. Nothing about the Cooke's had been stereotypical or cliche; Fiona liked that.

Jaime tossed TC's lunch bag on the coffee table in front of him and fell back into an overstuffed chair, opposite the small sofa.

"That bag is heavy, what did you order?" she teased.

He motioned to the empty chair next to Jaime offering it to Fiona.

"Please, have a seat." He opened the white paper sack and stuck his hands in; pulling out three cardboard containers stacked one on top of the other. "It doesn't matter what I order, Ralph sends whatever he wants anyway."

"It smells delicious," Fiona had the feeling she should say something, but she was still a bit awestruck by the relaxed environment; completely unpredicted.

"I don't mind sharing; Hey Jaime, grab some forks and paper plates from the cabinet, would you?"

"Oh, no thank you. I appreciate the offer, but my lunch looked a lot like yours. We had to take dessert to go; it simply wouldn't fit."

"Yeah, Ralph likes to feed people. Well, if you change your mind, let me know. Hey ladies, you don't mind if I eat while we talk, do you?" TC had already taken a huge bite of his sandwich and stuffed a few fries in his mouth as well.

"Nope, knock yourself out," Jaime answered as she got up and walked toward a large cabinet behind TC's desk. She pulled at the double doors, revealing a small set of shelves and another door to a refrigerated compartment. She grabbed a bottle of diet soda and a few plastic cups and returned to her chair. "Here, you're going to choke on all that pastrami if you don't wash it down."

"Thank you." TC poured himself some soda and slid the bottle a few inches in their direction. "You know, Ralph said something about wanting to retire when I was down there the other day." TC directed the small talk to both Fiona and Jaime. Fiona figured he was simply being polite and including her, but TC was fishing for signs of genuine interest from her. Fiona had no idea she was literally being interviewed. TC was secretly thrilled when she responded.

"I know I just met him, but if anyone deserved a little R and R, I would think it's Ralph. Jaime told me a bit about the wonderful things he does for others. If only he could find someone and train them as his apprentice to take over when he decides to retire. But, I would venture to guess, there aren't many like Ralph out there."

TC jumped up suddenly, sending his plate over the side of the coffee table.

"Fiona, that's it! That's how we can help Ralph feel good about his decision and still keep the deli thriving. And no offense, but you're wrong. There are a lot of great people out there; we just haven't met them all; yet."

His eyes were wide, and he paced back and forth; three steps to the right, three steps back to the left; over and again for about five minutes. Jaime picked up his plate and set it back on the table.

"Don't eat that," she scolded. For two people so close in age, they definitely had a mother and child dynamic. Jaime told Fiona; working with TC is exactly like having a child, or in her case, another husband; she said Joe and TC were a lot alike.

His pacing started to make Fiona feel uneasy, and she was grateful when he finally sat back down. TC looked at Jaime, then Fiona and back to Jaime again.

"Well, I thought this was going to take longer, but I had a feeling it would go well. Fiona? Would you be interested in working here at Cooke Industries? I could really use you on our team; you are one of those great people out there and I am so glad we met you."

It's Too Late; Baby

"I'm pregnant!" Meg Daly proudly announced. Of course, this was the kind of thing that she should have shared privately with Carter first, but that wasn't Meg's style. She stood up from the table in the restaurant where she and Carter were having dinner with her parents and youngest sister. Meg pushed out her stomach and modeled her non-existent 'bump'.

Mrs Daly gushed; "Oh honey, this is wonderful news, are you sure? Have you seen a doctor? How far along are we?"

Meg sat back down and rested her head on Carter's arm. He was trying to swallow his food that seemed to be stuck in his throat as it was suddenly void of any saliva. Carter was in such shock he couldn't even reason taking a drink of his water to help the situation. He literally sat there staring straight ahead; focusing on the space between Mr and Mrs Daly across from him.

"Yes; I saw the doctor this morning, and it's confirmed. I'm just about nine weeks along, so we have to work quickly on the wedding plans before I begin to show, for real." Meg's excitement gave way to her determination. She leaned up and kissed Carter on his cheek; "So, how happy are you, daddy?"

Without warning; Carter choked up his food and sent it projectile into Mrs Daly's plate. He gasped for air and apologized. His future in-laws were not at all amused. Carter heard a distinct buzzing in his head and felt like he was about to lose consciousness. His lack of enthusiasm; or any reaction for that matter disturbed Meg's parents and had put her on the defensive.

"Carter!" she screeched. "Say something for God's sake. I just made today the best day of your life. You're going to be a father, and we're going to be married. You'll officially be a part of the Daly family. Carter, you should regard that as a privilege."

"Uh; oh, yeah, wow. I'm good, I um, just, well, I'm surprised, How; I mean, I thought, well; OK, it's OK." He couldn't believe the stupidity of his own words; were they words, or a series of weird noises? Carter's head was still spinning; his thoughts raced so far away from being a father; and marrying Meg, he feared he would say something even more inappropriate if he tried again to speak. Instead, he feigned a smile and patted Meg's hand, where it rested on his arm. Carter barely processed Meg's announcement when her comment about becoming a Daly snuck into his already reeling thoughts. Wasn't she and the baby supposed to become Wyatt's? Isn't that how it typically works?

Meg and her mother immediately began brainstorming about the wedding; debating dates, colors, guests, and venue. The sound of their voices felt like fingernails scratching a chalkboard to Carter, who silently prayed for a way out of there. He sat quietly avoiding the outraged stares from Mr Daly. Oh, if looks could kill; Carter would have been a corpse. It seemed as though they had been sitting at that table for hours; when in reality only twenty minutes had passed before Mr Daly asked the server to, "Settle up."

Their server was a lovely woman in her early sixties. She was very proficient at her job, anticipating her guests' needs and knowing when to approach as well as when to not interrupt. Mr Daly beckoned her with a wave of his arm; and in an instant she was tableside, presenting him with their bill.

"I hope you all enjoyed your dining experience tonight; I look forward to being of service to you again, soon."

Without a word, Mr Daly handed her his credit card and waved her off. Before turning away, she leaned in and spoke to Carter.

"Hey hon, is everything OK? Can I get you some more water or something; you're looking a little pale."

Carter looked into her eyes, and shook his head.

"I'm good, thank you though." He was overly polite yet visibly shaken. She wanted to slip him a note or something; asking him to blink twice if he was being held against his will. Mr Daly chimed in; "Maybe you could bring him a big glass of mind your damn business. Yeah, that would be great!" It was evident that Mr Daly hadn't taken his daughter's announcement well. Although he rarely exhibited a pleasant side, his disrespect for their server was unwarranted.

Their server simply walked away.

"What an asshole!" she muttered to herself as she approached the register to run his card. She hoped he was at least a decent tipper. She waited until they had all exited before retrieving the signed receipt. He did tip well, no need to risk her job by calling him names out loud.

When they all returned to the Daly's, Meg begged Carter to stay the night, but he asked her to understand, he wanted to go home. He told her he'd like to be there in the morning, to tell his parents the news. Meg hated that he didn't refer to her pregnancy as good news; he simply said news.

"We should really tell them together, don't you think? Maybe we could get them a gift; something special for the grandparents to be?" She clung to his arm, despite his best efforts to get in his car. Meg backed up and leaned against the driver door; she pulled Carter closer and kissed him. "Aren't you happy; babe?"

"I think I just need a minute; you know, to breathe," he turned her around away from the driver door and opened it. "I'll see you tomorrow, OK?" Carter gave Meg a quick kiss and got in his car. As he backed down her driveway, she stood watching; embarrassed and enraged.

Carter hesitated at the stop sign at the end of Meg's street. His eyes began to sting, and the tears blurred his vision. He wiped them with the front of his shirt and opened all the windows for some fresh air. Instead of making the right toward home, Carter turned left and just drove. He kept driving for about fifteen minutes; relying on his car and instinct. His thoughts were fractured, but not as broken as his spirit. He wasn't sure what part of all this was most upsetting; becoming a father before he was ready, or being so selfish that he couldn't find it in his heart to be excited for Meg; the mother of his child. Oh, dear God. The tears kept burning, and Carter kept driving; until his tears turned to sobs. He pulled the car over to the side of the road and grabbed his cell phone from the console and dialed.

"Hey, little brother, what's going on back in old New Jersey?"

Sam's voice sounded like hope itself. Carter missed him; it had been too long. Sam joined the Army right out of high school; Carter had just turned thirteen. When his tour in the Middle East ended, Sam married and moved to California where his wife had been stationed. Sam and Shelly flew back east when they found the time, but since their son, Carter's nephew Noel was born three years ago; it had become more difficult for them to visit. Carter's parents flew out to California at least twice a year, but Carter was always too busy for his family; working for Mr Daly. The thought of every bad decision since meeting the Daly's made Carter sob even harder. He tried to collect himself before speaking, but to no avail.

"Sam, I am so sorry."

"Are you crying? Carter, what the hell? Are you OK? Are Mom and Dad OK? I just spoke to them two days ago! What's going on?" Sam's voice went from hopeful to frantic in an instant.

"Oh, God, I screwed up; so bad, I can't fix it. I'm so sorry. Please don't hang up; I need you."

"I'm right here kiddo, I'm not going anywhere. Breathe Carter."

"Sam," he paused to force the words from his mind out of his mouth. "Meg's pregnant." There was complete silence for a few seconds. Carter thought for sure Sam had in fact hung up on him. "Sam?"

"Wow, OK. Yeah, I'm still here. What did Mom and Dad say?"

"I haven't told them yet; I just found out at dinner."

"Carter, where are you?"

"Um, I'm in my car, parked on the side of a street." Carter looked around to find himself in front of Fiona's house. "Sam, I'm at Fiona's. I'm not sure why I drove here."

"Little brother; stay in the damn car. Do not go to her. If you think you're confused now; it will be so much worse if you see Fiona. Not to mention, you'd be breaking her heart all over again. You know better than anyone; Fiona doesn't deserve that. If you ever loved her, brother, stay away from her."

"Sam, please, don't be upset with me. I won't go to her, but I need to just stay here for a while; will you stay on the phone with me?"

"I already told you; I'm not going anywhere. What do you want to talk about; stupid shit or the serious stuff? I'm good with either." Sam wished his wife had been home. Shelly would know what to say to Carter. However, he was on his own, and this particular subject between the brothers was very unexpected and unprecedented.

Carter did his best to gather his thoughts. He wiped his eyes and tear-stained cheeks.

"Sam?"

"Still here," Sam was still searching for something to say that would put his brother at ease. It was obvious that Carter was in emotional distress, and Sam being thousands of miles away was more than frustrating.

"I know. Thank you. Listen, I want you to be honest. When I met the Daly's and started hanging out there, did you or Mom and Dad have concerns? I always wondered why no one ever asked me why Fiona and I weren't together anymore."

"Carter; we did ask. And yes, we were all confused and worried about you. It was so out of character for you to impulsively leave a relationship you coveted. You told me that you were saving for a ring, and wanted to marry Fiona someday. All of a sudden, you were with Meg and acting differently. Your whole life changed Carter, of course, we were all very concerned."

"Oh, I don't know how it happened. I felt so much pressure to live up to Mr Daly's expectations. I thought he recognized my skills, but that wasn't it; he basically bought me for his daughter, and I was a bargain. I sold my soul. Look, I'm not blaming anyone, but the guys didn't help matters. They had me convinced that my life would be better; bigger with Meg. And Mr Daly kept saying things like, he always wanted a son, and now he had one. He told me I'd run the business someday; and I was too stupid to realize, his daughters were the ones who would inherit everything, and unless I was attached to Meg, I'd have nothing. Now, I will be permanently attached to her, and I feel like I've lost everything. I lost myself, and the love of my life. Sam, I don't love Meg; I never will. I never stopped loving Fiona."

"You know; people get tempted; distracted all the time. Dangle something shiny in front of them, and they will blindly follow wherever that leads them. But every shiny object isn't treasure or even valuable. Sometimes shiny simply means cheap and flashy." Sam tried to sound paternal, but Carter took his comment as if he were referring to Meg as a hooker.

"Cheap and flashy, huh?"

"Carter, I meant no disrespect; I'm having a hard time getting my point across. My kid is only three; I'm not great at dad speeches yet."

"It's OK, I think our dad will agree with you. I am dreading having to tell mom and dad about the baby, but I am more afraid to tell them that Meg will be their daughter-in-law."

"Hey kiddo, let's table the marriage thing for just a little while. You know, I'm all for doing what's right, but marrying someone you don't love, can't be right. I think you should talk to our parents before worrying about a wedding. You can love your child, even if you don't live with the mother. People do it all the time."

"I know you're right. I have a lot of thinking to do. Thank you for being there for me. I don't know that I'd have gotten through this last hour without you."

"Are you feeling better? Can you drive home?"

"Yeah, I am going to turn around and head home as soon as we hang up. I'm so damn tired."

"Good deal. Listen, give me a call after you talk to mom and dad. If they get weird, I've got your back. But, I think you'll be just fine."

"Yeah, and thanks again Sam, I'm gonna go. Say hi to Shelly and give Noel a hug from me, OK?"

"You got it, talk soon."

Carter hung up and started the car. He drove to the end of the street to turn around. It felt weird to pull into one of Fiona's neighbor's driveways to do so. He was acutely aware that he no longer belonged here; on her street, in her neighborhood, among her friends. Still, he couldn't stop thinking about her. As Carter drove to the top of the street, he slowed down while passing Pete's. He couldn't help looking at the back door; the very place he had first met Fiona. Carter contemplated pulling into the side lot for a minute or two, but it was getting late, and he was exhausted. He turned to take one last look toward Pete's kitchen door; that's when he noticed the smoke.

At first glance, Carter figured the haze was nothing more than residual blurred vision from his surge of emotions. He grabbed the front of his shirt, and once again attempted to wipe away the sorrow. But the haze quickly became thicker, and his suspicions were confirmed; it was smoke. He pulled his car into the easement between the house behind Pete's and the dumpster and slowly approached the back door. It certainly could have been nothing more than Nick burning off the flat top grill to clean it and Carter wasn't prepared to explain to Nick why he happened to be driving by the pizzeria at midnight.

As Carter got closer; he could see a glow through the small window over the sink in the kitchen. He thought quickly and realized there was no logical explanation; other than an actual fire in the building. He quickened his pace; rushing through the back entrance.

"Nick!"

Carter grabbed one of the aprons hanging on a hook just inside the doorway. He made his way to the sink and soaked it in cold water; draping it over his head before venturing into the dining area. Once again, he called out.

"Nick… Nick, are you here?" The smoke was significantly thicker in the dining room, but Carter didn't see anyone, nor did he hear any response. It occurred to him that Nick would leave the building at the first sign of trouble. It would explain why the back door was left open; but not why help hadn't yet arrived. Carter pulled out his cell phone and dialed 9-1-1.

"What's your emergency?"

"Hey, Pete's is on fire; has anyone else called it in?" Carter made his way to the bar entrance. He placed his hand flat against the door before pushing it open. It was warm but he had to check. The dispatcher responded, "Pete's Pies?"

"Yes, this is Carter Wyatt; I'm in the building. I need to make sure everyone got out; please send the fire department; now!"

"Carter; Station 44 has already been dispatched; you should hear them coming to you any minute. Please get out of the building, help is coming to you. You have done your part Carter, you're already a hero."

Station 44 was a volunteer firehouse located less than a half mile from Pete's. Many of the members hung out in the bar and Nick was always sending pizzas to them; especially on weekends when the firefighters were on call. Carter knew it was only a matter of minutes before they would arrive. He turned to leave the way he had come in when he heard a woman's voice from the far side of the bar.

"Help. I'm in here."

Carter swung the door open.

"Lin? Is that you?"

"Yes, I'm behind the bar. Carter? I can't move, I'm so afraid." Linda was literally frozen with fear. "Where is the fire?" she asked.

"I'm coming, Lin. Just walk out from behind the bar; I'm having trouble seeing; the smoke is getting worse. Linda, can you hear me?" Carter felt his way around the corner of the bar. He then noticed the glow coming from under the restroom doors. The fire, he surmised, must be in the wall between the bar and kitchen. He knew he needed to get Linda out as quickly as possible before the fire escaped the confines of the restrooms. He took a few cautious steps forward. Carter could hear the sirens now; the trucks must have reached the parking lot in front. Linda followed his direction and within seconds, he could make out her image moving toward him through the smoke-filled bar. "Here, I'm here, just keep walking Linda, just a few more steps, honey."

"I see you."

Carter grabbed Linda La Salle by her shoulders and pulled her close to him. He took the soaked apron from over his own head and draped it across Linda's shoulders, pulling the bib by its strap over her head.

"Let's go."

He guided Linda through the dining room, and kitchen, heading for the back door. They could see the flames at the far end of the kitchen had burst through the wall between the bar and pantry.

"Don't look, honey, just walk out that door with me, OK."

Once outside; Carter and Linda made their way to the front of the building where the firetrucks and paramedics were just pulling in. He called out to a first responder.

"Hey, over here she needs help, now!"

Linda was having a hard time catching her breath, but otherwise unharmed.

"I'm fine. Carter, I'm ok, thanks to you." She gave him a playful swat on the arm; "And I will be asking you later why you were here tonight; but for now, I am just so grateful that you were."

The first responder sat Linda down on the back of the ambulance; "I got her, you should wait over there for someone to check you out too," he said to Carter.

"I'm not leaving her. I'm OK, really." He looked at Linda, "I'm staying right here."

She told the EMT.

"He's family; I want him to stay with me, at least until my brother gets here."

"Have you called Nick?" Carter asked.

"No, I assumed you did. We need to call him, right away."

Carter told Linda he would take care of it. She should just rest and let the first responder make sure she wasn't injured or needed to go to the hospital.

"Focus on you; I will worry about telling Nicky."

Carter took a few steps toward the front of the ambulance; making sure he could still see Linda. He didn't want her to hear what he was about to tell Nick, in fear of upsetting her even more. He held his phone in his hand for a few seconds; how the hell was he going to tell Nick that Pete's was on fire? And, would Nick even answer his call? He wouldn't blame him if he didn't.

However, Nick answered.

"Carter? Hey man, what's going on?"

"Nick; listen, it's important for you to know; Linda is fine, but the pizzeria is not. There's a fire; it's pretty bad, they're working on putting it out, but it's hard to tell how much damage has been done."

"Jesus! Are you sure my sister is OK? I knew I shouldn't have left her to close on her own. Oh, I can't believe this is happening, this is literally my worst nightmare. Carter, what the hell are we going to do? Is my restaurant completely gone?"

"I'm sure Linda is going to be fine, just a little smoke inhalation and she's pretty shaken up, she's being checked out now. As I said, it's too soon to tell how much damage has been done. Nick, where are you?"

"At Rob's place."

"Hey, man, let me talk to Rob, OK?"

Nick handed his cell to Rob. Carter quickly filled him in and asked if he would drive Nick back to the restaurant. He agreed.

"Hey Carter; what are we walking into? How bad is it? I really need Nicky to be prepared."

"I'm not sure. There was a lot of smoke, and when we were making our way out the back; we could see flames at the far end of the kitchen. They seemed to be coming from the pantry behind the restrooms which I know doesn't make sense, but maybe there was an issue with that wall. Honestly, the fire department got here in mere minutes, but until we can get in the building, we won't know how bad the damage is. Rob, it's not looking good. There's no way they can reopen any time soon, or even at all."

"Thanks, we're on our way. See you in about thirty minutes."

Carter hung up and returned to Linda's side.

"Is she OK?" he asked the first responder again.

"Yeah, and refusing to go to the hospital. I recommend it; just to be on the safe side. Maybe you can convince her to go."

Carter sat beside Linda.

"Lin honey, let's take a ride to the hospital. I'll go with you. We can have Nicky meet us there later. I need to know you're well. You know I love you."

"OK, I'll go, if you come with me. Call Nicky and tell him we will be at Regional Medical. Oh, and Carter, we will have that conversation about why you were here, so be prepared."

Carter helped Linda into the back of the ambulance. By then, some of the neighbors had congregated on the side street. One woman Carter recognized as the woman who lived directly behind Pete's walked over to check on Linda. She assured her friend that she was fine, and just going to get checked out. Carter mentioned his car was parked in the easement.

"Don't worry sweetie. It will be fine where it is, just take good care of our girl." The woman patted Carter on his shoulder before crossing the lot to return to her home.

Linda leaned over and took one last look at her family's pride and joy. The building was veiled in smoke. She nodded in agreement when the EMT asked if he could shut the doors. She asked to borrow Carter's cell to call her mother, who was visiting family upstate.

"I'm so glad Mom isn't here. I hate seeing her cry." Linda made the call; assuring her mom she was fine. She told her there was no reason to return early, and actually suggested she stay a bit longer. "Mom, there's nothing you can do here. Please, enjoy your time with Uncle Bobby and the kids." She hung up and handed the phone back to Carter. "Hearing her cry is no picnic either."

Unlikely Hero

ER nurse Liz Hall was grateful for a slow night in the emergency room. She was just about to take a break when she was informed of an incoming ambulance; a woman with smoke inhalation. She grabbed her stethoscope and draped it around her neck as she approached the bay doors. The ambulance had just pulled in, and the EMT was escorting the woman through the doors. Liz met them with a wheelchair.

"Hi there. And who do we have here?"

"Linda, Linda La Salle," the woman offered.

"Well, Linda, let's get you comfortable and make sure you're doing well tonight." Liz wheeled Linda into an exam room. She listened to her heart and lungs with little concern for what she was hearing. "Sounds good Linda, but I'm going to find a doctor just to make things official, OK?"

Liz noticed Carter standing just outside the doorway.

"Hey handsome, how about we give a quick listen to you as well," she gestured to a metal chair on the opposite side of the hallway. "Sit, relax."

Carter insisted he was fine, but Liz noticed the soot smudges on his face, hands and clothing, indicating he had spent some time in the building as well.

"Better safe than sorry. Besides, What else are you doing right now? May as well get checked out by a gorgeous older woman, right?"

Liz's comment made Carter smile. He knew she was just trying to add a little levity to his night, but he had to admit, she was really pretty.

"You convinced me. Should I strip right here?" he teased back.

"Oh, handsome and charming; well aren't you the total package?" Liz crouched down in front of Carter and listened to his breathing. She was just as relieved to find no real concern with his condition either. "Now, that wasn't so bad, was it? "

He thanked her and asked if he could sit with Linda while she waited for the doctor. Liz escorted Carter to the exam room.

"Hey Linda La Salle, does this doll face belong to you?"

Linda smiled.

"He's my hero."

Carter sat on the bed next to Linda and held her hand.

"You have no idea how grateful I am that you weren't hurt."

"I'm the one who's grateful, Carter. Now, are you going to tell me why you were at Pete's, to begin with? I need to know before someone suggests you had something to do with the fire."

"You know I didn't, right?" Carter felt the blood drain from his face at the mere thought of Linda not trusting him. "I would never hurt your family."

"Oh, honey, I know, but other people don't."

It hadn't occurred to Carter that it did in fact seem suspicious. A former employee happens to be in the area at midnight when the building catches fire.

"Oh, this does look bad, doesn't it?" He continued to tell Linda about Meg's pregnancy, and his subconscious drive to Fiona's. He told her that he had been sitting in his car on the side of the road talking to Sam for over an hour until he felt calm enough to drive himself home. "That's why I was driving past Pete's," he concluded.

"Carter, I'm so sorry. You had one hell of a night, didn't you?"

"Kind of. The last thing I need is to be arrested for arson. Just promise me, Lin, that you'll tell them I'm not a disgruntled former employee with a grudge."

"You have it all wrong. I was worried that the authorities would speculate that we hired you to set the fire for an insurance payout. My worry is that you'd get sucked into this when in reality, you're the one who saved me and probably our building."

Nurse Liz returned with the doctor. She couldn't help but overhear the last part of Linda and Carter's conversation.

"I bet you'll know the cause by morning. The inspectors usually get their reports done immediately. Tonight, you two deserve some rest."

The doctor, who had been reading Liz's notes, offered.

"If either of you think you may need a little help sleeping, I can send you home with a very mild sedative. Just something to settle your nerves."

Linda didn't hesitate, "Yes, please," but Carter respectfully declined. He knew he still had to drive home. Linda, however, had a better idea.

"Carter, your car is by the pizzeria which is by our house. Why don't you just stay with us tonight? I'd hate for you to have to drive this exhausted."

"You know, that's not a bad idea. As long as Nick is ok with me being there, I just might do that. Thanks, Lin."

"Carter, you'll always be family. I know Nick will be happy to have you there. He's going to need some support too," Linda asked Liz if she wouldn't mind checking the waiting room for Rob and Nick. "My brother will be the one nervously and incessantly talking," she told her.

Liz returned within minutes followed by Nick and Rob. Carter stood and approached Nick.

"I'm so sorry," he began. Nick embraced his friend and assured him there was nothing to be sorry for.

"You saved my sister. Nothing else matters."

Family First

Fiona nearly fell down the stairs as she raced from her room.

"Mom!" she called out again. "Mom! Where's Wanda's leash, I gotta go!"

Susan stepped out from behind the kitchen door.

"It's on the hook, where are you taking her? And why the hurry?"

"Nicky just called. There was a fire last night in Pete's kitchen. He asked me to come over. I thought Wanda would be a good distraction, like a therapy dog for PTSD. Now, where the hell are my shoes?"

"Holy shit, Fee! Is everyone all right? Was anyone in the restaurant?"

"Yeah, I guess Linda was there, closing up but she's OK. I'll know more when I get there."

"Let me know if the La Salle's need anything. I know Maria is still upstate with Bobby. I wonder if she knows? Oh, this is devastating news. Are you walking over, or driving?"

"Walking, as soon as I find my shoes, and yes, Nicky said Linda called Maria last night."

Susan bent down and picked up Fiona's shoes from behind the bench where she always left them.

"Here."

"Thanks, I will call you when I know more. Check on Maria."

Fiona and Wanda made their way to Nick's. It was a beautiful day, and the walk did them both good. Wanda enjoyed sniffing every rock, leaf and twig, while Fiona daydreamed about starting her new job with Cooke Industries. She thought of calling Laurel and letting her know about Pete's; maybe there was something she could do. Fiona quickly dismissed the idea; in fear of sounding like she was taking advantage of Laurel's financial status and evident generosity. However; a universal connection had already been established. Fiona always believed that people were brought together intentionally in life, but since meeting the Cooke's and of course, Jaime, she not only believed in spiritual connections; she felt them. Just daydreaming about being a part of their greatness had her feeling like she could accomplish anything. She no longer felt alone. She suddenly became acutely aware that she had felt this way before; with Carter; complete and invincible. Maybe there was something to TC's theory after all.

Fiona and Wanda had just started up the walkway in front of Nicky's house when her cell phone rang. It was Laurel.

"Hey, Laurel; um, I was just thinking about calling you. This is so weird."

"Oh, that *is* weird, and a little creepy. Is everything OK?"

"No, I'm at Nicky's now, I was just about to go in. How did you hear about the fire?" Fiona assumed Laurel's reason for calling was the same as Fiona's reason for calling her.

"What fire?" she was genuinely shocked. "I was calling to ask you about Monday; but that can wait, what fire?"

"Oh, I'm so sorry, I assumed you knew. Pete's caught fire last night. Everyone is safe, but I understand the building sustained a lot of smoke and water damage."

Laurel's voice lowered and became somewhat authoritative and serious.

"Oh my God, Fiona, I had no idea; listen, I'm on my way. Please tell Nick not to worry; we will deal with this together. I will see you soon."

"Thank you; I'll text you Nick's home address. He will be really happy to see you."

Fiona let herself in; as always. She found Rob and Linda sitting at the kitchen table.

"Linda, honey, how are you?" She hugged her friend and picked up Linda's empty coffee cup to refill it for her. She replaced the full cup in front of her and turned to Rob. He had his hand over his coffee cup indicating that he didn't require a refill. She kissed his cheek and sat in the empty chair next to Linda.

"I'm OK. Really. It's Nicky I'm worried about."

"Where is he?" Fiona asked looking around the room

Rob gestured toward the back porch.

"Outside smoking."

"Damn, he was doing so well; I really thought he'd quit for good this time."

Linda jumped to her brother's defense; "Give him some grace guys. This has been pretty devastating for all of us."

"I'll give him a minute before I go out there. So, what are we chatting about besides the obvious?"

Linda perked up at the opportunity to change the subject.

"Well Rob was just telling me that he had planned to ask Nicky to move in with him. He was going to do it last weekend before you were all invited out to Long Island. So, he booked a room for tonight, down the shore. He planned a romantic dinner and everything. The question is, given our current circumstances, should he still ask Nicky to go, or reschedule *again*?"

"Yeah, what she said," Rob joked.

Fiona gave Rob a wide-eyed stare.

"Am I weighing in here, or just observing?"

Rob appeared defeated.

"Please, tell me your thoughts. You two know him best; probably better than I ever will. A little help would be very much appreciated right now."

Fiona smiled slyly at Linda, knowing they had the same opinion.

"Robert, man up! Tell Nick what he's doing tonight. Do not let him talk his way into staying home and feeling shitty. There's nothing either of you can do here anyway; not for a while. You both deserve some time away; just to be together; to talk about the future. You know Rob, that's the issue, isn't it? The future. I think you're apprehensive for nothing though. I happen to know that when Nicky looks into his future; you're the first thing he sees."

"Thank you for that, Fee, and you're right, you both are."

Fiona excused herself and headed toward the back porch. She had to pass through the

La Salle's living room, and when she did; she couldn't help notice the snoring coming from someone face down on their sofa. She took a few cautious steps closer only to discover the sound sofa sleeper was Carter. One word escaped from her mouth; quietly and slowly like a valve leak.

"Shhhhhiiitttttt." Fiona backed away as stealthily as possible and returned to the kitchen. She sat back down next to Linda without a word.

"Oh, Fee, I should have told you; Carter is here. He's asleep in the living room."

"Yeah, I saw that. A 'heads up' would have been very helpful, Lin." Fiona felt numb and a little nauseated. She began to break out in cold sweat. "I just need a second," she whispered as she put her head down on the table. Linda continued her conversation with Rob, as though it was perfectly normal having Carter asleep in the other room. Fiona waited for a lull in their conversation.

"Lin? Wanna tell me why he's here? I mean, he hasn't been around in years. It's a little odd, don't you think?"

"Nicky didn't tell you? It was Carter that got me out of Pete's last night. He went with me to the hospital too. By the time we got home, it was early this morning. He and Nicky talked for a while, and he fell asleep on the sofa. I didn't have the heart to wake him." Linda finished her coffee, and brought her cup to the sink. "He's earned some good sleep, don't you agree?"

"Wow, that's a lot to process; I have so many questions."

"And I will tell you everything later."

While Fiona attempted to collect her thoughts in the La Salle's kitchen, Laurel was doing a bit of research from her tablet as Charlie drove her back to where this all began. She subconsciously began to convey her thoughts aloud. Charlie mistook her ramblings as the conversation between them and kept asking her to repeat herself. Although Laurel wasn't actually directing her thoughts to Charlie; she did reiterate each time he asked.

Not unlike Fiona, Charlie felt that connection to something great. He wasn't just a driver; he was a significant and coveted player on team Cooke. Laurel trusted him implicitly; she knew whatever was said in the car was in confidence. His continual loyalty was implied and reinforced by several years of keeping Laurel's trust. He listened to fractions of a million thoughts as Laurel articulated; while trying to help Laurel create one cohesive idea.

"Didn't you tell me that Pete's Pies was a participant in the *Can You Cooke* initiative?"

"I did." She placed her tablet beside her and leaned up in her seat as best as she could without causing herself discomfort from the tightening seat belt. "Go on, Charlie; what are you thinking?"

"Well, it will likely take a few weeks for any insurance money to be disbursed, right?" He didn't wait for Laurel to agree before continuing. "In the meantime, we could get a rebuild started with the special project fund from *Can You Cooke?* Couldn't we?"

"We could. I like to keep that fund as padded as possible as it's usually used for food in emergency situations. I'm wondering if I could squeeze a little more from our contributors, now instead of during the holidays. That way we have a few months to find a little extra by Thanksgiving."

"Well, OK Charlie, your idea is a front-runner for sure. Let's see where Nick is at this point. Then you can talk to him about our options."

"Wait, me? You want me to talk to him?"

"Of course. It was your idea and besides, it seemed as though you and Nick became friends last week. He may feel more comfortable talking to you."

"Yeah, Nick and Rob are cool. We have a lot in common. I mean Rob and I both drive and well Nick loves superhero comics and memorabilia almost as much as I do." For a moment Charlie sounded like a little kid, but his excitement over having new friends paled in comparison to the seriousness of wanting to help them.

"Charlie, how much longer until we get to the La Salle's? I have a few things to look into."

"Oh, just about twenty minutes."

"Perfect. Thank you." Laurel picked up the tablet she had placed on the seat. She sat back and got to work accessing the foundation information she'd need to illustrate Charlie's proposal. Laurel sent Fiona a quick text letting her know they were almost there. She checked her phone and slid it back into her pocket without telling Nick that Laurel was on her way. Fiona sat silently next to Nick on his back steps. He held his head in his hands and occasionally rubbed at his tired eyes. The two sat for a while; Fiona kept waiting for Nick to say something; anything but there were no words for what he was feeling. Finally, she broke the silence; "Nick, Laurel Cooke should be here any minute. She called me this morning and I told her what happened. She insisted on coming down to be with you."

"Fee; I'm exhausted. We'd better go in and make coffee."

"Good idea." She stood and offered her hand. "Come on, sweetie, let's get you washed up and caffeinated."

Fire and Ice

Meg was furious. She stormed into the kitchen and threw a wrapped gift box into the trash can.

"He doesn't deserve me!" she screamed to anyone who happened to be within earshot. Meg's sister Mare heard her scream. She sauntered into the kitchen and poured herself a cup of coffee.

"I told you he was an urchin when we met him. You insisted he'd clean up well. Meg, your baby daddy is nothing more than a set of pretty eyes and a nice ass."

"He was out all night! I've been calling his cell; he's not picking up. I called his parents, and they told me they assumed he was here with me last night. He was supposed to be going home to tell them about the baby; and the wedding. Where the hell could he have gone?"

"Track his phone. Or better yet, the car. Dad has a GPS tracker in all our vehicles. You know that. I'm more than sure there's one in Carter's car as well."

"I shouldn't have to track him down. He should have been here with me!" Meg was still screaming.

"Wow, Meg you know, all this stress isn't good for the baby; and red is so not your color," she said referring to the flush on Meg's face.

"Jesus Mare, can't you be a little supportive?"

"Nope."

Meg dialed Carter's cell again. This time it woke him. He picked up his phone from the coffee table; looked at his screen display and panicked. It took him a few seconds to collect his bearings, and finding himself passed out on the La Salle's sofa made him a little queasy. He knew he was in some deep shit. He assumed she had tracked his phone by now and knew he spent the night at Nick's. There was no use in coming up with a story; he would have to tell the truth. The hardest part would be explaining what he was doing in this neighborhood last night when he was supposed to be home talking to his parents about Meg's pregnancy. His anxiety was getting the best of him when he realized he hadn't been alone on the sofa. Tucked in the corner where his feet had been his old friend, Wanda. He leaned down and hugged her.

"Oh, I have missed you so much, beautiful," Wanda responded with a few affectionate licks to his face.

Carter stood; stretched and grabbed his phone and keys. He headed into the kitchen to find it filled with people; when he was only expecting to see Fiona; assuming she had brought Wanda with her. Instead, he found a kitchen full of chatting; laughing people, some familiar, some not. They were all drinking coffee and eating donuts from a huge purple bakery box in the center of the little kitchen table. Linda was the first to notice Carter standing in the doorway.

"There he is; my hero! Can someone get Carter some coffee and a plate?"

Charlie was leaning up against the counter near the sink and was closest to the coffee pot and cupboards.

"Got it," he turned to Carter and asked. "How do you take your coffee, man?"

Carter didn't mean to be rude or ignore Charlie's hospitality, but he couldn't take his eyes off of Fiona. Her gaze met his, as she searched for something to say.

"Light and sweet," she told Charlie, in response to his question to Carter. As soon as the words escaped; Fiona wished they hadn't. She inadvertently made the situation more awkward than it already was.

Laurel squeezed Rob's leg under the table. It startled him and caused him to laugh out loud. Of course, everyone in the kitchen turned their attention to Rob. Fiona was grateful.

"Sorry. Um, my phone went off in my pocket; I wasn't expecting that," he lied.

Carter accepted the cup of coffee from Charlie; who eagerly introduced himself to Linda's hero.

"You're the man of the hour my friend. I'm really glad to meet you."

Nick had rolled the desk chair up to the table from the other room and offered it to Carter. He told Nick he really should be going, but Nick reminded him with a whisper; "You're already in trouble with her; might as well stay for coffee and get to know our guests."

Carter joined the group, as well as their conversation. Charlie happily reiterated his thoughts on getting Pete's rebuild started as soon as possible. Nick seemed more hopeful than he had been earlier that morning, but his mind wouldn't quiet. He thought about what he and his family would do if they were to choose not to rebuild at all. He decided to talk to Rob and Linda about it later when everyone had gone.

Fiona's mere presence left Carter feeling at ease; relaxed and comfortable. He was enjoying the company and conversation; he hadn't smiled and laughed so much in a very long time. He kept one hand under the table; rubbing Wanda's ears as she nuzzled his hands with her nose.

"I wonder what Meg would say if she knew I woke up this morning next to another girl?" he said aloud.

The entire room could have done without the mention of Meg and Fiona had the perfect retort. She caught Laurel's stare and decided to simply let it go. Laurel was relieved and proud of Fiona's grace. She attempted to get the conversation back on track.

"I suppose we will have a better perspective as soon as we hear from the fire inspector. If you and your family decide to move forward with Charlie's plan, just let Fiona know. She and I can start things rolling on Monday."

"Oh, that's right," Rob exclaimed. "You start your new job on Monday. Fee, that's so exciting! Would you like me to drive you in on your first day?" he offered.

Before she could respond, Laurel piped up.

"Could you? I actually have something I'd like to run by you, Rob. We could meet for breakfast if you have time on Monday," Charlie let a low squeal escape from his throat; as though he was a child holding a juicy secret. Rob gave him a quizzical stare and then turned to Nick, who nodded in approval.

"Yeah, of course."

"I think we should all keep busy; you know life doesn't stop because of one unfortunate incident. No need to worry about us; Linda and I are good, and knowing our friends are happy makes us happy, right Lin?"

"Right," she agreed. Linda directed her response to Carter. She feared he would never be happy if he continued on this path yet somehow she knew his integrity; his character wouldn't allow for any other alternative.

Carter stood and walked over to the sink. He placed his empty cup inside and started to wash the few dishes that had been sitting there. At one time, not very long ago, this house was his second home. He slept here many nights after a long shift at Pete's. He and Nick would stay up playing video games and sleep in the next day before they went back to work together. Being in the La Salle's home felt like reliving a wonderful memory. He knew he was simply finding excuses to prolong that feeling. Carter dried his hands with a dish towel and said his goodbyes.

Fiona made her way past Laurel and Rob.

"I'll walk you out."

Carter held the door for Fiona, who stepped onto the front porch and froze. Carter hadn't yet noticed what made Fiona stop walking, and bumped into the back of her. He laughed as he steadied himself by grabbing both her shoulders. As he looked over her head toward the driveway, Carter realized why Fiona stood frozen in her footsteps. Meg had indeed tracked his car and was now propped against the front bumper. Her arms were crossed over her chest and although her sunglasses masked her expression, he knew from experience she was giving them the death stare. Fiona whispered without moving her lips; "Please let go of my shoulders."

Meg steadied herself and began to walk toward the house.

"So, you spent the night here? I really thought your slumming days were behind you, Carter."

Fiona moved to the side and took two steps down from the porch; "Give him some grace, Meg. It was a long and stressful night."

Meg exploded; "You don't get to speak! You don't get to say anything to me; ever! You are freaking whore! Did he tell you I'm pregnant? Do you have any idea what you have done?" It was obvious Meg assumed they had spent that long and stressful night together. Fiona opened her mouth to try and diffuse the situation when, of all people Charlie burst through the front door.

"Hey, you, crazy lady! You need to leave. It's you that doesn't get to speak to my friend that way; are you hearing me? You need to go."

Fiona stepped in front of Charlie.

"OK, time to go back inside." She took his arm and gently guided him backward toward the door. Fiona managed their way back to the kitchen and closed the door behind them. They could still hear Meg's voice as she continued to berate Carter at the top of her lungs. Fiona sat down next to Laurel who had just finished a text to Jaime. *Bringing Fiona back with me; 9-1-1. Girl's night at my house, copious amounts of wine necessary. We can send the guys to your house! You in?* Jaime responded immediately; *I'm on it.*

Laurel hugged Fiona.

"Girl's night, tonight?" she offered. "I think we should invite Linda, and would your Mom want to join us?"

Fiona was still feeling the shock of Meg's announcement. She heard Laurel, but there was no real comprehension.

"She's pregnant."

"I know, honey, I heard. Everyone did."

Many Worlds; One Family

Laurel sat up front with Charlie on their way back to Long Island to make room in the back for their passengers; all four of them. Girl's night had to also include Wanda who was perfectly comfortable with her head in Fiona's lap. Laurel knew by her initial reaction that Susan Lasher wanted to accept the invitation, but had reservations about leaving Wanda. Of course, Laurel suggested she pack a bag for her as well. Linda and Susan were absolutely giddy on the drive. Charlie politely asked if he could raise the glass partition between the front and back seats. No one objected; they were enjoying the ride.

"Forgive me, Laurel, but I was having a hard time concentrating. I'm so used to having only one passenger, maybe two. It doesn't usually get rowdy in here."

"No apologies necessary. I would feel the same if I were driving. And, thank you, Charlie, for everything. What you did for Fiona was kind of amazing, and very chivalrous."

"I lost it. I was brought up to have respect for everyone, and as antiquated as it may seem; I believe men should be there to defend women. Especially women who are innocent. That crazy lady accused Fiona of something she didn't do; she wasn't even there last night. She flipped my switch, that's for sure. If anyone ever spoke to my Mom or sisters, or worse; Kay that way I would have to borrow bail money!"

Laurel laughed.

"And I would make sure you had bail money," she assured him. "Hey, Charlie, speaking of Kay, do you think she'd like to join us tonight? It would be so great for Fiona to have someone her own age to hang out with."

"I think she'd love it! I'll give her a call. Thank you Laurel, for thinking of her. Kay hasn't been herself lately. If you ask me, she's the one who needs friends to hang out with. I'm working all the time, and my mom is too. Kay is with the girls a lot. It might be getting to her only having two hormonal teens to talk to. Even when she's at work, the only person she has is Mr Franks and he's not the best conversationalist."

"Is Kay interested in finding another job, Charlie?"

"She'd love to, but it hasn't been easy to find something that allows her to be home for my sisters after school."

The proverbial lightbulb suddenly lit up over Laurel's head. Sweet Kay may just be struggling to fit in. It would explain her evident and sudden change in character. There were no regrets in her decision to have Charlie call Kay about girl's night. Laurel felt like something good would inevitably come from getting everyone together.

"Call her, Charlie. Let's at least give her a little notice."

Charlie spoke into the air, activating the hands-free option on his phone.

"Call Kay." She was thrilled to get the invite and accepted without hesitation. Laurel told her to get a few things together, and they'd see her soon. Before Charlie ended the call, he told Kay he loved her. She said back with a sincerity in her voice he hadn't heard in a while.

Laurel thought of Carter and couldn't help wondering why a guy like him would choose someone like Meg. She hadn't even met her, but that didn't seem relevant. Laurel was never the type to pass judgment on others. She rarely expressed her opinions if they were negative in any way. She believed what we say about others, we speak into existence. If we fuel the negative, it grows, not only in ourselves but in the people we are speaking of as well. Admittedly, she felt a little guilty discussing the recent changes in Kay with Jaime and TC. But, now, with a new perspective, she would work to make it right. She cared about Kay and Charlie; she didn't know Carter or Meg, but still felt trepidation for their future.

Meg feared for their future as well. Carter was not the man she wanted him to be; the man she tried to make him into. Now, as they sat in the Wyatts' living room, Meg realized she would have to expand her manipulation tactics to include her future in-laws. They were simply not responding the way she wanted them to, and she feared their influence over Carter would present her with more obstacles.

Carter sat idly by and allowed Meg to deliver her rendition of his recent betrayal to his parents. Her voice was shrill, and her words harsh. She not only blamed Carter but accused his parents of raising him improperly.

Somehow, this became all their fault. Mrs Wyatt held herself together as best as she could while taking fire. Meg was intentionally hurting her, choosing which words would inflict the most pain. She was ruthless and didn't stop until she finally broke Carter's mother. Once Mrs Wyatt allowed her tears to escape; they became an uncontrollable deluge. Carter's dad wanted nothing more than to toss Meg out on her ass. His face was hot, and his fists were clenched as he too tried to control his emotions for the sake of his son. He rose from his chair; crossed the room to where Carter was seated on the sofa. Mr Wyatt sat next to him and put his arm around his son's shoulders, as a gesture of support. This infuriated Meg even further; Mr Wyatt thought to himself.

"Mission accomplished."

Carter's father had always told both sons that no matter what they have done; no matter what kind of trouble they were in; he would be there for them. It was easy to make and keep that promise as Sam and Carter were both good kids, good men. But the Wyatts were the kind of parents who would honor that promise even if trouble was familiar to them.

Meg continued to spew her venom; this time aiming directly at Mr Wyatt.

"Oh, you think your son is so perfect, don't you?"

"Yes, I do," he answered calmly.

"Well, you couldn't be more wrong about him. Believe me, there are big changes coming." She shot Carter a look and pointed her finger in his face. "I own you now!"

Meg placed her hand on her abdomen; "We own you; *All* of you." She picked up her handbag and stormed down the stairs and out the front door. Seconds later, they could hear the dramatic squeal of her tires as she pulled away from the house.

The Wyatts sat quietly with their individual thoughts; each searching for solutions that simply didn't seem to exist. Finally, Carter spoke:

"Please, before either of you say anything; I need to tell you where I was last night," with tears in his eyes, he told his parents everything. He started with dinner and finished his story in the La Salle's driveway. While he gave details of the fire, Mrs Wyatt began to cry again. She interrupted to ask if everyone was OK and if there was anything she could do for the family. It made Carter so proud to be her son to know she was thinking of others even at a time when no one would fault her for thinking of herself.

Mr Wyatt waited for Carter to finish speaking before confessing that Sam had called him last night and told him about Meg's pregnancy. He asked his father to keep it between them for the time being. Carter seemed surprised to hear of Sam's call, but Mr Wyatt reminded him that Sam assumed Carter was already on his way to tell them.

"There was no way Sam could have anticipated your delay in coming home."

"I'm not upset with Sam; he was preparing you; he was being a good son and brother. But let me ask you; if you thought I was on my way, where did you think I was when I didn't come home?"

"Well, I assumed you went back to Meg, but secretly, I hoped you went in to see Fiona," Mrs Wyatt confessed.

"Oh, poor Fiona! She got blindsided this morning. It was horrible, and I did nothing. I stood there and let Meg accuse her; blame her, and she did nothing wrong," Carter confessed.

Mrs Wyatt sighed deeply; "So, where do we go from here? I cannot sit back and let Meg ruin your life, Carter. You're a hero, after all." That was her attempt to lighten the mood, and for a few moments, it worked. The Wyatt family shared a smile, and Carter's parents took the opportunity to let him know how proud they truly were. Mrs Wyatt wasn't convinced that Meg was indeed pregnant. She was more concerned with the well-being of her own child at the moment. However, if there was a baby on the way; they'd deal with that when the time came; as a family.

Carter's phone chimed, notifying him of a text message. Ironically, it was from Fiona.

I hope all is well; I am honestly happy for you and Meg; may life continue to bless you. He placed the phone back on the table without responding. Fiona's text made him regret leaving her even more than he already did.

"I pressed *send*," Fiona told Kay
"Do you think he'll respond?"
"No."
"Well, maybe he thinks you're being insincere, facetious even."

"I don't do facetious things; he knows that. I text him because I truly care about him; I want nothing more than to see him happy. He won't respond, Kay because he no longer feels anything for me. It's fine; I'd rather have nothing than a disingenuous response, you know?"

"I do. And, I am so glad you and I got a second chance to get to know one another. I can only imagine what your first impression of me was like. I am truly sorry. If anyone was disingenuous, it was me when you and I first met. I suppose I was having some sort of identity crisis of my own."

"No apologies, Kay. I was so out of place; and honestly, very skeptical about the Cooke's. I couldn't imagine why they would want to meet me. If anything, I was the one giving off weird vibes that day. What a difference a week can make, huh?"

"You're being very kind, Fiona." Kay reached over and gave Fiona's hand a gentle squeeze. "You and Laurel are a lot alike; whether you realize it or not. You're both really special people; because only wonderfully special people naturally put others before themselves. I'd like to be more like the both of you."

"You're selling yourself short. We just had a conversation about you and Charlie's family. Kay, you lit up talking about those girls. I know you say you want more. Believe me, I admire you for wanting a bigger life; but I can't imagine anything bigger than being a role model for Charlie's sisters. I know they have their mom; however, you give them a look at their near future; they can see themselves at your age much easier than seeing themselves as mom's."

"I never thought about that. Thank you."

The two continued to trade stories; of their teenage years. Fiona's mom would chime in now and again with her rendition. Susan was having the time of her life. She and Linda kept Jaime's attention with stories of their own.

"Oh, Maria would have had a blast with us tonight."

Linda agreed.

"Yes, my mom's two favorite things to do are telling old stories and drinking wine. Should we call her? Oh, let's call her!"

Maria La Salle was happy to hear from her daughter. She had been worried since she got the call about the fire. It made her heart happy to know Linda was with Susan; and not home alone, stressed and worried.

"If I can't be there with you my darling, I'm so glad Susan is."

"Mom, I really wish you were here; this has been such a great night. I feel like a celebrity."

Maria asked Linda to send her some pictures so she could have faces to go with names. She told her daughter she'd see her in a few days, and they had a lot to talk about.

"Family meeting when I get home. But, tonight, just enjoy yourself, honey. Put Susan back on, I'd like to say goodbye."

The two friends spoke for a few minutes before Susan returned to the conversation happening in Laurel's living room. Maria told Susan she had just received the call from the fire inspector, and it had, in fact, been an accidental incident caused by faulty wiring. The news gave Maria peace of mind, as it pained her to think her children may be accused of setting the fire themselves. Maria asked Susan not to mention anything about the fire to Linda and let her enjoy the weekend.

"My poor daughter has been through enough; she deserves to laugh and be around her friends."

Susan promised and hung up. Linda asked her if everything was ok with Maria.

"Oh, your Mom is fine. She just feels bad for not being here. I told her we had everything under control for now, and not to worry." Susan was not exactly lying but hadn't given up the entire truth. It was more important for Linda to continue feeling carefree; even for just one night.

While Jaime and Laurel shared college stories with their new friends, Wanda made a new friend of her own. She and Laurel snuggled on the floor; as if they belonged to one another. Jaime reminded her friend that dogs were excellent judges of character.

"You know, dogs are more in tune with energies than people. They are not jaded; they have no preconceived expectations; just their instincts to know who is worthy of their unconditional love."

Laurel leaned down and kissed Wanda's head.

"She's a sweetheart. Just think, if not for Wanda; none of this would be happening. And, look around Jai, something amazing is brewing among these wonderful people; I'm just not sure what it is yet."

Rising from the Ashes

"Well, this is most unusual and unexpected." Nicky glanced around his living room; no one but Rob shared the space with him. His mother and sister were both gone, and the house was exclusively theirs for the night.

Rob thought of his reservation for the hotel on the beach; the one he canceled yet again. Despite the advice from the girls earlier that day, Rob thought it best to give Nick some time to process the fire without offering another life-changing decision.

"Feel like talking, or would you rather I find a movie and call out for Chinese food?"

"Yes, let's do all of that. We can order dinner and talk while we eat. Then we can find something entertaining to watch; a comedy would be awesome."

"Sounds like the perfect plan," Rob agreed as he picked up his phone to call for their favorite take-out.

They ate their dinner with little conversation. It was such a rare occasion when Nick La Salle didn't have something to talk about. Rob knew him well, but tonight he was in uncharted waters. Finally, Nick pushed his cardboard container of Lo Mein aside and turned to Rob.

"I don't know how to say this; I feel like the worst person in the world, but there's something I need to tell you."

"Jesus Nick, are you breaking up with me?"

"God no! I wanted to tell you; I'm thinking about not rebuilding Pete's. Rob, what would make you think I was breaking up with you?"

"Uh, Nick, take a second and think about what you just said to me."

"Wow, yeah, I hear it now. I'm sorry. I seem to be having difficulty getting the words out. It's not you, I'm really confused. I've been thinking; now would be the perfect time to make some changes, you know, try new things; experience life a little. But, this isn't just my life; what would it do to Mom and Lin if we didn't have Pete's?"

Instead of reinforcing Nick's concern for his family, Rob kept the conversation focused on his boyfriend. As much as Nick wanted to do right by his mother and sister because he loved them; Rob wanted to give Nick what he needed for the very same reason.

"If you could do anything; what would it be? Tell me what you're thinking. You know, nothing is impossible."

"Anything?" Nick's voice clearly expressed his excitement.

"Of, course. Go crazy."

Nick began sharing his hopes and dreams with Rob. It was immediately evident that he had given this subject a lot of thought, and Rob felt a little like he was meeting a part of Nick he hadn't before.

"I have always wanted to get out of New Jersey. I know that's crazy, but I feel so alive when we go to your parent's house. The air is fresh and it's so green and lush. It feels like vacation. As much as I appreciate my home; I always feel a bit depressed when we get back from Long Island."

Nick adjusted himself on the sofa. He leaned forward and stuffed a throw pillow behind him.

"I've been making pizzas since I was twelve years old. Before that; bussing tables and sweeping up in the bar. It would be my dream to learn something new; I'd love to go to school and become a paramedic."

"Really? I had no idea you were interested in working in the medical field. Nick, I think you'd be perfect. You're compassionate, composed and smart as hell."

"Thank you. I think about it all the time; but afraid to say it out loud. I don't want to disappoint anyone. I've always been a family-first guy."

"I know that, Nick, but as much as you love Lin and Maria; is as much as they love you. I think it will be worth it to talk to them about this. I cannot imagine your family being unsupportive of your dreams."

Rob listened while Nick shared every detail of his ideal future. They talked for hours, and Rob no longer regretted his decision to stay home. This was so much better than any weekend at the shore. Romance wasn't about where you spend your time together, but the quality of time spent wherever you are. He decided to hold off on asking Nick to live together. If Nick was serious about pursuing a new career in a new town; it made more sense to wait. He did wonder if Nick's desire to move to Long Island had more to do with the Cooke's than his own family. Nick's obsession with the Cooke's hadn't gone unnoticed, however, Rob too had to admit that life got more interesting since they met.

TC joined his wife in their living room. Her overnight guests were more than gracious and didn't leave her home in disarray, but Laurel was a habitual tidier when she was brainstorming. TC pretended to fluff pillows while Laurel refolded the throws for the second time. TC asked.

"Did you by any chance ask Rob to meet with you on Monday?"

"I did; how did you know?"

"You must have mentioned it to Charlie. Joe asked why Rob and Nick hadn't joined us on 'guys night'. Charlie explained they had other plans, but Rob was driving Fiona in on Monday and meeting with you."

"Guys night? Is that going to be a thing?" she teased.

"Well, yeah, what else would you call a bunch of guys drinking beer, watching sci-fi movies and passing out in Joe's basement before midnight? Maybe next time, it will be our basement, who knows?" he teased.

"Ah, sounds like fun, actually."

"It was fun, which is why it needs to be 'a thing' as you so eloquently put it. Hey, Charlie also told us what went down with that guy's girlfriend. I'm thinking we were so wrong about him. Fiona is great, but she's better off without 'blue boy'." TC was referring to the color emanating from Carter in the photo; Laurel knew he had forgotten his name entirely.

"Hon, 'blue boy has a name; Carter. Carter Wyatt and I have a feeling we haven't heard the last of him."

"Laurel, you know I love you more than nanites, but I'm sensing a personal attachment here."

"Yeah, me too. There's a reason I feel this attachment, I just can't pinpoint the details yet. I trust that whatever is supposed to come from these new relationships will reveal itself when the time is right. For now, I'm excited for Fiona to join Cooke Industries, and I do hope Rob will be open to my offer."

"Offer? Why do I feel like our HR department is about to get really busy?"

"You're probably right. I have an idea I'd like to speak to Linda and Nick about as well. Maybe something temporary while they rebuild Pete's Pies."

"Not everyone *wants* to work for Cooke Industries, Laurel. Not as much as *you* want them to. However, I trust your process; it hasn't failed us yet. So, what arena are we about to expand into this time?"

"When I know; you'll know. For now, my goals are getting Fiona acclimated; talking to Nick, Rob and Linda about potentially joining us in already established positions."

"I wasn't aware that we were currently hiring."

"We are always hiring, TC. What's the point of owning a company and having infinite resources if we can't utilize them to benefit others? Having good people work with us only strengthens the company as a whole. It's just good business practice"

"In sports, this is called, 'stacking your team'," TC called out to his wife as she walked toward the hallway. Laurel finally put the throws back in the hall closet; and returned to the living room. She sat next to her husband and patted his knee.

"Well, it's a damn good thing we aren't playing games, then. Look, if things don't work out the way I imagine, no one will be worse for the wear."

He knew better than to debate with Laurel. She was so much better at presenting and winning her case; no matter the subject. Few people were aware of Laurel's law background; she was in fact a licensed attorney in the state of New York. Soon after passing the *bar*; Laurel went to work for a small but reputable law firm in the city. She lasted less than a year before deciding she could do better for more people on her own. All the formal education in the world paled by comparison to real-life experience for Laurel. Ironically, she's an advocate for education and is very active with their intern and scholarship programs. She and her sister-in-law, Emma have changed the lives of many young people who dreamed of a college education but never thought it possible. Laurel realized what a walking contradiction she would seem to others if everyone knew she had a degree in law that she chose not to use. However; it seemed prudent to keep her license current just in case Cooke Industries ever needed her expertise.

"So, I take it, your sleepover went well, then?"

"Uh, ten-year-olds have sleepovers, hon, we had a girl's night, you know, like your guy's night, but classier."

"You look tired, Laurel. I'm assuming your sleepover didn't include much sleep," he teased, intentionally using the term sleepover again.

"I'm wiped out," she confessed.

"I have an idea of my own; why don't you hang out by the pool for a while; relax, and I'll go pick up something for dinner. We can call it an early night, and worry about everything else tomorrow."

Laurel wrapped her arms around TC's shoulders.

"And, that is why I love you; you're a freakin' genius."

Part 2
Doubling Down:

"Thanks for coming ladies. I really need your help." Fiona and Kay sat in the chairs opposite the small sofa in TC's office. He was perched on the very edge; leaning forward over the glass coffee table. Kay thought he looked like a squatting umpire; ready to catch a fastball; she just hoped they had one to throw.

It had been nearly three months since she and Fiona started working together. Kay felt renewed; purposeful and happy. Charlie took care of the girls twice a week, giving her two days in the office. TC was more than happy to set her up with everything she needed to work remotely the other three days a week. On occasion, Fiona would come to the house to work with her; which was always more fun than actual work.

Their new schedule was made possible since Rob joined the team and could take Charlie's shifts on his days with his sisters. Everything was running like clockwork, but Kay still felt unnerved when they were called to TC's office. Fiona, on the other hand, took being summoned in stride. She was used to his dramatic flair and each time they met, the outcome was far less daunting than the anticipation. Fiona walked to the mini fridge hidden in TC's cabinet and grabbed a bottle of water.

"Anyone else?" she offered.

TC waved his hand, declining the water, but Kay's throat was dry from feeling anxious.

"Yes, please," she croaked.

Fiona returned to her chair next to Kay and handed her friend the water.

"Well, boss, what can we do for you?"

"First of all, I want to thank both of you for the amazing work you've done with Chris and the vendors. When we decided to pair the two of you on this project, Laurel and I were curious as to how you'd work together as well as with someone who is established here and knows the ropes. It turns out; you're a dream team! I'm so impressed with the execution of Chris's idea to incorporate and make each vendor a shareholder. They now have medical insurance as well as owning a piece of their own company. The sense of pride they must feel is nothing compared to my feelings for the entire initiative. I know there are a few more details to work out, but soon you will both have some time to focus on your next project."

"And, what might that be?" Fiona asked.

"You're going to tell me. Laurel needs a new directive; she's driving me a little insane these days. I think you two are perfect for any humanities-based projects that may arise, and that's Laurel's arena of expertise. So, tell me, what do people need? What do they want? How can we assist?"

Fiona sat up in her chair.

"Actually, I have a few ideas."

Before she could elaborate, TC told them to take a few days to write a proposal for every idea that comes to mind; and have them ready by Friday.

"Nothing too professional, just an outline or summary will do for now."

Kay turned to her friend.

"This will be so much fun."

TC was pleased with their enthusiasm.

"Oh, and Fiona, I'm sure Chris will still want your input on the ongoing vendor project, so no worries about spending less time with him," he winked at her, awkwardly.

Confused, she asked.

"What was that wink about? Was it an implication that I enjoy spending time with Chris on a personal level; which I do. He's awesome, but I'm confused as to your interest," Fiona tried sounding professional, but TC knew she was just playing along.

TC cleared his throat.

"Fiona, that man has a crush on you, and you know it."

She and Kay couldn't contain their amusement. Both women broke out into laughter.

"If you were any other boss, you know this conversation would be insanely inappropriate, right? And I must say, you are way off the mark here. Chris is seeing Linda La Salle."

"Damn, well that would also explain why he was bragging about his Jersey Girl. I guess I better start paying attention at the water cooler." TC appeared to be a bit embarrassed about his misguided assumption. It was refreshing to see someone with his intellectual preponderance show humility and humanity without viewing those traits as weakness. Fiona couldn't imagine there were many people like TC on this Earth. She felt fortunate to be working with him; and even luckier to know him.

Kay was eager to ask Fiona what she had in mind. She waited until they were in the elevator; Fiona pushed 'L' sending them down to the lobby.

"Where are we going? I'm really excited to hear what you are thinking for our next project."

"And you will! Let's talk over lunch though; I'm starved."

Kay followed Fiona's lead; knowing she had something more than lunch on her mind. Admittedly; she hadn't yet thought of an idea on her own, but hoped she could collaborate with Fiona to come up with something brilliant.

It was later in the afternoon and Ralph's deli wasn't as crowded as it had been just an hour before. Fiona asked the hostess if they could be seated in Silvie's section. The hostess; who's name tag read, 'Mo' was happy to accommodate.

"Sure, girls, right this way."

Mo seated them at a table near the front of the deli; next to the glass wall with a perfect view of the lobby. Fiona noticed Jaime at the information desk and waved but Jaime turned too quickly to see Fiona.

"Oh, well, I'll catch up with Jaime later. Right now, we should decide what to order."

Within a few minutes, Silvie was standing tableside.

"Hey, ladies, so great to see you both. Mo said you asked for me personally, I'm flattered."

Fiona smiled.

"You're the best, but you know me, I do have another reason for wanting to see you today. Let's order first, and if you have a few minutes when you come back, I'm hoping you can help me fill Kay in on what we discussed last week. TC just asked us to come up with a few new project proposals, and I want so badly to make our idea into your reality. Well, yours and many other people as well, but you know what I mean." Her enthusiasm was evident.

"Oh, you are fired up about this, aren't you?" Silvie teased.

Fiona and Kay ordered their lunch and Silvie told them she'd make sure she had a little time to spend chatting when she came back with their food.

"You may want to start without me, Fee, there's a lot to catch Kay up on."

While Fiona and Kay waited for their food to arrive, Fiona began the conversation by telling Kay why she asked Silvie to join them.

"A week or so ago, Silvie and I got to talking in the ladies' room, of all places. She told me she had finally found a decent apartment she was sharing with a friend. Collectively, the women have five children; and they would both love to become foster parents."

"Wow, That is amazing."

"I know, right? However, their apartment is small; barely able to accommodate both families, and even with free child care from the older siblings and extra shifts; things are still tight for them."

Kay was already invested in Fiona's story.

"Please, go on."

"Anyway; with real estate being astronomical here in the city; I was thinking, what if Cooke Industries were to acquire an old building and renovate to help families who would foster if they had the room and resources. I would bet there are others right here in our company that would love to."

Kay lit up; "Oh, wouldn't it be so great to find a building with a small yard, or roof access, for a community garden."

"Kay, that's a wonderful idea." Fiona's mind was immediately racing with possibilities.

Silvie returned with their lunch and pulled a chair over to the table to join them.

"I told Ralph I would be on break for a few minutes. I let him know I'd be here with you two if he needed me."

"He's such a great guy," Fiona interjected.

"He is. This is the best job I have ever had." Silvie confessed.

"How are things working out with Linda? Have you had the chance to get to know her?"

Silvie gushed; "She's wonderful. And if you didn't know any better; you'd swear that Linda was Ralph's daughter or something. They work so well together."

"That's so good to hear. Well, you know Linda worked her family business practically all of her life; it's no surprise to hear she's bringing that dynamic into Ralph's kitchen."

"Kitchen? She's the heart of this whole place! Whoever hired her should be really proud of themselves." It was clear that Silvie as well as the other deli employees viewed Linda as an asset.

Kay opened her mouth to tell Silvie that she and Fiona collaborated with Laurel on that very decision, but Fiona shook her head ever so slightly, indicating to Kay; it wasn't the time to get into that particular subject. She feared they would never stay on subject if the conversation derailed this early in the game.

Silvie crossed her legs and leaned in on her elbows; "OK, what have I missed so far?"

Fiona reiterated; and continued to brainstorm with her friends.

"I have no idea if it is in the realm of possibilities to find and purchase an entire building, but that's where we come in ladies. I'm just not sure where to start. Do we research people or places first?"

Silvie suggested they split their focus; she happily volunteered to start with people.

"I can write an email; sort of tell my story, and ask for input or ask if anyone ever thought of fostering?"

"Good idea. Let's include that email in our proposal to TC before you send it out company-wide though, agreed?"

"Absolutely. I wouldn't want to jump the gun."

Kay offered to research places; "I know nothing about real estate, but I love old buildings. I think they have such charm and history. Let me find a few preliminary options, just for example. I'll pull the info and pictures from the internet to present to TC."

"Well, what does that leave me to do?" Fiona quipped.

Silvie got serious for a moment.

"Fiona, would you work on ways to get potential foster's the information they'd need to become certified? It would help to know the process before we ask if anyone is willing or interested."

"Yes, absolutely. And good thinking; Silvie. We could send that information in a follow-up email. Having it all compiled and ready to send shows our commitment to this project."

Kay took a bite of her sandwich and held up one finger, indicating she needed a minute before continuing.

"I am all for this, believe me, but do either of you think that TC will see this as forming a commune, or like a foster parent cult?"

Fiona smiled at the thought of a cult of do-gooders living in a walk-up and raising children to grow their own food on the roof, but she knew what Kay was getting at.

"It's possible that TC won't share our vision, or possibly perceive it as ambitious but not conceivable. If that happens; we go over his head."

Kay laughed loudly and Silvie seemed confused.

"Who could possibly be over his head?"

Fiona and Kay answered in perfect unison; "Laurel!"

TC wasted no time at all, and had Laurel on the phone, likely before Fiona and Kay even reached the elevator. He told her about the meeting with her friends and Fiona's immediate enthusiasm.

"I could see her wheels turning. I'm expecting great things from Fiona."

Laurel seemed pleased.

"Tell me, how's Kay doing? This corporate atmosphere is all new to her. You didn't intimidate her, did you?"

"Laurel, I only intimidate people who need to be intimidated. Kay is fine. She and Fiona work well together. Clearly, Kay is a team player, whereas Fiona has leadership qualities that I hadn't expected. I'm really impressed."

"I saw it, from the first time I met her. I knew she would excel in whatever she put her efforts into. I am really curious as to what they come up with for this next project."

"Well, I set our follow-up for Friday at three p.m., why don't you join us? Then you and I can go to dinner here in the city."

"That actually sounds wonderful. What time are you getting out of there tonight?"

"Leaving in an hour. See you soon."

Kay and Fiona finished their lunch, thanked Silvie for everything, and asked if she would be free to meet with them on Friday morning, prior to their presentation. She agreed, and the two women made their way back up to their office. Kay pulled out her phone to read some notes she had been typing during lunch.

"Look, I wrote as much as I could in my notes section, so we didn't forget the details."

Fiona was impressed.

"Kay, I didn't even notice you typing. Wow, I must have been on a roll."

"You were, and that's a really good thing," Kay suddenly stopped talking, and all the color drained from her cheeks.

"Honey, what's wrong?"

"Um, nothing. I just thought for a minute I had deleted my notes." It was obvious that Kay was lying. She wasn't very good at it.

"OK, I will respect your decision to not tell me the truth; but you are a lousy liar."

Kay took a deep breath and let it out slowly.

"Fee, if I don't tell you, someone else will, and I'd rather you hear it from me, would you rather it be me?"

"I think that depends on what it is. Please tell me everyone is ok, no one is hurt or anything, right?"

"No, nothing like that. I'm probably being dramatic. I got a text from Charlie to look at my social media. There's a post from someone who tagged you and Nicky. It's shitty, and just mean and I don't want to be the one that makes you feel bad, but I do want to show you," Kay was rambling.

"Show me. I'm a big girl, I can take it, whatever it is." Fiona had no idea what it could be or who would want to upset her never mind Nicky.

"OK," Kay pulled up the post on her phone and handed it to Fiona. It was from Meg's account. There was a picture of her and Carter standing near a tree, both with their hands on her growing belly. The second picture was of an ultrasound. The caption read:

" Was yours; Is mine; forever will be theirs; I just doubled down! We're having twins!"

Fiona was justifiably confused. Her heart broke for Carter, yet she had to question why Meg was so emphatic about hurting him; claiming him, and not focused on the joy of having children. This was not, in Fiona's mind, a competition. She sat quietly for a moment; which made Kay visibly anxious; squirming in her chair. Finally, she asked; "Are you OK?"

Fiona smiled at her friend. She knew Kay was concerned for her.

"I'm fine. Thank you. This whole debacle really has nothing to do with me or Nicky. We didn't get her pregnant!" Although Fiona appeared to find the post humorous, her heart ached. Meg knew just which buttons to push for maximum damage. The truth was, Fiona did suddenly feel as though there was no longer hope. She and Carter would never be; despite everyone believing the contrary.

Kay laughed loudly; partially due to her nervousness in regard to her friend's feelings. She was also relieved to hear that Fiona wasn't affected by Meg's ignorance and obviously noxious demeanor, or so she thought.

"It's not really my place to comment, I mean, I don't know Meg, but she seems to be the worst kind of attention seeker."

"It does appear that way, doesn't it? I don't know much about her either, to tell you the truth. She and her family live a few towns over. Her father is a big shot in the automotive industry, but we had never crossed paths until she met Carter. Even then, Meg did a great job of keeping him far away from me and everyone we knew. You know; they have been together for years. I can't help wondering why she's still so insecure. Anyway, you and I have work to do; important work. We can't afford to let someone else's drama distract us."

"You're right. I shouldn't have shown you that post." Kay symbolically turned her phone over, screen down.

"Kay, like you said; I would have seen it eventually. It was better you showed me; honestly. Now we can move forward. There's nothing I can do to help Carter, anyway. But you and I can help a lot of people if we do our jobs well, and I know we will."

Fiona's phone chimed. She looked at her notifications and there was a message from Nicky. He sent her a screenshot of Meg's post and wrote; *What the hell is this? We didn't knock her up! So why tag us? Do we care?"*

Fiona showed Kay the message; *Great minds do think alike.*

Losses and Gains

Susan Lasher sat alone at her kitchen table. She had been there for hours; just sitting, wondering who she should call, what she should say, and where she would get the strength to do so. The tears had finally subsided, and Susan made the decision to call Maria first. As she dialed; another wave of despair came over her. She was just about to hang up when she heard her best friend's voice.

"Hey, lady; what's up?"

Susan sobbed uncontrollably; no words would come. Maria asked her if she was home; and Susan managed an audible.

"Yes."

"I'll be right there."

By the time Susan composed herself long enough to walk across the kitchen and unlock the back door, Maria was already on her steps. She opened the door for her friend, who without a word came in and hugged her. Maria managed to get Susan back in her chair. She went over to the counter and began making a pot of coffee; all the while keeping her composure, yet she couldn't help but speculate as to what may have happened. Maria concluded someone must have passed; otherwise, Susan would not be so complacent. If someone was sick or hurt, she'd be anxious to get to them, and her friend was clearly at a loss. Susan took the coffee cup from Maria and nodded in appreciation. Her eyes still filled with tears; she began telling her friend what had her so distressed.

"My mom passed this morning."

"Oh, sweetie, I am so sorry." Maria felt guilty giving her best friend such a definitive response but there wasn't much more to say that would make a difference. She continued; "Have you called Fee yet?" Susan shook her head.

"OK, do you need me to do that for you?"

"No, I can. I just need another minute. Thank you."

"What about flights? I can look that up for you."

"Oh, yes, please. I hadn't even thought about that. Of course; we need to get to Florida."

"I'm on it. I'll go grab your laptop and you need to call your daughter."

"Maria, thank you. I know how busy you are with packing and moving. I really appreciate you being here with me." Susan reached for her friend's hand.

"You are more important to me than anything else I have to do. I'm here for as long as you need me to be."

Susan gave Maria's hand a squeeze.

"I need to call my kid."

Fiona and Kay were just putting the finishing touches on their proposal for TC. They had asked Laurel to look it over before their meeting. She told them TC had invited her as well, but if they would like to video chat and give her the highlights beforehand; she'd be happy to listen. Kay made the call and put Laurel on the sixty-inch monitor in the conference room.

"Well, hey there ladies; how's the dream team today?"

Kay told her they were waiting for Silvie.

"We asked her to sit in with us this morning; you know, she is the real inspiration for this project proposal."

Laurel spoke like a proud parent; "I couldn't be more excited; not only for the proposal but for all of you as well. It makes my heart swell with pride knowing we are fortunate enough to have such compassionate and innovative people on our team; as well as a part of our very large extended family."

Kay beamed. She needed this more than anyone; a win in her book. It was an extraordinary feeling to have gained acceptance from her peers as well as Laurel and TC, both personally and professionally.

"Thank you so much for the opportunity, Laurel. You have no idea how much this means to me."

As Silvie made her way into the office, Kay grabbed the written proposal from the top of Fiona's desk and presented it to her as if it were a birthday gift she knew Silvie had been wishing for. Laurel greeted Silvie from her rather omnipotent position on the large screen overlooking the office.

"Hello, Silvie, so happy you're joining our meeting of the minds this morning."

The waitress felt a little overwhelmed and simply smiled without a word. She had never been included in something so important, and relevant; never mind credited for her contributions. She began leafing through the hard copy that Kay had printed specifically for her. There were copies for each of them as well as a PowerPoint presentation for TC. Kay knew it wasn't necessary, but she had a dream a few nights before that the internet failed just as they were about to present to TC, so she wasn't taking any chances.

Silvie whispered to Kay.

"Where's Fiona?"

Kay told her she had a call just before they got started and would be back shortly. The women made some small talk to pass the time but Laurel's concern for Fiona's absence increased.

"Kay, can you please check on Fee? I have a strange feeling that something is wrong."

"Of course." Kay exited the office into the hall where she found Fiona standing, staring blankly with her phone in her hand. She asked if everything was OK, but Fiona just smiled weakly and began walking back into their office. She nodded to Silvie who was sitting in Kay's desk chair and then looked up into Laurel's image on the monitor. "I have to go," she said. Her voice was weak, and all the color had drained from her face. "Um, that was my mother who called. My Grams passed away this morning."

Kay's eyes welled with tears as she hugged her friend.

"I'm so sorry Fee, what do you need? I'm here for you, we all are," she offered.

Laurel was unnerved by her lack of emotional reaction. She feared Fiona was in shock; and tried to anticipate the best way to assist her friend.

"Let's get you out of there. I'm calling Rob; he will drive you home. I'm sure he is in the building this morning. I'll also let TC know we are postponing the meeting; so no worries." Laurel grabbed her cell to call Rob.

Fiona's thoughts came back into focus; "No, it's fine, Kay can do the presentation as scheduled," she turned to her friend who was frantically shaking her head in protest. "Yes, you got this. You're well prepared; and the sooner we get TC to sign off on our proposal, the sooner we can get started. I may be gone for a week or so. My Grams lives; um, lived in Florida. I'll need to fly out with mom as soon as possible."

Kay panicked; "No, oh just no, we can wait."

Laurel took charge; "Kay, we are going to do this together. You asked Fiona what she needed, and she told you. She needs to know you have everything covered while she's with her family. Silvie; can you join us this afternoon?"

Silvie nodded in agreement. Kay pulled herself together, knowing Laurel was right. This is how she can help; "OK, I will handle everything; you have nothing to worry about, Fee. Just please, take care and I will text you later, if that's OK?"

Fiona had gathered her things and thanked her friends.

"I will look forward to hearing from you later, and Kay? Thank you." She hugged her and Silvie and blew Laurel a kiss before making her way down to the lobby where Rob was waiting to walk her to the car.

Everything changes

Fiona's cousin Kylie was waiting in the common area of Orlando airport. She greeted her family with hugs and kisses, grabbing the carry-on bags from both her aunts; Susan and Stephanie. Kylie was the eldest daughter of the eldest Lasher sister; Fiona's aunt Sandra. She and Fiona were only eighteen months apart, with Fiona being just that much older. The girls grew up looking forward to summers and holidays together at Grams' house. Sandra and her two daughters lived only a few streets away, and may as well have lived with Grams. Fiona always wondered why they didn't. Grams certainly had room for everyone.

The women made their way over to baggage claim; and retrieved the rest of their luggage. Kylie and Fiona caught up while they waited; each had so much to tell the other. It occurred to Fiona that it had been entirely too long since they spent time together, and this was such a bittersweet reunion. She thought about Grams and knew she'd want the girls to enjoy their time together, and not just grieve. As if Kylie were reading Fiona's thoughts, she hugged her; again, because she could.

The drive from the airport to Grams' house was a little over an hour. Aunt Steph teased that Kylie wasn't old enough to drive; "This is crazy, my baby niece is driving," Kylie jokingly reminded her that she had been driving for years, and if she wanted to really feel old; her younger sister drives now as well. "You think this is crazy? Wait until you get in the car with Jade."

It wasn't until they arrived at the house; and stepped in Grams' front door that Fiona felt her absence. Seeing her cousin sort of kept the idea of Grams alive; as she always equated time with her cousins with time spent at Grams'. But now, walking into the house, knowing she wouldn't be traditionally greeted with the smell of brownies baking; the sounds of pots and pans clanging together in the kitchen made Fiona melancholy. She took her mom's hand as they walked through the front door together.

Aunt Sandra was in the kitchen, but there were no sounds of pots and pans. She had ordered some deli platters for everyone and had set everything out on the breakfast bar. She appeared exhausted; but greeted her family with warm hugs and tears of joy. She did her best to focus on the pleasure of having her family all together, but it was evident Aunt Sandra was deeply grieving.

"You know the drill ladies, drop your bags in the rooms and come out by the pool. I figured we'd eat and chat a bit before having to go over Mom's will."

Stephanie shuddered; "I really hadn't given that much thought; do we have to Sand?"

"Later. Mom's attorney sent over copies of the last execution. I guess Mom had made some changes about ten years ago. I didn't even know she had a will, never mind an updated draft. But yes, we really need to read through it as a family as there's a copy for each of us."

Fiona came back into the living room and joined Kylie on the oversized and overused sectional.

"Where's Jade?" she asked

"I have no idea," Kylie called to her mother. "Mom, where's Jade?"

Aunt Sandra stepped back into the house from the pool area.

"Oh, I sent her for ice. She was driving me crazy. I had to give her something to do. She should be back any minute though."

Kylie reminded Fiona of the last time they were all together in Gram's house. It was right after she and Carter broke up; and right before Wanda became the Wonderdog.

"Do you remember when Grams told us she wanted to replace this old couch?"

Fiona laughed; "Yes, we protested so much. The three of us have been sleeping on this old thing for as long as I can remember. I'm so glad she kept it."

The cousins sat quietly for some time; just breathing in all the memories Grams' house held for them. Aunt Sandra asked if they would join the sisters by the pool, and Kylie responded.

"We'll be right out. We're going to wait for Jade to return."

Once the cousins were reunited, they joined the three sisters outside. There was a slight but pleasant breeze blowing through the screened-in pool area. Aunt Sandra had set out enough food for twenty people and enough wine for twice that. While the Lasher sisters reminisced; their daughters chatted about Fiona's new job with Cooke industries. Her cousins were obviously happy for her and a little envious as well.

"You've actually met Anthony and Laurel Cooke?" Jade gushed.

"Yes, I've met them, I work with them. They're amazing people. You wouldn't guess they're insanely wealthy." Fiona regaled her curious cousins with the story of Laurel wanting to meet her and being invited to their home. She also told them about Carter and Meg, leading to their girls' night with Laurel.

Kylie teased.

"That's it; I'm moving to New Jersey so I can hang out with you all the time."

"You're both welcome to come any time, you know that, right?"

Aunt Sandra got up and went back into the house, only to return a few moments later with the envelopes containing the copies of her mother's last will and testament.

"It's fine if you all would rather not read these just yet, but would anyone have an objection to me reading my copy? I have to rip off this band-aid before I have a freaking anxiety attack. I've had enough wine to handle it; I think."

Susan and Stephanie agreed that Sandra should be the one to read through it first. Steph told her oldest sister.

"Just let us know what we need to know; or not. I'm OK with sitting out here drinking all night; everything beyond that is up to you."

Sandra looked at her girls and niece; "Anyone want to join me?" They all agreed, they weren't ready either but had no objections to Sandra reading through. As Sandra poured through the pages of her mother's last wishes, the cousins continued to catch up over another glass of wine. Kylie and Jade told Fiona they'd trade beach life for city living any day, but the truth was, they both envied their cousin for other reasons. She had a sense of confidence they hadn't seen in her the last time she visited. Fiona's post Carter trip to Florida had her feeling exhausted; defeated, and insecure. Despite Kylie and Jade's best efforts to pull the party girl out of their cousin, Fiona wanted nothing more than to hang out by the pool and relax. Grams' was even concerned for her granddaughter's state of mind. It was so uncharacteristic of the Fiona she knew and loved from the moment she held her for the first time.

This Fiona was so much more like her old self, even through her grief, she remained positive and hopeful. Sitting beside them, wearing torn jeans, a Green Day t-shirt and her ratty old Converse, she looked like a rockstar. Jade concluded it was definitely her sense of self, probably cultivated by her new job and friends.

"I'm just so happy that you're happy Fee. I can't explain it, but it's like you love life again."

Fiona smiled.

"I do love my life. I spent a lot of wasted time mourning my old life, with Carter. It was time I focused on myself, I guess. Although had it not been for a stupid picture of Carter and me, I wouldn't have met the Cooke's, or have my awesome job. So, I suppose everything does happen for a reason."

Kylie couldn't seem to keep her thoughts from coming out of her mouth; like her sister, she knew it was the wine, but poured herself a third glass.

"Do you still love him?"

"Who, Carter?" Fiona asked.

"Yes, Carter. I know what you told us, but none of that necessarily means you don't still love him. I was just curious because you haven't mentioned another guy, nor told us anything about dating."

"I always will, I don't believe when you love someone, that love goes away completely even when the person does." Fiona leaned forward, resting her elbows on the glass patio table. She took a moment to tune in to the conversation between her mother and Aunt Stephanie. They were giggling and playfully hitting one another; it was nice to see them happy even if it was a temporary alcohol-induced state.

Stephanie straightened the bamboo placemat under her plate; "Oh, wouldn't it be fantastic to all move in here together? I mean, there's no rule stating we have to sell Mom's house is there? We can just come down and spend the rest of our lives with Sandra and the girls, enjoying the weather, and being beach bums. It would be like having our own little sorority."

Fiona was secretly grateful for Aunt Stephanie's subject change. Although she had no idea what Fiona and the girls were just talking about, she was just the distraction Fiona needed.

Sandra stopped reading and looked over her glasses at Stephanie then at Susan.

"Well, you'll have to ask Fiona about that idea."

Susan seemed confused; "Of course, I wouldn't make that decision without her, and certainly not for her. But I think Steph was just kidding around."

"Kidding or not, that's not what I meant." Sandra was visibly agitated and slammed her copy of the will onto the table. "Mom left the house to Fiona," she announced.

Fiona choked on her wine and nearly spit it across the table; which would have resulted in Sandra getting even more angry, considering she was in the line of fire.

"What? No, there must be some mistake. The house belongs to all of us now. Aunt Sandra, are you sure you read that right?"

Sandra's tone changed as she realized this was not her niece's fault; "It's yours, Fee. There are other assets that are delegated to the rest of us; you do get the same share of her savings and life insurance as my girls, but it's specifically stipulated; this house is now in your name only."

Fiona's cell buzzed with a text notification. She apologized for the interruption and read the message Kay had just sent.

"I know you're with your family, and Laurel told me to leave you alone, but I just wanted to let you know I'm thinking of you. No need to text or call unless you want to. Sending love." Kay's text made Fiona feel better and worse at the same time. She knew why Grams left the house to her. Fiona loved it and would always tell Grams she would live there with her someday. Of course; that hadn't happened, and this was Grams' way of telling Fiona to live her dreams. It was amazing to be here with her entire family around her. She felt safe and very much at home. But Kay's text reminded her of the new family she also loved; and the job she couldn't wait to get back to. Fiona made up her mind about the house, but decided to not have that conversation until after the funeral tomorrow. She took a minute to answer Kay before reading Grams' will for herself.

"Thank you; miss you all. So much to tell you. I know you rocked the proposal today, can't wait to hear all about it. Love u."

Susan took a different approach to the subject at hand. She didn't want her daughter to feel badly for something she had no control over.

"Fiona, how do you feel about forming our own sorority?"

"Well, I think it's worth having a conversation over. But, not tonight, OK? Let's just try and get through tomorrow. We'll have time after the funeral to talk about the will."

Kylie got up and hugged Fiona. She whispered.

"Do what you want, don't listen to my mother or anyone else. I know you don't want to live here anymore, but Grams didn't know that."

The next morning; all six women showered, dressed and readied themselves with little conversation. Fiona felt like she was in a bad movie; playing a role that she could step out of and back into her real self any time she wanted. But this movie demanded more of her than she cared to give. Her heart broke for her mother and aunts as they fussed over one another with little regard for their own appearance. Kylie doted over Jade as they tried on earrings together in front of the vanity mirror. Sandra told Stephanie to change her shoes and literally took off the pair she had on, and gave them to her youngest sister. Susan made coffee for everyone, and delivered a cup to Sandra in Gram's room as she rummaged through her mother's closet for another pair of shoes for herself. It occurred to Fiona that her family was already a sorority and should be together. She just hoped Mom would understand that she had to go back; she had a new life and she had only just begun to live it.

The service was boring as far as Fiona was concerned. She didn't know what to expect, but that was not it. She had hoped for the chance to say a few words about her Grams', maybe others would have liked to do so as well. But Aunt Sandra kept things short and simple, and the funeral was over before she knew it. Fiona was impressed with the turnout though; everyone loved her Grams; even her mailman came to pay his respects. A few family members came in from the west coast. Susan told Fiona they were Grams' second cousins who lived near the west coast. She addressed them as aunt and uncles; however technically her third cousins. She and her sisters invited them back to the house afterward to join them for dinner which Sandra had catered in from Gram's favorite seafood restaurant. The delivery guy arrived right on time at six p.m. As usual, Sandra overdid it with the food order; and the entire kitchen was loaded with bags and containers. Fiona offered her help, and Sandra graciously accepted.

"You know Fiona, I'm not upset with you. I'm sad and hurt and I don't want to feel either way. It's just hard to think that my mother wasn't fair to my girls; it's quite evident that you were her favorite; just like your mother was."

Although she said she wasn't upset; Fiona couldn't help but take her words personally.

"Aunt Sandra, would you and the girls live here if that was an option? I mean, along with my mom and Steph?"

"Oh, I don't know; I suppose if my sisters were serious; that would work out to everyone's benefit financially; that is if we could afford to buy the house from you."

Fiona had had enough; "Now I know why Grams left the house to me. She knew I would do the right thing. I'm sorry Aunt Sand, but it seems as if you already had plans for it. What would you do if you were me, sell it and keep the profit? Or, would you make sure every one of us was satisfied with your decision? I've been giving this a lot of thought, believe me. I just figured today was not the day to have this conversation, yet here we are."

Sandra stopped unpacking the food and stared at her niece.

"I'm sorry."

Fiona joined Kylie and Jade in the living room. The three cousins huddled together on Grams' old sectional couch, trading 'remember when' stories. For a few moments, Fiona entertained the idea of living in Florida; in Gram's house, her house, with her family. The illusion seemed so natural and so comforting.

Nicky and Rob were doing a bit of dreaming as well. They had been pouring through the real estate websites hoping to find the perfect new home on Long Island. It was Nicky's last weekend in his childhood home, and he and Rob had been helping Maria pack up the rest of their belongings. The La Salle family unanimously voted to move on from owning Pete's Pies several months ago. Maria feared for some time that working in the family business had greatly repressed her children's opportunities to experience life and fulfill their own dreams. She had been entertaining the idea of moving upstate with her brother and sister-in-law for some time; the fire was the perfect catalyst to make that happen. Knowing Nicky and Linda both had aspirations of their own also made it easier for Maria to start packing. She felt guilty for holding her adult children back; keeping them loyally tied to the business. But when she tried to apologize to her daughter and son; they thanked her. Linda told her mother that if not for their business, she would have never been given the opportunity to take over for Ralph when he retired next year. Nicky expressed his gratitude for the business cultivating his leadership qualities as well as cooking skills. He assured his mother the family business had given them more than they gave to it. Maria felt an immense sense of pride that overwhelmed her guilt. The La Salle's were going to be OK.

Nicky stopped scrolling and turned his laptop toward Rob.

"Look at this house. It's so perfect, but the price is not so perfect. Do you think Fiona would want to live with us? The three of us could possibly swing a mortgage; Oh, and maybe Linda would want to rent a room while she looks for something more permanent. I'm going to text Fiona the listing link."

Maria threw a roll of packing tape in Nicky's general direction to get his attention; "Don't you dare text that poor girl. Whatever you're cooking up in your head can wait until she gets back. Let her be with her family, Nicky. For God's sake, her grandmother just died."

Maria was well aware of her overreaction, but when she spoke to Susan earlier in the day, she promised her friend she wouldn't discuss Fiona's inheritance with Nicky. They both knew he would want to help, but may inadvertently cause Fiona even more confusion. Susan's exact words were; *It's her story to tell, and you and I both know Fiona will tell Nicky when she's ready; let's not force her to be.*

"OK, jeez Ma, you could have knocked me out with that tape roll. I won't text her, but why am I getting the feeling you know something you're not sharing with me? Is Fiona OK?"

"She's fine, hon. I can tell you this; Fiona has a lot on her plate down there, I just don't want you to give her any more to handle. Everything changes when someone you love leaves this Earth. Everything certainly changed for Fiona, and you know when she's ready, you're going to be the first person she calls. So for now, just take care of Wanda and be here for Fiona when she gets back."

Fiona ducked into the bathroom while the rest of the family ate. She was anxious to call Kay and find out what had happened with her presentation to TC. Kay answered on the first ring.

"Hey, oh, hello. I'm so happy you called! How are you?"

"Hi, honey, I'm OK, thanks. I only have a few minutes, so tell me in twenty words or less; how did everything go?"

Kay gushed.

"Fiona, it was amazing! With Laurel and Silvie's help, we totally blew TC away. He couldn't stop talking about the garden idea, especially. Oh, Fiona, we have so much work to do when you get home. How many words was that?"

Fiona laughed.

"Who cares how many, that is amazing news. I knew you could do this without me."

"Wait, Fee, I don't like the way you said, 'without me', please tell me you're coming home."

"I'll be back in a few days, no worries. In the meantime, you're steering the ship; keep your eyes on the horizon, OK? Listen, I gotta go, I'll call you again soon." Fiona ended the call and as she made her way back into the living room to join her family, she couldn't help but focus on Kay's words 'come home'.

The next few days were so surreal. As much as the Lasher women tried to enjoy the remainder of their time together; their grief was what bonded them, not joy. Stephanie decided to stay a few extra days and asked Fiona if she could do so at Grams' house. She hated that her aunt felt it necessary to ask permission.

"Of course," was all she could muster.

Susan and Fiona finished packing and waited for Sandra to arrive to take them back to the airport. Fiona took one last long look around, knowing it would be some time before she returned. She could see the tears in her mother's eyes and instinctively knew it was the perfect time to share her decision in regard to the house.

"Hey Mom, can I have a dollar?"

Susan reached into her handbag and pulled out a five-dollar bill.

"This is all I have, take it."

Fiona took the bill and stuffed it in her pocket.

"That's actually perfect; now I have one dollar from all five of you, so be sure and collect your buck from Steph, Sandra and Kylie and Jade as well. It's been a pleasure doing business with you, Mom. Welcome to your new home."

Last One to Leave;
Please Turn Out the Lights

TC spotted Fiona standing in the hall just outside her office. She appeared to be focused on her phone screen but when TC got a closer look, her phone was off. He couldn't help worrying that Fiona's heart was still in Florida with her family, and he knew from experience, the heart is more powerful than the mind. He considered trying to console her, but he knew Laurel was much better equipped to do so. Emotional scenarios were not exactly in his wheelhouse; however, TC felt it was imperative to let Fiona know how valuable she was, not only at work but as a friend.

"Hey, how's it going?"

"Oh, sorry, I think I zoned out for a minute. I'm OK, thanks. Just a little preoccupied today; I'm really sorry, I will try and stay focused." She was overly apologetic for no reason. TC wasn't concerned with her focus, not today anyway. He genuinely cared for her well-being, and her sadness was evident.

"No need to apologize, Fiona. Why don't you hang out with me for a while? I suck at knowing the right thing to say but I am a very good listener. Besides, Kay isn't in the office today; wouldn't it be better to have someone around?"

"Thank you, but I'm sure you of all people have much more important things to do today other than babysit my sorry self. I'm really ok, just a lot on my mind I suppose."

"Fiona, this may sound insensitive, but believe me, it's not meant to be, I just hope you'd let me know if you're considering moving to Florida with your mother." TC's tone was more paternal than authoritative, or at least that's what Fiona imagined a father would sound like.

"I would tell you, but I'm not considering that at all. I do feel a bit guilty for that, but my life is here, and I know my Mom understands. It's always been the two of us, and now I have to figure life out on my own. Just a little overwhelmed today. I mean, what do I do first? I need a place to live; do I find a rental, or invest and purchase a home? Do I take Nicky up on his idea to live together, or should I spend time with just me? Anyway, I don't expect answers to any of that, I simply wanted to put your mind at ease by sharing what's in mine. Have no doubt, I'm not going anywhere any time soon"

Without a word, TC took Fiona's arm and led her down the hall and into his office.

"Sit, I'll make coffee."

She indulged her boss and sat on the little sofa. Fiona noticed a printed copy of their proposal lying on the table in front of her. She picked it up and opened the presentation folder to discover TC had made notes on nearly every page. She was thrilled to see such support for their ideas as well as his expertise for executing a plan, all written out in fairly legible writing.

"Hey boss, I have to say, you have decent handwriting for a guy, I'm impressed."

"Ha, yes, so I've been told. So, what do you think of my notes? I'm eager to get your team going on this project. I was hoping you were staying because my plan is for you to take the lead. What do you think of my recommendations for the team?"

"Oh, is that what this list of names on the inside cover is about?"

"Yes." TC handed Fiona a cup of coffee and took a seat across from her.

"I think it's completely your decision, but you're asking for my input, and I tend to believe the right people will present themselves at the right time."

"Well, that's exactly what Laurel said. You may want to give her a call when you're up to it and get together. Certainly, you two are on the same page; now we just have to get you to begin writing, so to speak."

"I agree. I was planning to call her later today. I could use a bit of advice on my living situation also."

"Where are you staying now?"

"Wanda and I are still in the Jersey house; it hasn't sold yet, but we have several showings this weekend. Our agent feels we will have an offer very soon. So, I'm pressed for time; and I need to find a solution that allows Wanda and I to stay together, no exception."

TC had to laugh.

"You know, Wanda is always welcome in our home. Laurel is very attached to her."

"I do know that, and I may have to ask that big favor if the Jersey house sells quickly. Knowing I have an option for Wanda does alleviate some stress. TC, you and Laurel are truly too good to be true. I feel very fortunate to call you my friends." Fiona began to cry. She knew it was residual emotion escaping but TC became visibly uncomfortable.

"Oh, Fee, please don't cry, I can't handle it. We aren't all that great, believe me. Laurel and I are happy to have met you as well, you're like family but remember, we both come from dysfunctional families; so it stands to reason we honestly have no idea what we're doing."

"All families are dysfunctional, but you two make everyone in your extended family feel extraordinary. Thank you for talking with me; I'm feeling better, and the caffeine is kicking in. I better go and get some real work done today. I'll give Laurel a call later; we have a lot of brainstorming to do."

Fiona left TC's office and returned to her own. There were dozens of memos and messages on her desk, all arranged in small piles, neatly lined up in front of her keyboard. At first, she couldn't decipher the theory behind the organization, but slowly, Kay's process became clear. Fiona was grateful for her partner's efforts to keep things structured in her absence even if it was an unnecessary endeavor. TC had made a note in the proposal suggesting an assistant for Kay and her, but unless the right person somehow magically materialized, Fiona was inclined to leave things as they were. The thought of Kay training an assistant made her laugh out loud; and although it would be fun to watch, time was a big consideration.

Fiona opened her playlist and adjusted the volume on her laptop. She had a proclivity for eighties classic rock, even though that was more her mother's genre. Somehow the nonsensical lyrics mixed with the head-banging instrumentals reminded her of innocence and security. Maybe she was too young to have lived through that time, but still, the music was so reminiscent of the best time of her life. If she were to be honest with herself; many of the songs from that era made her think of time spent with Carter.

She rifled through the messages on her desk and continued to wonder why Kay hadn't just saved them on their voicemail. It occurred to her that she may not have taught Kay how to do so, their phone system training never went beyond listening to incoming messages; maybe they needed that assistant after all.

One of the messages in the third little pile was filled with writing. The tiny scrap of pink paper held more words than the rest of her notes put together. Fiona picked it up and attempted to decode Kay's rendering. *Nicky left a voicemail here because he didn't want to call you in Florida. Said it was not urgent, but a Mrs Wyatt called him for your number, heard about your Grams and is sorry. Nicky said she sounded very sad, and it's up to you whether you want to speak with her, and this is her cell number, you know house phone, it's the same. Nicky said, ``She's very sweet for calling, but it's strange.* Kay followed all of that with six question marks, which Fiona found amusing. She could only surmise that Kay herself was expressing her own confusion with the exaggerated punctuation.

Fiona decided to call Nicky for some clarification before even entertaining the idea of reaching out to Mrs Wyatt; but first, there was work to be done. She turned up the volume ever so slightly on her laptop and dug into the email from TC containing his revisions and notes on their proposal. There was a short blurb on the very last page which read; *We have no need for adequate and affordable housing, but please add the Cooke's to your list of potential fosters. Thank you.* As Fiona reread the note, her heart felt as though it would explode. She couldn't think of anyone better to care for children who needed a family.

The day seemed to dissolve quickly as Fiona submerged herself in a myriad of preliminary research. She dreaded the train ride back to New Jersey, but Wanda was waiting patiently for her to return. What was once a joy, had become a chore; reminding Fiona that she was now officially a commuter. She decided to pass the time by making that call to Nicky, who would likely be home from class by then.

"Hey, Fee, how are you? I'm so glad you called."

"I'm OK, on my way home, I hate the train; never thought I'd say that, but I do. Anyway, I was hoping you had some time to catch up; you'll make my commute so much easier."

"I do. I just got home myself, rather back to Rob's parent's house; for now, that is. We need to buy a house."

"You and Rob? Yeah, you do. He's been wanting to do that with you for some time now. Have you been looking for one?"

"We have, but I think you should consider living here too. Maybe we could find something all together, even temporarily. I've been wanting to ask you, but the timing has been really bad, you know?"

"I know; listen, that is a definite possibility, and we can discuss our options soon. Right now, my main concern is Wanda; so an apartment might be out of the question. Let's get together this weekend though; do you guys have some time to hang out?"

"Of course, we can drive down to you, that might be easier. Oh, and Fee, did you get my message about Mrs Wyatt?"

"I did. Your message was actually my main reason for calling, well, other than I missed you terribly."

"You were gone for less than two weeks, and you missed me? Honestly, when my mom told me you had extended your stay by a few days, I worried you weren't coming back at all. I was freaked out."

"Well, don't think I hadn't considered it; but there was just entirely too much to deal with; my aunts, the will, the house. I'm really grateful that Grams had everything in writing, but damn, it was still a lot to contend with, especially after a loss, you know?"

"I do, and I'm just glad things seem to have worked out for everyone. Now, it's time to get you where you want, and need to be; with me!"

"I agree. Let's talk on Saturday, just come down at whatever time works for you and Rob, I'll be there. Oh, and Nick, what should I do about Mrs Wyatt? I want to thank her for her condolences and concern, but do I really want to open that wound right now? What if she wants to talk about Carter?"

"I don't know, Fee. This one is up to you. I have a feeling you'll know how to play this; just let it sit with you for a bit. So, Rob's home, I have to go. See you Saturday, love you."

"Love you back, say hello to Rob for me, and I can't wait to hear all about your classes when I see you!"

Nicky laughed.

"Not much to tell, it's only day three, but yeah, so far so good. I'll give you the details when I see you."

The drive home from the train station was exactly fourteen miles, but it may as well have been fourteen hundred. Even with the radio to keep her focused, the drive had Fiona feeling fatigued. The thought of going home and being alone depressed her. Nicky wasn't even down the street anymore; and for the first time since her return from Florida, Fiona felt the entire weight of her situation. She had no regrets about leaving her mom to live with her sisters. She knew her life would be so enriched by her family; the weather and atmosphere. Living there must feel like a permanent vacation, and her mother more than deserved that. However, the life Fiona once regarded as perfect; here in New Jersey; in the only home she ever knew now seemed strange and dismal.

As soon as she put her key in the back door, Wanda began to whine; and as the door opened, the poor dog raced past Fiona and into the yard. This situation wasn't working for either of them. Once back inside; Wanda snuggled next to Fiona on the couch; clearly she missed her and didn't care to be alone for that long every day, and Fiona hated leaving her.

"I know baby, I'm going to fix this for both of us, soon. I promise." She rubbed Wanda's ears with one hand and reached for her cell with the other, contemplating the return call to Carter's mother. Instead, Fiona dialed Laurel. "Hey, do you have a minute? I need your help. I want to buy a house on Long Island; know anyone in real estate?"

To the Rescue

Carter drove from work to his parent's house; Eddie in tow. They had been friends since second grade. There was a deep sense of loyalty between them but sadly it had been very one-sided of late. Carter was well aware that his feelings of devotion to his family and friends weren't always reciprocal; Eddie was no exception. All their young lives, the boys, along with Keith, did everything together. They shared a love of cars as well as the mechanics involved. However, as they got older Eddie was more about competing with Carter than being a true friend. Mr Wyatt's theory was that Eddie must have had a tough home life, and he wasn't wrong.

Keith, Eddie and Carter were inseparable, and it always seemed the boys' were most comfortable hanging out at the Wyatt's. Having two sons, Mrs Wyatt was used to a house full of boys; hungry, dirty, crazy boys. New faces graced her kitchen on a regular basis, but the one constant throughout their childhood, teen and adult years was Eddie. One summer when the boys were twelve, Eddie stayed three weeks in a row, without going home even once. Mrs Wyatt tried to tactfully ask Eddie why he hadn't gone home, but she was afraid of the answer. She knew it would all come out eventually, and eventually, it did.

Eddie's mom was never home. She worked three jobs to support her children, as she was the sole supporter. He had a father; when he remembered to come home, and an older brother and sister. Eddie's siblings were five and six years older than he; with little to no interest in their baby brother. He was left alone a lot. His mother would assume her older children were keeping their eyes on Eddie, but as soon as she would leave for work, they were out the door, leaving him to fend for himself, even as young as five. His father left for 'work' and wouldn't return for weeks, sometimes months. Eddie preferred it that way because when his father was home, he wasn't very kind to his wife and children. As a direct result of all the neglect and verbal assault; Eddie grew up with an enormous chip on his shoulder. People no longer mattered, only money and material things. He vowed to make more of his life than his father, but his idea of success was skewed. Eddie didn't know the difference between working to succeed and self-serving manipulation; very much like Meg's father. He saw Mr Daly as the perfect role model, and Carter's relationship with Meg was what kept Eddie in Mr Daly's good graces. As far as Eddie was concerned; the twins were his insurance policy as well as Carter's. He not only wanted to keep his job but hoped he and Meg's sister Mare would wind up together. However she, like her father, was a master manipulator, and used Eddie when she had nothing better to do; knowing he continued to misread her affections. Carter often thought they made a good couple, and never wondered what it was about Mare that attracted Eddie, yet he often questioned his own attraction to Meg.

"Are you staying tonight, Ed?"

"I think so, my roommate has a new girlfriend and it's just awkward there. I need a new place to crash."

"Well, you're welcome to stay with us for a while. I'm sure mom won't mind. Just remember, it's been a little tense around my place lately, I mean with the babies on the way and my parents worried about my future as well as theirs. Sometimes the conversations get pretty serious. I don't want you to feel weird if it comes up, and it will."

"Eh, it's fine. I can be there to help them see the positives of you and Meg getting married. You are going to ask me to be your best man, right?"

"Not now, Ed. It's been a day, can we talk about something else, or just not talk?"

"Yeah, but Carter, you're gonna blow this if you're not careful."

Carter wanted to believe that his friend had his best interest in mind, but that simply wasn't true. Eddie was looking out for Eddie.

As they pulled down the street, Eddie noticed a strange car in the Wyatt's driveway.

"Hey, man, whose car is that?"

"I have no idea. Maybe a friend of my mother's?" Carter pulled in behind the vehicle.

"Oh, it's a rental. Now, I am curious."

The two young men walked up the front steps and opened the door. Carter called out to his mother.

"Mom, you home?" but the responding voice clearly did not belong to Mrs Wyatt.

"Nobody's home, go away!"

Instantly, Carter recognized that brand of sarcasm and raced up the stairs into the living room.

"Sam, Oh my God, you're here!

Carter greeted his brother with an enthusiastic hug that nearly knocked them both to the floor. Sam's timing couldn't have been more perfect, as Carter truly needed his big brother to guide him into fatherhood. A tiny voice sounded from the kitchen.

"Hi Uncle Carter." He turned to see his mother holding his nephew Noel who was now almost too big to be carried.

"Hey, little man." Carter took Noel from his mother and hoisted him up on his shoulders. "Look how crazy big you've grown."

Shelly had been in the kitchen as well, and stepped into the living room for her turn to hug her brother-in-law.

"You almost whacked his head on the ceiling fan, now put my kid down so I can hug you!" she joked.

"So, how long can you guys stay?" Carter asked.

"You're stuck with us for two weeks. I'm hoping that's long enough for us to help you sort out this freaking mess," Shelly answered.

Carter shot his sister-in-law a wide-eyed look and subtly shook his head. She immediately caught on and changed the subject, but it was too late.

"What freaking mess?" Eddie asked

"The situation he's in with Meg. This is a total shit show." Sam didn't seem to care what Eddie thought; Carter was his brother and he wanted to protect him from what could be a truly unhappy life.

Eddie clapped back.

"You don't know what you're talking about. Our boy Carter is set for life, man. The Daly's are loaded. He'll always have a job and money as long as he's with Meg. Now, being the kids' dad and all, he's really set for life."

"Shut up Eddie, please." Sam made a dismissive gesture with his hand and rolled his eyes.

Carter attempted to diffuse the situation before someone exploded.

"Hey Ed, why don't we call Keith and see if you can crash with him tonight? I haven't hung out with my brother in so long, it would be cool to have some family time, you know?"

Eddie immediately became defensive.

"Oh, so now I'm not family? Screw you, Carter, I've been more of a brother to you than Sam has; you want me to leave? Fine, but believe me, I'm the one you need in your corner, not Sam!" Eddie stormed out the front door.

Mrs Wyatt peered out the window to witness Eddie sitting on the curb, taking on his cell. She really hoped Keith would agree to come and pick him up. Sam shook his head.

"Damn, Carter, that guy's brain was put in upside down."

"I don't disagree," Carter said and began to tell his brother and sister-in-law about Eddie's abnormal obsession with the Daly family. Carter told his family how Eddie continually pursues Mare, and her indifference only spurs him on. He described Eddie's fascination with Mr Daly and how he has been emulating his behaviors. "That man is an ass. I mean, he's utterly cruel sometimes, and good old Eddie wants to be just like him. It makes no sense considering his own father's history of verbal abuse and total disrespect for, well, everyone."

Shelly interjected.

"It actually makes perfect sense from a psychological standpoint, even the bit about him living vicariously through your situation with Meg."

Carter sighed.

"I wish we had a better word for what's going on than my 'situation', but I guess that's basically what it is for now."

"So, the first order of business, while we're here, is for us to meet Meg," his sister-in-law wasn't making a suggestion, she was making a plan. "What about dinner tonight? Let's put these wheels in motion. "

Carter seemed a little confused but agreed to ask Meg over for dinner to meet his family. Mrs Wyatt offered to cook, but Shelly suggested they call for take-out.

"What's her favorite, Carter?"

"Um, I'm not sure. These days, it varies. I could ask her what she'd like?"

"Yes, do that. I want her to feel comfortable meeting us. I know it can be a little overwhelming." It was becoming increasingly evident that Shelly had an agenda that went beyond just meeting Meg.

What Carter was not yet aware of, were the prior phone conversations between Shelly and her mother-in-law concerning Carter and Meg. Mrs Wyatt felt overwhelmed and outnumbered and wished Shelly could be with her to confirm her suspicions. It wasn't easy being the only woman in a house of men. She told her daughter-in-law during one of their phone conversations.

"Women know when other women are lying, and playing games. This girl has something to hide; she's not truthful with Carter, I just know it."

Her daughter-in-law agreed.

"Based on what you've been telling me, I have to say, things just don't seem to add up. Carter's in big trouble here if we don't intervene. We have vacation time accumulated, so hang in there Mom, I'm on my way."

Mrs Wyatt was grateful for Sam and Shelly's visit; not only to spend time with them and her precious grandson, but for the familial support. She had always hoped Carter would fall in love with someone like Shelly; someone who valued family above all else; someone like Fiona. Meg was the curveball she did not see coming, and she was grateful for Shelly coming in as her pinch-hitter.

Meg arrived at the Wyatt's thirty minutes early. Carter and Sam had gone to pick up dinner; leaving Mr and Mrs Wyatt to make the awkward introduction. Shelly stepped into the living room from the kitchen as she heard Meg call up the stairs; "Hey everyone, we're here."

Mr Wyatt followed Meg as she waddled into the room. Shelly leaned in and whispered to her mother-in-law.

"Well, I guess she's really pregnant," referring to Meg's evident belly.

Mrs Wyatt suppressed a giggle and made the introductions.

"Good to see you, Meg, I'd like you to meet Shelly, my daughter-in-law and this is Noel, my grandson.

Noel gave Meg a shy smile and toddled off to his father's childhood bedroom to watch cartoons. Shelly extended her hand.

"Great to finally meet you, Meg. Sorry, Noel is a little quiet around new people, but it doesn't last long. He'll be back, talking your ear off in no time."

"He's a cutie. I'm looking forward to him getting to know his Auntie Meg."

Meg's awkward phrasing was a clear indicator for Shelly to pay attention to her narcissistic tendencies. She couldn't help but think, the more appropriate thing to say would have been that she couldn't wait to get to know Noel. After all, he's just a baby; with very little interest in getting to know her simply because she's in the same room. Shelly reminded herself to try and split her focus between being a therapist and being Meg's future sister-in-law, but the very thought of Meg joining the family made her shudder. She was being unfair; judging solely on what she had heard from the family, and a conscious effort was needed to form her own opinions, both personally and professionally.

"The guys should be back soon," Shelly announced. "Meg, would you want to help me set the table?"

"Oh, not really, I'm very tired today, I think I'll just relax until dinner arrives."

Shelly was quite taken back by her response but had to admit, at least Meg was honest. She and Mrs. Wyatt grabbed the glasses, dishes and cutlery from the cabinets and set places for everyone at the dining room table. Mrs Wyatt seemed nervous, and Shelly asked her if everything was OK.

"Mom," she whispered. "You seem anxious. Remember, this is your home, she's a guest, nothing more, not yet anyway."

By the time the guys got back with their dinner, Shelly and Mrs Wyatt were seated at the table; fixated on Meg still lounging on the couch, completely disengaged. She hadn't stopped playing on her phone since she arrived. Shelly had tried on several occasions to include her in conversation to which she responded each time with a disingenuous smile and gesture to her phone as if to say.

"Don't bother me, I'm busy."

Meg spent the next hour and a half preoccupied with her phone and whoever was on the receiving end of her messages. Much to Shelly's surprise, Meg didn't give Carter much attention; and continually sidestepped any conversation regarding her pregnancy. Shelly made mental notes of her behaviors to discuss with her in-laws after Meg left. She was more curious than she had been before as Meg's lack of interaction and interest was quite the opposite of what she was anticipating. Even when Sam tried to lighten the tension with his infamous corny jokes, Meg had no natural response; not a giggle, smile, or even a disapproving eye roll; nothing.

Carter seemed relieved when Meg announced she had to leave. There was no explanation; nor did anyone ask for one. She simply got up from the table and told the Wyatt family there was somewhere she needed to be.

"I'll walk you out," Carter offered. He made it to the landing before Meg turned to him and said.

"No need, I can make it down the stairs and out the door all by myself." Her tone was neither pleasant nor sarcastic, and Carter had no idea how to react. He leaned in to kiss her goodbye, but Meg turned her cheek, avoiding lip contact. As she made her way down the stairs to the front door, Carter stood wondering what the hell had just happened.

Shelly handed a stack of dirty dishes to her husband.

"Sam, help your mom clean up, I'm going to have a talk with Carter. It looks like he could use a friend right now."

"Want me to talk to him?" he asked

"I got this. Maybe a woman's perspective would be more insightful." She kissed Sam on the shoulder and asked Carter to join her in the living room. "Hey kiddo, wanna talk?"

"Yeah, thanks. I'm really confused; what the hell was up tonight Shel? It's not my imagination, is it? Meg was really weird, I mean I know you don't know her, but that was not her. I have no idea who that was! Is it a hormonal thing?"

Shelly laughed.

"No, Carter, I think it's a deceitful thing. My professional assessment or my personal assessment; which would you prefer?"

"Both."

Carter took a seat in one of the recliners while Shelly settled in on the sofa; tucking her left leg under her so she could face her brother-in-law.

"Carter, let me ask you this, do you love her?"

Without hesitation, he answered.

"No, Shel, I don't. I never did. But, I love the twins. I mean, not just the idea of them, I love the people they will become. Does that make sense?"

"Of course it does. And, that's how an expectant parent is supposed to feel."

"Meg doesn't seem to feel that way, does she?"

"No, honey. She's much too self-absorbed and that worries me. She didn't even have a maternal response toward Noel. Basically, her attitude regarding your adorable nephew was more obligatory than anything else."

"How so?"

"Well, there aren't any rules when it comes to reacting to a child, but given the fact she's about to become a mom herself, she really had no interest in Noel. Actually, she wanted him to be more interested in her. It was weird, by anyone's standards; not just because I think everyone should love my kid."

"So, what does this all mean? Now, I think I might need your professional opinion."

"Well, I'm used to dealing with PTSD, depression, anxiety and addiction at the VA, this is a little out of my wheelhouse, but I'll try. Carter, please don't get upset, but I don't imagine Meg loves you either. Between what I've been told and what I just witnessed; You are more of a conquest than anything else. She wanted you; she found a way to have you, and now she's bored with you. The chase; the challenge was her obsession, not the person. You mentioned Meg having sisters, maybe this had to do with being competitive as well. You know, first one to the altar and all."

"That seems about right. But, what happens with the twins? Meg and I are bonded forever, whether we like it or not."

Shelly saw the tears begin to well in Carter's eyes. Her heart broke for him as she searched for comforting, yet truthful words.

"Dads aren't always husbands. Carter, you're going to be an amazing father; but your loyalties are with those babies, not necessarily Meg. Let me ask you; how did she respond when you told her you weren't ready to get married?"

"She threw stuff at me. She grabbed everything that wasn't nailed down in her room and chucked it all at my head."

Shelly couldn't help her laughter, but Meg's response was very telling.

"Basically, she wanted to hurt you physically. She needed that power over you, so you couldn't hurt her emotionally."

"I'll take your word for it. After that night though, she never mentioned marriage again. I even brought it up once; referring to the future and she told me not to worry about it."

"*What?*"

"Yeah, I said something about the twins having my last name; and then I said, by the time they're old enough to realize, we'll be married, and all have the same last name. I was just worried they'd be confused."

"And, she told you not to worry about it?"

"What, Carter, getting married or having different last names?"

"I'm pretty sure she meant both. She just shrugged it off."

"Carter, honey, is there any chance, even the slightest, that you aren't the twins' father?"

"There's a chance, yeah. I don't know for certain that Meg has been with someone else, but like I told mom and dad, she and I were careful. The odds of her getting pregnant were slim, but of course, it does happen even with protection. I just don't understand why she'd lie. I'm so invested in becoming a father; I already love them. It would be devastating to find out they weren't my babies."

"I have a theory. But, first let me tell you, no matter what happens Carter, you're going to be fine. I know this may seem harsh, but it would be better to know now. It's easier to overcome the loss of something you never had than to lose your fatherhood after you've met the twins, held them and cared for them. Please remember Carter, you have a family who loves you and will be supportive no matter what life gives you to endure, you know that, right ?"

"Yes, I do. But Shel, you have me all nervous now, what's your theory?"

"I think Meg told you the twins are yours, or at least she hopes they are because you are 'daddy approved'. I imagine it was much easier to tell her father that you knocked her up, knowing how much he likes you. He took such an interest in your talent and seems to respect you as a man. It's possible, she chose you, rather than you actually being the biological father. It's even possible that Meg was already pregnant before you two were intimate, but she knew her father would accept you over whoever she had already been with."

"Mr Daly is tough, for sure. He really doesn't like many people; I'm not sure why he likes me so much, but your theory makes sense. How can we know for sure, though? Is there a way to find out? You're right Shel, I can't start being their father and have the Daly's take that away from me."

"Well, in my experience, the truth always comes out, eventually. If, and it's a big if, you aren't the father, Meg is ready to let you know. She's bored with this game, so to speak. She's ready for someone else to take the responsibility, someone who will do what she says without question; if not the biological father, then someone else she can manipulate. The twins are her bargaining chip; not only with men but her parents as well. Now, she can tell 'daddy' the truth knowing he won't do anything to jeopardize his grandchildren. My professional opinion is, you'll know more very soon. If I'm wrong, we can order a paternity test when the babies are born. We can always say it's for insurance reasons because you two aren't married."

"She isn't due for another three months. By then, I may not want to know the truth."

"Oh, sweetie, I can't imagine how hard this is for you. But it's essential that you know your rights, options and the truth."

Carter wiped his eyes with the back of his hand.

"Thanks, Shel, I don't know what makes me sadder to think about; the babies not being mine, or Meg, for the rest of my life."

Shelly got up and hugged her brother-in-law.

"It's all going to work out, I can feel it."

Carter was grateful for Shelly; not only for her expertise but her love and support. He remembered when she and Sam first started dating, Shelly was so kind to him. She treated him like a person, not just Sam's kid brother. Back then Carter wondered if he would ever have a girlfriend like Shelly; smart, sweet, strong and loving; then he met Fiona.

Shot in the Dark

Fiona ducked into the little convenience store around the corner from the Cooke building. She had a few minutes to kill before Rob was ready to drive back to Long Island. It was getting late, and she was starving. Dinner seemed so far away, and the snacks were right there, so Fiona decided to stock up for the drive home. As she made her way down the center aisle toward the chip bags, hanging from an old metal rack. She noticed a young girl standing off to the side; leaning on the rickety shelving which held various cleaning products that had likely been there for years. Very few people come into a store like this one for some overpriced dish soap or toilet bowl cleaner.

She smiled at the young girl, who by Fiona's best guess was about thirteen or fourteen years old. She wasn't a typical teen, trying to look or act older than her age, but there was a sense of maturity that couldn't be denied.

"Hello."

The young girl just nodded and kept her eyes on the front of the store. Fiona grabbed her chips and a few other pre-packaged snacks and headed back up the center aisle toward the register. She noticed the girl eyeing her armful of goodies and was just about to offer to purchase something for her as well when the girl let out a gasp; pointing toward the door. She whispered to Fiona.

"He has a gun."

Fiona looked toward the register to see a man with a bandana tied around his face, covering everything but his eyes; pointing a gun across the counter at the clerk. He was yelling.

"Open the damn register!" Over and over, making the clerk even more nervous and incompetent. Fiona whispered back.

"Just stay behind me," to the young girl.

The clerk fumbled with his register, and the third failed attempt to open it sent the gunman into a panic. He slammed his hands on the counter, startling not only the clerk but the young girl as well. She screamed. He turned and fired. Just as he pulled the trigger, Fiona instinctively shielded the girl by turning her body toward her and grabbing her around the shoulders and head. The snacks tumbled to the floor as Fiona tried to guide the girl down as low as she could. It was too late; the gunman's bullet sailed down the center aisle and struck Fiona. She felt an intense burning sensation on her left side, right above her hip. Her knees buckled and she and the young girl fell to the floor. The gunman began yelling once again that time was up; he needed all the money now.

Fiona whispered.

"Are you hurt? Do you feel pain anywhere?"

The young girl answered.

"No, but I have blood on my hand, I think it's yours."

Fiona remembered her com and for the first time was grateful for TC and his insistence on wearing the insane devices. She slowly reached for her ear.

"Rob, can you hear me?" There was no response for a moment, then TC's voice answered.

"Fiona?"

Her voice was barely audible, and TC had to concentrate to understand.

"I'm around the corner, in the convenience store. We are being robbed; I've been shot. Call 911, no sirens or lights, this guy is jumpy."

"Oh my God, Fiona! Calling now, where were you shot? How bad?"

"On my side and I can't tell."

"Stay quiet, help is coming, I'm going to keep talking; I'm right here Fiona, you're not alone."

Ignoring TC's advice to stay quiet, Fiona answered.

"I'm not alone. I have a friend holding my hand." She gave the young girl's hand a squeeze; as she couldn't help thinking how afraid she must be.

Within minutes, the first police cruiser arrived, pulling along the side street; undetected by the thief still inside. A teenage boy walking his dog stood on the corner watching the scene unfold. He stopped an officer and asked what was happening.

"Hey, what's going on?"

The officer replied.

"Please step back, there's a robbery in progress; I'm asking you to stay on this side of the building, for your own safety."

The young man took a few steps backward, pulling his dog by the old rope tied around his neck.

"Come on boy." He wasn't in a position to have any attention called to him or the dog, but couldn't help asking. "Hey, is everyone OK?"

The officer held up one hand, gesturing for the teen to stay back.

"Don't know yet, multiple calls have come in reporting shots fired. Just stay the hell on that side of the corner."

He took yet another step back, but when the police officer rounded the corner, he followed. He leaned up against a parked car just out of view. The driver lowered the window.

" Hey man, everything OK?"

Startled, the young man apologized.

"I'm so sorry; I didn't think anyone was in the car. I didn't scratch it or anything, I swear."

"Oh, no, you're fine. I was honestly making sure you were ok. There's been a shooting in that store."

"Yeah, I know. My friend is in there. You don't happen to know who was shot, do you?"

"Actually, I do. My friend is in there too. Her name is Fiona, and as far as I know, she's the only one who's been shot." The driver got out of the car and leaned next to the young man; extending his hand. "I'm Rob and you are?"

The two shook hands.

"Nate and this is Harry. We have had a hell of a night. My friend Wendy is in the store. I told her to wait for me, thinking she'd be safe. It's a long story, but I really hope she's OK."

Rob smiled.

"Hang on, let's see if we can't get you guys some info." He turned on his com, "Fee, can you hear me? I'm right outside the door honey. The police are coming in right now."

She answered, this time at regular volume.

"Rob, I'm OK."

"Listen, honey, there's a young man out here worried about his friend. She's thirteen, blonde hair, green jacket. Have you seen her?"

Fiona looked down.

"Yes, she's right here. She's fine."

Rob conveyed the information to Nate who began to cry; "Thank God." He continued to tell Rob about Harry being stolen from Wendy, and how she sought his help. He told Rob how he was able to track down the dog thief and what he did to rescue Harry for her. "Kids like Wendy need protection out here. I just had to get Harry back for her, you know? Damn, she's just a kid."

Rob's com was still transmitting, and Fiona heard everything Nate had told him. She could hear the paramedics coming through the front door; "Wendy? Listen to me; I know you're afraid right now. You're going to have to trust me and follow my lead. As soon as the paramedics get in here for me, pay very close attention to what I am saying. OK?"

"I can't go with the cops. I have to find Nate!"

"I know; if you do what I say, everything is going to be ok, I promise."

The paramedics arrived and helped Fiona onto the gurney. They were so preoccupied with protocol no one even heard her; "Rob, stand by and follow my lead, we're coming out and we need your help."

"Copy." Rob felt as if they were in a movie; it all seemed so surreal. He wasn't even sure why he responded with the word, 'Copy'.

As Fiona was being wheeled to the ambulance, a police officer approached.

"We're going to need statements from both of you."

Fiona answered.

"That's fine. My sister is going with my boyfriend and our brother. They can meet us at the hospital," she motioned to Rob. "Honey, take good care of Wendy. I'll see you all in a bit."

Rob nodded and put his arm around the young girl.

"You OK?"

"I'm not hurt. I'm scared though. I don't want to talk to the cops."

"Let's take one thing at a time. Nate is in my car; he has Harry and they're waiting for you. I promise you're safe with me."

"Your girlfriend saved my life, you know?"

Rob opened the back door for Wendy. She climbed in and began to cry. As he looked through the rearview mirror, he saw her hugging Harry around his thick neck. He couldn't stop licking her and wagging his entire backside with excitement. Nate looked relieved; tired, but relieved.

Once they were on their way, Rob told them he wasn't really Fiona's boyfriend.

"I'm her best friend's boyfriend, actually. We're roommates, and we also work together. I'm trusting her judgment here, so please don't make any bad decisions, like running when we park the car."

Wendy agreed but Nate was still visibly nervous.

"We need to just go. Believe me, man, it's better for you and for us. I know you're trying to help, but people don't help kids like us, not really. Something always goes wrong, and we end up in worse situations. We can take better care of ourselves."

"No!" Wendy demanded. "I want to see Fiona. I need to know that she's ok. I'm tired of hiding, Nate. I'm tired of being afraid. Maybe she really can help us, or maybe I can help her. I don't know, but it's really important that I see her. After that, if you still think we're going to be in trouble, I'll go with you."

Rob became concerned with the entire situation; "Guys, please, I'm asking that you trust us. I know that's a really big ask. You don't know us, but I promise you, if Fiona says she can help, she will do just that. We're almost there. Listen, we are going to walk in, ask for Fiona and act like we are family, all of us. OK?"

They both agreed. Wendy was much more hopeful than Nate. He was older and had been through his own hell since he was just nine years old. He knew what being put into the system could mean, for both of them; and he also knew their chances were better on the street. But if there was a third option, especially for Wendy, he was willing to give it a chance.

"OK, we're family, for an hour."

Rob approached the admitting desk in the emergency room.

"Hi, we're here for Fiona Lasher. She was brought in by ambulance with a gunshot wound, I'm her brother, I mean, I'm her boyfriend. This is her brother and her sister. I'm so sorry; I'm just really nervous and freaked out."

The nurse behind the desk peered over her glasses at Rob. He was so clean-cut, well dressed and good-looking, she couldn't imagine he wasn't telling the truth.

"Have a seat, hon. Let me see what's going on with your girl."

Rob escorted them to a row of empty seats in the waiting area. He leaned over and whispered to Wendy.

"No one noticed Harry. He's so well-behaved; you're lucky."

Harry had tucked himself between Wendy and Nate with his rear end under the chairs. He rested his head on his folded front paws and lay silently and obediently. Wendy was so proud of him. She began to tell Rob the story of finding and saving Harry when the nurse reappeared.

"OK, kids. You can come back and see Miss Lasher. She's waiting for the doctor to see her; I bet she'd love some company."

Rob got up first and attempted to distract the nurse with questions regarding Fiona's injury. He gestured for the kids to walk through the doors ahead of him, but the nurse was paying closer attention than he anticipated.

"Sweetie, you can't bring that dog in here."

Wendy let her street smarts take over; "He's my emotional support dog. I need him with me at all times. I have an anxiety disorder. I know he isn't wearing his vest, but he was stolen from me a few days ago. My brother Nate found him and rescued him. His collar and vest were gone. That's why we only have a rope to lead him with. His name is Harry, and I promise, he won't be of any trouble." Both Rob and Nate were surprised at the fluidity of her story; the truthful bits as well as the blatant lie blended so well. Wendy was so convincing, they almost believed her.

The nurse seemed skeptical.

"Gentlemen, is this true ?"

Rob was quick to answer.

" Every word."

The nurse took a long look at each one of them; "OK, here's the deal; My only obligation is to Fiona and her medical care. However, my concerns are for all of you. If anyone feels they are in danger or are here against their better judgment, come find me at the nurse's station right outside this door. Just give me a sign, and I will alert the proper authorities, got it?" She knew they weren't telling the truth simply by the discrepancies in appearance. Fiona and Rob were dressed smartly, and properly groomed. The kids on the other hand wore ill-fitting clothing and hadn't bathed in some time. She couldn't imagine someone like Fiona allowing her siblings to be so unkempt when she was obviously prideful in her own appearance.

Wendy's eyes welled with tears.

"I want to be with Fiona." She looked over to Nate for some sort of approval. He smiled at her and nodded in agreement. "Please, it's been a long night. We just want to see our sister." Neither teen realized that the nurse suspected they were in some trouble, simply by their appearance. Her diligent scrutiny, however, made them uneasy as she continued to try and read the situation.

The nurse turned her full attention to Nate; "Don't I know you?"

He panicked; "No, I'm sure you don't. Uh, we don't even live around here."

"I do!" she declared. "You're 'hit by car', kid. Yes, I remember last year sometime in the fall. You were brought in by a witness; hit and run. You were pretty banged up. I treated you and you bailed before the doctor came in."

"It wasn't me. Maybe someone who looks like me, but I've never been hit by a car," Nate broke into awkward nervous laughter. "That's just crazy." However, the truth was; he had.

She furrowed her brow.

"Yeah, maybe." She watched as Nate leaned closer to Rob and placed his hand on Wendy's shoulder. The nurse had speculated, Rob and Fiona were involved in some type of nefarious dealings involving the two teens. But, the more she paid attention to their interactions, the more she doubted her first instinct. The teens weren't afraid of Rob and Fiona; they were afraid to be away from them. She knew something wasn't adding up, but her primary concern was for their well-being, and it was becoming clear they were better together.

"Well then, let me see if I can't scare up a doctor and get you all on your way home." She turned to Fiona, widened her eyes and smiled. They seemed to finally understand one another. Despite the inconsistencies; the nurse trusted that everyone was at least safe. She didn't yet know the circumstances regarding the shooting and the thought of someone intentionally targeting the teens made her feel physically ill. She could only go with her instincts and believe that Rob and Fiona were protecting the children from something.

Fiona simply mouthed.

"Thank you." She would have loved the opportunity to explain, but this was not the time or place. Fiona did, however, appreciate the nurse's concern. It was reassuring to know there were people like her looking out for kids like Wendy and Nate. Too many people turn a blind eye to the obvious ills in the world. No one ever seems to want to get involved, yet this particular nurse was more than willing to pay attention to the details of the situation.

The nurse walked through the door, and quickly turned back in.

"Hey, there's an officer waiting to speak with all of you, is that OK? I can ask him to leave."

Fiona answered.

"It's fine. We're OK. Let's get that over with."

She sent the officer in and told him he would have to step back out when the doctor arrived to examine Fiona's wound. He agreed and went inside.

"Hello, all. Just a few quick questions and I'll be on my way. This is just a formality, as the shooter is in custody." He never looked up, just opened his phone and began to type. He asked Fiona and Wendy what they saw, heard, and experienced. They answered honestly with no discrepancies in their stories. The officer was more than satisfied with their basic statements. "Thank you both, oh, and take care young lady. It looks like you got lucky. That could have been a lot worse," he gestured to Fiona's side.

Just as he walked out the door, the doctor came in. He was very soft-spoken and moved slowly and methodically. She was sure that his demeanor was soothing to his patients, but Fiona was rather agitated by it and would prefer to move things along at a much quicker pace.

"We've been here for more than two hours. Can we please just figure out what to do with me so I can go home? I'm very uncomfortable, and in a lot of pain. And, I'm freezing and super thirsty."

The doctor giggled which was again, very unsettling to Fiona.

"Well, we can proceed with a few stitches, but you're going to have one heck of a scar. I'd like to admit you and call in a specialist."

"Specialist. For what?"

"A plastics specialist. He can make sure scarring is minimal. Your wound isn't typical of a gunshot, or a bullet graze. It's like a hybrid between them. Very unusual."

"Yeah, I can believe that Doc; nothing that happens to me is ever typical or usual."

He giggled again.

"Good, you have your sense of humor."

"Can we just stitch me up and slap a bandage on this? I'm not worried about scarring, not in that area anyway. I mean, who looks at the fatty part of your side?"

Rob interjected.

"You got shot in your love handle!"

Fiona was clearly annoyed.

"Really? You think this is funny?"

Rob apologized.

"Sorry, Fee. You must be in pain. I was just trying to make you smile."

"Rob, shit, I'm sorry, I am. It's an intense burning sensation like my whole side is on fire. I just want to get all of us out of here and back to the house. Hey, can you do me a favor please?" She was trying to be as polite as possible. Rob didn't deserve to be the recipient of her frustrations.

"Yeah, anything."

"Make some calls. Nicky, TC, and Sarah."

"OK, but why my sister?"

"Ask her if she has any clothes she can bring to Wendy. We need everything, so if she has anything she saved from when she was younger, maybe she would lend us a few things. Please explain our situation to everyone and let them know we should be home soon."

"I know Sarah has stuff, and I also know she will be thrilled to help. You know, Nate and Nicky are about the same size, I bet we can take care of Nate as well. I'll be back in a few."

Fiona told Wendy she had just given a lot of clothing to charity when she moved a few months ago.

"Now I wish I had saved it all, but Sarah has amazing style; you're probably better off with her stuff anyway."

Wendy lowered her eyes.

"You don't have to do anything, I'll be OK. Nate and I are used to having nothing. We aren't here to try and get anything from either of you. I just had to know you were going to be OK."

"Yeah well, that's not how we do things in this family. Someone needs; we find a way to make things happen, you'll see. Wendy, I know you don't expect anything. I'm not offering out of a place of obligation, or pity. You and Nate are not going back out on your own, not if I can help it. I was in that store tonight for a reason, and I think you're it. I don't believe much in coincidences; not anymore. Nate, would you please find Rob and make sure he tells Nicky to have food ready when we get home? I don't care what it is, I am starving."

Nate smiled.

"OK, I'm on it, be right back."

The doctor returned with the nurse and a suture tray. The nurse cleaned Fiona's wound again and gave her a few shots to numb the area.

"Can you feel this, hon?" she asked, poking Fiona all over her side.

"Nope, I'm good. Let's do this."

Once she was stitched up and her wound properly dressed, the nurse began the rundown of continued care.

"You're going to have to keep this super clean, and the dressing will need to be changed at least twice daily."

"As luck would have it," Fiona explained. "My roommate is studying to become a paramedic. I have the best help there is."

Wendy piped up.

"I can totally help her too; I'm not even grossed out by blood or anything."

Fiona thanked her.

"You know, Nicky can teach you how to dress the wound, and then when he's in class, you can help me."

Wendy loved the idea of being useful. For the first time since she found Harry, she felt like her life had meaning. Fiona spoke as though she wanted Wendy to stick around. She was genuine and caring, not like the foster families that only wanted homeless kids for the monthly check, or to do their dirty work. Fiona and Rob were the kind of people Wendy once believed didn't exist.

"OK, I can totally do this," she said aloud.

By the time Rob and Nate returned, the nurse had printed out Fiona's instructions and had her prescriptions ready to go.

"You guys take good care of her."

The three answered in unison.

"We will."

Nate sat up front with Rob on the drive back to Long Island.

"Where are we going?" he asked, noticing they were leaving the city. Nate's thoughts began to go dark. What if they were kidnapping them? How would he escape and protect Wendy?

"We live on Long Island. It's about a forty-five-minute drive without traffic. It's pretty nice out there."

"I've never been."

"Nate confessed, now feeling even more apprehensive.

Nate glanced in the back seat to find Fiona, Wendy and Harry all fast asleep.

"They're out like lights," he told Rob.

"Good, because usually Fiona drives me crazy on the ride home. It will be nice to enjoy the drive for a change."

"Rob?"

"Yeah?"

"Are we going to be OK?"

"Absolutely."

"Listen, I've been in bad situations before, but Wendy is so young, I'd hate for anything to happen to her. If you and Fiona are thinking of using us for something bad, or illegal, just take me and leave Wendy alone."

"Oh my God, Nate! I swear that is not what's happening right now. I'm so sorry, man. I didn't mean to freak you out. I should have told you before that we didn't live in the city. Oh, Nate, I cannot imagine what you must be feeling." Rob was both mortified and impressed. He couldn't imagine ever hurting the kids and felt nauseated at the thought of Nate thinking so. However, Nate's bravery was astonishing, and Rob was determined to do what he could to help them both.

"I can't help it. Kids like us are used for a lot of crazy shit. Maybe you two are good people, but we aren't used to that. I didn't mean to accuse you of anything, I just figured we were in deep trouble when I saw you were driving us out of the city."

"You have every right to question us, but I promise, our intentions are to help you, both of you; not to hurt you. I'll make you a deal, if you're uncomfortable when we get to the house, say the word and I will drive you right back, OK?"

Still feeling uneasy, Nate had no choice but to try and trust Rob's word. "Deal."

Our Kind of Family

It was after eleven p.m. when Rob, Nate, Wendy, Harry and Fiona pulled into the driveway.

"You live in a mansion?" Wendy squealed.

"Hardly," Rob answered. "It's a big house for sure, but it's no mansion."

It took all three of them to help Fiona into the house. She was groggy from the pain medication the doctor had given her before she was discharged and exhausted from the unimaginable events of the evening. Try as she might, it was hard for her to stay focused; but she knew Nate and Wendy were depending on her. As they entered the house, she told Rob to please just get her to the couch in the living room. Her oversized, overstuffed and overly comfortable sectional was the first purchase she made after buying her house. It reminded her of Grams' couch, and she absolutely had to have it. Now, it seemed her oasis from the pain.

Fiona settled herself in the corner. Rob asked her what she needed, and she asked for pillows and a blanket, and Wanda.

"Oh, Wendy, Oh my God, I forgot to ask, does Harry get along with other dogs?"

"He loves dogs. Do you guys have a dog?"

"Yeah, Wanda. She's probably in my room," She asked Nicky to get Wanda so the two could meet. "First things first; my best girl needs to meet your best boy."

Wendy sat on the very edge of the couch, holding Harry's rope tightly in both hands.

"Please be good," she whispered in his ear. "Please!"

Wanda meandered down the hall behind Nicky. She seemed unphased by the voices coming from the living room until she heard Fiona. The sound of her voice had Wanda quicken her pace. She jumped on the couch and pushed up against Fiona's legs, laying her head in her lap. Wanda instinctively avoided Fiona's left side, sensing her pain.

"Hi, baby. I'm so happy to see you." Fiona felt instantly comforted.

It took Wanda a few minutes to realize Harry was just a few feet away, sitting silently between Wendy's knees. She jumped off the couch to greet her new friend. The two sniffed one another for a few seconds. Harry let out an adorable whine and Wanda responded with a shrill bark. Wanda jumped back up on the couch next to Wendy. She reached over to pet her, and Wanda licked her hand. Harry wouldn't take his eyes off of Wanda and pulled against the rope to try and get closer.

Nicky sat next to Wendy.

"Go ahead, let him off the rope." She hesitated, but eventually leaned down and loosened the rope. Once again, she pleaded with her four-legged friend. 'Please be a good boy."

Harry carefully climbed up on the couch. He had never been in a house, never mind on furniture before. He seemed confused at first but took his lead from Wanda. Harry stood on the cushion; too nervous to actually lie down. She looked up at him and gave a quick, "Yip." Harry obeyed, and cautiously lay down next to her. Wanda put her front paw on his and let out a sigh. The two relaxed and quickly fell asleep as though they had been friends forever.

"That's the most amazing thing I have ever seen," Nate exclaimed. He sat next to Wendy and put his arm around her shoulder. "Well, if Harry approves, I guess you and I can give this a shot, at least for tonight."

Wendy yawned.

"Is there a place for me to sleep?" she asked.

Fiona sat up as best as she could manage.

"Yes, you can sleep in my room, or if you'd like, you and I can camp out on the couch tonight. I think I'll be better off sleeping here so I can sit up a bit."

"I'll stay here with you if that's OK."

"I'd love that. Sarah is on her way over with some things for you. You can use the bathroom in my room to shower and change. I'll show you where it is."

With Nate's assistance, Fiona carefully got to her feet. She led Wendy through the living room, past the kitchen, and down the hallway to their right. She told her the room to the left was the main bathroom, and to the right was a spare room that they hadn't decided what to do with yet, and at the very end of the hall was Fiona's room. She opened the door, and Wendy expected it to look like a magazine. Instead, there were clothes hanging from the chair; the bed was unmade and there were dozens of mismatched throw pillows on the floor. It made Wendy feel more comfortable knowing this house was for living in, not just for looking at it.

Fiona's bathroom was huge. There were double sinks in the vanity, a shower and a separate tub with jets. It was painted a very light violet with darker purple accents and trim.

"I love this bathroom," she told Fiona.

"Me too. It was one of the reasons I fell in love with this house, actually. Well, that and it was totally cheap."

"Knock, Knock?" Sarah was standing in the doorway holding three large plastic bags full of clothing. She didn't wait for a response and joined Fiona and Wendy. Sarah dropped the bags on the floor and flopped onto the bed.

"Hey, you must be Wendy. I'm Sarah, Rob's sister."

"You're so pretty," Wendy told her.

"Thank you, and so are you," Wendy had never been told she was pretty. She blushed and looked down at her ill-fitting clothes, then ran her fingers through her matted blonde hair.

"Oh, trust me, girl, you're beautiful! Give us a chance and we will have you believing you can be a supermodel. Let's start with a shower and some good conditioner for your gorgeous hair."

Sarah winked at Fiona who had thrown her clothes to the floor to sit in her chair.

"I'm sorry girls, my ass is kicked. Wendy, Sarah will hook you up with everything you need. I'm just going to rest her for a while." She leaned back in an attempt to get comfortable, but the pain in her side was stronger than her desire for comfort.

Wendy followed Sarah into the bathroom. She gave the young girl some body wash, shampoo and conditioner as well as a clean t-shirt and a pair of sweatpants she pulled from one of the bags.

"Take your time sweetie, and just yell if you need anything. I'm going to go sit with Fee for a few minutes. Oh, there are clean towels right here." She pointed to a small shelf next to the shower stall. Wendy thanked her and closed the door.

Sarah sat on the bed and began to unpack the bags of clothing.

"Where should I put these?" she asked.

"Oh, shit, OK, um, let's just leave everything folded on the bed for tonight. Wendy and I are going to sleep on the couch anyway. I'll figure all that out tomorrow. And Sarah, thank you so much. You went above and beyond."

"Are you kidding? She's a little doll. I can't wait to dress her up."

"I'm glad you feel that way. I think the guys are much more skeptical about Wendy and Nate. How are they doing out there by the way?"

"Oh, when I came in, Nicky was giving Nate some clothes to sleep in and showed him where the main bathroom was. So, where's Nate sleeping?"

"You ask really hard questions, you know that?"

Sarah laughed.

"No really Fee, it's not like you guys have this place fully furnished yet. Oh, I have an idea, what about the sofa in your office, just for now."

"That is actually a really good idea. I was thinking if Nate decides to stick around; we could fix up the loft room for him. He'd have some privacy and at least his own half bath I mean, there's a shower, sink and toilet up there, what more would he need?"

"You think he should live here? Can you just keep people who don't belong to you?" Sarah realized that Fiona was thinking long-term in regard to Wendy and Nate. This was not just an overnight solution. Sarah feared that Fiona was in way over her head.

"They have no place else to go. Sarah, I didn't think this all the way through, but I know I can't just tell them to go live on the streets again. We have room and a lot of people willing to help. They would both benefit from a family like ours."

Sarah sighed.

"I'm with you, Fee, truly. Whatever you need, I will do what I can." Still, she couldn't help the feeling of dread in the pit of her stomach, something wasn't right.

"Thank you, honey, I appreciate that more than you know. And the clothes are an awesome start."

'Oh, wait til you see all the cute stuff I found. I hope Wendy likes it."

Wendy emerged from the bathroom, looking and smelling one hundred percent better. Sarah and Fiona could tell by the smile on her clean face, she felt better too.

"Thanks for the sweats, Sarah, and I love this T-shirt!"

"You are so welcome. Everything in the bags is for you. You don't have to use all of it. Just go through it all tomorrow and the stuff you don't like, we can donate."

Wendy began to cry. She hugged Sarah and then Fiona.

"OK, I'm so starving right now. Who's going to help me out of this chair so we can go get some food?" Fiona tried to lighten things up as she felt herself get teary and saw Sarah's eyes begin to swell. She knew what was on everyone's mind, but she also knew it couldn't be wrong to care for a child in obvious need.

Nicky had covered the entire dining room table with food. There were pots, bowls, platters and serving spoons in the middle, plates and silverware set at each chair.

"I cooked everything we had in the fridge. I had no idea what you guys would like; I hope there's something here that interests you. I know you said to order in, but I had all this nervous energy; so I put it to good use."

Sarah sat down and patted the chair next to her.

"Wendy, come sit and eat. Nicky is a great cook." She began to fill her own plate, offering each dish to Wendy who said yes to everything on the table.

Nate took some pasta, a little salad and a piece of bread.

"Thank you for this."

Nicky reacted.

"You better eat more than that. I didn't make all this food for you to go to bed hungry. Please don't be shy, we certainly aren't."

As they ate, Rob and Sarah entertained everyone with stories of their childhood. Nate imagined what it would have been like to have a family, go on vacations and go to school. He wanted so badly to be a high school graduate and maybe even go to college. It pained him to allow himself to dream of such things, and he forced his thoughts back to reality. He told himself to simply be grateful for right now, and tomorrow he'd go back to the only life he knew. He hoped Fiona and her friends would continue to take care of Wendy and Harry, but he felt he'd only be a burden they didn't deserve.

Fiona watched as he picked at his food, and noticed he wasn't as engaged in the conversation as everyone else.

"Nate, did the guys tell you where you'll be sleeping, well for tonight anyway?"

"Yes, thanks. Nick told me his old couch was in your office. I appreciate that."

"It's not that old," Nicky teased. "That couch pulls out into a bed. I don't think we have sheets to fit, but I'll get a regular flat sheet for you. I had that thing in my room growing up so my friends could crash. When we moved, I just couldn't part with it, too many memories, I guess. Now I'm really glad I brought it with me."

Fiona laughed.

"Yeah, and somehow it ended up in my office! Oh, there's also a huge bean bag chair in there, if the sofa is uncomfortable. So, Nate, you have options," She joked.

Rob and Sarah cleared the table while Nick gathered sheets, pillows and a blanket for Nate. Wendy and Fiona joined the dogs on the couch.

"Is it OK if I turn the television on for a bit?" Fiona asked her houseguest.

"Yeah, it's your house. You shouldn't be asking me if it's OK."

"I just want to make sure you can fall asleep, and the sound won't bother you."

"Thanks, I'm almost asleep already. It won't bother me a bit.'

Fiona watched as Wendy's eyes grew heavier with each passing second, and within minutes, she was peacefully sleeping. She hoped Nate was comfortable in the other room as well. Sarah said good night and she'd be back sometime tomorrow afternoon. Fiona asked her to peek in on Nate on her way out.

"Please make sure he's OK in there." Sarah walked down the hallway toward the front door, and as she passed Fiona's office on her right, she could hear Nate snoring. All was well, for now.

The next morning, Rob was up bright and early before anyone else in the house. He had received a call from Laurel to be on standby; she would need him in the morning. He meandered into the kitchen to make coffee when his text notification on his phone sounded. It was from Laurel; *Can you come by when you're ready? I need to talk to you.*

He replied, *Let me grab a quick cup of coffee and I'll be on my way, see you in thirty minutes.*

The smell of brewing coffee woke Fiona. She joined Rob in the kitchen with her head in her hands.

"I have a killer headache," she whispered.

Rob seemed concerned. He poured her a cup, and sat her down at the table.

"Be right back," he told her. Rob went into their room and woke Nicky. "Hey, I know you have a late class, but I need you to get up and look after Fiona. She's complaining of a headache. I'm not sure that's normal, considering she was shot in her side."

Nicky sat up and rubbed his eyes.

"Yeah, actually, it could be a reaction to her pain meds. I'm up, give me a few and I'll check it out. Where are you going?"

"Laurel needs me. I told her I'd be there soon, but I'm going to hang out until you come to take a look at Fiona."

"I'll be right out."

Rob sat at the table with Fiona and his second cup of coffee.

"Honey, Nicky will be right out. He thinks your headache may be from the pain medication."

She squinted and wrinkled her nose.

"It feels like the worst hangover ever."

Nicky joined them in the kitchen; and took a chair across from Fiona.

"Good morning, head hurts?"

"Yeah, like splitting open kind of pain."

Rob handed Nicky a cup of coffee and kissed him on the forehead.

"I gotta go, you got this?"

"We're good. See you tonight after my class. Have a great day." Nicky smiled at his boyfriend. He knew how lucky he was to have found Rob. Not everyone would be so supportive of having Fiona and her current chaos in their lives.

Nate stopped Rob in the hallway on his way out.

"Hey man, could you give me a ride back to the city?"

"I'm actually sticking around town today, but can I ask why you want to go back?"

Nate leaned in.

"I'm feeling like I should go. I don't want to be any trouble. You can check the room if you want. I didn't take anything."

"Oh my God, I didn't think you would. I don't think anyone would suspect you took anything. Nate, what's this about? I mean, I know this whole situation is off the wall but give us a chance. We all want to help if we can."

Nate looked over Rob's shoulder.

"Is Wendy OK?"

"Yeah, she's still sleeping. Fiona doesn't feel well though. Nicky is with her, but he has class later. I was hoping you'd look after the girls today. But, if you really need to go back, I can arrange it."

"Well, not if Fiona needs my help. I don't want to leave her and Wendy alone if she isn't well. Wendy may not know what to do if there's an emergency."

"Be the man, Nate. I would appreciate it. I'll be back in a while. There's coffee in the kitchen if you drink coffee."

"I'd love some. Thanks. Oh, and Rob, I really do appreciate all of you."

"We know."

Nicky offered to whip up some breakfast for Nate and the girls who graciously accepted.

Wendy worried about Harry who seemed right at home.

"I hate to ask, but is there something I can feed Harry? Leftovers maybe?"

Fiona smiled.

"Wanda will happily share her dog food with Harry. Why don't you let them both out back to do their business and get some exercise? I'll find a bowl and get them some breakfast."

Wendy called out to the dogs who eagerly followed her to the sliding glass doors of the kitchen which led to the backyard. She opened the doors and stepped onto the brick patio.

"You have a pool!" she squealed.

"Yeah, we haven't been in it yet though," Nicky told her. "Fiona just bought this house last month, and it was kind of late to open the pool, so we left it closed for now. But next summer, we will be totally splashing it up."

"You guys are so lucky. I hope I can live in a house like this someday."

Fiona sighed. She wanted so badly to just tell Wendy she could stay with her forever, but there were so many big issues to consider. The first and most concerning was, she was only twenty-four and knew nothing about raising a teenager beyond the recent memories of being one herself. Another concern of course, was that Wendy wasn't a stray dog she could just feed and play with, and Fiona needed real guidance as to the right way to help her.

Nicky handed Fiona a bottle of water, two ibuprofen and a b-12 vitamin.

"Stay hydrated today, and take two ibuprofen every six hours. Your headache should ease up soon. Oh, and do not continue to take those pain meds. You're just going to have to tough it out, lady."

"Just my luck; even my issues have issues." Fiona stared out the glass doors. Wendy was running around the yard in her pajamas, playing with the dogs; throwing Wanda's ball high in the air for Harry to catch. It was endearing to see Wanda graciously sharing her toys and the attention; but even more satisfying to see Harry play like a real dog for the first time in his life. Although she knew things would eventually change, Fiona found such joy just outside her kitchen doors. She knew at that moment she'd be a great mom someday and for the first time in a long while, she thought of Carter.

The Truth Does Hurt

Mr Daly called out to his assistant who was busy at her desk; just outside his office door.

"Helen, I need you in here, now"

Helen rolled her eyes and sighed deeply. If not for the decent pay and great medical benefits for her and her family, she'd choose to work anywhere else, for anyone else. Mr Daly was entirely too demanding, and his tone was often rude and disrespectful. She hated when he bellowed and wished he'd just leave her to her work. Helen got up from her desk and walked inside his office.

"What can I do for you?" she asked in the nicest tone she could muster.

"I need Carter Wyatt; ASAP," he answered without looking up from his file folder.

"OK, I'll call down to the shop." Helen turned on her heels and left his office. She sat back at her desk, and tried calming herself before picking up the phone. Calling the shop and asking for Carter is certainly something he was capable of doing himself, and it would have taken less time than it did to ask her to do it for him. She had been working for Mr Daly long enough to know it was a control issue; and not blatant laziness, which, in Helen's opinion, was even worse.

John, the shop manager answered.

"Hey Helen, to what do I owe the pleasure of your call?"

"Mr Daly needs to see Carter, ASAP. and I quote."

"Ah, OK, well, I can't spare the kid right now, he's going to have to wait."

"Oh, no John, then you'll be calling Daly yourself to tell him. I'm not in the mood for gunfire."

"All right, I'll send him right over. You hang in there Helen. Try and have a nice day."

John hung up and left his office to find Carter in the garage. He knew Carter was to become Mr Daly's son-in-law and assumed his presence was being requested as a personal matter.

"Hey Wyatt; the old man wants to see you up in his office."

"Now?" Carter asked, wiping his greasy hands on a shop cloth.

"Helen said ASAP. So you'd better get moving."

Carter, like John, assumed this was personal, as there was nothing he could think of that he'd be summoned for regarding his work.

"Be back in a few."

As he made his way from the garage to the main building Carter tried texting Meg who had been ignoring his calls and messages for a few days.

"Hey, your dad asked to see me, you know what for?" he wrote. Still, no response.

Mr Daly busied himself with the file in front of him, making notes, or so it appeared. Carter walked in through the open office door and greeted his boss.

"Hey, Mr Daly. You wanted to see me?"

Without as much as a second of eye contact, Mr Daly delivered his purpose for wanting to see Carter.

"Mr Wyatt, it is with a considerable amount of regret that I must inform you of your termination. Please collect your belongings and leave the property in a timely manner. Should you choose to protest verbally or physically, I am prepared to have you formally escorted from the premises."

Carter stood in the doorway stunned.

"I'm sorry, what?"

"I believe I have made myself blatantly clear. Thank you for your time and services."

Carter slowly made his way back to the garage to clean out his locker and say his goodbyes. He tried texting Meg once more but to no avail. He knew somehow this was all personal, and couldn't help but think of his conversation with Shelly just a week before.

"So, what did the old fart want?" John called out as he met Carter in the locker room.

"I've been fired."

"What? Why? He can't do that. Let me go talk to him; don't you leave!" John was obviously agitated by Carter's news.

"No, John, please don't. I am pretty sure I know what this is all about, and believe me, you're better off staying out of it. I couldn't live with myself if something happened to your job as well, because of me. I appreciate you; I do, but this is probably for the best."

"Damn, kid. I'm gonna miss you. You're an excellent mechanic, but an even better person. They just don't make many like you; you remember that. If you need a reference, Carter, just let me know. I doubt Daly would step up, but I certainly will."

"Thank you, John, I may take you up on that."

"Any time kid."

As Carter said his goodbyes to the guys in the garage, he couldn't help to notice Eddie's obvious avoidance. They hadn't been the same since the day Sam and Shelly arrived, but this was different. Eddie went out of his way to look too busy to speak to Carter as he passed him in the garage.

"Later, Ed," he called out. Eddie held up one hand, but never looked up from the engine he had his face buried in. It was as if he already knew why Carter was leaving Daly Motors in the middle of the day.

Carter's drive home was a blur, as he could not stop himself from running all the possible scenarios through his thoughts. What if Shelly's theory was correct? And what if the tension between him and Eddie had nothing to do with asking him to leave the day Sam and Shelly arrived? His perplexity rivaled his sadness at the thought of the twins not being his children after all. Carter's heart felt crushed under the weight of such deceit. He could hardly wait to get home where it was safe and comfortable and filled with people who would help him understand. Carter found himself talking aloud; "Almost there, just a few more miles." What he wasn't counting on was Meg waiting in his driveway.

"Why is she here?" Shelly mused as she peered out of the front window, hoping to stay undetected. Mrs Wyatt was just as confused as her daughter-in-law. "It's the middle of the day, who is she waiting for?"

Carter pulled into the driveway behind Meg's car. He jumped out and ran to her.

"Meg, what the hell is going on?" his voice was frantic: he reached out to kiss her. Meg stepped to her left, avoiding his attempt at affection.

"Carter, I wanted to tell you this in person, even though my family feels I owe you nothing."

"Come in, we can talk downstairs."

"No, here is fine. I'm not planning on staying long. Listen. I know what happened at work today and you have to believe me; it's for the best. I've been wanting to tell you for some time now, and I just can't take it anymore. You were supposed to marry me; be a father and buy us a house; not necessarily in that order. But your family has really screwed things up for me by putting doubt in your mind; although, they aren't entirely wrong. Carter, the babies are not yours; you're off the hook."

"Off the hook?" he yelled. "What the hell does that even mean? Jesus Meg, why would you do this to me?"

"Carter, you just don't get it. I need someone who will fit into my family. Someone who will do what I tell them to; what my father tells them to. That was supposed to be you, but that didn't work out as planned. So, I have to have a new plan now."

"How do I know you're not lying about the twins? I want a paternity test."

"I already had one done. I suspected they weren't yours all along, and I was able to get a DNA sample from the actual father, and it's an undeniable match. Here, see for yourself," she said as she handed him an envelope.

Carter opened it and read the results; *Father: Edward Simmons.* The results were not entirely a surprise, but he still felt as though he'd been hit by a train. For a few seconds he couldn't breathe, his head spun, and a wave of nausea rushed in. He looked at Meg who refused to make eye contact.

"Can I keep this?" he asked

"Yeah, that's fine. I have to go; can you move your car?"

For a moment, ever so brief, Carter felt sorry for Meg.

"Good Luck with everything, I hope life is good to you and to your children." As Carter pulled back into his driveway he noticed his mother and Shelly in the front window. He waved and smiled. Part of his heart filled with joy knowing he had an amazing family to depend on for love and support, but another part seemed to be suddenly missing; he was not a father anymore, and although he and Shelly talked about the possibility, the hurt was more than he could have imagined.

Can We Keep Them?

Rob arrived at the Cooke's a little later than he anticipated. He rang the bell, and heard Laurel yell.

"Come in". He opened the door and stepped inside. "I'm in the kitchen," she informed him, rather loudly.

"Hey Laur, sorry I'm late. I had to convince Nate to stay with Fiona today. He wanted a ride back to the city."

"It's fine. We have a few errands to run but I need to speak with you first, coffee?" she offered.

"No, thanks but I had two cups before I left. I'm good for the day. So, what's on your mind, boss?"

"The obvious. Tell me what the hell is happening at your house. Has Fiona lost her mind, or what?"

"Actually, I'm 'team Fiona' on this. I wasn't at first, but those kids need help. Laurel, they have nothing, no one, and nowhere to go. That's a whole lot of empty life, you know?"

"So, what's her plan? Do they stay with you guys forever? How can the three of you afford to care for two kids? What about school; food, and clothing? Not to mention medical care if needed."

"Laurel, I'm not going to pretend this is an optimal situation for any of us, or them; but I think you need to meet Nate and Wendy before you get in Fiona's shit over this. I totally understand your concerns; Nicky and I have them as well. However, you're the one who saw that special something in Fiona when you met her, correct ?" Laurel nodded. "So, please help us if you can because we won't give up on two kids in need, not without a fight."

"Well, Rob, I'm going to be honest here. I did not expect our conversation to start this way. I am in awe of your loyalty and compassion. And, you're right, I believe in Fiona, and I have to have faith in her. But, make no mistake, I am still worried."

"Me too," he admitted

"Let's start by making a list. First on the agenda, we need to pick Susan up from the airport in two hours. Fiona called her this morning, and she called me. I couldn't give her any more information than she already had, but I got her on the first flight into Newark from Orlando. She wants to spend a few days with Fiona while she is recovering. Then, we shop. What do they need?"

"Well, my sister had a bunch of clothes for Wendy, so she's OK for now, but Nate could use a few essentials. Nicky mustered up some sweats, a pair of jeans and a few T-shirts, but guys don't keep clothing like girls do. He doesn't have all that much to spare."

"Are they the same size? Can you shop for Nate?"

"Yes, no problem at all. I even know his shoe size. He told Nicky when he asked. Neither of us are the same size shoe; so we could definitely start there. Poor kid; his sneakers are literal shreds."

"Got it," she said, scribbling notes on a post-it. "Food! Now, I know feeding two teenagers is going to get costly, and with Nicky in school, yours and Fiona's income need to cover all the expenses. I'm thinking of doing a monthly subscription. They will even deliver an extra freezer to store everything. We can put it out in the garage. I have the website here if you'd like to take a look." She turned her laptop toward Rob. "There's a one-month trial, let's sign up for that until we know what the future holds."

"Wow; that's a lot of food, Laurel. Even the smaller packages are huge. I know that's kind of an oxymoron, but you know what I mean."

"Yeah, but totally cost-effective. So, pick one and we will have it delivered this weekend."

Rob poured through two pages of options, hoping to make the right decision. After seeing Nate and Wendy eat the night before, he surmised Nate as the pickier of the two.

"Here, this one looks good," he told Laurel, pointing to a moderate package at the bottom of the first web page. It contained equal parts healthy proteins and vegetables as well as frozen snack foods such as chicken tenders and pizza bites.

"Perfect." Laurel grabbed her credit card from her wallet and placed the order, "I opted for next-day delivery. It will all arrive tomorrow. Now, all we need is basic essentials, like milk, bread, cereal, and whatever else we can think of."

"You're pretty amazing, boss."

"Yeah, yeah, just don't tell anyone," she teased. "Let me grab my things and we can head to the airport. We'll have more time to talk in the car."

"Laurel, I have nothing stocked in the car for Susan. No water or snacks."

"We'll stop on the way, it's no problem. I should have told you we needed to run out to New Jersey for Susan. Everything is just happening quickly. Oh, do you think Fiona is OK with the kids for a while?"

"I do. I know everyone's biggest concern is that these two are a pair of grifters and they're going to rob us blind, but trust me, they aren't. I think Fiona is in good hands today. Both Wendy and Nate seem more concerned about taking care of Fiona than themselves; it's rather endearing."

Nate and Wendy seemed content watching television and cuddling with Harry and Wanda. Fiona imagined this must be like a vacation to them; not having to worry about anything. She thought of her own childhood and how easy she had it; safe, loved and normal. She was so glad her mother was coming to spend a few days with her; now more than ever before, she needed her. Fiona placed her phone down on the coffee table in front of her. She felt guilty for being occupied with it for the past few hours, ignoring her house guests.

"I'm so sorry guys, are you all right? Is there anything you need?"

Wendy sat up and sheepishly asked.

"May I have something to eat? I'm kind of hungry."

"Oh, absolutely sweetie. What can I get for you?"

Nate stood.

"I got this; you rest Fiona." He went into the kitchen and opened the refrigerator, "What would we be allowed to make?"

His question took Fiona by surprise. She had to stop herself from answering as though he should know better; because he didn't.

"Nate," she began in the most compassionate tone she could muster. "In this house, everyone can have whatever they like. If it's in the pantry or fridge, it's yours. There is no need to ask; not ever."

"OK, I was just thinking maybe Rob and Nick wouldn't want us to eat their food; so I thought I'd check."

"You're very polite, but their food is my food, is your food. Did that make sense? Anyway, we shop for the house, not for ourselves." She turned her head toward the kitchen. "Wendy, grab whatever you want, and Nate can help you cook it, or warm it up or whatever. Oh and Nate, you and I have a video conference call in thirty minutes, OK?"

Nate was confused, but he agreed and proceeded to take a few leftover containers over to the microwave.

"Wendy, how about some pasta for lunch?" he offered. "Oh, hey Fiona, can we get you anything?"

"Thanks, kiddo, but I'm OK for now. My head feels better but my stomach isn't right. I can't wait to feel normal again."

Nate laughed.

"It's been a day, give yourself some time. Remember, you were shot!"

Fiona sat back and closed her eyes, she felt herself begin to drift off; when the smell of food snapped her awake.

"Damn, I need caffeine, I think."

Nate walked in and handed her a soda.

"Will this help?"

"Yes, thanks. When you're finished eating, would you help me to the office? Once I'm on my feet I'm OK, it's getting off the couch that hurts."

"Sure."

Fiona was so preoccupied with her own thoughts, she failed to notice how nervous Nate had become since she invited him on the conference call. His hands shook as he tried to place the lids back on the plastic leftover containers. Wendy leaned in and whispered.

"What do you think is going to happen to us?"

Nate just shook his head.

"No idea, but I'm not going to let them send you to foster care. If that's what they want to do with us, I have a plan to get us the hell out of here."

Fiona called into the kitchen.

"OK, let's do this." as she struggled to get herself off the couch. Nate rushed to her side and offered his arm to steady her. They made their way up the hall and into her office. Fiona sat at her desk and flipped open the laptop. She pulled up her email and clicked the link TC had just sent her. A voice prompt sounded. *Please wait while your host connects your call.*

Nate pulled a folding chair over next to Fiona.

"Cool," he remarked.

Within seconds, TC's face appeared on the screen, followed by Chris.

"Hey Firebird," Chris quipped. "Looks like you're rising up again. How ya' feeling?"

TC smiled and adjusted his glasses.

"Hey Fee, is Nate joining us?"

Nate leaned in and looked at the screen.

"Holy shit," he said aloud.

Fiona had to laugh, "You know who that is?" she asked.

"Yeah, I'm homeless, not a cave-dweller, that's Anthony Cooke."

"And he can hear you," Fiona reminded him.

"Oh my God, sorry. I just wasn't expecting, well, I don't know who I was expecting. I really am sorry."

TC, as usual, was multitasking and typing on another screen.

"It's fine, sir, I get holy shit a lot. I've got something going on here, an issue at the labs so I'm going to let Chris get this party started, OK?"

Chris began with a rather formal introduction. He told Nate about his role with Cooke Industries, his own past and his experience with homelessness and the vendor project.

"Nate, in my personal as well as professional opinion, Fiona acted according to not only her personal ethics but those shared with our Cooke Industries family. Therefore, it is my honor to do what is in my power to help make things easier for you as well as Wendy. Now, we have a proposition for you, but we all want you to take some time and make the best decision for you. Although we're here to facilitate, no one wants to make life-affirming decisions on your behalf. May I ask for your full legal name?"

Still confused and a bit starstruck by TC's video appearance, Nate responded.

"Nathan James Morrow."

"Wonderful. I'd like to look into getting you a social security number, Nate, do I have your permission to do so?"

"Oh, I have one of those. I was in the system; we had to have a social. Here, I have my card." Nate opened his tattered wallet and produced his social security card. It was worn and torn, but the number was legible. He read it to Chris.

"This is very good news, Nate. I will do what I can from my end to get things rolling, provided you accept our proposal. I'm not sure if Fiona discussed this with you yet, Fiona?"

"I haven't," she answered.

Chris shook his head.

"No problem, Fee. I can imagine you've been a bit pre-occupied over there. I'd be happy to fill Nate in on our idea, but feel free to jump in. Oh, and TC, are you still with us?"

"I am. Sorry guys, this is important, but so are all of you. Just yell my name if you need my undivided attention."

Chris continued; "Nathan, we have a position open with Cooke Industries and we'd like to offer it to you. Would you be willing to work with us?"

"Like, get paid?" Nate was clearly caught off guard. He had been expecting to be hauled into Child Services or worse. Instead, these people are offering him a job. His emotions ran the gambit between cynical and grateful all within about thirty seconds.

"Yes, it is a paying position as Fiona and Kay's assistant. They will be training you and getting you up to speed on their current project. We have been holding off on filling this position at the request of your new friend Fiona who insisted she and her partner didn't need an assistant. But in light of our current situation, it's time to fill it. Seems to me, you were in the right place at the right time, son." Chris knew the best way to save Nate from returning to the city and his life on the streets was to give him a purpose larger than the one he gave himself among the homeless kids. He wanted nothing more than to rescue every child in need, but for now, he'd focus on Nate and Wendy.

Fiona piped up; "I think it would be great for Nate and me to meet with Kay and see how that chemistry works, for all of us."

Chris agreed, and asked that he be kept in the loop, so he could help to get things situated if Nate agrees to accept the job.

"OK guys, I'm signing off for now. Nathan, it was good speaking with you, sir. I look forward to meeting you in person soon."

TC looked up from his work and adjusted his glasses.

"Chris gone?"

Fiona laughed.

"Yep. So, would you like to add anything before I sign off and confer with my future assistant?"

"Yeah, see you tonight. I got a text from Laurel to meet her at your place. Oh, hey, you must be Wendy," he said, focusing over Fiona's right shoulder.

"Hi." Wendy smiled and waved at the screen, and somehow, in one millisecond, captured TC's heart. Fiona hadn't noticed her come in and seemed surprised when TC greeted her. She leaned her head toward Wendy, who patted it as if she were Harry or Wanda. TC found her gesture very endearing and made him even more curious about this young girl who happened her way into their lives.

"OK guys, gotta run, see ya' later." His screen went black.

Nate stood.

"So, Anthony Cooke is coming here? I have to get busy."

"Doing what?" Wendy asked.

"Cleaning up. No offense Fiona, but the place is really messy. I don't want Mr Cooke to think I'm a slacker, or an ungrateful guest in your house."

"So, you're considering our offer?"

"Just let me clean up for now. OK?"

Nate left the office and Wendy turned to Fiona.

"He's so nervous all the time." She shrugged her shoulders and left to return to the couch and television. Fiona wondered if she had imagined TC's reaction to Wendy. He was kind of adorable when he spoke to her. She couldn't help considering the idea of TC and Laurel caring for Wendy; what a perfect scenario that would be for everyone.

TC finished putting out his proverbial fires, making certain his laboratory staff were no longer agitated by the new safety protocols. There was no effective way to give them what they were demanding, but some monetary incentives had them in compliance in no time. He had the brainstorm to offer cash bonuses if the entire lab went accident and incident free following the new protocols for one month; problem solved. Both TC and Laurel hated throwing money at any problem as a way to quickly extinguish it; but realistically, TC knew it was optimal. He gathered his things and made his way down to the lobby where Charlie was waiting to drive him home.

"Hey man, are we waiting for the girls?"

Charlie shook his hand.

"Nope, Kay and Jaime are waiting in the car for us. We've all been summoned to Fiona's house," He joked.

"Let's get this show on the road then."

TC sat up front with Charlie, as he usually did. He hated his driver's feeling like an actual chauffeur, and unless he needed the room of the back seat to work during their trip home, TC preferred the front seat and friendly conversation.

Kay and Jaime were up to speed, thanks to the calls Laurel had made during her ride to the airport earlier in the day. Jaime was excited to show Kay what she had purchased during her lunch break.

"I bought them a game system," she gushed.

Charlie chimed in.

"Yeah, which one?"

Jaime held the box above the seat.

"This one. Joe told me to get it."

"Good choice." Charlie gave her a thumbs up.

Kay was quiet.

"I didn't know we were buying gifts. I have nothing to bring them."

"Yeah, you do. I have three more bags full of crap they don't need, and maybe even don't want, but I got it all anyway. This is from all of us, me, you and Charlie and Joe."

Kay smiled.

"You're the best!"

TC turned down the radio.

"Ladies, doesn't it seem like we're all missing the big picture? We're focused on the two teens and our Fiona was shot."

Jaime held up a pink shopping bag.

"I didn't forget our girl. I got a few things just for Fee, to make her feel better."

Kay piped up.

"Charlie, before we get to Fiona's, stop at the liquor store. I'll bring the wine."

"Great idea," Jaime agreed.

Susan Lasher waited patiently in her daughter's living room for Fiona to return from the bedroom where Nick was assisting with a bandage change. Charlie, TC, Jaime and Kay had just arrived, bearing bag after bag filled with gifts for Nate and Wendy. Jaime held on to the pretty pink shopping bag meant for Fiona while the others eagerly unpacked the rest, sprawling their contents across the coffee table.

"Is it Christmas already?" Susan joked.

Jaime hugged Susan and showed her Fiona's bag.

"I got the cutest things for Fee, where is she?"

"She and Nicky are in her room, changing her bandages. I'm sure they'll be right out. How have you been? We have so much catching up to do."

"Yes. I can't wait to hear about Florida life, I'm so jealous. Kay brought wine, let's start there."

Susan followed Jaime into the kitchen and joined Kay who was already uncorking and pouring.

"This is the best, not party I've been to," Susan said, happily accepting the glass of Pinot Grigio that Kay offered to her.

"Where did Laurel go?" Kay asked, holding the glass meant for her.

TC called in from the living room.

"Laurel and Rob are in the garage; don't ask!"

Laurel poked her head through the garage door and yelled into the house.

"Nate, can I see you out here for a moment please?"

Nate jumped up.

"Yes, Ma'am," he answered, stumbling over the bags on the floor to get to the door. Nate joined Rob and Laurel in the garage where they had been pushing boxes aside to make room for the freezer being delivered the following day.

"Nate; there's a delivery coming tomorrow between noon and four. Let them in through the garage door and ask them to put the freezer here." She pointed to the far-left corner, under the bicycle racks mounted to the wall, which had been left by the previous owners. She continued, "I have no idea if it will be readily stocked, or the contents will be brought in separately, so please just stay with the delivery people in case they need a hand, OK?"

"Sure, is this my first official assistant duty?" Nate joked.

"Actually, yeah."

While Laurel coordinated the freezer delivery with Nate and Rob, Susan entertained Jaime and Kay with stories of once again living with her two sisters.

"It's like nothing has changed," she told them. "My older sister is still bossy and demanding, while my younger sister refuses to accept any responsibility for anything. I'm always in the middle. Don't get me wrong, it's been fun, and Sandra and Steph don't fight; but they are so different. I had forgotten how much Sandra is like our mother until I had to live with her again. Oh, and my nieces are wonderful; they do keep Sandra grounded, and us entertained."

Jaime refilled Susan's wine glass; "You miss Fiona though; I can hear it in your voice and see it in your eyes."

"Oh, so much," Susan began. "I am so proud of her, and so grateful for all of you being in her life, but God, I miss her. I am a little envious, but I understand why she chose to come back to be with all of you."

"Oh, Susan, you have it all wrong," Kay chimed in. "Fiona didn't choose us over *you*. Fiona chose Fiona. She wanted so much to give this life a chance, her job, her friends; I mean it just began when she lost her Grams; I know she simply wanted to try before making another big decision. Fiona and I talk a lot about you; she misses you too and sometimes regrets telling you to stay in Florida, even though she knows that life is so much better for you. You have your sisters and nieces and a beautiful home."

Susan began to cry. She looked down the hall to make sure Fiona wasn't on her way back into the kitchen.

"Thank you for telling me that Kay. I do love my sisters, but I love my daughter more. It's been the two of us for so long, I honestly don't know how to enjoy my life without her." She wiped her tears and took a long sip of her wine, "I'm here among all this crazy chaos, and I know my daughter is loved and looked after, but I want to be a part of her life, her insane, dramatic, movie-worthy life."

Kay leaned over the table toward Susan.

"Tell her!"

"I agree," Jaime smiled at her friend. "She needs to know that her mom wants to be with her. Honestly Susan, we love her and will do anything for her, but you are the only one who can truly help Fiona right now. You know her; you know how to speak to her, get through to her, and support her like no one else can."

"Thank you, girls, maybe I can talk to Fee about sticking around a little longer; that is if you all don't mind," She asked with a giggle.

"Mind? We need you. Your daughter is a lot to deal with," Kay quipped.

As if taking her queue from Kay, Fiona entered the kitchen.

"Hey, wine? Where's mine?"

"Can you drink?" her mother asked.

"Yep. I am not on any medication other than ibuprofen; which means wine can be my friend." She smacked the table in front of her, as if she were attempting to get the attention of the tender at a bar.

Kay got Fiona a glass and poured her some wine.

"Still, Fiona, alcohol is a blood thinner, so please be careful."

Fiona finished her wine in just a few sips, and motioned for Kay to refill her glass.

"Thank you but to be honest, I need this; I'll take my chances." Her friends as well as her own mother couldn't come up with a valid argument against Fiona's statement. It was easier, and rather harmless to let her drink.

Wendy sauntered into the kitchen and asked if she could join them at the table.

"The guys are being crazy; can I stay in here with you?"

Jaime jumped up and grabbed a soda from the refrigerator. She poured it into a wine glass and handed it to Wendy.

"You're officially one of the girls now," she teased. "We are, however, still missing Laurel who should be joining us any time."

Nate and Rob walked past the kitchen on their way to the spare room where TC and Charlie were setting up the game system that Jaime had purchased. Nate was pleased to see Wendy sitting with the women, engaged in conversation, feeling like a part of the family. He secretly hoped he'd feel the same way eventually and his anxieties would all subside. He wanted to smile, laugh, work, sleep in on weekends and learn to play video games. Nate wanted even more for Wendy.

It was so surreal to see Anthony Cooke sitting on the floor among a pile of wires, trying to hook up the gaming system to the monitor he dragged in from Fiona's office.

"She uses her laptop anyway, right? She won't miss her monitor for a few days, will she?"

Nicky laughed.

"Well, we've been thinking of making this room into a game room eventually, so when we are able to buy a TV, we'll give Fiona her monitor back. I'm sure she won't mind."

TC seemed confused.

"Nick, instead of a game room, do you think offering this room to Nate would be a better idea? It would be nicer than the pull-out in Fiona's office."

"Oh, actually, we were thinking of fixing up the loft for Nate if he decides to stay with us. It's a huge space with more privacy and he'd have his own bathroom." Nicky turned to Nate, "Today just got away from us, but if you'd like to see the loft, I'll show you now before we get all into playing video games."

"There's a loft? How did I miss that?" Nate asked.

"Come on, I'll show you."

Nate followed Nick down the hall, through the living room and to the right. He hadn't noticed before, the arched doorway on the side of the fireplace behind the couch.

"Wow, I never even noticed this," he confessed.

Nick switched on the light just inside the archway to reveal a staircase.

"After you," he offered.

Nate followed the stairs up to a huge empty but finished attic room. It would only be defined as a loft due to the opening to the far right which looked out over the garage. It was an amazing space filled with potential.

"It's awesome up here."

"Yeah it is. I wonder why the builder left the opening over the garage though, and didn't completely enclose the whole room? That got my curiosity when we came to look at the house before Fiona bought it."

Nate shrugged his shoulders and continued to explore. He called back to Nick.

"What exactly does Fiona do at Cooke Industries? This house must have cost a fortune."

Nicky leaned against the wall.

"Actually, this house has a cool story if you want to hear it."

"Sure."

"Well," Nick began. "Rob and I were looking for a place out here to rent, and Fiona was looking for a house to buy. Her grandmother had just passed and left her a little money. We had been driving in from New Jersey to the city and out here on the island, and all decided it was best to find something here. Fiona asked Laurel to help her find a house; and Laurel suggested she buy something that we could sort of share. I mean, it did make good financial sense. Anyway, a few weeks of looking at houses, and we thought we'd never find one we could afford. Then, Laurel goes to a yard sale she saw listed online to look for old furniture. Oh, yeah, she loves repainting old furniture, but anyway; she goes to this yard sale and the guy recognizes her. They start talking and he tells her that he's selling his house. His wife cheated on him, they're getting divorced, and the house must be sold so she can have half the proceeds as part of the divorce agreement."

Nate seemed to have lost interest and suddenly Nick felt as though he was talking to himself.

"Oh, stay with me, this is the good part, and the end, I promise."

Nate's eyes widened and he shot Nick a fake smile.

"I'm with ya," he lied.

"So, Laurel asks the guy what the sale price is on the house. She tells him about us and Fiona wanting to buy in the area. He says, 'How much does she have for her down payment?' Laurel tells him and he says, 'It's her lucky day, I'm only asking half of what your friend has in cash'. OK, so we know this house is worth like ten times that amount, but the guy doesn't want his wife to get a lot from the sale. So, Laurel has the guy put the deal in writing; Oh yeah, she's an attorney by the way. She tells Fiona; we come to look at the place, fall in love and bam; Fiona buys the house for cash."

Nate tried feigning interest.

"Wow!"

"I know, right?" Nicky wasn't even out of breath. "I know you think we must be rich or something, but this house is nothing short of a miracle. OK, so yeah, the taxes are really expensive, but you know, it's not like we can complain."

"It's a little warm up here, can we go back down now?" Nate asked

"Of course, yeah, So, if you want to stay, we can get a ceiling fan; so it doesn't get so warm." Nick felt a bit embarrassed. It didn't occur to him at first that a seventeen-year-old had less than zero interest in stories about buying houses; never mind a seventeen-year-old who hasn't lived in a house since he was nine.

"It's up to you, Nate. No pressure, just let us know when you've made a decision." Nick tried redeeming himself, but couldn't get past his inadvertent lapse in compassion.

Just as Nate and Nicky returned to the spare room; TC announced that he had successfully connected the game console and it was ready to go.

"I see that Jaime bought two games; one looks like a trivia game, and the other looks very violent. Maybe tomorrow you boys could go online and order something somewhere between the two."

Rob laughed.

"Hey, she tried."

Charlie clicked on the trivia game icon.

"This actually looks fun. Any takers?"

TC surrendered the control he had been holding to Nate.

"I'd love to stay and play, but it's time Laurel and I went home. Get some better games and give me a call; I'll come back to play."

Charlie hadn't noticed Kay standing in the doorway.

"Charlie, I hate to be the responsible one here, but we have to go as well; we're everyone's ride home! And, the girls are home with Nana tonight, you know they take advantage of her. We're probably going to walk into a couple of sugared-up teenagers having a dance party."

Nate leaned in and whispered to Rob.

"They have kids?"

"No, well, yeah but no. Charlie and Kay help take care of Charlie's sisters."

"Oh, I was thinking they are so young to have teenagers."

"Yeah, but they are kind of amazing." Rob was thinking of their own situation and how he found himself becoming attached to Nate. He too was entirely too young to have a teenage son, but the thought of being a brother figure to Nate was becoming increasingly more appealing.

As everyone said their goodbyes, and made plans to get together in the upcoming week, Nate and Wendy stood back and marveled over the relationships between the group of friends. Wendy imagined that holidays and special occasions in regular families were much like tonight. She'd have to ask Fiona about that someday; or maybe if her luck continued, she'd find out for herself.

The Long Game

Fiona picked up her phone and checked her messages. She thought she had heard her notifications sound as she was letting the dogs back in after their morning romp in the yard. Indeed, Chris had left a message for her to call him as soon as she had some time to herself. She responded, *Give me thirty minutes.*

"Where's Wendy?" she asked Nate as she cleared her dishes from the breakfast table.

"Oh, I have no idea. I'll go check on her though."

"I have to call Chris in a few minutes, so I'll be in my office. You OK?"

"Yes, thanks. I hope you don't mind, but I borrowed some paper and a pen from your desk. I'm going to make a list of everything I need to do while I'm here."

"Take whatever you need, Nate. Let me know if there's anything you can't find. We are certainly not the most organized household."

Nate walked down the hallway toward the spare room where he guessed he'd find Wendy. Instead, he heard her muffled voice coming from Fiona's room. The door was open; he poked his head through, but Wendy wasn't there. As he stepped further into the room, he heard her voice again.

"Oh, and this is from our Fall Collection."

Nate tried his best to muffle a giggle as he realized what was happening in the bathroom. Wendy had dragged the bags of clothing from Sarah in with her and was conducting her own fashion show in front of the vanity mirrors while Susan sat perched on the edge of the tub, pretending to be a fashion critic.

"Yes, I agree, the fabric is perfect for Fall," she stated in some crazy accent; Nate could only guess the attempt was French.

He slowly backed out of Fiona's room; hoping Wendy or Susan hadn't heard him come in. Nate made his way back to the kitchen thinking how wonderful it was for Wendy to just be a normal teenage girl; if normal teenage girls put on their own fashion shows in the bathroom. Susan seemed to play along quite naturally, and Nate wondered if Fiona had done the same when she was younger.

"Hey, Fee," he called out, eager to tell her what he had seen. But Fiona had already retreated into her office. Nate stopped right outside Fiona's door as he could hear her greeting Chris on video chat. "Hey there, tell me something good," she sang.

"Hey, Firebird! How's the recovery progressing?"

"I'm good; I got lucky I suppose. If I had to get shot, at least it's in a non-threatening location with little damage to my body. I'm still sore, but managing better each day. Having the kids around certainly makes my life easier."

"Glad to hear it. Well, Fee, I have some good news and some well, just news I guess. I have been corresponding with my friend Tia over in Child Services. She and I have collaborated before on a few cases. I trust her, and explained our situation with Nate and Wendy."

"Why do I suddenly feel sick?" Fiona's throat became dry, and her hands began to tremble, anticipating worst-case scenarios, despite Chris' 'good news' statement.

"No need to feel sick, let's talk about all the good stuff first. Maybe that will help put your mind at ease." he began.

Fiona glanced over her laptop screen. She could see Nate's shadow on the far wall and knew he had been listening.

"Nate, it's cool, come in. You should be here for this call."

"Um, Fiona? Are you certain that's wise?" Chris cautioned. Although there were no consequences to deliver, Chris didn't want to risk Nate inadvertently misunderstanding anything he was about to say.

"Absolutely."

Nate entered the office and took the folding chair from the side of Fiona's desk and moved it closer so he could see the screen.

"Hi, Chris."

"Hello, sir, and how are you today?"

"I'm OK. I think, well, you tell me?" Nate was visibly anxious; he was pale and wringing his trembling hands.

"You're fine, Nate. Listen; Child services do have a file for you. However; when I spoke to Tia, she informed me that no one is looking for you; either of you. You only have eight months until your eighteenth birthday; you have a place to stay and no criminal record. Believe me, Nate, child services would rather you be here than go through the system for only a few months or worse, back on the streets."

Fiona and Nate both let out sighs of relief. Chris continued.

"I know Fee, Rob and Nick all want you to stay and we are working on making you an official employee with Cooke Industries, but Nate, there are things we all require you to accomplish. Fiona and I discussed it, and we'd like your input, obviously."

"Name it; what do I need to do?" Nate looked at Fiona who shot him a sly smile.

"Well, Chris and I would like to set you up with an online course to help you study for your GED. As much as we'd love to see you graduate from high school in the traditional sense; you'd be required to start from your Freshman year which would have you graduating at twenty-one. Your GED will allow for college admission if you so choose to go in the future, and it shouldn't take more than a few months to prepare for the test."

Nate was elated.

"Wow, that's amazing, Let's do that!"

"OK, there's more," Fiona continued. "Rob offered to teach you to drive. We think it would be wonderful for you to get your license. First, to be able to drive, obviously, but for identification as well. Would you be interested? Oh, and we need to apply for your passport. I understand there may be some travel involved with your new position."

"Yeah. of course! Wow, it just keeps getting better and better. Thank you. I will do everything, I promise." He was hopeful for the first time, yet Nate couldn't shake the feeling that all of this wonderful news came at a price.

Chris held up his hand as if to ask permission to speak.

"Now, let's talk about Wendy. Did either of you know Wendy had a birthday last week? She turned fourteen on October first; two days before you met her, Fiona."

"She didn't mention it. I had no idea, did you, Nate?"

"No. Honestly, I had just met her. The only thing I knew was that she was homeless, and her dog was stolen." Nate couldn't help thinking of Wendy in the other room, not a care in the world, feeling safe and wanted.

Chris continued.

"As I mentioned before, no one is looking to claim Wendy; which is both positive and negative in our current situation. The neighbors who originally took her in never reported her missing or applied for assistance on her behalf. As far as Child Services knew, she was still living with them. Now normally, I would call those people every name in the book, but they may have done Wendy a favor by forgetting her altogether."

"Poor kid," Fiona sighed

"Not necessarily, Fiona. This leaves us with a very good option here. You and Kay have a list of newly registered fosters all within Cooke Industries, do you not?"

"Yes, we do."

"Tia suggested we try and handle this 'in-house' so to speak; rather than having Wendy placed by Child Services. We have a say in where she lives and with whom. However, if we can't work this out by the year's end, Tia and I will have to come to some sort of agreement. We don't want to risk Wendy returning to the life she just came from; Fiona, she'll have to be placed."

Nate's concern heightened.

"Why do we have to place her at all? And, I don't think a family in the city would be the best idea. The temptation to run would be stronger where she's most familiar. Besides, those guys who took Harry know who she is; she could be in danger there."

"I hear you Nate, and this decision isn't one we will make without your and Wendy's input. Fiona and I as well as our team is not in the business of ruling the lives of others. And, to answer your first question, Wendy will need to go to school at some point. Even if she is homeschooled, she will need to be registered, which means, legal guardians and an address."

Fiona chimed in.

"We're playing the long game here Nate, with and for both of you. The decisions we all make now will impact your futures. We just want what's best. I know I didn't think it all through the night I was shot, but I also know we can trust my friends; especially Chris."

"Thanks, Fee; I appreciate that. Yes, I can be trusted. I won't stop until everyone is safe and happy. Now, that being said; we do know of a good foster family right down the road from you, don't we?"

Fiona smiled and shook her head

"I'd like to get their thoughts on placing Wendy with them; even temporarily. Right now, we need some stability in this scenario. Fiona, would that make you comfortable?"

"Absolutely. I had the same thought run through my mind the other night. I wasn't sure how to approach the subject, but if I can leave that part to you, Chris, I'd be more than willing to jump in afterward and close the deal."

Nate leaned back out of camera range and mouthed to Fiona.

"Who?"

She held up one finger to pause his thoughts and said her goodbyes to Chris. Once the video chat was closed, she turned to Nate.

"The Cooke's."

His eyes widened and he nearly tipped back out of the folding chair.

"Are you serious? Do you think they'll agree? Oh, Fiona, wouldn't that be amazing?"

"Let's not get ahead of ourselves, but you can bet on Chris handling this the right way. And, I did notice TC getting all paternal around Wendy; it was really cute. OK, Nate, let's keep this between us for now. Are you hungry? I think we could all use some time out of the house; let's grab my Mom and Wendy and go out for lunch."

"Are you OK to drive?"

" My mom will drive; I'm still a little sore. There's an awesome diner not far from here, you can literally order anything you want, and right now I want a Swiss cheese omelet and gravy fries."

Nate wrinkled his nose and furrowed his brow.

"Hey, don't judge," Fiona joked

Travel and Trial

Fiona sat at her desk in the office with her head in her hands, waiting for TC to connect to their video call. She was feeling a bit drained but looking forward to getting back to work full-time. TC had insisted she work from home for the past two months and although she was grateful for the option, being home for that amount of time was making her anxious. Admittedly, she did enjoy having a house full of people including her mother who decided to stay through the upcoming holidays.

"Hey Fee, you there?" Fiona picked her head up and adjusted her laptop.

"Yes, I'm here. Sorry, just a bit of a headache this morning."

TC was concerned.

"Are you sure you're ready to get back at it? I can send someone else in your place, or we can find another resource for the project; something closer to home, perhaps."

"No, I'm so ready. Nate and I are really excited about going to London."

"Everything went well with his passport, correct?"

"Yes, he has it. All systems are a go."

"Good. I really think you two will get a lot of good information from this particular expo. I spoke to the project director, Philip yesterday, and he's arranged a private tour for the two of you on Monday morning before the day's lectures begin." TC knew this trip to the expo in London wasn't entirely necessary for their current project. It was his way of providing Nate with the opportunity to accept responsibility; not only for his position but for Fiona as well. He needed to know the two were bonding professionally before taking more of a risk on Nate.

"That's fantastic. I cannot wait to learn more about rooftop gardening. The three sites we have begun to cultivate are coming along beautifully, but we can use all the guidance we can get. I do wish Kay were going with us, though."

"I'm sure she does too. But, I have a business trip planned in early Spring for you two, or three, depending on where we are by then. She'll have her chance to do fun things; I promise."

"Good. She deserves some fun. Kay has come such a long way in the past few months. I am so grateful for her; she really stepped up after my injury. Listen, boss, I have to go; your wife should be here soon to pick up Wendy. Today is a big day for them."

"I know. To be honest, I cannot concentrate here at all. I should have stayed home but unfortunately; I had no choice. I am looking forward to coming home and hearing all about their afternoon."

"I just know everything is going to work out; I'm thrilled for all of you. Try and have a productive day; we'll chat later."

"Fiona? Thanks for everything."

"Go to work." Fiona closed her call and went to check on Wendy. She found her on the couch with Wanda and Harry; sitting silently and pensive.

"Wendy, are you ready? Laurel and Jaime should be here any minute."

"I am. I wish you were coming with us though; I feel bad leaving you."

"Oh, honey, I'm fine. You know I'm feeling well; and besides, It's not like I'm alone," she assured her gesturing to the two dogs lounging on the couch. I think my mom and I may go out later anyway. You'll have a great time with the girls; I'm sure. Do you know what Laurel has planned?"

"She said something about going to the salon, but I'd rather not. I'd be happy with lunch or maybe a movie."

"Then tell her. Be polite, but honest, I bet you won't hurt their feelings one bit."

'OK, I will. Thanks"

Fiona didn't tell Wendy that she, in fact, had been included in today's plans, but declined. Laurel and TC wanted Wendy to live with them; not as a temporary foster but as their daughter. They had been spending as much time with her as they could, but it was evident that the young girl had become extremely attached to Fiona. Together, they had made the decision weeks ago to not proceed with fostering but to work toward a more permanent solution. Chris' friend Tia from Child Services suggested giving Wendy more time to feel secure before rushing her into another living situation. Fiona, Rob, Nicky and Nate were all too happy to keep her around; but now was the right time to present more stable options. Tia's advice to have Wendy start school after the winter break encouraged the Cooke's to look into adoption immediately. With all the information gathered, it was time to present Wendy with their proposal.

Jaime pulled into Fiona's driveway a few minutes before noon.

"I'll wait here." She offered. Laurel took a deep breath and slowly exhaled.

Why am I so nervous? Is this what men feel right before they propose?" she asked.

Jaime smiled at her friend.

"I don't know honey, but you have nothing to worry about. Wendy loves you; both of you. She's going to be over the moon when you ask her to live with you."

"I hope so. I'm so glad you're here, Jai. If things go sideways, I'll need you to make sure Wendy is ok. I may be too emotional to keep a level head. Well, here I go, see you in a minute."

Laurel got out of the car and nervously approached Fiona's front door. Before she could ring the bell, Wendy opened the door and greeted her with a warm hug.

"I'm ready; where are we going?" Laurel put her arm around Wendy's shoulder, and called back into the house; "See you later; Fee."

Fiona responded from the kitchen with a loud.

"Have a great day!"

Jaime backed out of the driveway and asked Laurel; "Which way are we going?"

"I thought we'd do a spa day; so make the left."

Wendy chimed in from the back seat, taking Fiona's advice; "Thanks so much, but would it be ok if we just went to lunch or something? It's really great that you want to take me to a spa, but honestly, it's not my thing. I'd much rather grab a burger or see a movie. Is that something we could do?"

Laurel was grateful for Wendy's candor.

"Yes, of course. Let's go to lunch."

Jaime added.

"Oh, I know where to go. I'm taking you ladies to *Gateway*. It's this really cool restaurant by the water, and they happen to serve the most incredible burgers. It gets packed during the summer, but it's just as awesome to go there when it's cold and look out over the ocean while you eat. Joe and I love it there."

"That sounds perfect," Wendy and Laurel both agreed.

The women chatted about different schools in the area, hoping Wendy would interject; but she was too preoccupied with her phone. Wendy had been using social media not only to catch up with celebrity gossip and trending videos but for reading enrichment. She would read everything she possibly could before someone asked her to put the phone away. Although Laurel and Jaime wanted Wendy to engage in their conversation, neither could fault her for using the forty-minute drive to catch up with her favorite celebs.

Wendy thought the restaurant was the coolest place she had ever seen. It looked like a bait shop on the outside, but once inside, it was actually more upscale than she and Laurel had anticipated.

"Why haven't we been here before?" Laurel asked

"I don't know, I was just wondering about that myself. Joe and I drive out here every now and then when he's craving seafood. I admit it's odd that you and TC have never come with us. We'll have to change that. If you love it as much as we do, we'll make plans to all come back for dinner," Jaime requested a table by the window so Wendy could enjoy the ocean view. There were two people on the beach that they could see from their vantage point; one man standing in the surf with a rather large fishing rod stuck in the sand and another man walking closer to the dunes with a metal detector clamped to his right arm. Both sky and sea were hues of gray, yet the view was majestic in Wendy's eyes.

"I already love it here. This may be my new favorite place in the world," she told the woman.

"Ohhh, mine too, I just read, they have a surf and turf burger," Laurel exclaimed.

"What's surf and turf?"

Laurel was happy to explain; "And this one has crab and lobster on top of the burger patty. I know this is going to sound entirely stupid, but Wendy, I have to ask; have you ever had crab, shrimp, or lobster before? I'm not trying to be pretentious; I only ask because many people have an allergy to certain seafoods, and I do not want to find out the hard way if you do."

Wendy laughed; "I'm not allergic. I've had seafood before; many times. There were a few places that would save food for me sometimes; one was a Chinese take-out, and another was a seafood place. And besides, Fiona craves Chinese take-out, a lot! I've tried pretty much everything on the menu. I get why you asked, and I appreciate that, but I think I'll have that burger too. It sounds so good."

"Let's all get it," Jaime said as she folded her menu and gestured for their server.

Their server came to take their order and asked if anyone wanted anything from the bar. Laurel shook her head, but Jaime thought it may help her nerves to have a glass of wine before lunch.

"Would you please bring us a glass of your house white?" she requested. Their server returned minutes later and placed the wine in front of Jaime. She smiled and slid the glass from her place setting over to Laurel and whispered.

"Just in case."

Wendy was still enthralled with the ocean and hadn't even noticed when her diet cola was placed in front of her. Ordering diet cola was a habit she'd acquired from Fiona; it made her feel more adultlike than ordering regular soda. There were several little obvious quirks and habits Wendy had picked up from Fiona, and Laurel couldn't help thinking that if she had to emulate someone, Fiona was a good choice.

As they waited for their food to arrive, Laurel gathered her courage to start the conversation they were there to have. She took a grateful sip of her wine and dove in.

"Wendy, there really is something important I'd like us to talk about today if you don't mind."

Wendy's attention quickly turned back to Laurel.

"Why do I feel like I'm in trouble? Did I do something wrong?"

"Oh, God no, not at all. OK, let me start over, I'm so nervous. I feel like all my words are going to come out wrong." She took another mouthful of her wine; swallowed and tried again, " So, TC and I haven't stopped thinking of what we can do for you since the day we met you. We both think you're extraordinary and deserve all that is good in this life. But, your future is not up to us; not really. What I'm asking is, would it be OK with you if I tell you what we've been talking about? If it's something you agree with, we can move forward from there, but for now; I'd very much like to tell you what is on my mind and in my heart."

Wendy looked shocked, but she was very curious as well.

"I'm listening."

"We know how much you love living with Fiona and the boys. Believe me, they love having you around as well; especially Fiona. You know, we asked her to join us today, but she was worried that if she were here, you wouldn't give my ideas the proper consideration. She isn't here because she wants what is best for you. Fiona is amazing, but it's time to get her back to work. Both she and Nate are about to be really busy. It doesn't seem fair that you would be there, alone most of the time when there are so many wonderful things you could be experiencing. Wendy, you'll hear me talk about school, structure, and socializing which may all seem boring to you, but they are vital components to being a teenager; and becoming an adult. We want you to have the opportunities you didn't have before; like friends and sleepovers; school dances, maybe. But, as I said, TC and I know those decisions are not ours to make; they're yours. We were hoping you'd come and stay with us, and give TC and me a chance. Wendy, we don't want to be your foster family, we want to be your parents."

Just as Wendy was about to respond, their food was served.

"Enjoy Ladies, just give me a wave if you need anything," their server pleasantly offered.

Wendy looked down at her plate; "This looks amazing," she exclaimed. "But before we eat, I do have something to say."

Laurel downed the rest of her wine and Jaime put her fork back on the table. Wendy continued.

"May I bring Harry?" she asked innocently

"Of course." Laurel seemed relieved.

"OK, then I'd love to stay with you," Wendy stated, taking a huge bite of her burger.

Jaime took her phone from her handbag and sent Fiona a text from under the table.

"All is right in the world today, love you, see you soon, Oh, and I'm bringing you and Susan some burgers."

Fiona and Susan were just leaving the department store when she heard her phone. They had been shopping for essentials for Fiona's upcoming trip to England. It had been too long since mother and daughter shared a shopping day together. Susan was glad she decided to stay longer and shuddered when she thought of leaving. She and Fiona had always liked one another as well as loved each other. They shared a friendship; and now that Fiona was her own person, Susan liked her even more. Fiona stopped to read Jaime's text message.

"Things are going well for our girls," she informed Susan.

"I knew they would. How are you adjusting to the idea of Wendy staying with the Cookes? I know we have all gotten very used to that adorable girl being around."

"I don't know, Mom. I have learned so much about myself since she's been with me. Having both Wendy and Nate has been an extraordinary experience for all of us. But, if I had to write Wendy's story for her, I'd certainly write it exactly the way it's playing out. You know how I feel about Laurel and TC; they're perfect for Wendy."

"You know Fee, I've learned a lot about you, Nicky and Rob too. It's been a pleasure to be around the three of you these past few weeks. I'm able to literally watch you all grow from spirited kids into practical, level-headed, responsible and amazing adults. I've always been proud of you, Fee, but I am so proud of Rob and Nicky too. You can tell the three of you have wonderful mothers," Susan said as she jokingly patted herself on the back.

"We do," Fiona agreed. "And, I think we're all going to be excellent parents someday; when we're ready. But for now, I think we'd all agree; we aren't, and Wendy deserves ready; she deserves the Cooke's. Besides, we'll be able to see her and spend time with her. We will be in her life; it doesn't get better than that."

"It doesn't. Fiona, Wendy is a lucky girl, not because of the Cooke's, not entirely. She's lucky because it was you standing next to her in that store. Never forget that; never forget you are her hero."

"Mom?"

"Yeah, baby?"

"I'm so glad you're here."

"Me too."

No Promises

"Something smells great," TC announced as he walked into the kitchen.

"We made dinner, and baked bread," Wendy informed him.

TC set his keys and phone on the counter and kissed Laurel on the cheek.

"Hello, beautiful." He took a seat next to Wendy and kissed her on the top of her head." And hello to you too, sweet girl."

"Dinner is almost ready. Why don't you two set the table, or would you rather just eat here at the counter?" Laurel asked

Wendy looked over at TC, hoping he'd answer, so she could simply agree. She wasn't yet comfortable making decisions around Laurel. TC was much easier to communicate with; he had a way of making Wendy feel connected; accepted.

"Here is fine; why dirty the entire table?" he offered.

"Well then, let's start with some salad." Laurel did seem uptight which was, by TC's expertise on the subject of his wife, highly unusual.

"Laur, is everything OK?" he asked, grabbing the salad tongs and filling his plate.

"Yes, of course."

Wendy had been feeling apprehensive with Laurel all day. They had fun baking bread, and Laurel used the opportunity to teach Wendy fractions and measurements. She found it entertaining more than educational, and loved every minute. However, Laurel just seemed to be holding back as if she wouldn't allow herself to find joy in their time together. Wendy began to think Laurel was having second thoughts regarding becoming her parent. She wasn't surprised, but a bit disappointed; it would have been nice to be a part of this family. She did feel more confident now that TC was home and decided to say something. After all, she had nothing to lose; they weren't hers yet anyway.

"Did I do something wrong, Laurel? I feel like you're disappointed in me, and I'm sorry but I don't know why."

Laurel swallowed her food and nearly choked in the process.

"Oh, Wendy, no. Oh, honey, you have it all wrong; I feel like I have disappointed you. I want so much to tell you how I'm feeling; share my thoughts and plans with you, but at the same time, I don't want to rush you into this. Wendy, the truth is, I am so afraid I'm going to screw up and you won't want to stay with us." Laurel burst into tears. She hung her head and covered her eyes with her napkin.

Wendy and TC were stunned; neither knew what to say to console Laurel. Finally, after a long minute, TC broke the silence.

"Laurel, how long have you been feeling this way? I'm so sorry, my love, I did not pick up on your uncertainty. I'm an idiot for thinking everything was going so well. I suppose I wanted to believe that all our dreams were finally coming true, I blinded myself to your apprehensions."

Laurel shook her head but was unable to speak. Wendy knew it was time to tell both Laurel and TC how she had been feeling as well.

"Laurel? I'm just going to talk, and I'll keep talking until you know for sure how much I want to be here with you. OK?" Wendy didn't wait for an answer. "I have no idea how I got so lucky, no idea why you two want me, no idea what the future will bring, but I do know that when I think of my future, I'm with you. You make me feel wanted, and I've never been wanted. You want what's best for me and I never thought best was an option. Most days, I'm the one who worries that if I say the wrong thing, or do something stupid, you'll change your mind, call Chris and have me placed in foster care. That is my nightmare, Laurel. I should have told you both I was feeling that way, but I was so afraid. Afraid, I would put the thought of sending me away in your head. You two are so perfect, like parents on television shows. I guess that's normal, but nothing in my life was ever normal, so I wasn't sure, but I love being here. If this is how a normal family is, I want it, and I don't want to screw it up."

Laurel picked her head up and dried her eyes. She looked across the counter at her husband who appeared shocked and proud at the same time. She took a deep breath and feigned a smile.

"We are so not normal," she teased, attempting to lighten the heavy feelings between them.

Wendy managed to laugh between tears, and for the first time in his life, TC had to make a choice as to which person he should console first. It had been just him and Laurel for so long, and now he was a parent; maybe not yet legally but in his heart. He wrapped his arms around Wendy and held her while she cried. Laurel gave her husband an approving smile; suddenly she too felt like a real parent.

"You know, neither of us grew up with a traditional, or what you call 'normal' family; I don't know many people who have. I'd have to say Rob and Sarah come the closest to normal out of all our friends, and they too had their grandmother care for them while their parents traveled for work. TC and I had been considering expanding our family for some time before we met you, Wendy. We are registered fosters and were about to apply when Fiona brought you into our lives. It was an instant connection for us. TC couldn't stop talking about making your life better, and I wanted nothing more than to teach you to cultivate your strength, compassion, your independence and natural ability to read people and react. Basically, we fell in love with you; not just the idea of becoming parents."

"I love you both," Wendy managed as she began to compose herself. TC retracted, giving Wendy some room to breathe.

"Well, that's good to hear," TC began. "Now, can we discuss school? Christmas is almost here, and I'd like to get you registered before winter break. There's a wonderful private school not far from here; I was hoping you would agree to go and take a look at it with us." The subject change was just what they needed. Wendy no longer felt like this perfect life could be taken away from her at any moment, and began to allow herself to dream of her future.

"Is it an all-girls school?" Wendy asked

"No, honey, it isn't."

"Oh, well, it doesn't matter either way."

Laurel seemed a bit confused.

"Don't you want to meet boys?"

"Nope. I'd love to have friends, but boys are not necessary. I'm going to marry Nate."

TC couldn't help himself.

"Does Nate know that?"

Wendy shot him a look.

"He will. I'll tell him when we're older and ready."

Laurel had to keep herself from laughing.

"So, how's the bread?"

Are you Shore?

Carter took a sip of his beer.

"Man, that's cold," he informed his father. Mr Wyatt sat across the table at the tiki bar from his youngest son, enjoying their time together. The boardwalk was nearly deserted, but the bars were open, and the weather was mild for December. It seemed like a great place to unwind and finally have some serious conversation. Mr Wyatt knew his son was in need of his guidance, or maybe just his ear. He struggled with bringing up the subject of Meg and the twins. The last thing Mr Wyatt wanted was his son to feel that hurt all over again, yet he thought talking it out may be cathartic. Shelly recommended giving him some time to open up, but that hadn't happened yet.

"It's quiet at the house now that Sam, Shelly and Noah are back in California. I think your mother misses having them around. I know, I do."

"Yeah, that little guy is so smart and funny too." Carter admittedly missed his nephew.

"You know, we were thinking of flying out for Christmas. Shelly has been so busy at the V.A. The holidays are especially hard on so many people; she's been counseling non-stop. Sam said she even has video sessions during her off hours. Mom and I thought she could use a hand with shopping, cooking, decorating, well, you know."

"I think that's a great idea. Shelly was amazing when they were here. She helped me through a really bad time. It would be nice for you guys to be there for Sam and Noel; to help her out during the holidays."

"Why don't you come with us, Carter? You have the time."

"Dad, I really need to find a job. It's been a few weeks now, and I'm starting to feel useless."

"Carter, you are far from useless. And, if you ask me, I think you should take advantage of this time to be picky. Make sure you choose a place that will not only pay you what you're worth but give you something to look forward to every day. You said you have some money saved, and your mom and I will cover you if you need anything."

"So, what you really want to say is, find a place where the boss doesn't have a daughter my age," he joked.

Mr Wyatt felt encouraged by Carter's willingness to joke about Meg and losing his job. He knew all that had happened in one day was too much for anyone to handle without some struggle. He flagged down their server and ordered another round for both of them as well as appetizers to share.

"Hey Carter, isn't that your friend from the pizza place?" he asked, pointing to the opposite side of the outdoor dining area on the pier.

Carter stood in place and craned his neck to see over the people seated in front of him.

"Yeah, that's Nick and his boyfriend Rob. I haven't seen them in so long."

"Well, go say hello. Maybe invite them to join us."

"Nah, let them be. It looks like it might be a date day."

"I'm going over there." Mr Wyatt got up from his deck-style chair and made his way over to Nick and Rob's table. "Hello Nick, remember me?"

"Hey, Mr Wyatt, of course, how are you?" Nick stood and offered his hand. Mr Wyatt shook it rather enthusiastically as he asked Nick if they'd like to join him and Carter for a drink. "I'm sorry if I'm interrupting, but Carter sure could use a friend right about now. Would you two like to hang out for a while?"

Nick glanced over to Rob who had already pushed in his chair and was navigating around the plastic table. "We'd love to," he answered for both of them.

Carter was pleasantly surprised to see Nick and Rob following his father back to their table.

"Hey guys, how have you been?" he asked, greeting them with a mixture of caution and embarrassment in his voice. Nick and Rob both offered their hands and responded to his greeting warmly. "Have a seat," Carter offered.

Nick was admittedly happy to see his friend.

"So, your Dad invited us to join you, what are the odds of us all being down here today? I guess we were meant to run into one another."

Rob chimed in.

"I've been trying for months to plan a weekend at the shore, and something always comes up. This was an impulse trip; one last quiet weekend before the holidays. So, what brings you two to the beach in December?"

Mr Wyatt sensed his son's apprehension.

"Eh, we decided it was a good day for some guy time; you know, burgers, beers and beach. I happen to prefer the off-season; not as many people, and it's not hotter than hell. You can truly enjoy the view and the atmosphere." he wanted so badly to tell Carter's friends what was going on, but it wasn't his story to tell. Mr Wyatt hoped Carter would open up to Nick.

"So, what's been going on?" Carter asked. "I haven't seen you two since the fire."

Nicky couldn't resist the opportunity to tell a story.

"Wow, that's right. Oh, man, so much has changed since then. Rob and I moved to Long Island with Fiona. Yeah, she bought a house after Grams died and Susan moved to Florida to be with her sisters. I'm in school to become a paramedic, and my mom is upstate. Linda lives in the city with her boyfriend; nice guy, you'd like him."

Carter tried his best to follow. "Wait, so you live with Fiona?"

"Yeah, we're roommates. Oh, Carter, you should see the house, it's awesome and she got it for a steal! Crazy story, but the short version is, Grams left Fiona the Florida house, but she gave it to her mom and aunts. Our friend Laurel, oh, you remember her, right? Anyway, Laurel found this house for sale in her neighborhood; the guy didn't want his cheating ex-wife to get a lot of money in the settlement, so he sold the house for literally a fraction of its worth. Laurel made the deal and Fiona paid cash for it with Grams' insurance money that she inherited. Rob and I were looking for a place to rent, but it seemed like a better idea to live together. It's been so great, even with Nate there, we have so much room. We've all been working on fixing it up, and we're making one room into a game room. Nate has done a great job so far in his loft, that kid amazes me."

"Nate?"

"Oh, yeah, there's this whole other story with Nate and Wendy. I'll tell you if you're interested, but we could be here a while."

Carter had forgotten how much Nicky liked the sound of his own voice, and the enthusiasm he exuded when he was on a roll.

"Sure, it will be nice to talk about something other than my life falling apart."

Nicky switched gears.

"Hey, I'm so sorry for rambling, I should have asked what was happening in your life. I just assumed you were getting married soon, and the babies were on their way." Nick and Rob exchanged concerned looks.

"Carter, we're here for you, what's going on?"

Carter sucked his breath in through his teeth and let it out slowly, making a soft whistling sound.

"I'd rather hear about Nate and Wendy, but I'll give you guys the abridged version of what has happened. Basically, I made the decision to not marry Meg, well not anytime soon. She was not happy and iced me out for weeks. My guess is, she took that time to set up another scenario for herself; one in which she gets her way on every level. So, Mr Daly fired me; and when I got home Meg was waiting at the house to tell me the twins aren't mine."

"Jesus, Carter!"

"I know, right? It gets worse, Eddie is the father." Carter downed the rest of his beer and held the plastic cup over his head, signaling their server. "Another round?" Mr Wyatt, Nick and Rob all shook their heads in acceptance of his suggestion.

Rob spoke first.

"Well, that's one hell of a story, I'm so sorry Carter. However, I'm not sure it beats ours," he quipped.

"Are you serious?" Carter asked.

Nicky and Rob spent the better part of the next two hours sharing their rendition of the Nate and Wendy saga, from Fiona being shot to the present day.

"Oh, so Fiona and Nate are leaving tomorrow for London. They'll be there for five days. Why don't you come back with us for a few days and hang out?" Rob offered.

"Yes," Nick agreed. "It will be so great! Oh, as long as you're OK with Susan being there. She's been like our house mother since Fiona got shot. She'll be staying with us until January third."

"Thanks so much, but it sounds like you have enough going on up there without adding me and my drama to the mix." Carter was being polite; he truly wanted to accept their offer and get away for a while. He was relieved to know that Fiona and Nate were not a couple, and wanted to hear more about Fiona being shot; more specifically how she was recovering. Although it was reassuring to know his friends wanted his company, Carter still felt as though he had no place in their current lives. His insecurities got the best of him, and all he could think of was the negativity he might impart.

Mr Wyatt had a feeling his son wanted to take them up on their invitation.

"Carter, it would be good for you to go spend time with some real friends." He nodded in Nick's direction.

"I can swing by and pick you up on our way back," Rob offered. "You're basically on our way home. Let's say around six p.m. tomorrow?" Rob left no room for another declination.

"He'll be ready," Mr Wyatt answered for his son.

"Great, we'll see you tomorrow," Rob and Nick explained they had few more stops to make while they were in New Jersey, and left the Wyatt's to finish their father/son time.

"You're amazing," Nick told his boyfriend as they walked along the boardwalk.

"I know. But feel free to tell me why you think so."

Nick took Rob's hand.

"You didn't have to invite Carter to stay with us, you barely know him."

"But, I know you, and I know how close you two were. Besides, he can't be all bad, his dad certainly loves him. I felt sorry for Mr Wyatt, he seemed at a loss; not knowing what to do for his son. It's no accident we were there today, Nick. I believe we were the answer he was searching for. Carter needs to know he still has friends; people who won't betray him like that Eddie guy and the baby momma."

"Meg," Nick corrected. "The baby momma's name is Meg."

"I know, I just couldn't dignify her, not after what she did. Nick, that woman played dirty and nearly destroyed Carter. I get the part about Carter hurting Fiona, and Karma is a bitch, but I'm sorry, he did not deserve to be torn down like that, losing so much all at once. Meg was vicious; and deliberate. I just hope Karma was watching her as well."

Nick was amused at Rob's personification of Karma and played along.

"Oh, she's watching, I'm sure of it."

"Should we call Susan and let her know we'll be bringing a houseguest?"

"Nah, she'll be fine with it, I can always call her from the road when we know for sure Fiona isn't home." Nick hadn't thought of how Carter's visit might seem to Fiona. He realized Susan would eventually tell her, but he hoped by then, it would be a non-issue.

"OK, we'll play this your way. You know those Lasher girls better than I do," Rob teased.

First Flight; Long Night

Nate slumped in an uncomfortable plastic seat in the terminal, waiting for their flight to board. This was his first flight, and despite Fiona's coaching, Nate had no idea what to expect. He was nervous, fidgety and growing more impatient with each passing minute. Fiona was seated next to him, checking her phone for messages. She could sense his apprehension and tried to think of a way to calm Nate's nerves. She noticed a discarded magazine on the seat to her left and handed it to Nate.

"Here, read this. It will help pass the time."

"Why did we have to be here so early?"

"Just in case there was a long line through security. It is better to be early than to be running through a crowded airport, or worse, miss our flight."

"Oh, look!" Nate exclaimed as he opened the magazine. "It's TC." The article was short; hardly a feature, but it mentioned the recent acquisition of several dilapidated buildings throughout the city by Cooke Industries. The editorial speculated as to the reasons behind the purchases; leaning toward the theory of knocking them down in favor of high-rise offices. "They have it all wrong," Nate told her as he skimmed the article.

"They usually do," she agreed. "That's nothing more than bad reporting, just gossip."

"Why? What's the point of writing without doing any real research?"

"People love gossip. They'd rather make up stories than know the truth. For some, the truth is boring, and not worth reading. But, little bits of information that may have some validity can be twisted and added to in order to create something so much more exciting."

"I'd much rather know the truth," he declared.

"Me too, but we do know the truth, and it's so much better than the lie. Just think, by tomorrow, you and I will be reporting back to TC all the information we need to transform the roofs of those buildings into community gardens; growing food for those in need. There's nothing better than that. Nate, you have a lot to be proud of, and a lot to learn. I suspect you'll soon be running your own project, and we'll be hiring an assistant for you." Fiona was encouraging and meant every word. She believed Nate was meant for greatness. Fiona looked up at the monitor above the check-in counter as the status changed to *boarding*. "Oh, we're boarding, grab your stuff."

"Can I take this?" Nate asked, rolling up the magazine and stuffing it in his back pocket without waiting for Fiona to answer.

Fiona made her way onto the plane from the jetway, with Nate in tow. They had been booked to fly business class which simply meant a bit more leg room and no middle seat. Fortunately, they only had to navigate past a few rows before settling in.

"Here, let me have your carry-on," she offered. "I'll put it in the overhead with mine."

"Can I hang on to it?" Nate asked.

"Yeah, if it fits under your seat. Let's see." Fiona bent down and shoved Nate's bag under the seat in front of his own. "Just barely, but you'll be fine."

"I feel better when I can get to my things," he admitted.

Fiona had gotten used to the Nate that had been living with her; the version of him which felt more like her younger brother; often forgetting his past. Although Nate was adjusting to his new life, there were many moments when his reactions were still those of a homeless kid; afraid, paranoid, guarded and even angry at times. TC and Laurel were kind enough to secure therapy for both Nate and Wendy, but it would take more than a few sessions to transform this insecure kid into a confident man. Fiona reminded herself to be understanding and practice patience, even if she were frustrated as well.

"I get that," she assured him. "It's a long flight, so settle in and try and get comfortable."

"How long?" he asked, attempting to adjust the seat belt.

"Seven hours, and here, let me help." Fiona reached across Nate and pulled the buckle forward, letting out some slack before clicking the two halves together in his lap. "Better?"

"It's fine, but are you sure it's going to take that long? I thought flying was supposed to be a fast way to travel." Nate seemed confused.

"Seven hours is pretty quick if you consider the distance we're about to travel. Imagine if you had to drive thirty-five hundred miles? That would take three or four days if you didn't stop at all."

"Yeah, I guess. I'm sorry, there are some things I never learned, thinking it would only be like an hour or two seems pretty stupid."

"Nate, don't ever let me hear you say stupid; especially not when you're referring to yourself. I will kick your ass." Nate had no doubt that Fiona was serious. Her tone changed from sweet to authoritative in an instant. She continued, "You are amazing. You have an awesome job with Cooke Industries, and you're about to be an international traveler; how many guys your age are smart enough to be you ? Well, I'll tell you! Not many."

"None of that makes me smart, Fiona, just lucky."

"Wrong answer. You were smart enough to stay." Fiona was referring to that vey first day after the shooting when Nate felt as though he needed to get back to the city. He didn't believe the Universe had a greater plan for him; only that he'd bring trouble into the lives of those trying to help. But he did stay, for Fiona, for Rob and most of all for Wendy.

The plane began to taxi, and the engines whined.

"What is that?" Nate panicked at the sound of the engines powering up. He gripped the armrests and pressed his back straight against his seat.

"It's fine, that's normal. Try and relax. Hey Nate, if you feel like you're going to be sick, use this," she said, offering him a small paper bag she pulled from the seat pocket. "I also brought motion sickness pills just in case you and flying didn't mix. Just let me know if you need to take one."

"I'll be OK. I'm just a little freaked out."

"Yeah, as soon as we're in the air, you'll feel so much better, I promise."

Nate seemed horrified.

"We aren't in the air?"

"Not yet," Fiona stifled a giggle. "Hang on, here we go."

As the plane ascended, Nate admitted Fiona was right; he did feel better. His nerves gave way to his appetite as he dug through his backpack for his stash of snacks.

"Want something?" he offered.

"Yes, please. I'll take whatever you have. Sometimes a little food helps with the nausea."

"Oh, and you were worried about me."

"I was; still am, but I never said I was the perfect passenger either."

Nate ate his snacks and tried reading through the other articles in the magazine he picked up; while Fiona read the novel she purposely packed for the flight. It took less than forty-five minutes before he became bored and began to squirm in his seat.

"Wanna talk?" he asked

"Sure, about what?"

"I don't know, ask me anything."

Fiona closed her book and stuffed it in her handbag.

"OK, let's see, anything, huh? I got it; what made you want to help all those kids living on the street? Wendy told us a lot of them knew you and depended on your help to survive. Tell me what makes a kid want to take on that kind of responsibility."

"Wow, Fee, I thought you were going to ask my favorite color, or my favorite song; that's a deep question."

"You don't have to answer if it makes you uncomfortable, Nate."

"No, I should talk about my life; and I'd rather tell you than anyone else."

"I'm here to listen, but only if you are willing."

Nate thought about his life before meeting Fiona. It seemed so long ago, but in reality, only mere months had passed. He found it strange not being able to instantly recall the first time he knew it was essential that he stepped in on another kid's behalf; the first time he decided to get involved. How could he be the same person he was then, now seated in a plane on his way to England on an all expense paid business trip? His life suddenly felt very surreal. Nate lowered his eyes; and began to speak.

"When I was about twelve, I was hanging out with a group of kids like me; pretty nice kids too. We would go to the park during the day. Some of us panhandled, some picked pockets, and others dug through trash for anything still edible that we could share. It wasn't glamorous, but we managed. Anyway, one day a kid I knew, I think his name was Al, saw a man throw out an entire sandwich he just bought from one of the food trucks in the park. I guess they gave him the wrong order and instead of standing in line to return it, he just threw it right in the trash can; still wrapped. So, little Al walks over and snags it, but before he could get back to us, the man grabs him and slams him to the ground. Al starts to cry and covers his head. The man tries to get the sandwich away from him, screaming for Al to put it back in the trash. Then he cracks the kid right across his face. Fiona, people were just standing there, watching. No one tried to help. I don't know why, but I went running over to Al, and helped him up. I picked up the sandwich and the man screamed at me to throw it away. So I asked him.

"Is it going to hurt us if we eat it? He says no, but he will. I put my arm around Al, and we walked away. The man followed us but when he saw all the kids on the playground, he backed off."

"Oh my God, Nate. That's horrifying. Was Al OK?"

"Banged up and scared, but yeah, he was OK. So, after that, word got out that I was fearless and some of the older kids would invite me to stay with them and sometimes bring me food. They were pretty cool for the first week, but then they introduced me to a guy they called *Boss*. Total drug dealer, and I wasn't about it. I got the hell out of there, but they found me and beat the crap out of me. Fortunately, they were satisfied just seeing blood and didn't kill me. I was so pissed; I went to the cops and gave them all the information I knew about Boss."

"Nate, you are amazing. That was an incredibly brave thing to do."

"Yeah well, not really. The cops thought they were doing the right thing and got me into a new foster home. I really believe they wanted to help, but after the first few days, the foster mom was touching me and asking me to sleep with her. The dad, who I think was just her boyfriend, threw me out into the yard and told me I deserved to live like a dog. They hadn't fed me or even checked on me for days, so I left. It took me three days to find my way back to the park and my friends. I told them where I had been and what had happened, and we all decided to look out for one another even more to try and make sure we stayed out of the system. There were four of us guys out scrounging and stealing and feeding as many kids as we could."

"Like Robin Hood and his Merry Men," Fiona exclaimed.

"Huh?" Nate knew who Robin Hood was, but not his Merry Men. Fiona told him she'd buy him the book for Christmas.

Nate went on.

"One of my friends got involved with some other drug people and stopped coming around; and another guy went to jail for stealing a car. That left me and Leo for a while, but Leo was killed by a drunk driver who drove off a bridge. I would have been there that night too, but I found a necklace on the sidewalk and stopped on my way back to pawn it. When I got to the underpass, there were cops and firetrucks and a bunch of ambulances. I asked a fireman what happened and described Leo to him. He told me the car landed right where he had been sleeping. There was a tent city under that bridge; with fifty or more homeless people living there, I think they said ten were killed in the accident." Fiona had been crying through the latter part of Nate's story. She dried her eyes, but the tears kept flowing. "Anyway, I was alone again, but I had a reputation for being the go-to guy and I had a lot of good resources to get things done. By the time I was about fifteen, every kid on the street knew me, and so many of them needed me, like Wendy."

"Can I ask, did you ever have to hurt anyone, like in self defense? Are there things you regret having to do?" Fiona was genuinely interested and concerned. Nate, in the short time she'd known him had become a part of her family, and his well-being was important to her. She wanted to know everything, so she could protect him and provide for him, like he'd done for others. The irony was not lost on Fiona; barely able to take care of herself, but there was a strong, undeniable feeling when it came to Nate. If Fiona could help it, Nate would never have to live in fear again.

"Just once, and it wasn't bad. I shoved a guy to the ground for grabbing a girl I knew. He hit the pavement pretty hard, but he totally deserved it," Nate sighed. "Yeah, I have regrets, but in those moments when I broke the law by stealing or lying my way out of being hauled into Child Services, I had no regrets. I only regret my actions now that they are no longer necessary to my survival. I feel guilty about that; it's like living a big lie."

"How so?"

"Look at me! I'm dressed in nice new clothes, sitting on a plane with the nicest person in the world, and I'm getting paid to be here. Just a few months ago, I was basically a criminal; I don't deserve all of this. You and the Cooke's and the guys think I'm some kind of hero, but I'm not Fiona; you are all heroes, you all saved me, and I can't understand why."

"Nate, do you believe in a higher power?"

"Like, God?"

"Yes; or whatever name you're comfortable giving a force greater than anyone on earth."

"I want to. Sometimes I even try and pray; but I never know the right words."

"There aren't any right words, Nate. Just speak what's in your heart; that's what my mother taught me. I'm glad to hear you do believe, though."

"Do you? Believe in God, I mean."

"Yeah, I'm like you, I want to believe, and I do pray to God, but I also think everyone's version of a higher power is the same force. We all give it a different identity, depending on how people were brought up, or what they choose to believe is real."

"So, God and Budda are the same guy?"

"Yes and no. Your higher power is unique to your beliefs. It can be about religion, the way you were taught, or how you feel spiritually. This is a bit hard to explain, but the similarities are in the fact that one has faith in their higher power, God, Buddha, or whom and whatever. The differences come from the system of beliefs that is usually dictated by individual religions or types of spirituality. Who doesn't matter as much as the how; does that make sense? As long as you have faith, you and your higher power of choice can overcome your fears."

"I like that. I want to have faith; I just don't know where to look for it. Fiona, why did you ask me if I believed?"

"I suppose I was just curious. I grew up believing there is a God; someone, or something to have faith in, you know? I took it for granted that when I said a prayer, someone was listening. However, since the shooting I've found myself thinking about it more and more. Why was I there that night? Was it my destiny, or whatever to bring Wendy to the Cooke's? Was I there for you? Had it been someone else in the store, what would have happened to Wendy? I can't help thinking that a higher power is responsible for the circumstances that have brought all of us together. The more I contemplate, the farther back the story seems to go. It's as though we are all a part of that power and universally connected. Our lives have been predetermined to intersect, and then interact.

"How do you know this?"

"I don't know anything for sure, but I have witnessed it, and I can feel it. I guess my thoughts; my theory is only valid if I continue to have faith."

"I feel it too, maybe not as deeply as you, but I know what you mean. I still struggle with the why though. Why would anyone have kids just to leave them, or abuse them? I've lived with a lot of injustice and darkness; it's hard to believe those things happened for a greater purpose. Um, can we talk about something else now?"

"Of course. Just remember that you are such an important part of our story. I know it was hell getting here but I feel you're right where you are supposed to be. You have a family now, and we believe in you. OK, next subject; what *is* your favorite color?"

"Green."

Boys will be Boys

When Nicky La Salle was a kid, his neighbors gave him the nickname; The mayor. Not only was he personable and quite the talker, but he also had this way of making everyone around him feel like family. Nicky was that kid who would ride his bike through the neighborhood in search of people to converse with and lend a hand where he could. More often than not, he was accompanied by Fiona, who in her own right was well loved in the neighborhood. Many thought they'd grow up to become a power couple; as their love for one another was evident since they were mere toddlers. However, love isn't always synonymous with romance; and Nicky La Salle preferred to love Fiona in the same way he loved Linda, like a sister.

As they grew older, Nicky took it upon himself to be Fiona's protector; at least until she found someone worthy of her who would become her Knight in shining armor. But it was Fiona's fierce love for her friend that often became the issue. She knew it wasn't always easy for Nicky to meet boys, as ignorance hasn't yet been eradicated in the world. Friends at school, and people they met would often find it necessary to tell Fiona that Nicky was gay, as if she hadn't a clue. They used the word as an insult, when in fact it was one of the best parts of Nicky. He was honest, and true to himself and proud of who he was and how he felt in his heart. Fiona hated having to defend that, but did so with every ounce of love in her own heart. Eventually, Fiona learned to combat ignorance by not giving it her attention. She realized she was defending Nicky's right to be himself, and that was simply not necessary. People who didn't agree with who he was didn't matter. Fiona was certain that love; true love would find Nicky. And it did.

Rob loaded their overnight bags into the trunk of the car while Nick called Carter to let him know they were on their way.

"Well, we finally got our weekend at the shore," Nicky said as he climbed in the car.

"We did. You know the first time I tried to plan this, I was going to ask you to move in with me," Rob confessed.

"I know, and I would have said yes, even then. But, I really think the timing worked out the way it was supposed to. It's a lot less stressful without the restaurant to worry about, and my mom and Linda. Everything is as it should be."

"I agree. I would have stayed in New Jersey, you know. I was totally surprised to find out you liked it on Long Island. I honestly figured you and Fiona would want to live in the old neighborhood forever."

"We might have; but it seemed as though our lives got bigger around the same time, and it felt right to leave our small lives behind. Don't get me wrong, we grew up happy; riding bikes, swimming in that dirty ass lake, and camping out in our backyards. I just think we both want more for ourselves, our futures and our own kids someday."

Rob smiled.

"You want kids?"

"Yeah, maybe. I hadn't given it much thought until Wendy and Nate showed up. What about you?"

"OK, this is a weird time to have this conversation, but what the hell? Yes, I would be open to having kids; having a family with you."

"Good, I think we'd be great parents. Maybe after the first of the year, we can start looking into our options. For now, let's enjoy Wendy and Nate and be a part of their first Christmas with us. I cannot wait to make it as special as we can."

Rob felt as if his whole world just got bigger and brighter somehow. He understood in that moment what Nicky was referring to when he spoke of a bigger life.

"It will be the best ever, but for now let's see what we can do to help Carter."

"Last chance to rescind your invitation," Carter said, poking his head through the back door.

Nicky responded.

"Not a chance, climb aboard."

"Conversation, or radio?" Rob asked,

Nicky took it upon himself to make the decision.

"Let's use this time to finish catching up. That way, when we get to the house, we can just chill and hang out. Car rides seem to go faster when we talk anyway."

"How long of a drive is it from here?" Carter asked

"Maybe ninety minutes, but if there's traffic, it could be close to two hours. It's a damn good thing Rob loves to drive."

"That's more than enough time to get all your questions out of the way. Besides, I'm sure Susan will have questions of her own; this will give me a chance to practice," Carter chuckled nervously.

"Oh, you keep mentioning Susan, and personally I don't think you have anything to worry about, Carter. I bet she's just happy to see you," Rob offered.

"I hope you're right."

Rob continued.

"Forgive me if I'm overstepping here, I know I don't share the same history as you, Nick and Fee, but I think you're obsessing over a mistake you can't fix or take back. In reality, you should be moving on from it; stop letting your time with Meg define the rest of your life. I know it might be a while before you stop loving her, despite her betrayal, but…"

Carter interjected.

"Rob, I never loved her. That's the sad part of this story, I never felt love. I let myself be manipulated by her and the whole Daly family and my stupid friends."

"Hey, speaking of stupid friends, whatever happened to Keith?" Nick asked

"Good question. He just stopped coming around. I have a feeling he knew that Eddie and Meg slept together and when Meg got pregnant, Keith suspected Eddie as the father. He stuck by him, and completely cut me out."

"You know what I think of them. I'm sorry, Carter, but they were never that nice to Fiona when you two were together. They were jealous and the first opportunity that came along to ruin your relationship became their purpose in life. Those two asses were more than willing to help Meg bust up your relationship with Fee."

"You're right, Nick, and I sat back and let it happen."

Rob let out a loud sigh and slapped the steering wheel with his left hand.

"Carter, I'm feeling a little frustrated here. You continue to say the same thing over and over. Here's how I see it; It's time to get over yourself. The only person who clearly didn't contribute to this mess but was hurt the most is Fiona. You handled yourself badly, made huge mistakes, and still, the Universe is giving you a second chance to make things right. It's like going to Karma court and having your record wiped clean. No Meg, no babies, no obligations to the Daly's at all; this is a good thing, Carter. Stop feeling sorry for yourself and find a way to make amends to Fiona. I noticed you didn't even ask us much about the shooting, and I found that odd."

Carter let Rob's words sink in, and for the first time, Nick La Salle was at a loss for something to say. He respected Rob's honesty and felt proud that he'd defend Fiona in her absence.

Carter spoke.

"I can't dispute any of that, Rob. You're right. I've been wrapped up in my own feelings for so long, I have forgotten what it's like to put someone else first. I've been selfish, and pitiful. It's beyond time that I stop being sorry for what happened. I keep saying these things happened to me, but really, they happened, period. There is more to this than Meg hurting me. So, if you don't mind, I think I'll use my time with both of you to reset. I need to rid myself of any Daly residue."

Nick found his choice of words amusing.

"That's one way of putting it. But, yeah, I can see how all their negative influences could stick around longer than you'd expect, like a bad habit. Carter, it's perfectly understandable to mourn the loss of a life you thought was meant for you. I can't imagine being told I was about to be a dad, then find out that was just a horrible lie. But the Carter I know, and love would continue to search for his higher purpose, rather than wallow. Let's find that guy, OK?"

Rob glanced back at Carter through the rear-view mirror.

"It's settled then, no more pity, no more Meg, let's get you back to your original factory settings."

Nick agreed.

"The original Carter is a great guy, I can't wait for you to get to know him, Rob."

Rob put the car in park and stretched his arms above his head.

"Talking does make the drive seem shorter, but I'm so ready to get out of this car!" He opened the door and jumped out of the driver's seat. "I'll grab the bags, Nick. You go in first and make sure Susan isn't too surprised."

Nicky put his key in the door and turned the lock. He pushed it open and called to Susan.

"Hey, we're home!"

"In here, honey," She called back

Nick walked into the living room to find Susan and Wanda curled up on the couch.

"You two look comfy."

"Mmmm, we are, but I'm so glad to see you. I was feeling a little lonely, and about to call Laurel and ask if Wendy would come over to keep me company. I mean Wanda is great but not much of a conversationalist."

"Susan, we brought a surprise guest home with us, I really hope that's OK."

"Oh, Nicky, don't tell me, you and Rob rescued another kid?"

Carter and Rob were just coming up the hall when they heard Susan. Carter responded as he entered the room.

"Well, if you consider me a kid, then yes, they rescued me."

Susan put her reading glasses on the table and stood.

"Carter, it's so good to see you," she said, stepping around the table to meet him for a hug,

"You too," he admitted. Carter instantly knew he was wrong to assume Susan wouldn't be welcoming. She hadn't changed at all, and Carter was grateful for her warm greeting. It occurred to him that his perception was more than likely influenced by his own insecurity and regret. Rob was right.

"Well, now, let's get this party started," Susan announced. "Nicky, take Carter's things to Fiona's office. I think he'd be most comfortable there. Rob, honey, why don't you make a fire in the pit out back, and I'll grab a couple bottles of wine. It's chilly enough to enjoy the fire, and I've been wanting to use that thing since we got it."

"Me too," Nick confessed. "Another one of Laurel's yard sale treasures, in perfect condition. She's the queen of second-hand shopping."

"We could all take a page from that girl's book. I love how thrifty she is for someone who doesn't necessarily have to be," Susan said as she selected three bottles of wine from the hanging rack in the kitchen.

"I think she said she paid ten bucks for our firepit and convinced the guy to deliver it to us for free." Nick loved talking about Laurel. He admired her before they met, but now that they were friends, he adored her. Their newly formed extended family seemingly revolved around Fiona, but for Nicky, Laurel was their keystone. Nick ushered Carter to the back patio, still chatting away about Laurel Cooke. Had Carter not met her after the fire, he may have gotten the impression Nicky was name dropping or bragging about their friendship. But even the very short time Carter had been in her company, he could sense how truly impressive she was.

Susan didn't know exactly why, but having Carter there made her feel hopeful. She thoroughly enjoyed the boys' company and found their stories entertaining. Wanda too took advantage of their attention and snuggled with each one in turn. Nicky and Rob were happy to be home and Carter felt relaxed for the first time in a long while.

We Can Do Better

Fiona still felt queasy from the rather jarring plane landing and the line to get through customs seemed miles long. She propped herself against the wall of the terminal and slid along when the line began to move forward.

"Almost there," Nate informed her, craning his neck to try and count the number of people ahead of them before they reached the customs counter.

"Good. I'm starving and cranky. I need food and a nap." Fiona rubbed her tired eyes and kicked her luggage a few inches in front of her.

Not only was Fiona relieved to get through customs, but Nate was also as well. He tried to be patient, but his own frustration was exacerbated by Fiona's continual complaints.

"I love you Fee, but you really do need a nap."

They walked in the direction of the giant glass doors which led out into the street. Nate happened to notice a man standing on the walk holding a sign that read: *Cooke Industries {2}*

"Fiona, I think that guy is here for us," he said, tugging on her sleeve.

"Good eye, Nate. I'd have never noticed him. I mean, he's not even trying to stand out." She and Nate approached the man with the sign. "Phillip?" she guessed.

"Nope. George. You Cooke's people?" he asked in a very abrupt and unprofessional manner.

"Yes, thank you," Fiona answered politely

"Get in," George barked as he climbed into the driver's seat and popped the trunk.

Confused, Nate and Fiona stood on the walk for a moment, waiting for George to assist them, but he started the engine and rolled up his window, leaving them to load their luggage into the trunk themselves. Nate hoisted his bag in and reached for Fiona's.

"I don't mean to sound entitled, but that guy is sort of rude."

"Maybe they just do things differently here." Fiona offered as she slammed the trunk lid shut.

Both Nate and Fiona reluctantly got in the car with George, who did manage to deliver them safely to their hotel. He pulled up on the curb and announced.

"This is it." He sat with the engine running while Nate and Fiona unloaded their bags, and as soon as the trunk lid latched; George sped away without as much as a wave.

Nate opened the door for Fiona and gave her a puzzled look.

"Yeah, that was weird by anyone's standards," she laughed but had to agree. "Should we say something to someone about George?" Nate asked, obviously having trouble letting George's rude behavior go.

"No, we're here now, let's just get checked in and find some food. We'll both feel better after we eat and sleep."

Fiona approached the front desk of their hotel. The attendant was about her age with giant green eyes and gorgeous red curls. Fiona thought she looked like a movie star.

"Hi, hello, Fiona Lasher with Cooke Industries, checking in please."

The woman with the green eyes smiled.

"Yes, I have you in two adjoining rooms, third floor; three seventeen and three nineteen. Here are your key cards. Do you need help with your bags?"

Fiona was just about to take her up on the offer when Nate interjected.

"No thanks, I got it." He hoisted his duffle onto his left shoulder and took the handles of both his and Fiona's rolling bags, and set off toward the elevators.

"I guess we're good," Fiona said, taking the keys from the desk attendant. "Oh, is room service available?"

"Yes love, any time day or night, just give them a ring." Her hospitality was refreshing after their strange encounter with their driver, George. Fiona caught up to Nate who had already summoned the elevator to the lobby.

Fiona handed Nate his key.

"Slide it in face-up then push down on the door handle." He opened his door with ease and asked if they could have dinner together. "Of course, just come on over when you're ready, we'll order one of everything on the menu."

Fiona found an itinerary for the Rooftop Expo on the table in her room.

"OK, well, let's eat and pass out quickly, tomorrow is a very busy day. There's a lecture at eleven a.m I really want to hear."

"What's the lecture about?" Nate asked, stuffing a handful of fries in his mouth.

"Hydroponic systems. I know all of the manufacturers are local to London, but I'd like to get an idea about the builds; both traditional and hydroponics. My goal is to find a small business in the city to build the beds and irrigation for us at each site. So, when we're at the trade show, pick up all the brochures and information you can, OK?"

"Will do. Hey, maybe we could get some volunteers to help build the planter beds too; like a club, or kids that need community service hours. I was also thinking it would be a great idea to have our own rooftop gardens expo when we're ready to raise money for the project."

"Nate, I love your ideas. Now finish your food and go to bed."

Nate laughed.

"This time difference has me all messed up. I'm so tired, but I really want to hang out a little longer. Would it be ok if I went down to the lobby and looked around a little?"

"Oh, sure. Just do me a favor, please and don't leave the hotel. The last thing I need is to have to make a call to TC and let him know I lost you."

"No worries, I just want to explore. I'll give the door a knock when I'm back in the room."

Fiona knew she wouldn't be able to fall asleep until she was sure Nate was safely back in his hotel room, but she also knew he was old enough and certainly smart enough to spend time without a chaperone. Still, she couldn't help feeling responsible for Nate, not only as her assistant but very much as the younger brother she'd come to love.

Nate wandered the lobby of their hotel, looking in shop windows, and meandering down corridors to nowhere. He noticed the woman with red hair and green eyes heading for the front door. She was carrying two paper shopping bags and kept looking over her shoulder. He rushed over to open the door for her.

"Here, let me get that for you."

She thanked him and stepped onto the street; Nate followed. The woman quickly glanced in both directions and nervously paced back and forth in front of the doors. Nate noticed a young girl peeking around the corner of the building. By his best guess, she was twelve, maybe thirteen. He recognized the telltale signs of a homeless kid; the ill-fitting clothing, unkempt hair and wide-eyed stare; obviously on high alert. When the girl spotted the woman, she approached rather quickly; grabbed both bags and nodded. The woman warned.

"Next time sweetie, meet me around the back. If I lose my job, I can't be here to help. You take care."

The girl smiled.

"Thank you. Thank you so much."

The woman hadn't noticed Nate and was startled when he came up behind her.

"Hey, that was really cool of you."

"Oh, lord, you frightened me! Listen, you didn't see anything, OK?" She turned on her heels and went back inside; again, Nate followed.

The woman took her place back behind the check-in desk hoping Nate would retreat to his room, but Nate had an idea he couldn't let go. He approached the woman, whose name was Katheryn according to her tiny gold nameplate.

"How long have you been helping her?" he asked boldly.

Katheryn just shook her head; "Please, I really could be fired for that. Can we just forget what you saw?"

Nate leaned over the desk.

"Miss Katheryn, I was homeless until a few months ago, and if I told you my story, you wouldn't believe me. I think what you're doing is amazing, and I just want to help." Nate reached into his pocket and handed her thirty dollars. "This is for any time you might not be able to sneak food out to that girl. Please use it to buy whatever you can for her, and the other kids she's likely sharing with. It isn't much, but it's all I have with me at the moment. I hope I see you again before we leave in a few days, I would love to give a little more."

Katheryn's eyes welled with tears. She took the money from Nate's outstretched hand, and gave it a light squeeze.

"Bless you."

"I have been blessed, believe me. Thank you for being a blessing to kids like me."

As Nate headed back toward the elevators, Katheryn tried desperately to quell her emotions, but a few breathy sobs escaped. Nate turned and waved as the elevator doors closed.

The next morning, Fiona and Nate set out to find Philip, their contact. Fiona assumed he'd be somewhere in the conference room where the trade show was taking place. As they passed through the lobby, Nate noticed Katheryn leaving the building. He waved and she touched her right hand to her heart and smiled.

Fiona furrowed her brow.

"Uh, she's a little old for you."

Nate shook his head.

"It's not like that. She's just a friend."

Although Fiona's curiosity peaked, Nate offered nothing more as an explanation. She decided to leave it alone; it was obviously something Nate wanted to keep to himself. They made their way into the conference room where dozens of vendors tended to their display booths. Some were interactive, while others provided information on either their services or goods. Nate loved the vendors who gave away promotional items, and had collected nine key chains by ten a.m.

Fiona stopped to tie her shoe when she heard her name being called over the P.A. system. It was asking for her presence near the stage. She made her way to the front of the room where a young man in a gray suit stood, checking his phone. He finally looked up and asked.

"Fiona Lasher?"

"Yes, I'm Fiona, can I help you?"

He extended his hand politely.

"Philip Straton, nice to make your acquaintance."

Fiona shook his hand and explained she was on her way into the lecture on hydroponics. Philip seemed almost relieved as if she were nothing more than an untimely obligation.

"Good, good, enjoy the expo. Let's catch up tomorrow night after the reception; maybe for a drink?"

"Sure, I'd like that," she answered hoping she had read him wrong. "Aren't you going to be on the tour tomorrow?"

"Me? No, I'll be here making certain our vendors and other guests are being taken care of. However, I'm sure the rooftop tour will provide you with great insight and information you can bring back to Mr Cooke. I'll be looking forward to your thoughts when we meet."

"Great, see you then," she managed before he turned and left the stage area.

Fiona met Nate in the small banquet room intended for the lecture. It was nothing more than a dining area with the tables removed and the chairs arranged in rows. The lecture proved to be anti-climactic; as it consisted of one man with a monotone voice describing slides of a PowerPoint presentation. Nate yawned.

"Sorry!"

"Don't be, this is torture, let's get the hell out of here."

"Seriously?"

"Yeah, let's go see London."

"Fiona? I know we can do better."

"And we will."

They exited the banquet room quietly and slowly, but once they hit the lobby, the two of them sprinted toward the door like high school kids ditching class. Nate and Fiona spent the next eight hours looking for every opportunity afforded to tourists. Nate's idea of the perfect day consisted of taking hundreds of pictures and buying souvenirs for everyone back home. Although Fiona enjoyed the palace, museums and the bus tour; her greatest joy came from Nate's excitement each time he found another souvenir to buy for someone.

Meanwhile, Back in New York

Rob sat at the kitchen table with his morning coffee. He had a few hours before he needed to be in the city and everyone else was still asleep. It was rare for the house to be so quiet, and he found himself missing Nate and Fiona; especially Nate.

Susan eventually woke up and joined Rob for their morning coffee.

"Thank you for making coffee, Rob. Lord knows it's getting harder and harder to function without my caffeine."

"You're welcome. It's strangely quiet this morning, isn't it?"

"It is. What time is Nicky's class today?"

"Not until two. I have to be in the city in a few hours. I have a couple of local runs on my schedule today and should be back by dinner. Maybe we can have a cookout?"

"It's thirty degrees, Rob, let's just order in. Oh, and will you take me with you today? I have some shopping I'd like to do."

"Yeah, I wonder if Carter would like to go as well?"

"Dear lord, I totally forgot about Carter," Susan admitted.

"How could you forget about me?" Carter asked as he entered the kitchen.

"Oh, honey, I'm just not used to you being here. That means you'll have to stick around until you become a part of our routine."

"Or at least until Fiona gets back."

"Don't you worry about Fee. Anyway, grab some coffee, and let's talk about our plans for today. Rob has to be in the city soon and I was thinking of catching a ride in to do some shopping; would you like to join me?"

"I'd love that. Could we possibly go see Linda while we're there?"

"Yes! We can go to the deli for lunch. It will give me the chance to show you off to my friends in the Cooke building too."

"Oh, I don't know about all that, but I'm in for a day in the city. I haven't seen Linda since the fire, and I really want to."

"It's a date! Finish your coffee and get ready. I'll be out in a jiffy." Susan couldn't have been more excited to spend the day with Carter. She loved shopping in the city, especially at Christmas time, but to have the company of one of her favorite people was the icing on her cake.

Carter downed his coffee and rinsed his cup.

"Shower?" he asked Rob

"Down the hall, first door on your right."

"Thanks. I guess I'll see ya' in a bit then."

"Take your time; we have an hour or so before we have to leave. I need to make sure Nicky is awake before we go anyway; otherwise, he'll sleep in and be late for class."

Susan volunteered to sit in the back seat on their way into the city. She figured the boys would have time to talk while she checked in with Fiona via text message. Her daughter's reply was vague but positive; still, Susan had a feeling Fiona wasn't enjoying her business trip as much as she anticipated. Susan also took the time to text Laurel in regard to Carter's visit and their day together.

"By any chance, will you be at Cooke Industries today?" she asked. Laurel responded that she and Wendy would be staying local, but suggested Susan see Jaime while she was there.

"Jai will be happy to see you; she loves visitors when she's working."

Laurel couldn't help herself and immediately called her husband to let him know Carter and Susan would be in the deli for lunch.

"Now is your chance to meet Carter. I'm curious to know if you still think he and Fiona still have a chance. After all, he's part of the original story that brought all of us together."

TC responded.

"Tell Jaime to call up when Susan gets there. I'll make sure I happen to be in the deli at the same time."

Rob dropped Susan and Carter off in front of the Cooke building just after noon. He let them know he'd be headed back home around five, giving them plenty of time to shop, have their lunch, and visit with Linda. Carter teased.

"Thanks man, it's nice having a personal chauffeur, I could get used to this."

Susan and Carter stepped into the lobby of Cooke Industries to find it bustling with people. The holiday decorations were elegant and tasteful, and the piped-in music enhanced the feeling of Christmas. Carter felt as though he had stepped right into a movie.

"This is amazing," he exclaimed. "What a wonderful way to do some Christmas shopping; can we look around?"

Susan began to explain the vendor program to Carter.

"I had already planned on buying as many gifts as I can from our vendors. You know, Linda's boyfriend Chris initiated this program and continues to coordinate; as you can imagine, he's been busy lately." She and Carter walked through the lobby, pausing at each vendor station to admire their wares. "Each one of these talented people had been street peddlers before Chris and Laurel presented the idea of using the lobby to TC. Now, they're safe, warm and prosperous. Most people don't realize what Cooke Industries does for the community; the city, and the people. Some of them even sleep here if they have nowhere to go. Chris tries to get every one of his vendors into a safe place; either with roommates or in temporary shelters. The buildings TC just acquired will provide rooms and apartments for a lot of people in need that are connected with one of the Cooke programs."

"I'm in awe. I had no idea that Cooke was any more than a boring tech. company. Susan, I have already seen several items I will have to have while we're here."

"Go ahead, Carter, do some shopping. Let's meet in front of the deli in thirty minutes. I have a friend I need to chat with anyway."

Carter felt like a kid let loose in a candy store as he meandered through the lobby. Among other purchases, he selected a hand-wrapped gemstone necklace with a silver star charm. It reminded him of Fiona, and he could only hope for the opportunity to give it to her.

Jaime's concierge desk was swarming with people when Susan approached. She tried waving to get Jaime's attention but to no avail. Susan stood in line with the others, hoping to be assisted with either directions to the restrooms or a vendor map to aid in their shopping experience. Susan waited patiently and finally made her way to the front of the crowd.

"Hey, sweetheart. This is an impressive crowd!"

Jaime came around the front of her enormous desk and hugged Susan.

"Yes. It's been like this for weeks and we suspect it will only get better and busier as we get closer to Christmas. TC approved all overtime for everyone in administration. Not only are the vendors rocking it, but because of them we're making extra money as well."

"That's wonderful, I just hope you aren't too overworked to enjoy the holidays."

"You know Joe; he's been amazing. He's cooking, cleaning and even did some shopping this week. I got one of the good ones, that's for sure. If it weren't for his help, I'd never be ready for the holidays."

"Speaking of good ones, Carter is here with me. We're meeting for lunch in a few minutes. Would you have some time to join us?"

"Susan, I'd love to, but I doubt I can step away for more than a few minutes. How about I pop in for a quick introduction?"

"Perfect, see you in a few."

Jaime neglected to tell Susan she was to let TC know when she and Carter had arrived. She figured it was best for everyone to simply think it was a coincidence. No one wanted Carter to feel as though he was about to be interrogated, nor did anyone want Susan to be on the defensive. TC simply wanted to finally meet the other half of his 'convergence couple'. Jaime made the call and got back to work. This wasn't exactly a covert operation, but it reminded her of a spy novel and that amused her.

Susan and Carter met at the deli entrance and were seated immediately, despite the crowd of waiting patrons. TC had called ahead describing the pair with specific instructions to take care of them, VIP style, but not to tell Linda as their visit was a surprise for her. As luck would have it, Silvie answered that call and was all too happy to comply. She escorted them to their table and asked for their drink preferences.

"Coffee, please," Susan replied. Carter opted for a soda, and Silvie disappeared into the crowded deli to grant their requests.

Linda La Salle was lending her expertise in the kitchen when Silvie found her.

"Hey boss, there's a couple in the dining room asking for a manager. I tried to help them, but they're insisting on speaking with you." Silvie felt guilty for being so misleading, but she suspected it would be worth the surprise.

Linda wiped her hands on a dish towel and followed Silvie back to the table. Before she realized who was seated in her restaurant, she began to speak.

"Hello, I'm Linda, and how may I help you." She raised her eyes to meet those of her customers only to discover Susan and Carter's smiling faces. "Oh, what a wonderful surprise! Carter, my hero, what are you doing here?"

Carter stood and hugged her.

"Hey Lin, how are you?" he asked

"I'm so good now. I cannot believe you two snuck in here without anyone telling me. Let me inform the kitchen I'll be taking a break, give me a minute."

Silvie told her boss to take a seat; she'd be happy to let the kitchen know.

"Sit, visit, enjoy your friends. I got you covered."

Linda thanked her and asked that she bring the appetizer sampler to their table when she had a moment.

"This is the heroic young man who saved me from the fire."

Silvie smiled.

"Well then, I'll have that sampler right out for your hero."

Linda jumped into the conversation.

"Don't get me wrong, I am so thrilled to see you both, but does someone want to fill me in? You two are unlikely lunch companions, never mind here in the city. I am doubting this was an accidental meeting."

Susan lowered her eyes, deferring to Carter who began to explain. He told Linda about Meg and Eddie and losing his job with Daly Motors and running into Rob and Nick on the boardwalk. Carter tried to focus on the positive aspects of his story; however, Linda knew him well and felt his evident despair.

"Listen to me, Carter, this whole scenario stinks, but I believe it was all supposed to shake out this way. I know you and I know your heart, and it belongs to Fiona, it always has. Now, you two can get back together and set the world right again." She reached over and patted his hand. "Susan, back me up here. You know you're thinking it too, otherwise, you wouldn't be having lunch together."

Susan sighed.

"OK, I admit, I was thrilled when the boys brought Carter to the house and told me he'd be staying a few days. I was even more thrilled when he agreed to hang out with me today. But, as much as you and I want to see the kids together, Lin, it's ultimately up to them."

Linda rolled her eyes.

"Ha, that's not entirely true, not when it comes to our crazy family. We have some strong divine intervention going on, and Carter is now part of that; otherwise, the boys wouldn't have been at the boardwalk at the very same time as Carter and his dad. We all know Fiona and Carter are meant to be together; and honestly, Carter if you hadn't made your Meg mistake, none of us would be together now. Like I said, everything has a reason; and without Meg, there would be no picture for TC to have obsessed over."

Carter tried to speak several times, but the two women monopolized the conversation with their speculations as if he weren't even there. He rather enjoyed the story they were spinning and the future they wished for him. He too hoped Fiona would be as receptive to him being around more than he had in the past few years. Realistically, so much time had passed, and Carter couldn't be sure Fiona had any feelings left toward him. Just as he felt himself getting lost in his own thoughts, he heard a voice behind him ask; "May I join you?" Carter turned to discover Anthony Cooke himself standing behind his chair.

Now Carter's head felt as though it would explode. First, Linda mentions some pictures of him that TC has and then TC himself shows up at his lunch table. He couldn't help but think there was something to Linda's divine intervention theory after all.

Linda greeted TC with a smile and a quick wave.

"Sit, we'd love your company. Silvie will be right back with some food. Do you have a lunch preference, or should I order for you from the 'off menu' items today?" she asked.

"If Ralph trusts you, I do too. You know he's my food guru."

"We all love him," Linda agreed.

"I'm sorry, we haven't met, I'm TC Cooke, and you are?" TC addressed Carter with an extended hand. Of course, TC already knew who he was about to have lunch with, but it would prove prudent to allow Carter to believe this was in fact a coincidence.

"Carter Wyatt, Sir. Nice to meet you."

"Fiona's Carter?" he asked, already knowing the answer.

"I suppose at one time, yes."

"Well, then Carter Wyatt, I suppose we'll see if you are once again indeed worthy of our Fiona."

Carter blushed.

"Um, no disrespect to you, any of you, but don't you all think Fiona should be making these decisions for herself? As much as I'd love to see her again, she may not feel the same. I mean, chances are she doesn't. I don't want anyone here disappointed, especially me."

TC spoke.

"You're right Carter. And I am already slightly impressed with your willingness to consider her feelings. So, what is it that you do, Carter Wyatt?"

"Sir, I've been working as a mechanic, but recently lost my job. It's a long story, but I'd like to clarify that I didn't get fired for anything I did wrong, as far as my performance or ability."

"I wouldn't conclude you had, not without giving you the opportunity to explain." TC was testing Carter's integrity, as he already knew the story from Laurel. TC could be quite intimidating when he needed to be; it was a trait he typically reserved for board meetings and business disputes. However, he wasn't ready to let Carter know his true self; as that part of Anthony Cooke was reserved for family.

Carter graciously answered TC's questions and shared his personal life openly with his three lunch companions. There were details Susan hadn't yet heard, and of course, Linda wanted to be updated as well. Silvie brought more food than any four people could possibly eat; and as they enjoyed each of Linda's recommendations, Carter spilled his heart out directly onto the table.

When they finished eating, Linda informed them she needed to get back to her kitchen. Before she said her goodbyes she asked.

"Carter, you mentioned being out of a job; you know I could use an assistant manager here, interested? "

TC couldn't help himself and interjected.

"Why do all the women in my life want to employ every person they know?"

Susan and Linda laughed, knowing he wasn't wrong. Laurel was notorious for creating jobs within Cooke Industries just to make sure everyone she met had an income. Fiona, of course, had followed suit, and would likely continue to do so. Susan imagined Wendy would as well; expecting her soon to be father to employ all her friends as she grew up.

"Thank you, Lin. I'd love nothing more than to work with you again, but I will need some time to think about this. I hope you understand."

"I do, and I'll give you until Christmas to decide. I'm sure I'll be seeing you then." She gave him one more warm smile as she returned to her busy kitchen.

"Well, this was awesome, but I should get back to work also. Susan, it's great to see you, and I'm sure I'll see you again soon. Carter, nice to meet you. I must admit, you're more impressive than I figured. Thank you for the enlightening conversation."

Carter shook his hand and turned to Susan.

"Wow, that was the most interesting lunch I have ever had. Never in my wildest dreams did I think I'd ever be sharing a plate of gravy fries with Anthony Cooke."

"Oh, wait until he comes for dinner. He will steal your food right off of your plate. That man loves to eat!"

Everyone continued to speak as though Carter was a permanent fixture now, one of the family as Linda put it. Somehow, it should have all felt unnerving, but Carter's feelings were those of contentment. Their collective energy drew him in like a giant magnet, and the closer he felt to these amazing people, the closer he wanted to remain.

TC returned to his office eager to tell Laurel he had finally met Carter.

"Call Laurel."

"Hey sweets, how was lunch?"

"Great, I just got back to my office and couldn't wait to call you."

"And?"

"I'll fill you in when I get home, but Laur, he's a great kid. I think we're right; Carter and Fiona may have another chance."

Our Wanda

Nate waited patiently for any sign from the adjoining room that Fiona was awake. He had been up for hours listening intently for a bump or bang; maybe the sound of the television, so he could go in and ask how her date with Philip went. Finally, through the thin walls of their hotel room, Nate suspected Fiona was indeed moving about; he softly knocked on the door between their rooms.

Fiona opened the door.

"Good Morning."

"Hey, I made you coffee," he offered her a paper cup filled with black instant coffee.

"Thanks, but I thought we'd go down and get some breakfast together. There's something I'd like to talk to you about. I'll be ready in about five minutes, OK?"

"Sure, should I wait in my room, or can I hang out here?"

"Have a seat, I just need to brush my hair and my teeth, and we can head out."

Nate sat at the small table near the window in Fiona's hotel room. She had the drapes open, and he could see it was another cloudy, rainy morning in London.

"Is there a plan for today? Will Philip be joining us?" he asked, in an attempt to appear subtle.

"No plan, and just me and you, kiddo," Fiona called from the bathroom.

Nate stood as Fiona grabbed her handbag and room key from the table.

"Ready?" she asked, heading toward the door.

The two rode the elevator down to the lobby and made their way to the restaurant. The smell of real coffee was more than inviting, and Fiona wondered if they'd be willing to just leave a full pot on the table.

It was late morning and most of the hotel patrons had cleared out, leaving their choice of available seating. Fiona requested a table near the window. She loved the quaint feeling of the street and the roadside vendors;

it reminded her of the Cooke building lobby. The two were seated and their orders taken, and it became obvious to Fiona that Nate wanted to ask her about the night before.

"Go ahead, ask," she began

"I can't help it, I'm anxious to hear about your date."

"Well, let's just say; we won't be spending any more time in the company of good old Philip."

"Was he a jerk? He didn't hurt you, did he?"

"Yes to jerk, no to hurting me. I think he and I had very different preconceptions. I was hoping for a nice evening with a nice guy and well, Philip was hoping for an exciting evening with a naughty girl."

"Huh?" Nate seemed confused.

"I'm trying to keep this clean for you, but Philip basically wanted a physical encounter. He immediately invited me back to his room for a drink; of course, I declined. He told me his time was valuable and I was wasting it by playing games. Nate, I was mortified. You are getting this, right?"

"Yeah, I got it." His confusion gave way to anger. "I'm going to find that idiot and punch him in the face."

"No, we are going to simply move on from the whole Philip experience. As a matter of fact, I was wondering if you'd be open to leaving a few days early. I thought we could see if our tickets can be changed when we are finished with breakfast. I know it will cost extra, but there's only one day left of the Expo, and we did get to do some really cool stuff. I think I'd like to go home if that's OK with you?"

"Absolutely. And, Fee, don't worry about the cost. I have some money, I'll pay the difference for us," Nate offered.

"You're sweet. Thank you. Let's just see what it will be before worrying about how to pay. Eat your breakfast; we have a busy day ahead."

Nate figured it was his imagination, but somehow knowing they were going home soon made breakfast taste so much better. He even thought he saw a bit of sunshine peek from the overcast skies as he gazed out the window of their hotel for the last time.

Once they were back in Fiona's hotel room, she opened her laptop and checked the airline's website.

"We are in luck, there's a flight to New York in six hours. I can change our tickets and upgrade us to first class for two hundred bucks. I really thought it would be more expensive. Are you good with that?" she asked Nate who seemed miles away in his thoughts.

"Yeah, that works." He reached into his pocket for his wallet and handed Fiona his bank card. "Here, use this."

"Nate, you don't have to pay. I love the fact that you offered, but I'm ok with the added cost."

"Please, Fiona, let me do this. I've never had money, and there is no way I could ever repay you for all you've done. This is just a small part of what I owe you."

"You owe me nothing, Nate. But if you insist; I will accept your noble offer." She took the card from Nate and began entering their information. Fiona realized how important it was to dignify Nate's generous offer by accepting. He continued to impress her.

"I'm going to pack," he said as he disappeared through the adjoining doors. Nate took paper and an envelope from the tiny desk drawer in his hotel room. He quickly penned a note to Kathryn and slipped two twenty-dollar bills in the envelope with his message; *Katheryn, don't ever stop being someone's hero. I am glad I met you, Nate.* His intention was to deliver the note to her upon checking out, but it was Katheryn's day off. A very nice elderly gentleman promised he'd give the envelope to her when she came in for her next shift. He had kind eyes and somehow Nate knew he would.

Fiona breathed a sigh of relief knowing they'd be on their way home in just a few short hours. She decided not to tell anyone other than Charlie and Kay they were coming home early. Fiona sent Kay a text asking if they would pick them up from the airport.

Please don't tell everyone. It's been a crazy trip and I sort of want to just come home to a quiet house. Thank you, see you soon.

Fiona hadn't expected an immediate response due to the time difference, but Kay did write back almost instantly.

We will be there. Can't wait to see you. {hugs}.

By the time Fiona and Nate arrived at the airport, Nicky and Susan were enjoying their morning coffee in New York. Rob had left earlier upon TC's request to pick up several business associates and deliver them to

Cooke Industries. The house was quiet; Carter was still asleep in Fiona's office and Wanda hadn't come out for breakfast yet.

"I haven't seen Wanda this morning, have you?" Nicky asked Susan.

"No, I was just thinking she may be enjoying Carter's company, I know I have. It's been nice having him around."

"Yeah, I think he needed some time away; just to hang out with friends. Susan, you are a saint for putting up with the guys this week."

"Oh, more like you three are the saints for being so nice to me. It's probably not easy having an old lady around."

Nicky laughed.

"I'm going to check on Wanda. It's getting late and she needs to go out." Nicky walked through the living room, down the hall and made the right into Fiona's office. Carter had obviously just woken up. He stretched and rested his arm over Wanda who had fallen asleep next to him, but she didn't move. "Hey girl, rise and shine." Carter bent down and kissed Wanda's head. He quickly realized there was something wrong with her.

"Nick!" he yelled in a panic.

"I'm here, what's going on?"

"It's Wanda, she's barely breathing and not moving." Carter became frantic, and Nick called for Susan who rushed into the office.

"Susan, it's Wanda, something's wrong."

Susan checked Wanda's breathing as she gently stroked her back.

"Hey girl, Mommy is here, it's all right." Susan shot Nicky a terrified look. "Call the vet Nick. Tell them we are on our way, *now*!"

Carter picked up his clothes from the floor and ran out of the room to change. He could hear Nick speaking to the vet.

"Yes, her breathing is shallow, and she's not responding to our voices or touch. Yes, we're on our way now, thank you."

Nicky entered the office to find Susan holding Wanda and sobbing.

"Call them back, Nick. Let them know she has passed, and we will need their assistance, not medical treatment."

Nicky fell to his knees and broke into tears. Carter entered the hall to find his friend sitting on the floor, and immediately knew what had just happened. He placed a consoling hand on Nick's shoulder. Nick looked up and gestured into the office as if to ask Carter to check on Susan. Carter sat next to her on the fold-out couch, placing his hand over hers. They sat silently for a while, as did Nick. Finally, Susan regained her composure.

"Nicky, we'll need a blanket to wrap her in. We can call the vet on our way, but she needs to be properly taken care of."

Carter stood.

"I'll take her. Just give me the address. You two shouldn't have to do this," Susan thanked him, but Nicky offered to go as well. "I want to be with her. If you'll drive, I'll hold her on the way." His eyes were red and swollen and his hands shook. Nick reached into the hall closet and chose a blanket to wrap Wanda in.

Carter took charge.

"I'll get her in the car while you go get your wallet and keys. Susan? Are you sure you'll be OK by yourself for a while?"

"Yes, thank you, guys. I'm going to be fine. I do appreciate you both so much." She got up and hugged Carter. "It means the world to me to have you here right now. I just wish I knew how to tell Fiona." Susan waited until she was alone before she broke down again. The tears wouldn't stop, and she knew she needed a distraction. She picked up her phone and called Laurel.

"Hi, Susan. Is everything OK?"

"Laurel, Wanda died this morning. I'm so sorry to bother you, I just need to hear a friendly voice."

"Oh, Susan, I am so sorry. Where are the guys?"

"Carter and Nicky took her to the vet. I decided to have her cremated and her ashes returned to us. I think Fiona would want that."

"Poor Fiona. Have you told her yet?"

"No, she and Nate have a few more days in London, I think I'm going to wait until she comes home. She may be mad at me, but if I tell her now it will only ruin her trip and there's nothing anyone can do at this point."

"Feel like company? I can bring lunch."

"I'd love that, Laurel. I love the boys, but I could use some girl talk."

"I'll see you in a bit. Oh, Susan?"

"What, honey?"

"It's so good that you're here. We all love you, just wanted you to know that."

When Carter Met Wendy

By the time Nicky and Carter returned, Laurel and Wendy had successfully comforted Susan with food, a little wine and of course their company. Carter retreated to Fiona's office, figuring Susan would like some time with the girls. Losing Wanda was hard enough without Susan having to deal with his feelings of grief as well. It had been a long morning for everyone; Carter sat back in the oversized bean bag chair and closed his eyes. He expected to drift off, but couldn't shake the feeling that he wasn't alone. Carter turned his head to the left and opened one eye; his suspicions were confirmed. Harry stood just inches away, staring at him as if to say "Get out of my bed."

"Hey there. Is this your bed?" Harry took a few cautious steps closer.

"Well, come on, climb in, there's room for both of us," Carter offered, patting the bean bag. Harry was still a bit skeptical, and approached slowly, never taking his eyes off of Carter. Finally, he climbed in the chair and settled next to his new friend. Carter closed his eyes and put his arm around Harry; still, the feeling of being watched lingered.

"You're Carter, right?" he heard a voice say. For a second, Carter thought it was a dream and Harry was the one speaking. But clearly, this voice was feminine and coming from the doorway. He shook his head and sat up.

"Yeah, and you must be Wendy."

Wendy entered the office and took a seat in the folding chair next to Fiona's desk.

"That's Harry," she informed him. "He likes you, that's a good sign. I think he misses Wanda, and I wonder if he knows she's not coming back?"

"Oh, I believe he knows. Sounds like Harry and Wanda had a connection; and just like people, dogs can sense when a part of them is gone."

"They were good friends. Hey Carter, did you know that I found Harry in a dumpster, just the same way Nicky found Wanda? Do you think that has anything to do with their connection?"

"Maybe. It's possible that they had an understanding for one another because they had been through the same circumstances."

"Kind of like me and Nate, I guess."

"Nate and me; always put the other person first when you're speaking and writing," he corrected. "But, yeah, Harry and Wanda both knew what it felt like to be unwanted, and then rescued and loved more than anything. Every dog should be so lucky."

"Every kid too. But it's not like there's a lot of super-rich people just waiting around to meet a homeless kid to take care of. Harry and I both got lucky. Nate too, he loves being with Fiona and the guys. I know they aren't super rich, but they are super awesome."

Carter laughed.

"There's a really popular story that reminds me of you."

Wendy let out a loud sigh and rolled her eyes.

"Yeah, Laurel and I just watched the movie after we saw people posting about me on social media. They were calling me 'Little Orphan Wendy' and 'Wendy Warbucks'. I asked Laurel what that meant, and that's when she told me about Annie."

"The posts seem kind of rude, but you have to admit, there are similarities, right down to the dog." Carter tried to put a positive spin on her story. He wasn't sure if she knew enough to be insulted, but certainly, enough to resent the implications.

"Laurel told me to just ignore them, and eventually, I'd get used to it. It just sucked to finally have a phone, and be on social media apps like normal kids, only to see my picture with stupid comments being posted everywhere."

"Laurel must be very smart, and I would have to agree with her. You know, people will get to know you eventually and they will love you. Just do me a favor, and be careful what you post on social media; try and keep it all positive."

"She is really smart. TC says Laurel is never wrong, and I believe him. Oh, and I am careful, believe me. So, are you going to get back together with Fiona?"

"Wow! That is a really big question. I wasn't expecting to have this conversation, but I will tell you this; it isn't just up to me whether Fiona and I can ever be together again. I have no idea how she feels about that, or me."

"Do you love her; still?" Wendy stared Carter down as if she were interrogating a criminal.

Carter refrained from correcting her grammar for the second time and indulged her question.

"I do. I always have and always will. I made some huge mistakes that I'm sorry for, and Fiona has every right to hold them against me."

"She doesn't. Don't ask me how I know; it's a girl thing," She informed him. "I do know that Fiona still thinks you two were meant to be together. You need to let her know that she did nothing wrong. Fiona thinks you left because of her, and I know that cannot be true. She saved my life; has anyone told you that?"

"Yes. Rob and Nick told me the story. I understand why you feel so protective of her. Wendy, I never want to hurt Fiona again. Even if we cannot be together, I won't hurt her, you have my word."

"I'd better. Hey, wanna see something cool?" she asked, taking her phone from her back pocket. "I took this pic of Nate and me, is that right? Anyway, I took it, and it has the same weird color thing happening between us, just like the photo of you and Fiona. You know, the one that TC found on social media. Look!"

"What am I looking at exactly, Wendy? Other than a really cute picture of you and I'm guessing, Nate?"

"Look between us, there's a red streak near me and a blue one near Nate, and right where they meet, the color streak turns purple; just like the pic of you and Fee."

"Oh, I do see the colors now, but I have no idea what picture of us you're talking about."

"Here, I have it saved." Wendy pulled up the photo from the day of Wanda's miraculous rescue. There stood Carter and Fiona; and where they touch, a distinct purple hue formed from their individual colors.

Carter felt chills run up his back and a numbing sensation behind his eyes. He stared at the photo for a few minutes before scrolling back to the picture of Nate and Wendy. The very same occurrence was distinct in each image.

"Amazing," he managed.

"Wendy responded enthusiastically.

"Right? That's how we all know you and Fiona are meant to be. That's how I know I'll marry Nate someday. Pretty cool, huh?"

"Very cool. Thanks for showing me. You mentioned TC, how did he come across this old photo?"

"No idea. But, there is a picture of TC and Laurel that has the same weird color thingy between them; except theirs is yellow and blue and green where they meet. It's in a frame in their room. Laurel said her friend Jaime took it when they all first met."

"Wendy, that is really interesting and answers a few questions I have been afraid to ask. So, when you say everyone, you mean the Cooke's think Fiona and I should be together?"

"Yeah, they do. We all do. Rob, Nicky, Susan, and me. I wasn't sure but I might be now."

Harry stretched and rested both front paws over Carter's legs. He let out a sigh and a little snort and fell back to sleep. Wendy smiled.

"Well, Harry really does think you're a good guy, so for now, I will too. You should spend Christmas with us next week. It's my first one, ever. Imagine that. I'm fourteen and never had a real Christmas. I'm so excited! Laurel and I have been making gifts for everyone. I think you should stay."

Carter thought to himself.

"Wow, this kid has no filter at all. Whatever she's thinking comes right out of her mouth." He supposed it wasn't necessarily a bad thing, and people would certainly get along better if everyone was as honest as Wendy."

"I will give that some serious thought," he said. "I'm kind of hungry. Would you want to join me for lunch?"

"We brought so much food. I'll meet you in the kitchen," she said, jumping up from her chair and skipping out of the office.

"Wendy? Were you bugging Carter? "Laurel asked as her soon to be daughter strode through the living room.

"Basically," she quipped.

Feels Like Home

Nate and Fiona boarded their flight and settled into their seats. A flight attendant approached and offered beverages, snacks, pillows, blankets and headsets for the in-flight movie. They eagerly said yes to all.

"First class is so cool." Nate was squirming in the oversized seat. "Look how much room we have," he exclaimed.

"I know, it was so worth it, right?"

"Definitely!"

Admittedly, Fiona felt like a little kid, playing grown-up. She thought of all that had happened in the past year and how each piece of her story fit so perfectly into someone else's puzzle. Her thoughts wandered and eventually settled on Carter. Fiona wondered how he was doing when the babies were due, and when he and Meg planned to marry. Her heart ached to the point of breaking all over again. She knew she needed a distraction.

"Hey Nate, you never told me what your favorite part of our trip was."

"Oh," he began as he avoided choking on a tiny pretzel. "I really loved the tour of the rooftop gardens. I mean, all the touristy things are great, but kind of boring; except the double deck bus; that was awesome."

"It was, wasn't it? We need more of those in New York."

"The buses, or the gardens?" Nate asked.

"Well, both. There isn't much we can do about the cool buses, but we can help create more gardens. I'm excited to get to work. I hope Kay is doing well by herself this week. I really wish she could have come with us. You know, I really admire her; she takes such good care of Charlie's family."

"His grandmother is sick?" Nate asked, trying to clarify the few bits of overheard conversation between Kay and Fiona before they left for London.

"Sort of, she's showing signs of dementia. Although she insists she's perfectly fine, Charlie and his mom decided it was best to have some tests run, and for her to have help with the girls until they figured out what to do for her."

"That makes me sad. Is there anything we can do?"

"Yes, of course. We cover for Kay at work. If she needs time with her family, you and I will make sure we take up the slack on the project. Kay and Charlie both need to know they have a support system in their friends."

"Fiona?"

"Hmmmm?"

"What does it feel like to be in love?"

Fiona was caught off guard by Nate's abrupt change in subject. She paused for a few moments before attempting to answer.

"Well, I think it's different for everyone, so that may be difficult to explain, but I'll try."

Nate sat silently waiting for her to speak. Fiona turned to face her young friend.

"It feels like you are the only two people in the world. When you're together, everything else falls away, but at the same time, everything else matters even more. Somehow, food tastes better, music is sweeter, trees are greener, you get the picture, right?"

"I do."

"Nate, do you think you're in love?"

"I have no idea. I mean, yeah, but I shouldn't be."

"Wendy."

"If I say yes, you'll think I'm a creep. She's too young for me, I know. I just can't help how I feel. I want to be there for her, always."

"First of all; I already suspected that you've fallen for her, so no worries there. Second, you are not a creep. Third, yes, the age difference is an issue, but only for now. I know fourteen and seventeen seem unfathomable, but in a few years, eighteen and twenty-one will seem normal and twenty-one and twenty-five will be perfect; get my point? It's not so much her age that is concerning, Nate, but her capacity to understand love at her age."

"Do you think she could ever love me?"

"I think she already does, but there's a distinct difference between loving someone and being in love. You feel in love and Wendy doesn't even know what that is yet. She does love you, and more importantly, she trusts you. The best advice I can offer is to continue to cultivate this amazing friendship you two have; keep that bond strong. If and when she realizes she's in love with you too, you'll be right there, in her life, by her side. You know, I wasn't much older than Wendy when I fell in love with Carter. Had we met the year before, things might have played out very differently for both of us. We wouldn't have dated, and by the time I realized how perfect he was for me, he would have likely been dating someone else."

"I swear, Fiona, when Wendy starts dating, I won't survive."

Fiona couldn't stop herself from laughing; "I'm sorry Nate, I'm not laughing at you, it's just that I felt that way when I found out Carter was dating Meg. I thought for sure my entire life would implode; but it didn't. I survived and you will too. Try not to think about that, just focus on the positive and see where it takes you; both of you."

"She's really incredible. I can't help thinking of all she had to deal with just to survive. She was so young to be on her own, and yet she somehow knew that was better than being placed in a bad home. Her life could have been really difficult, or worse, over. It's like Wendy has been blessed; like she exists for a greater purpose, you know?"

"I agree, Nate, and I believe that about you too." Fiona's thoughts once again landed on Carter. She paralleled Nate's teen angst with her own. The thought of acting as if the world would end without Carter made her feel embarrassed, but she certainly didn't want Nate to regret telling her how he felt. He had endured more in seventeen years than most kids his age will over their entire lifetime. The last thing Fiona wanted for Nate was to think his feelings had no validity; that no one cared.

Fiona raised the plastic shade on the airplane window. She could see the city below them shrouded in grey smog and cloud cover. The high-rise buildings barely poked through the overcast skies, but Fiona was somehow comforted; they were finally home. Once the flight attendant permitted cell phone use, Fiona sent Kay a text.

Landing now; may be a while to get through customs, see you soon. Happy to be home.

Charlie had the advantage of parking in the taxi and limo area in front of the airport. He stood outside the car, trying to seem very official while Kay waited in the front seat. He noticed people staring at the car, then glancing toward the doors in an attempt to figure out if Charlie was in fact there to pick up someone famous. He was used to the public gawking, and usually they were completely satisfied to see Anthony and/or Laurel Cooke approach his car. Today, however, Fiona and Nate may prove to be a bit disappointing to the onlookers. Charlie decided he would give them something to talk about as he saw his friends about to exit the terminal. He rushed to their side, grabbing their carry-on luggage and bowed as if it were a respectable greeting for people of a higher status. Fiona shot him a look of confusion, but Nate caught on quickly.

"Thank you, Charles. Your service is always excellent." Nate reached for his sunglasses and put them on as he gave an awkward wave in the general direction of the small cluster of people watching from the walkway.

Charlie almost burst into laughter as he popped the trunk and loaded their larger bags. He opened the back door for his passengers; but before Nate climbed in, he turned to the crowd and waved again. Much to everyone's amusement; they all waved back.

"Oh, for God's sake, Get in the car!" Fiona demanded, giving Nate a shove on the shoulder.

Fiona and Nate were visibly exhausted, but all too willing to share stories of their London adventures with Charlie and Kay as they made their way out of the city toward home. Nate interjected.

"And that guy Philip was a total ass to Fiona, and I really wanted to find him and punch his teeth in."

"Ah, yes. And as much as I appreciated the sentiment, the decision to come back early seemed much more civilized." Fiona did appreciate Nate, and there would have been a level of satisfaction in seeing Philip knocked out. However, she knew it was her responsibility, both personally and professionally to teach Nate the mature way of handling difficult situations. Kay and Charlie kept rather quiet as to avoid undermining Fiona but secretly Charlie wanted to give Nate a high five.

"Almost home," Charlie announced as he pulled off the freeway.

"You two are going to stay for a while, right?" Fiona offered.

"Oh, honey, I know you are exhausted; we can just drop you off and head back to the city." Kay was being polite. She had hoped for an invitation to stay. After a week of caregiving, Kay was craving some socialization.

"No, really. I'd love it if you guys hung out for a while. Do you have to be back in the city right away?"

"Actually, no. Charlie's mom is off tonight; she has everything under control and I'm dying to get the details about that Philip guy."

"Then it's settled. We can get dinner, and just catch up."

Charlie and Nate unloaded the trunk while Fiona and Kay went inside. Fiona thought it was eerily quiet in the house despite knowing her mother, Nicky and Rob were all home.

"Hey, hello?" she called from the front hall.

"Fiona?" Susan asked

"Yeah Mom, we're home," she answered, stepping through the living room threshold. Fiona wasn't prepared for the somber scene of Laurel and Susan sitting silently on the couch; drinking coffee while Wendy rested her head in Susan's lap.

"Jesus, who died?" Fiona joked, but no one laughed, or responded to her rhetorical question. "Oh, Oh, no, I was kidding, did someone really die?" Fiona asked frantically. She began taking inventory in her head, "Nicky? Where's Nicky? Is he OK? Rob! Where are the guys? Mom, you're scaring me."

Wendy sat up, but stayed next to Susan who straightened her legs and turned to face Fiona. Kay, Charlie and Nate were standing behind Fiona trying to read the room.

"Sit down honey," Susan offered.

"No, I don't want to sit, someone tell me what happened!"

"Fiona, we lost Wanda. I'm so sorry."

Fiona's eyes welled with tears.

"No, no, no, no, no, not my girl," she sobbed.

Wendy stood and went to Fiona's side. She gently took her hand and led her to the couch. Wendy sat back down next to Susan and gave Fiona's hand a gentle tug. Fiona felt her legs buckle as she collapsed onto the couch.

"What happened?" she asked between sobs.

"Fee, she was almost fifteen yers old; she was just tired. She didn't suffer, and I was with her when she died." Susan told her grieving daughter. "The guys took her to the vet to be cremated. We will have her remains back in a few days. I hope I made the right decision there. I thought it's what you'd want."

"Yes, yes. I would have done the same." Fiona reached for a tissue and noticed Nate was gone. She turned to Wendy, "Go check on Nate. He's either in his room or the office."

Wendy obliged. She looked first in Fiona's office, but only Harry occupied the room. He had been laying on the fold-out bed in the spot where Wanda took her last breath. She went in and gave him a hug and kissed his nose.

"I know, boy. I miss her too."

She quietly ascended the stairs to Nate's loft room; and found him unpacking his bags.

"Hey, you OK?" she asked. Nate avoided eye contact. He didn't want Wendy to know he'd been crying, but she knew he had. "It's perfectly normal to cry, you know. I've been doing it all day. Wanda was like everyone's dog; our best friend and the start of our weird family. Feeling sad is good, Nate; it means you care. How amazing is it that you and I have so much to care about? I mean, just a few months ago, we had nothing and no one. Now, we have this crazy life with these crazy people, and we have each other."

Nate began to sob. Wendy went to him and wrapped her arms around his waist and rested her head against his chest. Nate hugged her back and secretly hoped she'd never let go.

"I love you," she whispered. It was sweet and comforting, much like a sister to a brother, but Nate hadn't been told by anyone in his life that he was loved. He hung on her words, and in that moment Nate felt content. If he never heard those words again, it wouldn't matter. She loved him at that very moment, and that's all he needed.

Reunion

Nicky peered through the glass doors from the back patio.

"Fiona's home early," he announced. Rob, Carter and Nicky had been talking outside on the patio for hours. They told stories, reminisced and drank beer in solidarity as each of them dealt with the loss of Wanda.

Carter panicked.

"Oh, I cannot be here! How are we going to explain this to Fee? She's been through enough; I can't just walk in and say hi." He ran in place for a moment, resembling a cartoon character; unable to decide on a direction. Rob tried not to laugh, but Nicky assured him she'd understand.

"Carter, I know Fiona and I really believe she will be grateful for you being here and helping Susan with Wanda. You don't have to say anything, I'll tell her why you've been staying with us. She's not going to be upset."

"Well, if she does get upset, she'll have every right," Carter was obviously worried.

"Let's go in and talk to her," Rob offered, sliding the glass doors open.

Carter cautiously followed Nicky and Rob back in the house. He stopped in the kitchen as they proceeded to join Fiona in the living room. She had turned around when she heard the sliding doors open and was surprised to see Carter, but still too distraught to respond. Nicky sat down next to her while Carter took a seat at the kitchen table.

"Fee, how are you honey?" he asked.

"I've had better days, Nicky. Thanks for being here for Mom."

"Actually, I wasn't much help. I kind of fell apart. However, Carter really stepped up, and before you freak out on me, let me explain why he's here."

"I'm not going to freak out."

Nicky leaned in closer.

"Rob and I ran into Carter down the shore. Seemed like he could use some time with friends, so we invited him here for a few days. In my defense, you weren't supposed to be back for another two days."

"It's fine, Nick. You live here too. I'm not upset, really."

"Fee, the twins aren't Carter's, they're Eddie's," Nick whispered.

"Ohhhhh, that is so not good," she whispered back, reaching for another tissue to blow her nose. "Poor Carter, he must be devastated."

"Yeah, so you can understand why he's here, right? If this is too weird for you, Rob offered to drive Carter back to New Jersey tonight."

"Not necessary. Let's all just take a breath. It's been a long damn day, and the last thing any of us needs is to make it even longer." Fiona adjusted her position on the couch and turned toward the kitchen, "Hey Carter, thanks for everything." Her words were sincere.

Laurel and Kay had been cleaning up in the kitchen. Kay caught Carter's attention.

"Go!" she mouthed, gesturing toward Fiona.

He stood and walked over to the couch. She looked up, right into his eyes, and he felt his insides melt. He couldn't stop staring at her. He wondered how he could have been so stupid; giving up the privileged of staring into her eyes every day for the rest of his life; and for what? Certainly, his mistakes brought no satisfaction, no reward. His life was no better, no richer, just empty and filled with regret. He never thought he'd see her again, never mind be here in her house, standing right in front of her; he wanted to tell her he still loved her, but no words came. Instead, he sat down quietly next to her.

"Nicky told me she slept with you," Fiona began

Carter seemed uneasy.

"We are talking about Wanda, right?"

Fiona chuckled.

"Yes, the dog. Oh, Carter, today is not the day to have that conversation," she assured him.

"Maybe that day doesn't ever have to come?"

"Maybe."

Fiona didn't want or need any explanation from Carter regarding his time with Meg. It was no longer a vital part of her story; not really. Losing Carter made her stronger, less vulnerable and more willing to take risks. If not for Carter making his choice to be with Meg, she wouldn't be where she was; both personally and professionally. Sometimes life works that way; the right people can be in your life at the wrong time. When that happens, the Universe has a way of removing them. If they were meant to be, then Fiona supposed, the Universe would bring them back. What a beautiful notion, she thought. If it has any validity outside of her own interpretations then maybe she and Carter could have another chance to be together. She thought of her conversation with Nate; their story was indeed being written long before she was shot.

Carter pressed his back into the corner of the sectional, carefully avoiding contact with Fiona. She was exhausted and in need of sleep; the idea of Carter being her source of comfort was so inviting, Fiona leaned in to rest her head on his shoulder. She tucked her legs up under her and closed her eyes. Carter reached for the blanket draped over the back of the couch and pulled it over her. Within minutes, Fiona was fast asleep, and Carter felt as though he was already dreaming.

Laurel and Wendy said their goodbyes, and once again headed home for the evening. Rob suggested Charlie and Kay stay the night instead of driving back into the city so late. They agreed, and Susan offered them Fiona's room.

"I didn't think I'd ever see my daughter this content again," Susan confessed as she walked Laurel and Wendy to the door.

Wendy interjected.

"Carter is so cute!"

The two women laughed, and Laurel had to agree.

"Yes, he's adorable. After spending some time with him, I understand why Fiona never stopped loving Carter."

"I believe he never stopped loving her either," Susan added.

Dumpster Dogs

Mrs Wyatt packed for their trip to California so she and her husband could spend Christmas with their oldest son and his family. She had hoped Carter would join them, but knowing he was with Fiona made her happier than anything. Carter had called to let her know he was extending his stay with Nicky, Rob and Fiona, and to give Sam and his family a hug from him when she got to California. He sounded better than he had in years; excited to go to the mall with the guys for a few last-minute gifts and some extra clothing for himself to get through another week or two. Mrs Wyatt raised her eyes as if to look to the heavens.

"Thank you for bringing happiness back into Carter's life," she said aloud.

On their way back from the mall, Carter noticed an animal shelter, just a few miles from Fiona's house.

"Hey, do you guys know anything about that shelter? Is it a reputable place?" he asked.

Rob was very familiar with the establishment; "It's a great place. That shelter has been around as long as I can remember. Every year at this time, our parents would take us to make a donation. Sarah and I would volunteer to play with the puppies and kittens and walk some of the larger dogs. When Sarah was around Wendy's age, she fell in love with a black and white kitten. There was just something about him over all the others that won Sarah's heart. Of course my parents adopted him."

"That's so cool. Is he still around?" Carter inquired.

"Yeah, he's only six, I believe. His name is Penguin, and he's still Sarah's best friend."

"Could we possibly go back there later? I'd like to make a donation."

"Sure, let's check in at the house and we'll go back in a while. I'll call Sarah and see if she'd like to go with us."

Carter thought for a moment.

"Maybe Wendy would like to go as well."

Nicky turned around in the front seat to address Carter.

"I think you may have just given us our first Christmas tradition together."

A few hours later, the five of them entered the shelter through the main doors. It was cheerfully decorated, with a fake tree in one corner. Under the tree were piles of blankets, towels, and bags of food for both dogs and cats. Off to the side was a cardboard box wrapped to resemble a Christmas present. Wendy looked inside to find toys, bones and smaller bags of food and treats. The abundance of offerings had them all feeling hopeful and filled with holiday spirit.

Rob and Sarah approached the customer service counter and explained that they'd like to make a monetary donation. The young woman asked if they wanted to donate in someone's name.

"Yes!" Wendy piped up.

The woman handed Rob a form to fill out.

"Go ahead and list your names and the name or names of those you'd like your donation to be in. You don't have to list the amount, just the names."

Wendy whispered to Sarah.

"Write in the name of our dumpster dogs."

Sarah smiled.

"I love that!" She continued to fill out the donation form listing everyone's name and at the very bottom Sarah wrote; *This donation is dedicated to Wanda and Harry; Mrs and Mr Dumpster Dog.*

She showed it to Wendy for approval.

"That's perfect."

The woman behind the desk read the form and looked up at her donors; "This is great. It's funny you mention dumpster dogs though, we had a litter of puppies come in last week that were found abandoned in a dumpster behind a department store."

Wendy and Carter exchanged glances as if they shared a thought.

"Can we see them?" Wendy asked.

"Sure. I bet they would love to have a little play time; would you want to take them into the visiting room for a while?"

Sarah and Wendy pleaded with the guys.

"Can we play with the puppies, please?"

Rob could never say no to his younger sister.

"Of course."

The shelter worker led them into the puppy room which immediately burst into loud choruses of barking and whining. So many little lives wanting attention; waiting for a home; it was heartbreaking. Sarah noticed the tears forming in Wendy's eyes and reminded her that being in a shelter is a hell of a lot better than a dumpster.

"These are the lucky one's. They will eat today and sleep soundly tonight. And, although they may not yet have a forever home, the workers here do everything they can to make sure they're all adopted."

Wendy shook her head; wiped her tears and followed Sarah into the play area where the shelter worker had just placed two Pitbull puppies.

"Oh," she sighed, Wendy was already in love.

"There were five pups in all," the woman explained. "Three of their siblings have already been adopted, and these two have grown very close to one another. I don't know of many families willing to adopt two spirited Pitbull puppies, but I do hope the little brothers are able to stay together."

Once again, Carter and Wendy exchanged looks. Carter asked.

"What is the adoption process?" He was more convinced than before as he watched the pups interact with Wendy and Sarah. They were gentle and affectionate and reminded him of Harry.

The shelter worker explained that an application must be submitted, and a home check performed before they could go to any home.

"We could schedule a home check for the day after Christmas," she informed them.

Waiting until then was not a deal breaker for Carter, but he was admittedly disappointed. He and Wendy were both hoping to surprise Fiona for Christmas.

"Thank you," he said. "would you give us a few minutes?"

Carter turned first to Rob and Nicky.

"Would either of you object to having these two dogs join your family?" Of course, neither objected, and immediately began making plans to accommodate the two pups. Wendy suddenly stood and walked into the hall. She whispered to Carter as she passed, "Give me a minute." She took her phone from her pocket and dialed Laurel. "Laur? I need a gigantic favor. It's so big, you can consider it my Christmas present."

"OK, I will do my best; what is it honey?"

"I know this is wrong, I do, but Carter wants to adopt puppies for Fiona for Christmas. The shelter lady told us they had to do a home check, and it would take days to schedule it; which means after Christmas. Carter is going to do it anyway, with Nick and Rob of course, but is there any way you could talk them into letting us take the puppies today? Oh, and if so, can they stay with us for two days until Christmas Eve?"

"That is a really big favor, Wendy! But, what good is being a Cooke if you can't use your name to get things done? Let me speak with the woman who works there, I'll see what I can do."

"Thank you!" Wendy handed her phone to the shelter worker. "Would you please speak with my mom?"

Laurel felt as though her heart would explode when she heard Wendy call her Mom. She quickly composed herself and presented their case to the woman on the phone.

"Hello, my name is Laurel Cooke and my daughter, and our friends would very much like to adopt the puppies they're visiting with. However, the pups would be a special Christmas gift for another friend, and we were hoping I could expedite the adoption process with my personal endorsement. My daughter will gladly provide our information on the application as well. I can tell you the puppies would have the best home they could imagine. The yard is fenced in, and there are three responsible adults, and one very responsible teenager in the home. Is this something we could work out?"

Wendy watched the woman pull up the application on her computer and begin typing. She hung up with Laurel and returned Wendy's phone.

"Go get the primary adopter, hon. We can have you out of here in a few minutes; all of you."

Wendy ran to get Carter.

"I need you. They're ours, today. Go fill out the application."

The drive back to the Cooke's proved to be a challenge, with five people and two squirming puppies crammed in Rob's car.

"I think one peed back here," Sarah informed them. Somehow, the puppy's accident lended to the excitement of their adoption and Fiona's pending surprise.

"No worries," Rob said. "It's all part of the process. Cars can be cleaned. The important thing is giving these cute little guys a great home." Although Rob was well aware that the pups were to be a gift for Fiona, he was already attached.

Wendy walked the puppies in on their shelter provided leashes, to find TC standing just inside the door. She smiled coyly, hoping he wasn't too upset.

TC took the leashes from Wendy and guided the pups inside. He couldn't help his prideful feeling, knowing Wendy was confident enough to use the Cooke name to her advantage.

"So, how does it feel to be a Cooke?" he asked her.

Wendy breathed a sigh of relief.

"You aren't upset?"

"Not even a little," he assured her. "You do know, that won't always work though. I prefer you not take advantage, but I do know this time your heart was in the right place."

"Thank you. I did this for Carter and for Fiona. I knew you and Laurel would understand."

"We do. Now, let's introduce these little guys to Harry."

That night, snuggled next to Harry and his tiny sidekicks, Wendy had an idea of her own. She wanted to give Fiona a special Christmas gift as well, something from her heart. She grabbed her laptop and began typing:

When she was just a little pup, the dog with one blue eye, met a horrible human who hurt her and made her cry.

He picked her up and carried her away. She thought he was there to save the day. All she wanted was to be loved and fed, but the human who first found her, left her for dead.

He opened the mouth of the metal monster and threw her tiny body inside; no one could see her, and no one could hear her as she began to cry.

It was dark and scary with no way to climb free, she whimpered, scratched, and barked for days until it happened, finally.

Another human came along; but this one was kind and good; he struggled and strained as it started to rain, but he did what a good human should.

He freed her from the monster and ran to get her help; grateful that she was alive, and that he heard her yelp.

Many years had passed; and the dog with one blue eye, met a friend who told her he was also cast aside.

"Do people think it's funny, or are people just that mean, to throw away our little lives; never to be seen?"

She gave her friend a sloppy kiss and nuzzled his handsome face, "Don't think about the trouble, forget about the pain, just remember the good human who gave you a life again."

You and I were lucky; so many dogs out there; may never know a place called home, with people who truly care.

So please be kind and patient and teach your new little friends to love; I promise you, I'll be there too, watching from above.

Wendy printed the poem and a picture of Wanda and Harry from her phone. She snapped a few of the pups lying beside her and selected the cutest of the bunch to print as well. Tomorrow, she thought, she'd look for a frame with three sides, one for each photo and her poem in the middle. Laurel had a stash of frames in her studio that she'd been collecting from yard sales and thrift stores. Wendy had already decorated one for Nate and was sure she remembered a three-sided frame in one of those boxes. Pleased with her gift idea for Fiona, Wendy fell asleep thinking of Wanda, and surrounded by her dumpster dogs.

Greatest Gifts

Christmas Eve morning was more magical than Wendy had anticipated as it began to snow. She felt positively giddy as she watched the puppies run around the yard with Harry biting at the falling flakes. Never before had she experienced the feeling of the holiday; but if this is what everyone meant by Christmas magic, it was worth the wait.

Laurel joined her soon to be daughter on the back patio and handed her a mug of hot chocolate with a candy cane and mini marshmallows.

"Seems like a hot chocolate kind of morning," she said.

"Thank you. This is perfect, all of it."

"All of what, sweetie?"

"Christmas. It's perfect. This has to be my best day ever."

"Wendy, I'm glad you're happy, but you do know, Christmas isn't even really here yet. We have the party tonight at Fiona's and of course Christmas Day here at our house tomorrow. There's a lot more Christmas to be had."

"Laurel, I can't imagine anything more than what I have right now. Although, I am crazy excited to give everyone their gifts. We really worked hard on them, and I know everyone will go nuts."

"I bet they will. I'm most excited to give Nate his gifts. They turned out amazing; you and I make a great team. Joe offered to bring them to Fiona's for us. His truck is much bigger than our vehicle."

"We do make a great team; our whole family. I'm going to get the little guys in before they get cold and give them some breakfast. I'm glad they're going to their real home tonight. If I spend much more time with them, I'll be too attached to give them up, even to Fiona."

"Oh, is that so? Are you trying to tell me that Harry may need another little friend of his own?"

"Maybe someday, but for now, it's all about these two. What do you think Fiona will name them? I've been calling them Red and Blue, you know, like the colors in the photo of Fiona and Carter."

"That's clever! But, I suppose it will be up to Fiona to name them."

"Laurel?"

"Yeah honey?"

"Can I start calling you, Mom?"

"I'd like that. We both would. But, when you call TC Dad for the first time, let me be there to see his face, OK?"

"Deal."

"Now, let's feed our boys and finish cooking for tonight."

Fiona's house was rather chaotic with Christmas Eve preparation. Although Susan was happy to lend her expertise, this was the first big event Fiona, Nicky and Rob had ever hosted. It was becoming increasingly more difficult to keep Susan's gift a secret, especially for Nicky who wanted nothing more than to tell her his mother would be coming to the party with Linda and Chris.

Every time Carter looked at Fiona, he had to quell his own excitement. He had moments of pure anxiety wondering if the puppies were the best gift idea. Was it too soon after losing Wanda? Would Fiona want the responsibility of two new pups? Was it too soon to give such a special gift? He tried to push all doubt from his mind, but couldn't afford to make any mistakes; not with Fiona, not so soon after their reconciliation. He kept checking his watch; time moved so slowly, and Carter felt as though five o'clock would never come.

Nate struggled with gift wrapping and almost completely gave up. He had no recollection of ever receiving a gift, never mind wrapping gifts for others. He rifled through the small pile of shopping bags on his bedroom floor, second-guessing each purchase. How could he ever properly reciprocate? Rob was teaching him to drive, Nicky was helping him study for his GED, and Fiona, well, she had given him the greatest gift of all; a home. Nate began to wish he had been more elaborate in his gift selections; a sweater, scarf, and bracelet suddenly seemed like meager offerings. However, time was up; it was Christmas Eve and all he could do was hope for the best. If he could manage to get his gifts properly wrapped, he'd feel more confident about giving them. Nate checked his handwritten list of names for the twentieth time, making certain he hadn't forgotten anyone. He even remembered a gift for Jaime and Joe, just something to show his gratitude for all the gifts Jaime bought when he first met everyone, and for

Joe's patience when Nate asked a myriad of questions during any sporting event on TV. The gift Nate was most worried about was the one he bought for Wendy. What do you give to the girl who suddenly has everything? Nate chose to give her his heart; well a heart anyway. He had spent nearly his entire paycheck on a gold necklace with a heart locket and had it engraved with Wendy's new initials.

"WC". As he tried one more time to wrap his gifts, Nate thought to himself, *I don't think Christmas is supposed to be this stressful*.

"Where's Nate?" Jaime asked, popping her head through the back door of Fiona's kitchen. Susan answered.

"Upstairs, why?"

"We have his gifts from the Cooke's. Joe and I can bring them back here for now. I think it will be easier to get them into the house later."

Susan was confused.

"OK, I guess. What kind of gift needs to be left in the yard? You aren't about to tell me they got him a pony, are you?" she teased.

"Ha, oh, no, nothing like that. Laurel and Wendy refinished two vintage dressers. They painted them and replaced the hardware. Susan, they're awesome, wait til you see them. Of course, they needed Joe's truck to get them over here. So, we were thinking we could leave them out back under a tarp until everyone arrives."

"I see. I have to tell you, Jaime. I'm relieved it really isn't a pony. Do you need help? Nicky's home, I'll go get him."

"Yes, please!"

Joe and Nicky managed to get the dressers against the house, under the overhang and covered them with two tarps.

"Just in case it starts to snow again," Joe said. He and Jaime explained they had more gifts and food at their house to bring over and would return in about an hour.

"I'm so excited for tonight," Susan confessed. "It's been so crazy over the past few months; we all need a night to be together and celebrate."

Jaime hugged her.

"I promise, we'll be back as soon as we can. I know TC, Laurel and Wendy will be here soon. They're also delivering a special gift for Fiona."

Fiona sat on the floor in her bedroom amidst piles of shopping bags and boxes from her online shopping deliveries. There were three different designs of wrapping paper strewn about, and somewhere among the flurry of paper, she was sure there were scissors and at least two rolls of tape. She dug in, pulling the contents from one of the shopping bags onto her lap. With just an hour left until everyone was due to arrive; Fiona knew she had to get the wrapping underway. She managed to wrestle a scarf for her mother into a tiny gift bag when there was a knock at her door.

"If you're my mother, do not come in. Anyone else is clear to enter," she called out.

"It's me, Carter."

"You may enter." she teased.

Carter slowly pushed the door open and peered inside Fiona's room. He wasn't surprised to see Fiona scrambling to wrap her gifts at the last minute.

"You know, I could help you if you'd like?" he offered.

"Yeah, sure. Just let me find yours and put it to the side. No one should have to wrap their own gift."

"You didn't have to get me anything."

"Oh, whatever, Carter," she joked, picking up a box and throwing it on her bed. "There, now, just grab, wrap and I'll tag, OK?"

"Sure. Listen, there's something I'd like to say though, I don't mean to get all serious, but I wanted to thank you for letting me stay, and for not killing me in my sleep."

Fiona laughed and tossed a roll of tape at Carter.

"The thought never even crossed my mind."

"Liar." Carter picked up the tape and secured his first wrapped box. "Ready for this?" he asked, handing it to Fiona so she could tag it.

"Yep, that was for Rob," she said, as she wrote on a little whimsical sticker that read, *from, Santa.*

"Fee, I know when the holidays are over, I'll be headed home. I was wondering if it would be ok to come back sometime?" Carter couldn't hide his insecurities; his eyes lowered, and his cheeks flushed.

"Carter, if I had things my way, you would just stay here with us, with me. I know that sounds crazy, given the time we have been apart, but I feel like things between us could be good again. It's way too soon, I know, and it's probably the whole Christmas thing that has me feeling this way, so take my words for what they're worth. I might just be wishing for something that isn't there anymore. You and I aren't kids; we've been through so much since we have been apart, and aren't the same people who fell in love, are we?"

"Fiona, I'd love nothing more than to stay with you forever. I want to just forget about the time we spent apart and spend every minute, starting now, loving you. You're right, we aren't those kids anymore, but that doesn't mean we aren't meant to be together. I want the opportunity to prove myself to you, so you can trust me, I really want to be the man you deserve."

Fiona stopped wrapping the box in front of her, and just sat with her thoughts for a moment. Carter felt as though an eternity had passed before she finally spoke; "I do trust you. As insane as that is; I believe you love me, and I believe you always have, and I trust you. Maybe I shouldn't, maybe I'm being overly optimistic here, but I just know I can. Carter, I'm just better when you're with me. I don't care about your mistakes or my mistakes; I only care about this moment. Everything that has happened to us has led us here, so who am I to deny the signs? My life got so crazy over the past few months, and you jumped right in all that crazy and made it your own; no questions, just blind faith. How can I deny that? I won't make you prove yourself over and again when you already have."

"May I kiss you?" he asked

"I think so."

He leaned over the myriad of packages piled on the floor between them and kissed her, ever so softly. She leaned back just a little, he moved closer and kissed her again. Every cell in her body reacted; it was as if they shared their very first kiss for the second time.

"Merry Christmas, Fiona."

"Carter."

"Hmmm?"

"Will you stay?"

"I never want to leave you again."

It's a Wonderful Life

Susan and Nicky busied themselves in the kitchen while Rob placed gifts under the tree, as per Susan's instructions. The first of their guests had arrived, and Christmas was officially underway. Kay, Charlie and his two sisters, Lexi and Erika made themselves comfortable in the living room. Kay offered her help to Susan who graciously declined; "You're our guest tonight, relax and enjoy. Can I get anyone anything?" she asked.

Charlie looked to his sisters as if to give permission to answer. Lexi, the older of the two, spoke for them both.

"May we have something to drink?"

"Hot chocolate, or a soda?" Susan offered. Lexi and Erika opted for the former. By nature, neither Wheeler's sister had a shy personality, but they were previously instructed to be on their best behavior. Kay couldn't wait for them to finally meet Wendy. She was thrilled when Laurel suggested she and Charlie include the girls.

"It will be so great for Wendy to start meeting kids her own age, you know making friends is so important." Laurel, however, wasn't just considering Wendy when she invited the girls; Charlie wanted them to be a part of the Christmas surprise they had planned for Kay.

The front door swung open with a bang, and Wendy ran into the house yelling for Carter.

"Oh, Carter, where are you? We need you. Has anyone seen Carter?" Her voice carried through the entire house, and Carter indeed heard her beckon. He stood from his place on Fiona's bedroom floor and told Fiona she'd have to finish wrapping without him.

"Um, I have to help Wendy with something, so I'll be back in a few to bring the gifts out for you."

"OK, I will venture to say, I shouldn't ask what that's all about."

"Good call. I'll be right back." Carter quickened his pace down the hall and into the living room where he found Wendy waiting impatiently.

"Where can we put the puppies?" she whispered.

Rob offered the small room next to his and Nick's bedroom.

"We're slowly turning that room into our den. There isn't much in there. I think the pups will be safe there for a bit."

"Thank you. Let's bring them in," Carter said. "I'll stand guard in the hall to make sure Fiona doesn't come out of her room."

TC and Laurel each ushered the puppies through the house and into the room next to Rob and Nicks. The Wheeler girls tried to contain their excitement but seeing two cute puppies walk by solicited a few muffled squeals. Wendy smiled at them.

"Don't worry, they'll be back out soon. Here, you can pet Harry for now," she said, gently pushing Harry in the direction of the couch. Lexi and Erika both called for Harry to join them and of course, he wasn't about to turn down a comfy place on the couch next to people who wanted to pet him. The girls fussed over him, and Harry turned on his back for belly rubs. "Awe, he's such a good boy," They gushed.

Jaime and Joe were the next to arrive; toting arms full of brightly colored boxes and bags.

"Merry Christmas!" Joe shouted in his best Santa voice. "Ho, Ho, Ho." Nate heard Joe's bellow and knew it was time to come downstairs. He struggled with his own offerings but somehow made it all the way to the tree without dropping a single box. Fifteen-year-old Lexi Wheeler nearly choked on her hot chocolate when she saw Nate. She turned to her younger sister and whispered.

"Whoa, that guy is gorgeous."

Satisfied with the temporary placement of the pups, Wendy joined the rest of the guests in Fiona's living room. She and Nate hugged, sharing a moment of gratitude for their newfound family.

"Merry Christmas."

"Merry Christmas, Nate, oh, wait till you see your presents. I'm so excited," she chirped.

Lexi immediately recognized their connection; "Oh well, looks like he's taken," she told Erika. Lexi's twelve-year-old sister was still in her 'boys are gross' phase and didn't pay much attention to her sister's comments. She was more interested in Harry and what time they would be eating. "I'm so hungry," was her only response.

Wendy took it upon herself to make the introductions.

"I'm Wendy, and this is my friend Nate. You must be Charlie's sisters," she assumed. Lexi and Erika introduced themselves and asked Wendy about the puppies. She sat down beside Erika and in a low voice began to tell them about Carter's surprise for Fiona. "As soon as everyone gets here, they will be the very first gift given," she explained.

"Who are we waiting for? Dinner is ready!" Susan announced.

Nick answered.

"My sister and Chris. I just heard from them. They'll be here in five minutes." He watched for a reaction, but Susan gave no indication that she knew about Maria joining them. Nick went to the front door and watched out the window, like a child waiting for Santa himself. "They're here!"

Carter and Fiona had managed to get her gifts out of her room and under the tree just in time for the last of their guests to arrive. Linda and Chris walked in ahead of Maria, shielding her from Susan until they could reveal their surprise.

"Susan, Merry Christmas!" Linda said as she stepped into the kitchen. As Susan looked up to return the greeting, Linda stepped aside.

"Merry Christmas my friend," Maria offered, holding out her arms.

"Oh, Oh, my God, you're here! Merry Christmas!" Susan immediately became emotional, embracing her best friend. "Oh, Maria, I've missed you," she sobbed. Everyone felt the love and warmth from the reunited friends and gave them a moment to simply enjoy the surprise.

"OK, I can't take it anymore. You all must be famished. Dinner is buffet style, so make your plate whenever you're ready. In the meantime; we have a few more special gifts that cannot wait. Carter, I believe you're up next," Nick announced. Admittedly, he was a bit worried about the puppies making a mess in his den.

Carter looked over to Wendy.

"Wanna give me a hand?"

She got up and followed Carter into the hall which led to Rob and Nick's side of the house. They both paused for a moment before opening the door.

"I hope they didn't trash that room!"

"Let's find out," he said, opening the door. Much to their relief, Carter and Wendy found two sleeping puppies curled up together in the corner of the room. "Awe, they are really amazing. Dumpster dogs are the best, aren't they?"

Wendy agreed as she picked up their leashes and handed them to Carter.

"Laurel and I got them proper leashes and collars. I didn't think you'd mind."

"Oh, thank you so much. I really appreciate that." He stopped for a second to hug Wendy. "I couldn't have done this without you."

Rob and Nick intentionally distracted Fiona with conversation while Carter ushered the pups into the living room. She noticed them out of the corner of her eye, but the reality took a moment to sink in.

"Wait! are those puppies?" Fiona stood and made her way over to Carter. "You have puppies?" she exclaimed.

"No, you have puppies," he corrected. "Merry Christmas, Fee." Still, in awe, Fiona sat back down on the corner of the couch. Carter walked the pups closer to her.

"They're brothers. They'll need names and you know what, Fee? These little guys were found abandoned in a dumpster. Wendy and I figured they were meant to be a part of your family."

Fiona began to cry; she thought of Wanda and couldn't imagine how anyone could toss puppies in the trash. She thought Wanda was in a unique situation until she met Wendy and Harry. Now, hearing these beautiful little souls had the same thing happen to them not only broke her heart but made her question the good of humanity she wanted so badly to believe in.

"They're really mine?" she asked

"Yes, they are. I know it's a huge responsibility, but Nate, Rob, and Nicky all agreed to help out. And, I'll be here too," Carter told her. "Let's get them outside first, then they can meet everyone."

"Oh wait." Wendy piped up. "First, can we bring Nate's gifts in?"

Nick, Rob and Joe agreed to carry in the two dressers that had been stashed just outside the glass doors.

"Merry Christmas, Nate. These are from the Cooke family," Joe told him.

The dressers were painted in hues of grey with black and white accents. The drawer handles were changed from the original design to sleek bright red pulls, giving them a very classy, yet masculine makeover. Wendy couldn't contain her excitement.

"Do you like them? Laurel and I painted them just for you. I thought we could start decorating your room now that you officially live here."

Nate was speechless. He never had his own furniture, or even enough clothing to warrant the need for one dresser, never mind two. He loved the colors and began daydreaming of all the things he'd like to have in his room. Wendy's voice reeled his thoughts back into reality.

"Well?" she asked impatiently.

"I love them. Thank you all so much. I can't believe you did this for me."

Chris and Joe offered to help get the dressers up the stairs into Nate's loft room.

"We can leave them here, but they're kind of taking up a lot of space and they won't exactly fit under the tree. How about we get them upstairs right away?" Joe said, pushing the first dresser closer to the staircase.

It was a bit chaotic as the men pushed through the living room; navigating two large dressers past a dozen people, three dogs and enough gifts to fill the North Pole. No one noticed Sarah Rosen as she made her way through the chaos to find her brother.

"Hey, Sarah, I thought you were going to a party with your friends tonight," Rob said as he kissed his sister on her cheek.

"I am. I'm on my way, but I had something I wanted to give to Wendy." Sarah found Wendy sitting with Lexi and Erika. "Wendy, I wanted to ask you something," she began.

"Oh, Sarah, Merry Christmas! This is Lexi and Erika, Charlie's sisters!"

Sarah greeted the Wheeler girls and knelt in front of Wendy.

"When we were at the shelter the other day, I asked about becoming a volunteer. I also asked if they allowed younger volunteers, and the woman told me they didn't. However, when she realized I was inquiring about you, she made an exception. As long as I'm with you, you'll be able to help the shelter dogs and cats while they wait for their forever homes. I already asked Laurel if it would be ok, and she thought it was a great idea. Would you want to volunteer with me?" Sarah handed Wendy an envelope with a small magnetic name tag inside, it read; " *Wendy Cooke, volunteer.*"

"Yes, I'd love that! Thank you, Sarah. I can't wait to spend time with the animals, and with you." Sarah was pleased that her young friend accepted her gift with such enthusiasm. She said her hellos and goodbyes and left to meet her friends.

Nate wanted to spend the rest of the evening in his room, marveling at his gifts, and loading them with his clothing that he had been keeping on some makeshift shelves. He sat on the edge of his bed for a few moments feeling grateful for having a family, a home and every other blessing that had been bestowed. He could hear the excitement building downstairs as Charlie announced the next big gift was for Kay. Nate knew his place was with his family, not only tonight on Christmas Eve, but every day from now on.

"Kay, you have already graciously accepted my proposal, and I cannot wait to marry you any longer," he began. Everyone became rather curious and stopped what they were doing to listen to Charlie explain his special gift. "You are the most amazing person I know and do so much for my family, our family. Now with your new job, there isn't much time left for wedding planning. We have put it off for far too long, so with Laurel's help, I have come up with what I hope is a solution. First of all, I've set the date with our church. How does May twenty-ninth sound?" He waited for her to respond, but Kay simply nodded with tears of joy filling her eyes. "OK, the date is set, now it's up to you." He handed her a small envelope with a business card inside. She seemed confused at first, but as she read the print, Kay realized he had hired a wedding planner. Charlie's smile lit up the entire room, "This is David Klein, he's a friend of Laurel's and has agreed to help you plan your perfect wedding. He knows you want something simple, and your first meeting with David is scheduled on December twenty-eighth; three p.m. at Laurel's house."

Kay stood and hugged Charlie. Her tears spilled onto his shoulder. She whispered.

"I can't wait to marry you. This is the most wonderful gift I could ever receive." Everyone broke out with thunderous applause; whistles and cheers. Lexi Wheeler exclaimed in jest.

"I am not wearing pink!"

Susan politely reminded everyone that dinner was ready and if they hadn't yet eaten, now would be the time to do so.

"There are literal mountains of gifts under that tree, and if you want yours, you'd better come and get your food first."

The Wheeler sisters would have been happy just being among the others; playing with the puppies and Harry. Neither had expected gifts under the tree with their names on them, but Laurel, Jaime and Fiona made certain everyone had a gift. Laurel and TC gave each girl a new laptop, Jaime had pashmina scarves embroidered with the sisters' initials and Fiona gave them hand-wrapped gemstone necklaces, much like the one Carter had purchased for her. Wendy was admiring Erika's necklace.

"That's beautiful," Carter asked Fiona if she had purchased one for Wendy as well, and she had.

"The reason I asked, I actually bought one very similar for you before I adopted the puppies. I would have given it to Wendy instead if you hadn't bought one for her. She really seems to like Erika's."

"That's so sweet, Carter. See? You keep proving my point about accepting all this crazy and making it your own. I love that you care about Wendy." Carter sat beside Fiona and watched as each person tore through their gifts, thanking their friends, exchanging hugs, spilling tears and sharing laughter. Carter wondered if he was the only one that felt as though something magical happens when these particular people come together.

The puppies continued to be the life of the party, and as the evening progressed, they became increasingly more comfortable with their surroundings. Fiona was in awe as she watched them interact with Harry, as well as one another. For being so young, and spending the majority of their lives so far in a shelter, both pups were very social and fairly well-mannered. Everyone took turns suggesting names for the little brothers.

"I've been calling them Red and Blue," Wendy offered.

Fiona immediately understood the reference.

"Oh, I like that," she told her. "But let's see if we can elaborate on your idea to maybe give them a little more personality."

Nate, who had been playing with one of the pups, suggested his name.

"What about Phoenix for this guy? You know, like your nickname," he teased.

Fiona agreed.

"Yes, I love it. From now on, you'll be known as Phoenix," she said, placing her hand on the puppy's head. "OK, so we have red fire, now we need blue ice! Oh, how's Yeti for an icy name?"

"Phoenix and Yeti, That works," Carter chimed in.

"It's settled, the puppies are named," Fiona announced. "Wendy, thank you for the inspiration, and Nate, great call with Phoenix."

TC cleared his throat, stood and raised his glass.

"Now that the newest additions to our family are officially named, I would like to propose a holiday toast, would everyone please raise a glass?" For the first time all evening, the house was quiet as everyone raised their glass and turned their attention to TC.

Wendy jumped up from her seat.

"Wait, Dad, wait!" She dove under the tree and began rifling through the unopened gifts in search of hers to Fiona. "Don't toast yet, I have to give this to Fiona," she exclaimed, holding the package up with her right hand.

TC couldn't have continued if he wanted to. The sound of Wendy calling him Dad for the first time left him with a lump in his throat the size of a watermelon. Laurel caught his eye and smiled. He just stood in place staring at his wife to keep from crying his own tears of joy. She mouthed.

"I love you."

Wendy handed her package to Fiona.

"I almost forgot. This is from me, Harry and the boys." Fiona tore the paper from the picture frame that Wendy had embellished with red and blue rhinestones. She took a minute to read her poem and immediately became emotional, "You wrote this?" she asked.

"Yep. I couldn't believe that so many dogs get left in dumpsters, I really thought Harry was the only one. Then you guys told me Wanda's story, and then we found out about the puppies. I was really sad, but I thought, why be sad when they all wound up being a part of our family? That's a good thing, right? It's like Wanda sent the puppies to us so we would remember to be happy." Fiona set the frame down and hugged Wendy. "You are truly amazing. Our very own Christmas Angel."

TC composed himself.

"Anyone else have a special gift or announcement to make tonight?" Everyone let out a chuckle, but the room was still filled with emotion. TC continued, "Let's try this again, shall we? Please raise your glasses." He paused for just a moment and began his toast once again.

"Merry Christmas to all. I want to thank everyone here for not only making this the most extraordinary Christmas but for being the most extraordinary humans I have ever known. Each of you has enriched my and Laurel's lives more than we could imagine, more than we possibly deserve. We have grown together so organically to become one family in such a very short time. Our bond, our story is nothing short of a miracle. We could not possibly repay each of you for what you have given to us and given of yourselves without expecting anything in return. With open minds, open arms and open hearts; we move toward a new year; together. I cannot wait to see what the Universe has in store for us. God Bless our family and Merry Christmas."

AFTERWARD

Wendy Cooke approached the podium center stage, adjusted the microphone and smiled for her audience.

"Welcome to the commencement ceremony for the class of 2025," She began. The crowd clapped, with the second and third row cheering loudly as if they were at some sort of sporting event. Wendy wasn't embarrassed by their obvious enthusiasm, but proud to know that everyone she's ever loved, and everyone who has ever loved her was in attendance for her big moment.

"My name is Wendy Cooke, and no, I'm not your valedictorian; he's much smarter than me," she quipped. "You'll very likely enjoy his words more than mine, but I am honored to have been asked by my classmates to speak to you all today. I'm not going to attempt to thank everyone who has helped me get here; for that would take entirely too long and I only have about five minutes with you. Besides, this is not the Academy Awards, it's our Academy Graduation."

More applause, Wendy smiled, paused for effect then continued.

"Four years ago, when I began my classes here, I was a year behind, and delayed in every subject but reading. I kept my reasons a secret; afraid of what my classmates might think of me if they knew. I hadn't counted on people filling in the blanks with speculation; making me seem as if I had problems they were simply not prepared to deal with, or had no interest in. After months of anxious encounters, I still hadn't made a friend at school. I remember coming home one day and begging my mother to let me quit school and take all my classes online. You see, I was being tutored virtually for two hours every day after school to try and catch up to my classmates, but no one knew that; not even some of my teachers. My mother, in all her infinite wisdom, told me, instead of quitting, why don't I tell my story? I thought she was kidding."

Her audience chuckled.

"She wasn't kidding. You see, my mother is an amazing person; she's never wrong! I trusted her suggestion and wrote my story as an English assignment. Now, for those unfamiliar with said story, don't worry, I'm not telling it today, but you can find it on our school website, right next to the picture of me standing at my locker in my underwear."

Again, her audience burst into laughter.

"That's what it felt like; letting a school full of strangers into my past, my personal space, my dreams and my nightmares, but I did it. I thought for certain, I'd be teased, bullied and cast even further out of any possibility of a social life; but, none of those things happened. Surprise! My mother was right, again, or still, depending on how you look at it. My classmates then, now my amazing friends, wanted to know more; they wanted to understand; not out of morbid curiosity, but out of compassion. You all wanted to help me; know me, and accept me into your

world."

Wendy took another pause and blew a kiss into the crowd.

"I wrote about Harry, and the next day my desk was covered in dog toys and treats; with a card signed by my entire homeroom *For Harry, may you never feel unloved*. I told of the days when I didn't have enough to eat, and you wanted to share your lunches with me. When I got confused, you offered to study with me. I invited our whole class to a pool party at the end of our Freshman year, and everyone showed up."

Wendy realized she'd gone down an unintended path, as her audience began to tear up. She knew it was time for some levity.

"Oh," she added. "Except for Jason who got the chicken pox from his little brother."

She pointed to Jason and winked. The young man stood, faced the crowd and took a bow. Everyone laughed. Wendy made a mental note to thank him later for the assist.

"My words today are meant to be our legacy; something we can leave for the future Academy students, which by the way will include my little sister in the Fall. I know our school will be as welcoming, supportive and accepting for Cassie as it was for me. This is not my story, it's ours. We have all contributed vital pieces that have fit so perfectly together. Let our experiences here become a roadmap, a guidebook for integrity, compassion, camaraderie, and higher education at what I like to call, The Academy of Extraordinary Humans.

"May your futures be as blessed as you have made my time here with all of you."